TRO¥

First published in the United Kingdom by Michael Joseph, an imprint of Penguin Books, in 2020.

Library of Congress Cataloging-in-Publication Data available.

ISBN: 978-1-7972-0707-0

Manufactured in China.

Designed by Maggie Edelman

10 9 8 7 6 5 4 3 2

Chronicle books and gifts are available at special quantity discounts to corporations, professional associations, literacy programs, and other organizations. For details and discount information, please contact our premiums department at corporatesales@chroniclebooks.com or at 1-800-759-0190.

Chronicle Books LLC

680 Second Street

San Francisco, California 94107

www.chroniclebooks.com

TRO¥

The Greek Myths Reimagined
Volume III of Mythos

By Stephen Fry

CHRONICLE BOOKS
SAN FRANCISCO

CONTENTS

INTRODUCTORY NOTE

The birth and rise of gods and humans is the subject of my book *Mythos*, whose successor *Heroes* covers the great feats, quests, and adventures of mortal heroes such as Perseus, Heracles, Jason, and Theseus. You do not have to know those books to enjoy this one; when I have judged it useful, I provide footnote references pointing to where fuller details of incidents and characters can be found in the previous two volumes, but no preexisting knowledge of the Greek mythological world is presumed or required for you to embark on *Troy*. As I remind you from time to time, especially early on in the book, do not think for a minute that you have to remember all those names, places, and familial inter-relationships. To give background, I do describe the founding of many different dynasties and kingdoms; but I assure you that, when it comes to the main action, the different threads turn from a tangle into a tapestry. A two-part Appendix at the back of the book addresses the issue of how much of what follows is history and how much myth.

Stephen Fry

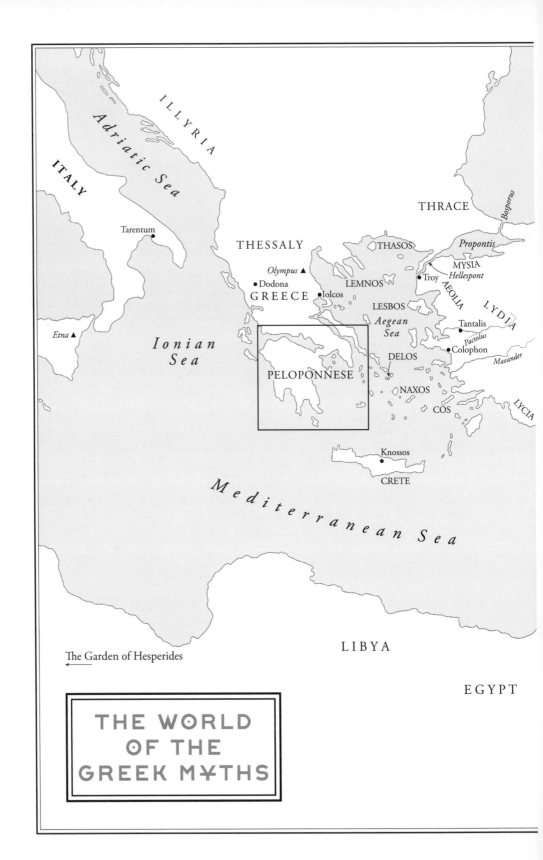

ITALY

ILLYRIA

Adriatic Sea

Tarentum

THESSALY

THASOS

THRACE

Bosporus

Propontis

Olympus ▲

MYSIA

Hellespont

• Dodona

LEMNOS

• Troy

AEOLIA

LYDIA

GREECE

• Iolcos

Etna ▲

Ionian Sea

LESBOS

Aegean Sea

Tantalis

Pactolus

• Colophon

PELOPONNESE

DELOS

Maeander

NAXOS

LYCIA

COS

Knossos

CRETE

M e d i t e r r a n e a n   S e a

The Garden of Hesperides
←

LIBYA

EGYPT

THE WORLD OF THE GREEK MYTHS

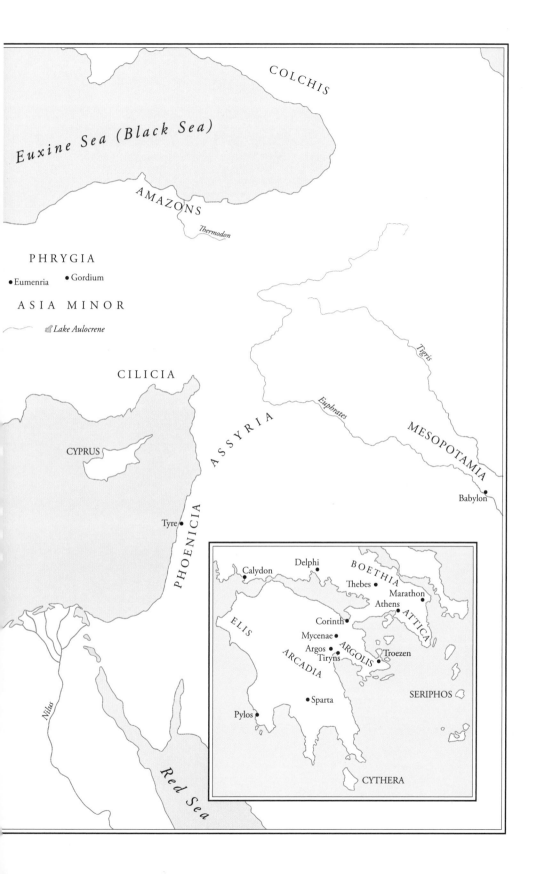

COLCHIS

Euxine Sea (Black Sea)

AMAZONS

Thermodon

PHRYGIA

• Eumenria   • Gordium

ASIA MINOR

Lake Aulocrene

CILICIA

Tigris

Euphrates

ASSYRIA

MESOPOTAMIA

CYPRUS

PHOENICIA

Tyre •

Babylon •

Nilus

Red Sea

Calydon •   Delphi •

BOETHIA

Thebes •   Marathon

Athens •   ATTICA

ELIS   Corinth •

Mycenae •

Argos •   ARGOLIS   Troezen •

Tiryns •

ARCADIA

SERIPHOS

• Sparta

Pylos •

CYTHERA

THE OLYMPIANS

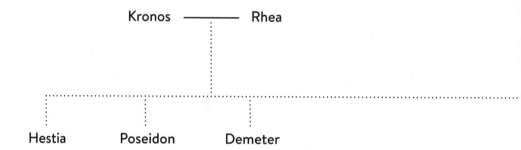

Kronos ——— Rhea

Hestia   Poseidon   Demeter

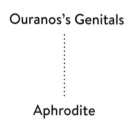

Ouranos's Genitals

Aphrodite

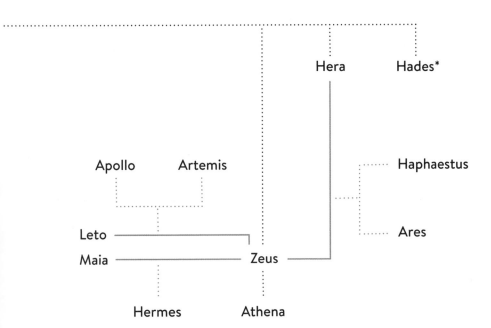

*Hades is not technically an Olympian, as he spent all of his time in the underworld.

TIMELINE

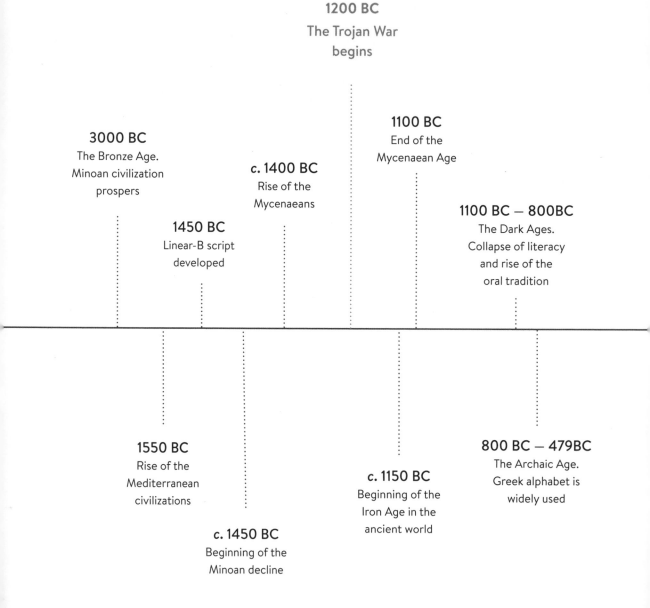

1200 BC
The Trojan War
begins

3000 BC
The Bronze Age.
Minoan civilization
prospers

1100 BC
End of the
Mycenaean Age

c. **1400 BC**
Rise of the
Mycenaeans

1450 BC
Linear-B script
developed

1100 BC — 800BC
The Dark Ages.
Collapse of literacy
and rise of the
oral tradition

1550 BC
Rise of the
Mediterranean
civilizations

c. **1150 BC**
Beginning of the
Iron Age in the
ancient world

800 BC — 479BC
The Archaic Age.
Greek alphabet is
widely used

c. **1450 BC**
Beginning of the
Minoan decline

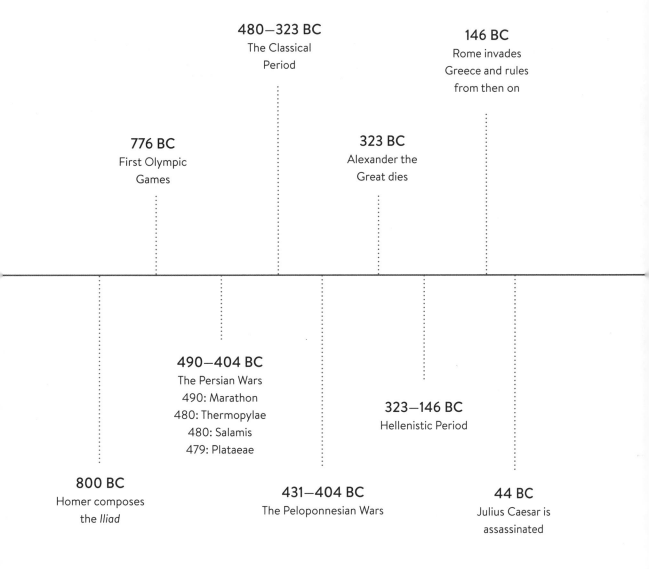

480–323 BC
The Classical
Period

146 BC
Rome invades
Greece and rules
from then on

776 BC
First Olympic
Games

323 BC
Alexander the
Great dies

490–404 BC
The Persian Wars
490: Marathon
480: Thermopylae
480: Salamis
479: Plataeae

323–146 BC
Hellenistic Period

800 BC
Homer composes
the *Iliad*

431–404 BC
The Peloponnesian Wars

44 BC
Julius Caesar is
assassinated

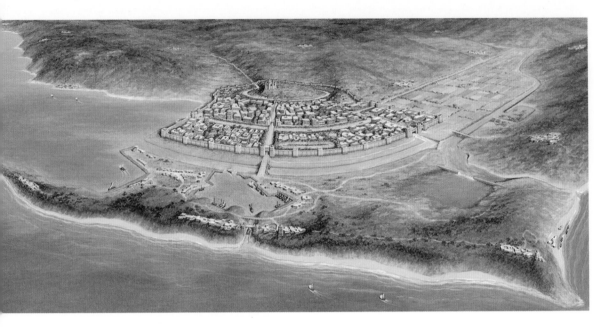

◆ The City of Troy

IT FELL FROM HEAVEN

Troy. The most marvelous kingdom in all the world. The Jewel of the Aegean. Glittering Ilium, the city that rose and fell not once but twice. Gatekeeper of traffic in and out of the barbarous east. Kingdom of gold and horses. Fierce nurse of prophets, princes, heroes, warriors, and poets. Under the protection of ARES, ARTEMIS, APOLLO, and APHRODITE, she stood for years as the paragon of all that can be achieved in the arts of war and peace, trade and treaty, love and art, statecraft, piety, and civil harmony. When she fell, a hole opened in the human world that may never be filled, save in memory. Poets must sing the story over and over again, passing it from generation to generation, lest in losing Troy we lose a part of ourselves.

To understand Troy's end we must understand her beginning. The background to our story has many twists and turns. A host of place names, personalities, and families enter and exit. It is not necessary to remember every name, every relationship of blood and marriage, every kingdom and province. The story emerges and the important names will, I promise, stick.

All things, Troy included, begin and end with ZEUS, the King of the Gods, Ruler of Olympus, Lord of Thunder, Cloud-Gatherer, and Bringer of Storms.

Long, long ago, almost before the dawn of mortal history, Zeus consorted with Electra, a beautiful daughter of the Titan Atlas and the sea nymph Pleione. Electra bore Zeus a son, DARDANUS, who traveled throughout Greece and the islands of the Aegean searching for a place in which he could build and raise his own dynasty. He alighted at last on the Ionian coast. If you have never visited Ionia, you should know that it is the land east of the Aegean Sea which used to be called Asia Minor, but which we know as Turkish Anatolia. The great kingdoms of Phrygia and Lydia were there, but they were already occupied and ruled over, so it was in the north that Dardanus settled, occupying the peninsula that lies below the Hellespont, the straits into which Helle fell from the back of the GOLDEN RAM. Years later JASON would sail through the Hellespont on his way to find the fleece of that ram. The lovestruck Leander would swim nightly across the Hellespont to be with Hero, his beloved.[1]

---

1. The stories of Helle, the golden ram, and Jason can be found in *Heroes* (page 154), and the tragedy of Hero and Leander in *Mythos* (page 285). Even later in history those same straits, now called the Dardanelles after Dardanus, were the source of terrible fighting in and around the peninsula city that the Greeks called Kalli Polis (Beautiful City), which over time had turned into the name Gallipoli.

The city Dardanus established was called—with little imagination and less modesty—Dardanus, while the whole kingdom took on the name Dardania.[2] Following the founder king's death, Ilus, the eldest of his three sons, ruled—but he died childless, leaving the throne to his brother, the middle son, ERICHTHONIUS.[3]

The reign of Erichthonius was peaceful and prosperous. In the lee of Mount Ida, his lands were fed by the waters of the benign river gods Simoeis and Scamander, who blessed the land of Dardania with great fertility. Erichthonius grew to become the richest man in the known world, famous for his three thousand mares and their countless foals. Boreas, the North Wind, took the form of a wild stallion and fathered a remarkable race of horses by the filly foals of Erichthonius's herd. These colts were so agile and light of foot they could gallop through fields of corn without bending a stalk. So they say. Horses and riches: always, when we talk of Troy, we find ourselves talking of wondrous horses and uncountable riches.

---

2. In some versions Dardanus annexed, absorbed, or even invaded an existing kingdom that had been founded by King Teucer, a son of the river god SCAMANDER and the oread, or mountain nymph, Idaea. This Teucer is not to be confused with the bowman of the same name whom we shall meet later. In later poetry and chronicles Trojans were sometimes called Teucrians.

3. The youngest of Dardanus's three sons, Idaeus, gave his name to Mount Ida, the greatest of the peaks lying to Dardania's south.

FOUNDATION

After the death of Erichthonius, his son TROS succeeded to the throne. Tros had a daughter, Cleopatra, and three sons, ILUS (named in honor of his great-uncle), Assaracus, and GANYMEDE. The story of Prince Ganymede is well known. His beauty was so great that Zeus himself was seized by an overmastering passion for him. Taking the form of an eagle, the god swooped down and bore the boy up to Olympus, where he served as Zeus's beloved minion, companion, and cupbearer. To compensate Tros for the loss of his son, Zeus sent HERMES to him, bearing the gift of two divine horses, so swift and light they could gallop over water. Tros was consoled by these magical animals and by Hermes's assurance that Ganymede was now and—by definition always would be—immortal.[4]

It was Ganymede's brother Prince Ilus who founded the new city that would be named Troy in Tros's honor. He won a wrestling match at the Phrygian Games, the prize consisting of fifty youths and fifty maidens, but—more importantly—a cow. A very special cow that an oracle directed Ilus to use for the founding of a city.

"Wherever the cow lies down, there shall you build."

If Ilus had heard the story of CADMUS—and who had not?—he would have known that Cadmus and Harmonia, acting in accordance with instructions from an oracle, had followed a cow, and waited for the animal to lie down as an indication of where they were to build what would become Thebes, the first of the great city-states of Greece. It may seem to us that the practice of allowing cows to choose where a city should be built is arbitrary and bizarre, but perhaps a little reflection should tell us that it is not so strange after all. Where there is to be a city, there must also be plentiful sources of meat, milk, leather, and cheese for its citizens. Not to mention strong draft animals—oxen for plowing fields and pulling carts. If a cow is taken enough by the amenities of a region to feel able to lie down, then it is worth paying attention. At any rate, Ilus was content to follow his prize heifer all the way north from Phrygia to the Troad,[5] past the slopes of Mount Ida, and onto the great plain of Dardania; and it was here, not far from where Ilus's great-grandfather's first city of Dardanus had been built, that the heifer lay down at last.

---

4. Indeed, the cupbearer lives *two* immortal lives in the night sky: as the constellation Aquarius, the Water-Carrier, and as a moon of his lover, Jupiter (the planets all take on the gods' Roman names).

5. Also in honor of Tros, the whole peninsula was beginning now to be referred to as the Troad (pronounced "Tro-ad," not to rhyme with "toad").

The Palladium

Ilus looked about him. It was a fine place for a new city. To the south rose the massif of Mount Ida and at some distance to the north ran the straits of the Hellespont. To the east the blue of the Aegean could be glimpsed, and through the green and fertile plain itself threaded the rivers Simoeis and Scamander.

Ilus knelt down and prayed to the gods for a sign that he had made no mistake. In immediate answer a wooden object fell from the sky and landed at his feet in a great cloud of dust. It was about the height of a ten-year-old child[6] and carved into a likeness of PALLAS ATHENA, a spear in one upraised hand and a distaff and spindle in the other, representing the arts of war and the arts of peace, over which the grey-eyed goddess held dominion.

The act of looking at so sacred an object struck Ilus instantly blind. He was wise enough in the ways of the Olympians not to panic. Falling to his knees he cast up prayers of thanks to the heavens. After a week of steadfast devotion he was rewarded with the restoration of his sight. Brimming with revived energy and zeal, he began at once to lay out the foundations for his new city. He planned the streets so that they radiated like the spokes of a wheel from a central temple which he would dedicate to Athena. In the innermost sanctum of the temple he placed the wooden carving of Pallas Athena that fell from the sky: the *xoanon*, the Luck of Troy, the symbol and assurance of the city's divine status. So long as this sacred totem reposed there unmolested, so long would Troy prosper and endure. So Ilus believed and so the people who flocked to help him build and populate this new city believed too. They called the wooden carving the Palladium, and after Ilus's father Tros they gave their city and themselves the new names of Troy and Trojans.[7]

There we have the founding line, from Dardanus to his sons Ilus the First and Erichthonius, whose son Tros fathered Ilus the Second, after whom Troy is also called Ilium or Ilion.[8]

---

6. Three ancient Greek cubits, roughly approximating to four feet six inches. A wooden cult object like this, carved in the form of a deity (usually a goddess), was known as a *xoanon*.

7. The liquid vowel "i" in ancient Greek and Latin often becomes a consonantal "j" in English: "Jason" for "Iason," "Jesus" for "Iesus," "Julius," "Juno," "juvenile," etc. The French have *Troyen* and *Troyenne*; in German it's *Trojaner* but pronounced "Troy-ahner." It's the same "y" sound in Italian and Spanish. The Portuguese spell and say it a bit like us, though: *Trojan* to rhyme with "explosion." Modern Greeks say *Tro-as*, rhyming with "slow ass."

8. Hence the name of Homer's epic poem, the *Iliad*.

CURSES

There was another royal line in Ionia which we should know about: its importance would be difficult to overstate. You may already know the story of King TANTALUS, who ruled in Lydia, a kingdom to the south of Troy. Tantalus served up his son PELOPS to the gods in a stew.[9] Young Pelops was reassembled and resurrected by the gods and grew up to be a handsome and popular prince and a lover of POSEIDON, who gave him a chariot drawn by winged horses. This chariot led to a curse which led to . . . which led to almost everything . . .

Ilus had been as outraged as anyone by Tantalus's depravity, enough to expel him by force of arms from the region. You would imagine that Pelops would have no objection to his father's expulsion—after all, Tantalus had slaughtered him, his own son, butchered him, and presented him to the Olympians in a fricassee—but far from it. No sooner had Pelops attained manhood than he raised an army and attacked Ilus, but was easily bested in battle. Pelops left Ionia, settling at last in land far to the west, the peninsula off mainland Greece that is called the Peloponnese after him to this day. On this remarkable piece of land grew up such legendary kingdoms and cities as Sparta, Mycenae, Corinth, Epidaurus, Troezen, Argos, and Pisa. This Pisa is not the Italian home of the Leaning Tower, of course, but a Greek city-state ruled over at the time of Pelops's arrival by King OENOMAUS,[10] a son of the war god Ares.

Oenomaus had a daughter, HIPPODAMIA, whose beauty and lineage attracted many suitors. The king was fearful of a prophecy foretelling his death at the hands of a son-in-law. There were no nunneries in which daughters could be shut up in those days, so he tried another way of ensuring her perpetual spinsterhood—he announced that Hippodamia could only be won by a man who could defeat him in a chariot race. There was a catch: the reward for victory might be Hippodamia's hand in marriage, but the price of *losing* the race would be the suitor's life. Oenomaus believed that no finer charioteer than he existed in the world; consequently he was confident that his daughter would never wed and provide him with the son-in-law that the prophecy had taught him to dread. Despite the drastic cost of losing the race and the unrivaled reputation of Oenomaus as a charioteer, eighteen brave men accepted the challenge. Hippodamia's beauty was great and the prospect of winning her and the rich city-state of Pisa

---

9. Zeus punished Tantalus with an eternal torment in the underworld: water and fruit were kept always just out of his reach, giving our language the word "tantalize." See *Mythos*, page 218

10. Pronounced "Ee-no-*may*-us."

was tempting. Eighteen had raced against Oenomaus and eighteen had been beaten; their heads, in varying stages of decomposition, adorned the poles that ringed the hippodrome.

When Pelops, ejected from his home kingdom of Lydia, arrived in Pisa he was instantly struck by Hippodamia's beauty. While he believed in his own skills as a horseman, he thought it wise to call upon his one-time lover Poseidon for extra aid. The god of the sea and of horses was happy to send from the waves a chariot and two winged steeds of great power and speed. To make doubly sure, Pelops bribed Oenomaus's charioteer MYRTILUS, a son of Hermes, to help him win. Motivated by the promise of half Oenomaus's kingdom and a night in bed with Hippodamia (with whom he too was in love), Myrtilus crept into the stables the night before the race and replaced the bronze linchpins which fixed the axle of Oenomaus's chariot with substitutes carved from beeswax.

The next day, when the race began, young Pelops dashed into the lead, but so great was King Oenomaus's skill that he soon began to catch up. He was almost upon Pelops, his javelin raised to strike a deathblow, when the waxen linchpins gave way, the wheels flew from the chariot and Oenomaus was dragged to a bloody death under the hoofs of his own horses.

Myrtilus went to claim what he thought was his just reward—a night with Hippodamia—but she ran complaining to Pelops, who hurled Myrtilus off a cliff into the sea. As the drowning Myrtilus struggled in the water, he cursed Pelops and all his descendants.

Myrtilus is not the best known of Greek heroes. Yet the part of the Aegean into which he fell is still called the Myrtoan Sea. For countless years the local people conducted annual sacrifices to Myrtilus in the temple of his father Hermes, where his corpse lay embalmed after his death. All this devotion for a weak, lustful man who had accepted a bribe and caused the death of his own king.

But the curse on Pelops. This curse matters. For Pelops and Hippodamia had children. And those children had children. And the curse of Myrtilus was on them all. As we shall see.

If this story, the story of Troy, has a meaning or a moral, it is the old, simple lesson that actions have consequences. What Tantalus did, exacerbated by what Pelops did . . . the actions of these two caused a doom to be laid on what was to be the most important royal house of Greece.

Meanwhile, the royal house of Troy was about to invoke a curse of its own . . .

King Ilus had died and the throne of Troy was now occupied by his son LAOMEDON. Where Ilus had been devout, diligent, industrious, honorable, and provident, Laomedon was greedy, ambitious, feckless, indolent, and sly. His greed and ambition included a desire to develop the city of Troy still further, to give it great protective walls and ramparts, golden towers and turrets, to endow it with a splendor such as the world had never known. Rather than plan and execute this himself, Laomedon did something that might seem strange to us but which was still possible in the days when gods and men walked the earth together: he commissioned two of the Olympian gods, Apollo and Poseidon, to do the work for him. The immortals were not above a little contract labor and the pair threw themselves into the construction project with energy and skill, piling up great granite boulders and dressing them into neat blocks to create magnificent gleaming walls. In a very short time the work was done and a newly fortified Troy stood proudly on the plain of Ilium, as grand and formidable a fortress city as had ever been seen. But when Apollo and Poseidon presented themselves to Laomedon for payment he did what many householders have done since. He pursed his lips, sucked in between his teeth, and shook his head.

"No, no, no," he said. "The ramparts are bowed, I asked for straight. And the south gates aren't what I ordered at all. And those buttresses! All wrong. Oh dear me, no, I can't possibly pay you for shoddy work like that."

They say a fool and his gold are soon parted, but they ought to say too that those who refuse ever to be parted from gold are the greatest fools of all.

The revenge of the cheated gods was swift and merciless. Apollo shot plague arrows over the walls and into the city; within days the sound of wailing and moaning rose up around Troy as at least one member of every family was struck down by deadly disease. At the same time Poseidon sent a huge sea monster to the Hellespont. All shipping east and west was blocked by its ferocious presence and Troy was soon starved of the trade and tolls on which its prosperity depended.

So much for the Palladium and the Luck of Troy.

The terrified citizens flocked to Laomedon's palace to demand relief. The king turned to his priests and prophets, who were of one mind.

"It is too late to pay the gods with the gold you owe them, majesty. There is only one way now to placate them. You must sacrifice your daughter HESIONE to the sea creature."

Laomedon had a large number of children.[11] While Hesione may have been his favorite, his own flesh and blood mattered more to him than his own flesh and blood (as it were), and he knew that if he ignored the instruction of the prophets, the frightened and angry Trojan populace would tear him to pieces and sacrifice Hesione anyway.

"Make it so," he said with a heavy sigh and an irritated flick of the hand.

Hesione was taken and chained to a rock in the Hellespont to await her fate at the jaws of the sea beast.[12]

All Troy held its breath.

---

11. One of whom, TITHONUS, married EOS, goddess of the dawn, and was granted immortality by Zeus. Immortality, but not eternal youth. As a result he withered away until Eos turned him into a grasshopper. See *Mythos*, page 256.

12. A fate identical to that which befell the Ethiopian princess Andromeda, who was rescued by HERACLES's great-great-grandfather (and half-brother) PERSEUS. See *Heroes*, page 42.

SALVATION
AND
DESTRUCTION

SEE, THE CONQUERING HERO COMES

At exactly this time, the very moment that Hesione, shackled to her rock, began to cast up prayers to Olympus for her delivery from Poseidon's sea dragon, Heracles and his band of followers arrived at the gates of Troy on their way back from his Ninth Labor, the acquisition of the girdle of HIPPOLYTA, Queen of the Amazons.[13]

With his friends TELAMON and OICLES by his side, Heracles was ushered into the royal presence. Honored by the visit of the great hero as the Trojan court was, Laomedon's mind was more on his plague-ridden and beleaguered city's depleted storerooms than on the privilege of playing host to Heracles and his followers, however famous and admired they may be. It was a small army that traveled with him, but Laomedon knew that they would all expect to be fed. Heracles alone had the appetite of a hundred men.

"You're very welcome, Heracles. Do you plan to honor us with your company for long?"

Heracles looked about the somber court in some surprise. "Why the long faces? I had been told that Troy was the richest and happiest kingdom in the world."

Laomedon shifted on his throne. "You of all men should know that we are but playthings of the gods. What is a man but the hapless victim of their petty whims and vengeful jealousies? Apollo sends us contagion and Poseidon a monster that chokes our sea channel."

Heracles listened to Laomedon's self-pitying and largely fabricated version of the events leading up to Hesione's sacrifice.

"Doesn't seem so difficult a problem to me," he said. "All you need is for someone to clear the seaway of that dragon and save your daughter—what did you say her name was?"

"Hesione."[14]

"Yes, her. The plague will blow through soon enough, I dare say, they always do . . ."

Laomedon was dubious. "That's all very well, but what about my daughter?"

Heracles bowed. "The work of a moment."

Laomedon, like everyone in the Greek world, had heard stories of the Labors that Heracles had undertaken—the cleaning out of King Augeas's stables, the taming of the CRETAN BULL, the trapping of the great tusked boar of

---

13. See *Heroes*, page 81.

14. Pronounced almost as "Hess irony" . . . but without the "r." Rhymes with "Hermione" and "Briony."

Mount Erymanthus, the killing of the NEMEAN LION, and the eradication of the Lernaean HYDRA . . . If this lumbering ox of a man with a lion skin for clothing and an oak tree for a club had in truth performed such impossible feats and defeated such terrible creatures, then he might be able to free up the Hellespont and rescue Hesione. But there was always the question of payment.

"We're not a rich kingdom . . ." Laomedon lied.

"Don't you worry about that," said Heracles. "All I would ask for in return is your horses."

"My horses?"

"The horses my father Zeus sent to your grandfather Tros."

"Ah, those horses." Laomedon waved a hand as if to say, "Is that all?" "My dear man, clear the channel of that dragon and restore my daughter to me and you shall have them—yes, and their silver bridles too."

Less than an hour later Heracles, blade between his teeth, had dived into the waters of the Hellespont and was breasting Poseidon's rising surge. Hesione, chained to her rock, the waters now coming up to her waist, watched in astonishment as a huge, muscled man, kicking hard, headed straight toward the narrowest part of the channel, where the dragon lurked.

Laomedon, Telamon, and Oicles, with the rest of Heracles's loyal company of Greeks behind them, watched from the shore. Telamon whispered to Oicles, "Look at her! Did you ever see anyone more beautiful?"

While Hesione did present a most alluring sight, Oicles had eyes only for the spectacle of his leader engaging a great sea dragon in the simple, direct, and violently confrontational manner for which he was celebrated. Heracles headed directly toward the creature, but far from showing fear the dragon opened its mouth wide and itself made for Heracles.

Oicles thought he had the measure of his friend and commander, but what Heracles did next was entirely unexpected. Without breaking stroke he swam straight into the monster's open mouth. The cheers from the shoreline were choked into a shocked silence as Heracles disappeared from sight. With a gulp and a snap of its colossal jaws the creature rose up with a roar of triumph before diving down into the deeps. Hesione was saved—for the moment at least—but Heracles . . . Heracles was lost. Heracles the greatest, strongest, bravest, and noblest of heroes swallowed whole, without so much as a struggle.

Oicles and the others should have known better, of course. From inside the animal's stinking interior Heracles immediately busied himself hacking hard with his blade. After what seemed an eternity, scales and chunks of flesh came bobbing to the surface.[15] Telamon was the first to see them and pointed with a

15. Some historians claimed Heracles was inside for three whole days, which seems unlikely. It is the same number of days Jonah is said to have been inside his big fish, so perhaps that is just the canonical duration in such stories.

great shout as the sea began to boil with blood and torn flesh. When Heracles himself at last arose with a heaving gasp, seawater streaming from him, the assembled Greeks and Trojans gave a mighty hurrah. How could they have doubted the greatest of all the heroes?

A short while later the shivering Hesione gratefully accepted Telamon's cloak and supporting arm as she and the cheering soldiers accompanied Heracles back to Laomedon.[16]

Some people are constitutionally unable to learn from their mistakes. When Heracles demanded the horses which had been agreed would constitute his payment, Laomedon sucked in through his teeth with a hiss, just as he had done with Apollo and Poseidon.

"Oh no, no, no," he said, shaking his head from side to side. "No, no, no, no, no. The agreement was that you *free up* the Hellespont, not leave it all clogged with blubber, blood, and bones. It'll take my men weeks to clean up the mess on the shoreline. 'Free up the Hellespont'—those were your very words and those the terms. Can you deny it?"

Laomedon jutted out his beard and gave a piercing glance around the room toward the assembled courtiers and members of his elite royal guard.

"His very words . . ."

"'Free it up,' he said . . ."

"As ever, your majesty is right . . ."

"You see? So I can't possibly pay you. Grateful to have Hesione back, of course, but I'm sure the dragon would have done her no harm. Could have collected her from the rock ourselves in due course, and certainly without making a mess like that."

With a roar of indignation Heracles took up his club. The soldiers of Laomedon's guard immediately drew their swords and formed a defensive circle around their king.

Telamon whispered urgently in Heracles's ear. "Leave it, my friend. We're outnumbered a thousand to one. Besides, you have to be back in Tiryns in time to start your Tenth and last Labor. If you're so much as a day late, you'll forfeit everything. Nine years of effort wasted. Come on, he's not worth it."

Heracles lowered his club and spat at the semicircle of soldiers behind which Laomedon was cowering. "Your majesty hasn't seen the last of me," he growled. Executing a low bow he turned and left.

"I didn't meant that bow," he explained to Telamon and Oicles as they made their way back to their ship.

"You didn't mean it?"

---

16. There are versions of this story that suggest the corrosive gastric juices of the dragon either completely stripped Heracles of all his hair or else turned it permanently white.

"It was a sarcastic bow."

"Ah," said Telamon, "I did wonder."

"Dear me, how uncouth these Greeks are," said Laomedon, watching from the high walls of his city as Heracles's ship hoisted her sails and glided away. "No manners, no style, no *address* . . ."

Hesione looked on the departing ship with some regret. She had liked Heracles and was quite certain in her mind that no matter what her father might say he truly had saved her life. His friend Telamon too was most polite and charming. Nor was he unbecoming to look at. She looked down at her lap and sighed.

HERACLES'S RETURN

King EURYSTHEUS of Mycenae and King Laomedon of Troy were cut from the same shabby cloth. Just as Laomedon had reneged on his deal with Heracles, so now did Eurystheus. On his return from Troy, Heracles undertook his Tenth (and, as he thought, final) Labor—the transportation across the Mediterranean world of the monster Geryon's enormous herd of red cattle—only to be told by Eurystheus that two of the earlier Labors he had completed would not be counted, and that the ten must now become twelve.[17] Thus it was that three full years passed before Heracles found himself free from bondage and able to turn his attention to the matter of King Laomedon's treachery, a grievance that had only grown and festered with time.

He raised a volunteer army and sailed a flotilla of eighteen penteconters, fifty-oared vessels, across the Aegean. At the port of Ilium, he left Oicles in charge of the ships and reserve troops and set out with Telamon and the larger part of his army to confront Laomedon. The wily Trojan king had been alerted by scouts to the arrival of the Greeks and managed to outmaneuver Heracles, leaving the city of Troy and wheeling round behind to attack Oicles and the ships. By the time Heracles had discovered what was happening, Oicles and the reserves had all been killed and Laomedon's forces were safely back behind the walls of Troy, preparing themselves for a long siege.

In the end, Telamon broke through one of the gates and the Greeks poured in. They hacked their way mercilessly through to the palace. Heracles, a little behind, came through the breach in the wall and heard his men cheering Telamon.

"Surely he is the greatest warrior of them all!"

"Hail Telamon, our general!"

This was more than Heracles could bear. One of his red mists descended. Roaring in fury, he stormed through to find and kill his deputy.

Telamon, at the head of his troops, was about to enter Laomedon's palace when he heard the commotion behind him. Knowing his friend and the terrifying effects of his jealous rages, he immediately set about gathering stones. He was in the act of building them up, one above the other, when a panting Heracles reached him, club raised.

"Sh!" said Telamon. "Not now. I'm busy building an altar."

"An altar? Who to?"

"Why, to you, of course. To Heracles. To commemorate your rescue of Hesione, your breaking of the siege of Troy, your mastery of men, monsters, and the mechanics of war."

"Oh." Heracles lowered his club. "Well, that's good of you. Very good. I . . . yes, very considerate. Very proper."

"Least I could do."

Arm in arm the pair ascended the steps of the royal palace of Troy.

The slaughter that followed was terrible. Laomedon, his wife, and all their sons were killed—that is to say, all their sons but the youngest, whose name was PODARCES. His salvation came about in unusual fashion.

---

17. The discounted labors were the Second—the Lernaean Hydra—and the Fifth—the Augean Stables. For further details, see *Heroes*, page 90.

Heracles, his club and sword dripping with the blood of half the royal line of Troy, found himself in Hesione's bedchamber. The princess was kneeling on the floor. She spoke very calmly.

"Take my life, so that I may join my father and my brothers."

Heracles was in the act of complying with her wishes when Telamon came into the room. "No! Not Hesione!"

Heracles turned in some surprise. "Why not?"

"You saved her life once. Why take it now? Besides, she is beautiful."

Heracles understood. "Take her. She's yours to do with as you please."

"If she will have me," said Telamon, "I will take her back home, to Salamis, to be my bride."

"But you have a wife," said Heracles.

Just then a sound from under the bed caught his ear.

"Come out, come out!" he called, stabbing there with his sword.

A young boy emerged, covered in dust. He rose up to what full dignified height he could manage.

"If I must die, then I do so willingly as a proud prince of Troy," he said, and then ruined the noble effect with a sneeze.

"How many sons did the man *have?*" said Heracles, raising the sword once more.

Hesione cried out and pulled at Telamon's arm. "Not Podarces! He's so young. Please, Lord Heracles, I beg you."

Heracles was not to be persuaded. "He may be young, but he is his father's son. A harmless boy can soon grow into a powerful enemy."

"Let me buy his freedom," urged Hesione. "I have a veil of gold tissue that they say was once the property of Aphrodite herself. I offer it to you in return for my brother's life and freedom."

Heracles was not impressed. "I can take it anyway. All of Troy is mine by right of conquest."

"With respect, lord, you will never find it. It is lodged in a secret hiding place."

Telamon nudged Heracles. "Worth at least taking a look, don't you think?"

Heracles grunted his assent and Hesione went over to a tall, intricately carved cabinet that stood beside the bed. Her fingers released a hidden catch at the cabinet's rear and a drawer slid out from the side. She drew from it a length of gold tissue and passed it to Heracles.

"Its value cannot be estimated."

Heracles examined the veil. It was marvelous how the material flowed almost like water through his fingers. He put an enormous hand on the boy's shoulder. "Well, young Podarces, you are lucky that your sister loves you," he said, and tucked the veil into his belt. "And your sister is lucky that my friend Telamon seems to love *her*."

Heracles and his forces left Troy a ruin. The ships of the Trojan navy were commandeered and loaded with all the treasure the Greeks could fit into the holds. Hesione, carried aboard by Telamon, looked back toward the city of her birth. Smoke rose up everywhere, the walls were breached in a dozen places. Troy, once so fine and strong, had been reduced to broken stones and smoldering ashes.

Inside the city, the Trojans picked their way over the corpses and rubble. Their attention was drawn to the sight of a youth, barely more than a boy, standing outside the temple of the Palladium, which had at least been spared. Surely, that was young Prince Podarces?

"Citizens of Troy," the boy shouted. "Do not despair!"

"How come he's still alive?"

"I heard he hid under his sister's bed."

"Princess Hesione bought his freedom."

"He was bought?"

"For the price of a golden veil."

"*Bought!*"

"Yes," cried Podarces, "I was bought. You may say it was my sister, you may say it was the gods. There is a reason for all things. I, Podarces, of the blood of Tros and Ilus, tell you this. Troy will rise again. We will build her up so that she is finer, richer, stronger, and greater than she ever was before. Greater than any city in the world in all mortal history."

Despite his youth, and the dirt and dust that clung to him, the Trojans could not fail to be impressed by the strength and conviction that rang in his voice.

"I am not ashamed that my sister bought my freedom," he went on. "It may be that time will prove me worth the expense. I prophesy that, in buying me, Hesione ransomed Troy itself. For I am Troy. As I grow to manhood so Troy will grow to greatness."

Ludicrous for one so young to be so self-confident, and yet no one could deny the lad had presence. The Trojans joined Podarces in kneeling down and casting up a prayer to the gods.

So it was that, from that day on, Podarces led his people and directed the rebuilding of their ruined city. He did not mind that everyone now called him "the One Who Was Bought," which in the Trojan language was PRIAM. In time that became his name.

We will leave young Priam, standing proud among the ashes and rubble of Troy, and travel over the sea to Greece. Things worth taking note of are happening there.

THE BROTHERS

We left Telamon sailing to Salamis with his new bride Hesione. Telamon and his family play an important enough role in the story of Troy to justify our going back in time to look at their origins. Once again I charge you not to remember every detail, but following these stories—these "origin stories" as we might call them now—is worthwhile and enough will stick in the memory as we go. Besides, they are excellent stories.

Telamon and his brother PELEUS grew up on the island of Aegina, a prosperous naval and commercial power situated in the Saronic Gulf, the bay that lies between the Argolid to the west and Attica, Athens, and mainland Greece to the east.[18] Their father AEACUS, the island's founder king, was a son of Zeus and Aegina, a water nymph who gave the island its name. The boys grew up in the royal palace as loyally close as brothers can happily be, and as arrogantly entitled as princely grandsons of Zeus can less happily be. Their mother ENDEIS, a daughter of the centaur CHIRON and the nymph Chariclo, doted on them, and a future of comfort and easy power seemed assured. As usual, the FATES had other ideas.

King Aeacus turned away from Endeis and consorted with the sea nymph Psamathe, who presented him with a son, PHOCUS. As aging fathers will, King Aeacus doted on his youngest child, the "consolation for my old age" as he lovingly called him. Phocus grew into a popular and athletic boy, the darling of the palace. Endeis could not abide the role of neglected first wife and became consumed by a jealous hatred of Psamathe and her child, a jealousy shared by the boy's half-brothers, Telamon and Peleus, now in their early twenties.

"Look at him, swaggering around the place as if he owned it . . ." hissed Endeis, as she and her sons, from behind a column, watched Phocus march down a corridor, making trumpet noises.

"If Father gets his way, he *will* own it . . ." said Telamon.

"Loathsome little brat . . ." muttered Peleus. "Someone should teach him a lesson."

"We can do more than that," said Endeis. She lowered her voice to a whisper. "Aeacus is planning a pentathlon in honor of Artemis. I think we should persuade little Phocus to enter. Now listen . . ."

Phocus had never been more excited about anything. A pentathlon! And his big brothers were urging him to take part. He had always imagined that they didn't like him very much. Perhaps it was because he had been too young to join

---

18. See the map on pages 10-11. The Argolid, or Argolis, is the name given to the (sometimes loosely confederated) city-states of Corinth, Mycenae, Tiryns, Epidaurus, Troezen, and Argos.

in with their hunting expeditions. This must be a sign that they now thought him grown up enough.

"You'll need to practice," Peleus warned.

"Oh yes," said Telamon. "We don't want you to make a fool of yourself in front of the king and the court."

"I won't let you down," said Phocus earnestly. "I'll practice every hour of every day, I promise."

From the shelter of a stand of trees Telamon and Peleus watched their little brother throwing his discus in a field outside the palace walls. He was disconcertingly good.

"How can someone that size throw it so far?" asked Telamon.

Peleus held up his own discus and weighed it in his hands. "I can throw further," he said. Taking aim, he turned, twisted his body round and released. The discus flew flat and fast through the air and struck Phocus on the back of the head. The boy went down without a sound.

The brothers raced to the spot. Phocus was quite dead.

"An accident," whispered the panicked Telamon. "We were all practicing and he ran in front of your throw."

"I don't know," said Peleus, white in the face. "Will we be believed? The whole court knows how much we resented him."

They gazed down at the body, exchanged glances, nodded, and grasped each other firmly by the forearms by way of sealing an unspoken bond. Twenty minutes later they were spreading dried leaves and twigs over the bare earth beneath which their young half-brother's body lay buried.

When word spread around the palace and grounds that Prince Phocus was missing, no one could have been more anxious to find him than Endeis and her sons. While Endeis patted the hand of her hated rival Psamathe and poured words of hope into her ear, Telamon and Peleus noisily joined the hue and cry.

King Aeacus had climbed onto the roof of the palace and from this high vantage point he called down in an ever more frantic voice the name of his beloved young son into the fields and woods on all sides. He was interrupted by a shy cough. A dusty and begrimed old slave was approaching him.

"What are you doing up here?"

The old slave bowed low. "Forgive me, lord king, I know where the young prince is."

"Where?"

"I come up to these roofs every day, your majesty. It's my job to keep everything watertight with thatch and pitch. Around noontide I chanced to look down and I saw it. I saw it all."

The roofer led the king to the spot where Phocus was buried. Peleus and Telamon were summoned, confessed their crime, and found themselves banished from the kingdom of their birth.

TELAMON IN EXILE

Telamon made his way to the nearby island of Salamis, ruled over by King CYCHREUS, whose mother, the sea nymph Salamis, gave the island its name.[19] Cychreus took a liking to Telamon and—as only kings, priests, and immortals could—he offered to cleanse him of his abominable blood crime of fratricide.[20] This done, he appointed Telamon his heir, giving him his daughter Glauce's hand in marriage. In due course Glauce presented her husband with a baby son of magnificent size, weight, and lustiness, whom they named AJAX, a name which would one day be known in every corner of the world (usually prefixed by the words "the mighty").[21]

We have already followed Telamon's later adventures and seen how he helped Heracles revenge himself on Laomedon. After the sack of Troy and the slaughter of the entire Trojan royal male line (save Priam), Telamon returned to Salamis with his prize, Hesione, by whom he had another son, TEUCER, who was to make a name for himself as the greatest of the Greek archers.[22]

We are more or less done with Telamon now. He featured as a kind of lieutenant to great heroes like Jason, Meleager, and Heracles, but his importance to us in the telling of the tale of Troy is in his fathering of those two sons, Ajax and Teucer. The same could be said of his brother Peleus. But the son of Peleus

---

19. Salamis was a sister of Aegina, which makes Cychreus, what . . . ? I'm so bad at kindred and affinity . . . Telamon's grandmother's sister's son would be his . . . ? A cousin of some sort, at least.

20. See the story of BELLEROPHON in *Heroes* (page 126) for a similar example of blood crime and its expiation through kingly intercession.

21. Other versions attest to Cychreus's daughter Periboea being the mother of Ajax by Telamon. There is also a source that makes Glauce, not Endeis, the mother of Telamon, and also, by him, the mother of Ajax. But we need not concern ourselves with all these variant and mind-fogging details. Suffice to say, Telamon fathered Ajax the Great. The name *Ajax*, incidentally, or *Aias* as the Greeks more commonly rendered it, derives from a word meaning "to mourn" or "lament" (a cross between those words of pain and despair "Aiee!" and "Alas!"), although the poet Pindar claims it derives from *aetos*, "eagle." To make matters more complicated, as we will discover, there were *two* warriors called Ajax/Aias who fought for the Greek side in the Trojan War: but more on that later.

22. Once more demonstrating the onomastic minefield that must be negotiated when tiptoeing around the stories of Greek myth, for the Trojans had a Teucer too—one of the founding kings of the Troad, Dardanus's predecessor.

was so much more important to our story, and the manner of his birth so remarkable, that Peleus himself deserves more attention.

PELEUS IN EXILE

When the brothers were banished from Aegina for the killing of young Prince Phocus, Peleus went further afield than Telamon. He crossed the Greek mainland and traveled north to the small kingdom of Phthia in Aeolia. It was no random choice: these were ancestral lands. We must go back in time to find out the connection between Aegina in the south and Phthia in the north.

You will recall that Peleus's father Aeacus was the son of Zeus and the sea nymph Aegina. HERA, as ever ragingly jealous of her husband's affairs, had waited until Aeacus grew to manhood before sending a plague to the island which wiped out the human population, all but Aeacus.

Alone and unhappy, Aeacus wandered his island praying to his father Zeus for help. Falling into a sleep under a tree he was awoken by a column of ants marching over his face. He looked around and saw a whole colony swarming about him.

"Father Zeus!" he cried out. "Only let there be as many mortals to keep me company on this island as there are ants on this tree."

He caught Zeus in a good mood. In answer to his son's prayer the King of the Gods transformed the ants into people, whom Aeacus called the Myrmidons after *myrmex*, the Greek word for ant. In time most of the Myrmidons left Aegina and made their home in Phthia. And that is the reason Peleus chose Phthia as a place for exile and expiation: to be with the Myrmidons.[23]

EURYTION, Phthia's king, welcomed Peleus and—just as Cychreus of Salamis had done for Telamon—cleansed him of his crime, appointed him heir, and gave him his daughter in marriage.

Marriage to the king's daughter ANTIGONE;[24] the birth of a girl, Polydora; high status in Phthia as heir apparent to the throne of the Myrmidons; purification from his crime—things looked good for Peleus. But he and Telamon were made of energetic, restless material, and the settled domesticity of married life suited neither. Over the coming years they distinguished themselves on board the *Argo* in the quest for the Golden Fleece, and afterwards, like so many of the

23. Here we say goodbye to Aeacus. It is worth noting, however, that after Aeacus's death his father Zeus rewarded him (if it can be said to be a reward) by setting him up as one of the three Judges of the Underworld, along with his Cretan half-brothers Minos and Rhadamanthus. See *Mythos* (page 133) and *Heroes* (page 144).

24. Not to be confused with the Theban Antigone, daughter of Oedipus: see *Heroes*, page 256.

Argonaut veterans, they flocked to Calydon to join in the hunt for the monstrous boar that Artemis had sent to ravage the countryside there.[25] In the heat of that legendary chase, Peleus's spear went wide and fatally wounded his father-in-law Eurytion. Accident or no accident, this was another blood crime, another kin-slaying, and Peleus once more found himself in need of royal expiation.

The king who offered to cleanse him this time was ACASTUS, the son of Jason's old enemy Pelias; and so now it was to Acastus's Aeolian kingdom of Iolcos that Peleus made his way.[26] Bear with me, reader.

By this time, Peleus had outgrown the unappealing characteristics that had caused him to play so monstrous a part in the killing of his young half-brother Phocus, and he was now recognized by all to be a modest, amiable, and charming man. So modest, so charming, so amiable—and so handsome too—that it was not long before Acastus's wife ASTYDAMEIA found herself overcome by desire for Peleus. She came to his bedchamber one night and did everything she could to seduce him, but with no success. His sense of propriety as a guest and friend of Acastus froze him in horror as she repeatedly pushed her body against his. Stung by the rejection, Astydameia turned her love to hate.

Those of you who know the story of Bellerophon and Stheneboea, or of THESEUS's son Hippolytus and Phaedra,[27] or indeed that of Joseph and Potiphar's wife in the book of Genesis, will be familiar with the mytheme or recurrent trope of the "woman scorned" and how it inevitably unwinds. Hot with mortification, Astydameia sent a message to Peleus's wife Antigone, who was home in Phthia raising their daughter Polydora.

"Antigone, this is to advise you that your husband Peleus, whom you thought so faithful, is now betrothed to my stepdaughter Sterope. I can imagine how painful for you this news must be. Peleus has made no secret of his distaste for you. Your figure since giving birth, he tells the court, is now as plump and squashy as an overripe fig and he cannot bear the sight of you. It is as well you hear this from me and not from one who wishes you ill. Your friend, Astydameia."

After Antigone heard this message she went out and hanged herself.

---

25. See *Heroes*, pages 167 and 225.

26. You will already be aware of how confusing it can be to have so many similar words and names in these stories. Peleus is not to be confused with Pelias or the mountain which was soon to be his home, Pelion. In fact, even though the mountain is called Pelion in the much earlier story of the giants who tried to heap it up on top of Mount Ossa (see *Mythos*, page 216), it is possible that it took its name from Peleus, which means "muddy." Perhaps Pelias, who came from this area, has a similar meaning. Maybe the Greeks thought Aeolia an especially muddy part of the world . . . Being a mountainous region it certainly gets more rainfall than most of Greece. Another potential and rather less charming meaning of the word is "the dark color of extravasated blood" . . .

27. See *Heroes*, pages 126 and 314.

Even such a terrible outcome was not enough for the vengeful Astydameia, who now approached her husband with bowed head and choked sobs.

"Oh, my husband . . ." she began.

"Whatever is the matter?" said Acastus.

"No, I cannot say. No, I cannot . . ."

"I command you to tell me what is troubling you."

The terrible story came tumbling out. How the lustful Peleus had come to her bedchamber and tried to force himself upon her. How she had repulsed the rape and written to advise Antigone of her husband's faithlessness. How Antigone in her humiliation and grief had taken her own life. How Astydameia had wanted to keep all this from Acastus, who seemed so fond of Peleus . . . But now he had pried it from her . . . Oh dear, she hoped she had not done wrong in telling him . . . ?

Even as Acastus comforted his wife, his mind set itself on an implacable course. He knew he had to be careful, however. It would be an infraction of the sacred laws of hospitality to kill his guest. Not only that, Peleus was a grandson of Zeus. To lay hands upon him would be foolhardy. Nonetheless, Acastus was determined to ensure the death of the wanton and depraved villain who had dared lay hands on his wife.

The next day he and his courtiers took their young guest out on a hunting expedition. In the late afternoon, Peleus, exhausted from the chase, found a grassy bank at the edge of a dark wood and sank into a deep sleep. Signaling for silence from his men, Acastus stole up to him and took his sword, a powerful weapon forged by HEPHAESTUS and given to Peleus's father by Zeus himself. Acastus hid it in a nearby dungheap and, grinning with delight, he and his men tiptoed away, leaving Peleus locked in sleep. Acastus knew that at night the region was made lethally dangerous by marauding centaurs, half horse, half human, who would surely find Peleus and kill him. Sure enough, not two hours later a herd of wild centaurs on the fringe of the wood sniffed the air and detected the scent of a human.

Now, everyone has two grandfathers.[28] On his father's side Peleus had Zeus and on his mother's side the wise, learned, and noble Chiron, the immortal centaur who had been tutor to ASCLEPIUS and Jason.[29] It happened, that evening, that Chiron was among the band of centaurs that emerged from the woods and cantered toward the sleeping Peleus. Chiron overtook the others at a gallop, awoke Peleus, and recovered his sword. After they had seen off the other centaurs, they embraced. Peleus was quite Chiron's favorite grandson.

---

28. . . . unless you are the issue of an incestuous coupling, of course.

29. Asclepius was the great healer who had been raised to divine status as the god of medicine. See *Mythos*, page 210.

Chiron and the Centaurs

"I have watched over you," said the centaur. "You have been the victim of a great wrong."

Peles learned from Chiron what Astydameia had done and wept with sorrow for the loss of Antigone and with rage at the injustice that had been practiced on him. He went back to Phthia, erected a tomb for his dead wife, and returned to Iolcos with an army of his best Phthian soldiers—the elite Myrmidons. Acastus was killed, the wicked Astydameia cut into pieces, and Thessalus—the son of Peleus's old friend Jason—installed on the throne. From that point on, Aeolia became known as Thessaly, as it is to this day.

Rather than return to Phthia and live the life of a prince and heir, Peleus accepted an offer from Chiron to spend time with him in his mountain cave in order to learn at the feet of that renowned centaur.[30] There was much wisdom and knowledge that Chiron could impart, and life on Mount Pelion proceeded for a year or so in a quiet rhythm. But Chiron began to detect in Peleus a new restlessness that amounted to something like sorrow.

"Something disturbs you," he said one evening. "Tell me what it is. You are not attending to your studies with the joy and zeal that you once did. You gaze down onto the sea and there is a lost look in your eyes. Do you still grieve for your Antigone?"

Peleus turned to face him. "I have to confess that I do not," he said. "It is another love."

---

30. "At the *hoofs*" would be more precise.

"But you have hardly seen anyone for a year."

"I saw her a long time ago. When I was sailing with Jason. But I have never forgotten her."

"Tell me."

"Oh, it is so foolish. I was leaning on the stern of the *Argo* one night. Have you ever seen how a green light shines from the sea sometimes?"

"I am not a practiced sailor," said Chiron.

"No, of course." Peleus smiled at the thought of Chiron's hoofs clattering and skidding on a slippery deck. "Well, take it from me, sometimes you see at night an enchanted light glow in the water."

"Sea nymphs, no doubt."

"No doubt. I think perhaps that particular night we were sailing over the sea palace of Poseidon himself. The lights were especially bright. I leaned out further and a creature rose up from the water. I have never seen anything or anyone so beautiful."

"Ah."

"She stared at me and I stared back. It seemed like an age. And then a dolphin broke the surface. The spell was gone and she dropped back down into the deep. I was in a dream . . ." Peleus stopped, reliving the moment.

Chiron waited. He was sure there must be more to come.

"You may know," Peleus said at last, "that the figurehead on the prow-beak of the *Argo* was carved out of timber that was taken from the sacred oak grove of Dodona and was endowed with the gift of prophecy?"

Chiron bowed his head to show that he was familiar with this well-known truth.

"I consulted it. 'Who was that creature?' I asked. 'Who was she?' The figurehead replied, 'Why, who else but THETIS, your future bride?' That was all the answer I could get. *Thetis*. I have asked around. Priests and wise men are agreed that there is a sea nymph of that name. But who is she, Chiron? Every night when I sleep, the image of her rises up before me just as she did from the waves."

"Thetis, you say?"

"Well? Have you heard of her?"

"Heard of her? We are family. Cousins, I suppose you would call it. We have in common TETHYS as a grandmother."[31]

"Is she . . . ?"

---

31. Tethys was one of the original twelve Titan children of the primordial divine beings OURANOS and GAIA; along with Pontus, Thalassa, and OCEANUS, she was an original deity of the seas and oceans (see *Mythos*, page 24). Geologists named the ancient Mesozoic sea that once covered much of what is now Europe and western Asia after her.

"Thetis is as beautiful and desirable as you remember. All the gods have at one time or another fallen for her matchless graces—"

"I knew it," groaned Peleus.

"Let me finish," said Chiron. "All the gods have at one time fallen under the spell of her beauty, Zeus in particular. But many years ago, mankind's champion, the Titan PROMETHEUS, revealed a prophecy about Thetis that has stopped all gods and demigods from daring to approach her."

"There is a curse?"

"For the gods it would be a heavy curse indeed, but not perhaps for you, a mortal. Prometheus foretold that any son born of Thetis would grow up to be greater than his father. You can imagine, I am sure, that no Olympian wishes to father a son who might eclipse, or perhaps depose, them. Ouranos, the first Lord of the Sky, was overthrown by his son KRONOS, who was in turn overthrown by *his* son Zeus,[32] who entertains, you may be certain, no desire for the cycle to be repeated. Despite Thetis's beauty and his own lustful nature, all these years the King of Heaven has let her be. Nor has any other Olympian dared to consort with her."

---

32. See *Mythos*, pages 33 and 50.

◈ The Procession of Thetis

Peleus clapped his hands in delight. "That is all? A fear that their son could rise to be greater than them? Why should *I* worry about such a thing? I would be proud to father a boy who might outshine me in fame and glory, why should I not?"

Chiron smiled. "Not all gods, nor indeed all men, are like you, Peleus."

Peleus waved the compliment, if compliment it was, aside. "It is all very well," he said with a touch of moodiness now, as the cold reality dawned on him, "but the seas are vast and wide. How could I ever find her?"

"Oh, as to that . . . Did your friend Heracles never tell you the story of his encounter with her father?"

"Oceanus?"

"No, Thetis is a Nereid.[33] It all happened when Heracles was sent to fetch the Golden Apples of the HESPERIDES, the Eleventh of his Labors. He had no idea where to find them. The nymphs of the River Eridanus told him that he should seek out Nereus, son of Pontus and Gaia. But like Proteus—like most deities of water, in fact—Nereus can change his shape at will. Heracles had to hold the old sea god tight while he turned himself into all manner of creatures. At last his energy was drained. He submitted and told Heracles everything he wanted to know. Nereus's daughter Thetis is the same. She will only yield to one who can hold her fast no matter how many alterations to her form she makes."

"I don't have Heracles's strength," said Peleus.

"But you have passion, you have purpose!" said Chiron, stamping a hoof in impatience. "What you felt when you looked down at the *Argo*'s wake and saw Thetis rise up—is that feeling strong enough to hold her?"

"Strong enough?" said Peleus, and then again with rising conviction, "Certainly it is strong enough!"

"Then go down to the shore and call to her."

THE WEDDING AND THE APPLE

Peleus stood on the shore of the Aegean and called for Thetis until his throat was raw. From the cliffs and mountains shadows slowly flowed onto the beach like a dark tide as HELIOS and his sun-chariot dipped down into the west behind him. Soon SELENE rode across the sky overhead throwing silver-blue

---

33. In Greek the *—id* or *—ides* ending denotes "descended from," indicating the paternal line. So the offspring of the sea god NEREUS are *NEREIDS*, of Oceanus *OCEANIDS*, of Heracles the *Heraclides*, and so on. Thetis's mother was an Oceanid whose name, although a perfectly good Greek name for a girl, will usually cause the modern reader to smile—Doris.

light from her moon-chariot onto the wet sand at Peleus's feet. Still he stared into the black waters and hoarsely cried out Thetis's name. At last . . .

Was he dreaming, or was that a pale form far out rising from the waves? It seemed to be growing in size.

"Thetis?"

She was close enough to land to be able to stand. Only ribbons of seaweed covered her sleek nakedness as she trod the sand toward him.

"What mortal presumes to summon me? Oh!" She came toward him so quickly that he cringed back in fear. "I know that face. You dared one night to fix me with a stare. What was in that look? It disturbed me."

"It . . . it was love."

"Oh, *love*. Is that all? I thought I saw something else, something I cannot name. I see it still."

"Destiny?"

Thetis threw back her head to laugh. Her wet throat, necklaced by a thin trail of seaweed, was more beautiful than anything Peleus had seen in the whole world. Now was his chance. He lunged forward and grasped her around the waist. Instantly he felt his arms widen and his hands slip. Thetis had disappeared and he was holding a twisting dolphin in his arms. He hugged so hard the blood sang in his ears and he almost fell as the dolphin suddenly became an octopus. Then it was an eel, a sea-eagle, a jellyfish, a seal . . . more different forms than he could count. Not wanting to be put off by the terrifying oddness of what he was seeing and doing, Peleus closed his eyes, braced his legs, strengthened his grip and held fast, feeling the different textures of spikiness, slipperiness, silkiness, and softness until there came a gasp and a cry. Drained by the enormous expenditure of energy that it took to change shape so many times and with such rapidity, Thetis had yielded. When Peleus opened his eyes, she was draped in his arms, flushed and finished.

"I was right," said Peleus in a tender voice. "It was ordained. You are not defeated. You are not in *my* hands, you are in the hands of MOROS.[34] We both are."

There, on the wet sand, he laid her down and as lovingly as he knew, he made her his.

There was relief on Olympus. The dangerous prophecy of Prometheus could now apply only to Peleus who—fine fellow as he was, noble warrior, excellent prince and all that—could hardly be counted in the first rank of mortal heroes, to be mentioned in the same breath as Theseus, Jason, Perseus, or Heracles.

---

34. The Greek personification of destiny: see *Mythos*, page 31.

He was welcome to father a child who might prove to be greater than himself. Besides, he was likeable, as was Thetis.

When the couple tentatively put out word that they were to be married by Chiron in his cave on Mount Pelion, every one of the Olympians—indeed all the gods, demigods, and minor deities—paid them the inestimable compliment of accepting their invitation to attend the last great gathering of the immortals that the world would know. All the gods, demigods, and minor deities? All but *one . . .*

There was seating room in Chiron's cave only for the centaur himself, the twelve Olympian gods, and the happy couple themselves. Perhaps "happy" is too strong a word, but by this time Thetis had accepted her fate. She was well aware of Prometheus's prophecy, but a maternal flame she had never suspected to harbor had flickered into life within her, glowed brighter, and was now blazing with a fierce heat. She felt exultant at the prospect of bearing in her immortal womb a child destined for greatness.

The divine guests of honor took their seats in two semicircular rows at the back of the cave, Zeus enthroned in the center, flanked on the one side by his wife Hera, Queen of Heaven and goddess of matrimony, and on the other by his favorite daughter Athena. The other Olympians jostled for position around and behind like spoiled children. DEMETER, goddess of fertility, less vain, sat quietly in the back row beside her daughter PERSEPHONE, Queen of the Underworld, who was there to represent HADES, who never ventured into the upper world. The twins Apollo and Artemis beat Poseidon and Ares to places in the front, and Aphrodite slipped determinedly next to Hera, who bowed her head stiffly at Hermes who had entered laughing with DIONYSUS and the limping Hephaestus. When the Olympians had at last disposed themselves with what dignity they could muster, senior demigods and Titans were ushered by Chiron into standing positions around the rest of the cave, leaving a kind of central aisle down which the bride and groom might process.

Outside, nymphs of the seas, mountains, forests, meadows, rivers, and trees sat on the grass at the mouth of the cave and whispered to each other, almost beside themselves with excitement. So complete a gathering of the immortals in one place had not taken place since the ceremony of the installation of the Twelve on Mount Olympus.[35] They were all here.

All but one . . .

The goat-footed god PAN skipped around his band of satyrs, fauns, dryads, and hamadryads, piping a tune so raucous to the gods' ears that Hermes was sent out from the cave to command his wild son, in Zeus's name, to stop.

---

35. See *Mythos*, page 108.

◈   The Marriage of Thetis and Peleus

"That's better," said Hermes, ruffling the coarse fur that curled between the horns on Pan's head. "Now we can all enjoy the privilege of hearing Apollo fumble with my lyre."[36]

The Oceanids and Nereids were closest to the cave's mouth. One of their own was being wed to a mortal hero, which was nothing—many sea nymphs had married Titans and even gods—but never had such an alliance been honored by the presence of all the deities.

All but one . . .

The gods had bestowed glorious presents upon the couple. Of especial note were a pair of magnificent horses, Balius and Xanthus, the gift of the sea god Poseidon.[37] Balius, the dapple grey, and Xanthus, his bay twin, were grazing outside the cave when the sound of a sudden clanging made them start up and whinny in alarm.

---

36. The lyre had been the invention of the precocious infant Hermes on the day of his birth: see *Mythos*, page 103.

37. Poseidon is generally considered to have "invented" the horse.

HESTIA, goddess of the hearth and home, was sounding the gong to announce the start of the ceremony. A hush descended. The gods settled themselves; those in the front row who had turned round to speak to those behind now faced forward and adopted expressions of solemn intent. Hera smoothed her gown. Zeus sat more erectly, his head and chin raised so that his beard pointed toward the cave's entrance. As if following, all within the cave turned their heads in the same direction.

The nymphs held their breath. The whole world held its breath. How glorious were the gods, how majestic, how powerful, how perfect.

Arm in arm Thetis and Peleus walked slowly in. The bridal couple, as bridal couples always do, outshone every guest—even the very gods of Olympus—for this, their brief starring moment.

Prometheus, at the back of the cave, was hardly able to watch. His prophetic mind could not foresee in detail what the future held, but he felt sure that this gathering would be the last of its kind. The very grandeur and glory of the ceremony could only betoken some kind of collapse. The moment when flowers and fruits are at their fullest and ripest is the moment that precedes their fall, their decay, their rot, their death. Prometheus felt the coming of a storm. He could not say how or why, but he knew that this wedding feast was somehow a part of it, and that the child of Peleus and Thetis would be a part of it too. The coming storm smelled metallic, as the air always does before thunder. It smelled of copper and tin. Mortal blood smelled of copper and tin too. Copper and tin. Bronze. The metal of war. In his head Prometheus heard the sound of bronze clashing on bronze and saw blood raining down over all. Yet outside the cave the sky was blue and every face except his own was bright with joy.

All but the twelve Olympians now rose to their feet as Peleus and Thetis came through the mouth of the cave, the one smiling proudly, the other with head cast sweetly down.

I think too much, Prometheus told himself. It's no more than a headache. Look how happy they all are, all the immortals.

All?

Prometheus could not rid his mind of the idea that there was one missing . . .

Hestia anointed the bridal couple with oils while Apollo's son HYMENAIOS sang in praise of the gods and the bliss of matrimony. No sooner had Hera sat down after blessing the union than a commotion was heard at the mouth of the cave. The crowd of nymphs and dryads outside tumbled apart in a flurry of confusion as the one deity who had not been invited strode through. The form was silhouetted in the entrance but Prometheus recognized her at once—ERIS, goddess of strife, feuding, discord, and disarray. He understood that to have invited her to a wedding feast would have been to court upset. But *not* to have invited her, surely that was to court disaster too?

The congregation parted as Eris stalked down to face the semicircle of enthroned Olympians. She put a hand inside her cloak. Something round and bright rolled along the ground and stopped at the feet of Zeus. She turned and left the way she had come, through the crowd of frozen and dumbfounded guests. She had not uttered a word. So swift and sudden were Eris's entrance and exit that some in the cave wondered if they might have imagined it. But the object at Zeus's feet was real enough. What could it be?

Zeus leaned down to pick it up. It was an apple. A golden apple.[38]

Zeus turned it over carefully in his hands.

Hera looked over his shoulder. "There is writing on it," she said sharply. "What does it say?"

Zeus frowned and peered closely at the golden surface of the apple. "It says, 'To the Fairest.'"[39]

"'To the Fairest'? Eris honors me greatly." Hera put out her hand.

Zeus was about to pass the apple obediently to his wife when a low voice murmured on his other side.

"The world will agree, Hera, that the apple must surely be mine." The grey eyes of Athena locked with the brown eyes of Hera.

A silver ripple of laughter came from behind them both as Aphrodite stretched out *her* hand to Zeus. "Let us not be foolish. There is only one to whom the words 'To the Fairest' could possibly apply. Give me the apple, Zeus, for it can be meant for no one else."

Zeus dropped his head and vented a deep sigh. How could he choose between his beloved and powerful wife Hera, his adored favorite child Athena, and his aunt, the powerful goddess of love herself, Aphrodite? He clutched the apple tight and wished he could be somewhere else.

"Cheer up, father." Hermes came before him, leading a reluctant Ares. "What you need is someone we can all trust to make the decision and award the apple on your behalf, yes? Well, it so happens that we met just such a person not long ago, didn't we, Ares? A young man of honest, impartial, and unimpeachably reliable judgment."

Zeus stared. "Who?"

---

38. One of the Golden Apples of the Hesperides. These magical fruits had played their part in the Eleventh Labor of Heracles and in the winning of ATALANTA by Hippomenes: see *Heroes*, pages 91 and 232. Since they were originally a wedding present from Gaia, primordial goddess of the earth, to her grandchildren Zeus and Hera, the appearance of one of them at this last great wedding of the Olympian Age offers a grim circular symmetry.

39. *Te kalliste*: "to the most beautiful." *Kalos* is the Greek word for "beautiful"—as in "calisthenics," "calligraphy," and so on.

THE QUEEN'S DREAM

To find out who, we have to travel across the Aegean Sea and back once more to the plain of Ilium. We left Troy, you remember, a smoldering ruin. The male line of Ilus, Tros, and Laomedon had been expunged by the vengeful forces of Heracles and Telamon. Only the youngest, Podarces, had escaped the slaughter. In letting Podarces live—or Priam, as the world now called him—Heracles had spared a remarkable prince who had grown into an outstanding ruler.

Within the magnificent shell of the great walls and gates constructed by Apollo and Poseidon, Priam had set about rebuilding Troy around the site of the temple of the Palladium which, out of respect for Athena, Heracles and Telamon had also spared. Priam revealed himself to be a natural leader with a passion for detail and a deep understanding of the workings of trade and exchange—what we would call today economics, commerce, and finance. The city's place at the mouth of the Hellespont—the straits through which all sea traffic to and from the east were obliged by geography to pass—afforded Troy tremendous opportunities for enrichment, opportunities that King Priam seized with acumen and an astute intelligence. The tolls and tariffs rolled in and the kingdom grew in greatness and prosperity. Even if it were not for the wealth generated from trade with foreign kingdoms, Troy would have been prosperous enough on account of the fertility of the land around Mount Ida. The cattle, goats, and sheep on its slopes provided milk, cheese, and meat, and the lowland fields fed by the rivers Cebren, Scamander, and Simoeis filled the barns, silos, and storehouses every year with more than enough grain, olives, and fruit to ensure that no Trojan ever went hungry.

The towers of Priam's new palace reached higher than the level of the walls and gleamed in the sun to tell the world that Troy, the Jewel of the Aegean, was the greatest city in the world, ruled over by a mighty king and prospering under the protection of the gods.

Priam's queen was called HECUBA.[40] In the early days of their marriage she had presented Priam with a son and heir, Prince HECTOR. Little more than a year later she was pregnant again. One morning, very close to the time of delivery, she awoke sweating and in great distress from a most vivid and unusual

---

40. Hecuba's origins are disputed. It was apparently a favorite game of the Roman emperor Tiberius to confound scholars by challenging them to name Hecuba's mother. "Ha! You can't!" he would crow—according to the historian Suetonius in his book *The Twelve Caesars*. It is in many ways a recognition of the apparent "completeness" of Greek myth that this story should proliferate. The expectation that every last genealogical connection in a *real*, historical dynasty could be known is asking too much—to expect such knowledge when it comes to a *mythological* family is on the face of it absurd, but such is the appeal of Greek mythology and its alluring sense of authentic detail . . .

dream. She related it to Priam who immediately called for Troy's most trusted prophet and seer, AESACUS, a son from his first marriage.[41]

"It was the strangest and most alarming thing," said Hecuba. "I dreamed that I gave birth, not to a child, but to a torch."

"A torch?" repeated Aesacus.

"A torch that burned with a great flame. Like a brand, you know? And I dreamed that I ran with this torch through the streets and alleyways of Troy and that everything around me was lit with fire. Does it mean that this birth will be more painful than the last? Or . . ." she suggested hopefully, "perhaps it means that my child is destined to light the world with a blaze of fame and glory?"

"No, majesty," said Aesacus heavily, "it means neither of those things. It means something quite different. It means . . ."

His voice trailed off and he twisted the hem of his cloak with nervous fingers.

"Do not be afraid to speak," said Priam. "Your gift is given you for a reason. Whatever you say, we will not be so foolish as to blame you for it. What does this dream tells us about our child and its destiny?"

Aesacus took a deep breath and spoke in a rush, as if trying to expel the words from his mouth and mind forever.

"It tells us that . . . that your baby will be the death of us all, the cause of the complete destruction of our city and our whole civilization. It tells us that if that child in your belly survives to manhood—for it is certain that it will be a male child—then Troy will burn to the ground, never to rise again. Ilium will be no more than a memory, a burnt page in the book of history. That is what the queen's dream tells us."

Priam and Hecuba stared at Aesacus.

"Leave us, my son," said Priam after a long silence. "Understand that you are sworn to secrecy."

Aesacus bowed his way from the room. He hurried out of the city gates without exchanging a word with a single soul. He ran and ran, deep into the countryside, to be with his beloved, Hesperia, daughter of the river god Cebren.

Aesacus never returned to Troy. Not long after Hecuba's dream Hesperia died from a venomous snakebite. Aesacus was so desolated that he threw himself from a cliff into the sea. The ancient goddess Tethys took pity on him, however, and, before he hit the water, transformed him into a seabird. A bird that in its grief would dive and dive into the depths, repeating its suicide forever.

---

41. To Arisbe, daughter of the seer Merops, King of Percote, a city to the northeast of Troy.

THE BOY WHO LIVED

Priam and Hecuba put Troy before everything. Before love, health, happiness, and family. They had not built the city up to be what it was only to risk its destruction. Aesacus's prophecy, if true, seemed cruel, random, and unwarranted, but the Fates had never been known for their mercy, justice, or reason. The future of Troy came first. The child must die.

Hecuba went into labor that very day. When the boy was born (Aesacus had been right, it was a male child), it twinkled, gurgled, and beamed with such engaging charm and unblemished beauty that neither had the heart to smother it.

Priam looked down into his son's smiling face. "We must send for AGELAUS,"[42] he said.

"Yes," said Hecuba. "It can be no one else."

Agelaus, the royal family's chief herdsman on Mount Ida, had the advantage of playing no part in city politics or palace intrigues. He was loyal and trustworthy, and he knew how to keep a secret.

He bowed before the king and queen, unable to conceal his astonishment at the sight of the baby in Hecuba's arms.

"I had not heard the happy news that a new prince or princess had come into the world," he said. "No bells were sounded, no heralds proclaimed the birth."

"No one knows," said Hecuba. "And no one must ever know."

"This baby must die," said Priam.

Agelaus stared. "Sire?"

"For the sake of Troy, he must," said Hecuba. "Take him away to Mount Ida. Kill him quickly and mercifully. Consign his body to the underworld with all proper prayers and sacrifices."

"And when you have done so, bring us proof that he is dead," said Priam. "Only when we know it is done can we begin to mourn."

Agelaus looked at his king and queen, both of whom were weeping. He opened his mouth to speak, but no words came.

"We would not ask you to do so terrible a thing," said Priam, laying a hand on the herdsman's shoulder, "you know we would not, if the survival of us all did not depend upon it."

Agelaus took the child from Hecuba's arms, put him in the leather bag he carried on his back and made his way up to his stone cottage on Mount Ida.

Looking down into the child's sweet face he found that he was no more able than Priam or Hecuba to kill something so entirely beautiful. So he climbed

---

42. Pronounced to rhyme with "badger-lay-us."

high above Ida's treeline and left the baby lying naked, squealing, and alone in a rocky cleft on the cold mountainside.

"The wild beasts will come soon enough to do what I cannot," he said to himself as he trudged heavily back down. "No one can say that Agelaus murdered a royal child."

No sooner had he disappeared from view than a she-bear—alerted by unfamiliar sounds and smells—lurched round the corner, sniffing the air and licking her lips.

As luck would have it—Luck? No, Fate, Providence, Destiny . . . *Doom*, perhaps, but not Luck, certainly not Luck. As Providence ordained, then, this bear had just that morning lost her newborn cub to a pack of wolves. She leaned down, gave the squealing baby one long lick with her huge tongue, picked it up, and pushed it to her breast.

Some days later Agelaus climbed back up to view the body and take some proof to the king and queen that their son was dead.

He could not believe his eyes when he saw the baby kicking and babbling, healthy and happy.

"Alive! Pink and plump as a prize piglet!" He took the child up and tucked him into his leather bag. "The gods want you to live, my boy, and who am I to fly in the face of the gods?"

As he slung the bag over his back and turned to go down the hillside, a huge bear reared up from behind a rock and blocked his path. Agelaus froze in fear as its growling rose into a roar, but the baby lifted its head from the bag with a gurgling chuckle and the bear dropped down on all fours, gave one long, loud, mournful howl, and lumbered away.

Back at his cottage, Agelaus placed the infant on the table and looked him in the eye. "Hungry, my little one?"

He took goat's milk from a pitcher and poured a small amount into a tightly woven woolen sack which he gently pressed to the baby's lips. He watched the child suck and guzzle until it could take no more.

There was no doubt about it, Agelaus would raise him as his own. But first he had to fulfill the promise he had made to Priam and Hecuba. They had insisted upon evidence that their boy was dead.

It so happened that Agelaus's best sheep-herding bitch had given birth to five puppies that very morning, one of which was struggling feebly, too sickly to fight for the nipple and certain to die before the day was out. Agelaus found this runt, drowned it quickly in a water trough, and cut out its tongue.

He took one last look at his new charge before starting back down for Troy. "You stay here, my little backpack boy," he whispered. "I shan't be long."

Priam and Hecuba looked at the severed tongue and their eyes filled with tears.

"Take it and bury it with the rest of him," said Hecuba. "You made all the correct sacrifices?"

"Everything was done according to the proper laws."

"It shall be given out that a royal prince died in childbirth," said Priam. "Funeral games will be held in his honor on this day every year in perpetuity."

THE TWINKLING HERDSMAN

Agelaus told his friends and fellow herders that the baby he was rearing had been left on the steps of the small temple to Hermes that stood in the foothills of the mountain. The story was easily accepted; such occurrences were common enough. Unable to think of a name for his adopted son, Agelaus continued to call him "little backpack." The Greek for backpack is *pera*, and the boy's name as he grew up was somehow mangled over time into PARIS.

On the slopes of Mount Ida, Paris grew into a beautiful and highly intelligent boy, youth, and young man. No herdsman fought better to protect his livestock or indeed his father and fellow pastoralists. No calves, lambs, or kids fell to the wolves and bears when he was in charge, no poachers or bandits dared trespass on his pastures. Among the people of the area he earned another name, Alexander, or "defender of men."

Before long, Paris met and fell in love with the oread, or mountain nymph, OENONE, a daughter of the river god Cebren.[43] They married and a paradisal idyll seemed destined for the pair.

Paris's passions in life were simple and few: the beautiful Oenone and the welfare of the flocks and herds he looked after for his father (as he thought) Agelaus. He was especially proud of the bull of his herd, a huge white animal with perfectly symmetrical horns and the most marvelous thick and curly forelocks.

"You," he told the bull, fondly slapping its flank, "are the best bull in the whole world. If ever I saw a finer, I swear I would bow down and crown it with gold. Even the gods don't have a bull as beautiful as you."

Now it so happened that the god Ares, who had a great fondness for Troy and its people, overheard this boast and told Hermes about it.

"Foolish mortal thinks his bull is more beautiful than any one of ours."

---

43. Which made Oenone a sister to Aesacus's beloved, Hesperia.

"Oh!" said Hermes, "I sense a lark."

"A lark?" said Ares.

"A jest, a jape, a joke. All you have to do is turn yourself into a bull and let me do the rest."

Hermes explained the outline of his prank and a smile spread over the war god's face.

"That'll teach the brat," he said, as he set about his transformation. Ares had no time for shepherds and agriculturalists. They lazed in fields when they could be fighting and killing.

At that moment, on the grassy lower slopes of Mount Ida, Paris was indeed lazing in a field. He was, in fact, fast asleep. A shadow falling over his face woke him. He looked up and saw a young herdsman gazing down, eyes twinkling.

"Can I help you?"

"Paris, isn't it?" said that herdsman.

"That's right. And who might you be?"

"Oh, just a humble drover of cattle. I hear you have a prize bull that you believe to be matchless?"

"That I *know* to be matchless," said Paris.

"I even heard it said that you will crown with gold any beast that's finer?"

"I did say that, as it happens," Paris admitted, puzzled. "But I didn't know anyone was listening."

"Oh, if you didn't mean it . . ." The herdsman turned to go.

"I meant it," said Paris. "Stay where you are and I'll fetch mine," said the herdsman. "I think you might regret your boast."

Hermes—for it was, of course, he—went down and drove his bull up the hill to Paris, deriving great pleasure from slapping its rump and flicking its back with a switch, not something any Olympian would normally dare to do to the combative and short-tempered god of war.

The instant Paris saw Ares-the-Bull, he conceded that this beast was broader, whiter, finer, and altogether more handsome than even his own prize animal.

"I can't believe it," he said, marveling at the thick coat and shining horns. "I thought mine could never be beaten, but this fellow . . ." He fell to the ground and began gathering all the celandines, aconites, and buttercups he could find in the grass. "My crown of gold is nothing more than a wreath of yellow flowers," he said to Hermes, arranging a garland around the horns. "But give me time to make my fortune and I will find you and reward you with real gold."

"No need," said Hermes, putting his hand on Paris's shoulder and smiling. "Your honesty is reward enough. It's a rare and beautiful thing. Even rarer and more beautiful than my bull."

JUDGMENT

Time passed and, beyond mentioning in passing to Oenone the remarkable beauty of the strange bull as an example of how there are more wonders in the world than can be found on the slopes of a mountain, Paris thought no more of the incident. He was most surprised, therefore, to be woken from a pleasant sleep one afternoon not long afterward by a shadow once more falling over him and for the shadow, after he had sat up and peered with shaded eyes against the sun, again to reveal itself to be that of the young drover.

"Oh dear," said Paris. "I hope you have not come for your gold crown already?"

"No, no," said Hermes. "I have come for something else. I bring a message from my father Zeus, who calls upon you to do him a great service."

Paris knelt in wonder. He saw now—how had he not noticed it the first time?—that the young man's face shone like that of no mortal. And how could he have missed the live snakes that writhed about his herdsman's staff, or the wings that fluttered on his sandals? This could only be Hermes, the messenger of the gods.

◈ The Judgment of Paris

"What can I, a poor herdsman and shepherd of the fields, do for the King of Heaven?"

"You can get up off your knees for a start, Paris, and come with me."

Paris scrambled to his feet and followed Hermes through to a sparsely wooded copse. The god pointed to a clearing, dappled with patches of sunlight, where Paris could make out three shining female forms. He knew at once that these were immortals. Great immortals. Goddesses. Olympian goddesses. He stood transfixed, trying to speak, but all he could do was drop to his knees.

"He does that," said Hermes. "Up, Paris. Your honesty and unclouded judgment have been noted. We have need of them now. Take this apple. See those words inscribed on it?"

"I can't make out those marks," said Paris, flushing. "I never learned."

"Not to worry. It says, 'To the Fairest.' It is for you to choose which of these three is worthy to receive it."

"But I . . . I'm just . . ."

"My father wishes it."

Hermes was still smiling, but something in his tone of voice made it clear that he would countenance no denial. Paris took the apple in trembling hands. He looked at the three female figures. Never had he seen such loveliness in all his life. His Oenone was beautiful, the daughter of an immortal herself. He had thought no beauty could ever match hers. But then he had thought the same of his bull.

The first goddess stepped forward. He knew from the purple silk, the peacock feathers lining her headdress, the fine cheekbones, the grandeur, and the proud majesty that this could only be Hera, the Queen of Heaven herself.

"Give me the apple," said Hera, coming close and gazing deep into Paris's eyes, "and power and sovereignty over all people shall be yours. Kingdoms and provinces across the wide world shall come under your rule. Imperial sway, riches, and dominion such as have been given to no mortal. Your name will ring down in history—Emperor Paris, respected, honored, and beloved of all, obeyed by all."

Paris was ready to put the apple straight into her outstretched palm, so clearly was hers the prize. Her beauty filled him with awe and reverence, and the reward she offered would give him everything he had ever dreamed of, and more. He had always felt, somewhere deep inside, that he was destined for greatness, for power and fame. Hera would give it to him. The apple must go to her. But he realized that he had to be fair and allow the other two goddesses at least to make their claims, absurd as they would certainly be beside those of the Queen of Heaven.

Paris looked toward the second goddess, who was now coming toward him, a grave smile playing on her lips. In the very surface of the shield she bore—by some artifice he could not understand—he could make out the furious and frightened scowl of Medusa. This aegis alone told him that the goddess now before him was Pallas Athena, and her words confirmed his conviction.

"Present me with the apple, Paris, and I shall give you something more than powers and principalities. I offer you wisdom. With wisdom comes everything else—riches and might, if you choose; peace and happiness, if you choose. You will see into the hearts of men and women, into the darkest corners of the cosmos and even into the ways of the immortals. Wisdom will earn you a name that can never perish from the earth. When all the citadels and palaces of the powerful have crumbled into dust, your knowledge and mastery of the arts of war, peace, and thought itself will elevate the name of Paris higher than the stars. The power of the mind shatters the mightiest spear."

Well, thank goodness I didn't give the apple straight to Hera, Paris thought. For here is the prize above all prizes. She is right. Of course she is right. Wisdom first, and power and wealth will surely follow. Besides, what use is power without insight and intelligence? The apple must go to Athena.

He stopped himself from giving it to her when he remembered that there was one more contender for the prize to be heard.

The third apparition stepped forward, her head tilted demurely down. "I cannot offer you wisdom or power," she said in a soft voice.

She lifted her face and Paris was dazzled by the sight. Never had such transcendent radiance met his eyes.

"My name is Aphrodite," said the vision, looking shyly up at him from under her lashes. "I am not wise or clever, I'm afraid. I cannot win you gold or glory. My only realm is love. Love. It seems so small next to empires of the land and sea, or empires of the mind, doesn't it? Yet I think you might agree that so insignificant and silly a thing as love—why do we need it after all?—might be worth considering. My offer to you is this . . ."

She was holding a scallop shell which she passed to him. When he hesitated, she nodded encouragement.

"Take it and open it, Paris."

He did so, and inside the shell, moving and alive, there shone the shimmering image of the most entrancing, captivating, enthralling, and bewitching face he had ever seen. It was the face of a young woman. Even as he stared into the shell she raised her chin and seemed to look directly into his eyes. She smiled, and Paris almost lost his balance. Flames leapt to his cheeks; his heart, throat, head, and stomach pounded so hard that he thought he might burst apart. The sight of Aphrodite was astounding, but it almost hurt his eyes and he had wanted to look away. This face inside the shell made him want to dive inside.

"Who . . . who . . . who?" was all he could say.

"Her name is HELEN," said Aphrodite. "If the apple is mine, she will be yours. I will dedicate myself to ensuring that you are together. I will protect you both and defend your union always. That is my oath to you and it cannot be broken."

Without a moment's thought Paris pushed the apple into Aphrodite's hands. "The prize is yours!" he said hoarsely, and, turning to the others, added, "I am sorry, I hope you understand . . ."

But Hera and Athena, the one scowling, the other shaking her head in sorrow, had risen up into the air and were now vanishing from sight. When Paris turned to thank Aphrodite, he saw that she too had gone. There was no scallop shell in his hands. He was not standing. He was lying on the grass, the sun scorching his cheeks. Had it all been nothing but an afternoon dream?

But that *face* . . .

Helen. Helen. Helen.

Who in the world was *Helen*?

FAMILY FEUDS

Who in the world was Helen?

We are Icarus and Daedalus, soaring west on feathered wings, or perhaps we are Zeus the Eagle, bearing the Trojan Prince Ganymede to Olympus in our talons, or we are Bellerophon, striding the air on his winged horse PEGASUS. Far below us, the blue Aegean crawls. We break the coastline not far from Mount Pelion, home of Chiron the centaur. We pass over the peak of Mount Othrys, home of the first gods. In its shadow we see the kingdom of Phthia, where Peleus rules over the Myrmidons. His new wife, the sea nymph Thetis, is pregnant with a male child. We will return to them soon enough. Bearing southwest, we overfly the Saronic Gulf; looking down we can make out the island of Salamis, home of Telamon, where his sons Ajax and Teucer live. Ahead of us lies the great peninsula of the Peloponnese, home to some of the great kingdoms of the Greek world. Corinth and Achaea to the north, Theseus's birthplace of Troezen to the south. Further west lie Pylos and Laconia, but directly below we can make out Argos and its neighbor Mycenae, the mightiest of all the king-doms. We should take the time to find out who lives there.

◈ Helen

Pelops, son of Tantalus, you remember, having failed to regain his father's kingdom of Lydia from King Ilus of Troy, came west to Pisa to win King Oenomaus's daughter Hippodamia in a chariot race.[44] Pelops won the race, but he and his line were cursed by Myrtilus the charioteer, whom he had cheated.

Pelops, having killed Oenomaus and won Hippodamia, ruled in Elis, and established there, in the kingdom of Olympia, a four-yearly cycle of athletic contests (which continue to this day as the Olympic Games). He and Hippodamia had two sons, ATREUS and THYESTES.[45] By the nymph Axioche, Pelops also fathered another boy, CHRYSIPPUS.[46] Prince LAIUS of Thebes, who had been given refuge in Elis from the internecine violence that was raging in his home city, fell in love with the beautiful Chrysippus and abducted him, thus earning the curse that was to ruin the house of Laius and Laius's son Oedipus and their descendants. This curse, augmenting the original curse cast on Cadmus, the founder of Thebes, and running down through to the children of Oedipus, might be seen as a mirror image of the curse on the house of Tantalus.[47]

Bear with me. A blizzard of geography and genealogy has already blanketed these pages, but—as ever with Greek myth—there are some essential strands in the tapestry, if you'll forgive the change of metaphor, that must be picked out in bright colors if we are to follow the lines of the story clearly. It is not necessary to know the location of every city-state in the Peloponnese, mainland Greece, and the Troad, nor every cousin and aunt in the great families that ruled there and which were to play prominent parts in the drama to come, but some are very much worth our time and trouble. The royal house of Troy, Priam and Hecuba and their children, for example. Telamon and Peleus, and their offspring, are important too. And so is the house of Tantalus, which, down through Pelops to his sons and their sons, casts a shadow over the whole history of the Trojan War and its aftermath. The curse on Tantalus was doubled with each succeeding generation, a cascade of curses whose force propels us to the end of everything.

So, pausing for breath, we find ourselves in the Peloponnese again. Laius has abducted Chrysippus. Pelops curses him and sends his two legitimate sons, Atreus and Thyestes, to rescue their half-brother Chrysippus. Instead they kill

---

44. Not the Italian Pisa, if you recall. The Greek Pisa lies in the northwest of the Peloponnese, capital of the kingdom of Elis.

45. A third son, Pittheus, went on to rule Troezen. Pittheus was the father of AETHRA, Theseus's mother, who features in *Heroes*, but whom we shall meet again soon in relation to the story of Troy.

46. Literally "golden horse."

47. The curse of Ares was on Cadmus for his slaying of the Ismenian Dragon and the curse of Dionysus on the next generation for their snubbing of the god's mother, Semele. For these, and for the unfolding of the curse on the house of Laius, see *Mythos* (pages 189 and 196) and *Heroes* (page 237).

him.[48] Whether out of jealousy, as Peleus and Telamon had done with their brother Phocus, or out of some other motive, is not quite clear.

You will know well by now that when a blood crime has been committed, only an immortal, a priest, or an anointed king may cleanse it. Kings Eurytion and Acastus had done this for Peleus, King Cychreus for Telamon. In earlier times, after Bellerophon accidentally killed *his* brother, it was King Proetus of Mycenae who had performed the necessary purification.[49] And it was to Mycenae that Atreus and Thyestes fled in search of expiation when Pelops expelled them from Elis for their fratricide.

What happened next to Atreus and Thyestes is so complicated and insane that I cannot in all conscience submit you to every detail. If I piece together a paragraph that attempts to explain it, we will emerge with three names of importance to the furtherance of our tale.

The brothers Atreus and Thyestes settled in Mycenae, deposed the king there (Eurystheus, the despot who had set Heracles his Twelve Labors), and then set about betraying each other in as many grotesque ways as they could fashion, each vying for the throne of Mycenae, winning it, losing it, and winning it back again. Thyestes stole away Atreus's wife Aerope. In retaliation Atreus served up Thyestes's own sons to him in a feast.[50] Thyestes was told by an oracle that the only way he could revenge himself on his brother Atreus for this crime would be by fathering a son by his own daughter—a son who would grow up to kill Atreus. So Thyestes bedded his daughter Pelopia, who duly bore him a son, AEGISTHUS. Thus adultery, infanticide, cannibalism, and incest all followed each other in swift and juicy succession. Pelopia was so ashamed of the incest that, as soon as Aegisthus was born, she abandoned him deep in the country-side. In traditional fashion the baby was found by a shepherd, and, in a somehow inevitable twist of fate, the shepherd took the baby to its uncle, King Atreus, who—unaware that the child was his brother Thyestes's son and prophesized to slay him—adopted Aegisthus and raised him along with his own three children by Aerope: their two sons AGAMEMNON and MENELAUS, and daughter Anaxibia.

If you are with me so far I am greatly in awe of you.

Only when Aegisthus had grown to manhood did his "uncle" Thyestes reveal to him that he was in fact *his* son (and grandson) and that he had been born to be an instrument of vengeance. Aegisthus, rather than being horrified to discover that he was the offspring of so noxious a union, obliged his father/grandfather

---

48. By throwing him down a well, according to some sources. Other versions have him killing himself . . .

49. With epic results: see *Heroes* (page 125).

50. As their grandfather Tantalus had done with their father, Pelops.

Thyestes and slew Atreus, whose sons Agamemnon and Menelaus fled Mycenae, leaving it under the control of Thyestes and Aegisthus.

Where did Agamemnon and Menelaus go? They went south, to the Lower Peloponnese, and to the prosperous kingdom of Laconia (or Lacedaemon), which we know these days by a name that still stirs the blood—Sparta.[51] The young princes were welcomed by Sparta's king at this time, TYNDAREUS,[52] who was married to LEDA, a princess from the kingdom of Aetolia, on the Gulf of Corinth's northern side.

THE EGGS

One afternoon Tyndareus and Leda made love by a river. When Tyndareus had finished, he departed—as men will—leaving his wife lying back with her eyes closed, the sun shining down and warming her happy afterglow.

She was surprised moments later to feel her husband back on top of her. It was unusual for him to replenish his stores of amatory energy so rapidly.

"You're very frisky this afternoon, Tyndareus," she murmured.

But something wasn't quite right. Tyndareus was hirsute, but no more hairy than the average Greek male. He certainly wasn't furry. But, no, this wasn't *fur* that she could feel all over her flesh, it was something else. It was . . . Surely not? . . . Could it be *feathers*?

Leda opened her eyes to see a great white swan lying on her. More than lying on her. The bird was forcing itself into her.

Who else but Zeus? Leda was beautiful and—looking down on Sparta that afternoon—the sight of her lying naked on a riverbank had been more than he had been able to resist. In order to have his way with beautiful girls, boys, nymphs, and sprites of one kind or another, the King of the Gods had transformed himself in many extraordinary ways over the course of a long lustful career. Eagles, bears, goats, lizards, bulls, boars—even a shower of golden rain in one case. A swan seems almost routine by comparison.

---

51. Lacedaemon, a son of Zeus, had been an ancient King of Laconia. He renamed the realm after Sparta, his wife (and niece). The Spartan people in classical times were known for their terseness and directness of speech. They (like stereotypical Yorkshire people, perhaps) didn't hold with all the book-learning and southern metropolitan nonsense that was found in Athens and other such soft places. There is a story that King Philip II of Macedon (father of Alexander the Great) besieged the city and threatened them thus: "If I defeat you, we will raze your city to the ground. We will kill every man and boy in the city and take every woman and girl into slavery." The Spartans sent a one-word reply. "*If* . . ." This is often thought to be the original *laconic* reply.

52. Pronounced "Tinder-*ay*-us," but "Tin-*dahr*-yus" is possible.

Those familiar with the story of the birth of Heracles will be aware of the concept of *heteropaternal superfecundation*.[53] Common enough in littering animals like pigs, dogs, and cats, this biological phenomenon is rare, but not unknown, in humans. There was a well-documented case in 2019.[54] It is a form of what is known as *polyspermy*—the fertilizing of the same egg as a result of different acts of sexual congress, causing a set of twins to be born, each of whom has a different father. In the case of Leda, this crazed zygotic quirk was even more remarkable, for she gave birth to two sets of twins. Actually, that is not strictly true. It was odder even than that. When she came to term, Leda *laid two eggs*, each of which contained a set of twins.

I know. But stay with me.

From one egg came a girl and boy whom they named CLYTEMNESTRA and CASTOR, from the other a girl and boy whom they named Helen and POLYDEUCES (also known as Pollux). Tradition has it that Zeus was the father of Polydeuces and Helen, and Tyndareus of Clytemnestra and Castor. Castor and Polydeuces were brought up together as loving twin brothers, inseparably devoted each to the other. Helen and Clytemnestra grew up to make the fateful matches that determined the main outlines of this whole story.

There is an older version of this myth that maintains Zeus fathered Helen another way. They say he pursued NEMESIS, daughter of Night, goddess of divine retribution, punisher of *hubris*, bringer down of those whose pride and vanity causes them to overreach and insult the order of things. Through rivers, meadows, and mountain passes the god pursued her. She changed her shape into a fish and darted into the ocean, but still Zeus chased on, until—when she had taken the form of a goose—he turned himself into a swan and finally coupled with her. In the fullness of time, Nemesis laid an egg which was found by a shepherd who brought it to his queen, Leda. She incubated it in a wooden chest and, when it hatched, raised the human child that emerged, Helen, as her own daughter.[55]

---

53. See *Heroes*, page 54. In the same afternoon Alcmene had sex with both Zeus and her mortal husband Amphitryon causing her to give birth to the twins Heracles and Iphicles. Heracles was fathered by Zeus, Iphicles by Amphitryon.

54. https://www.dailysabah.com/asia/2019/03/29/chinese-woman-gives-birth-to-twin-babies-from-different-fathers-in-one-in-a-million-case

55. This is the version preferred by Roberto Calasso, who writes about it with great drama and poetry in his book *The Marriage of Cadmus and Harmony*. There is indeed something poetic about the idea of Helen being a child of Nemesis, who, as a daughter of Night, is a sister of Eris. There is uncertainty about the origins of the name ("torch," "light," "fire," "sun" are some possible meanings), but it is generally agreed that its similarity to "Hellenic," "Hellenes," and other words for "Greek" is coincidental.

◈ Leda and Zeus

In either case, Zeus was Helen's father, but she was raised by Leda and
Tyndareus as their own, along with her sister Clytemnestra and their brothers
Castor and Polydeuces.

Castor and Polydeuces were decidedly handsome. Clytemnestra's looks drew
admiration from all who saw her, but *Helen* . . . From the first it was clear that
Helen's beauty was of the kind that is seen once in every generation. Less often
than that. Once in every two, three, four, or five generations. Maybe once in the
lifetime of a whole epoch or civilization. No one who beheld her could remember ever having seen anyone a tenth as lovely. As each year passed, her attractive-
ness grew such that none who looked on her ever forgot her. Before long the
fame of Helen of Sparta was as great as that of any mighty ruler, brave warrior,
or monster-slaying hero—or of any mortal that lived or had lived.

Yet, for all her jaw-dropping beauty, Helen managed to avoid being spoiled
or self-regarding. Besides skill at many of the arts in which women were encouraged in those days, she had a bright and lively sense of humor. She loved to play
jokes on her family and friends, and was helped in this by a remarkable gift of
mimicry. Many were the times she confused her mother by calling to her in her
sister Clytemnestra's voice. Many were the times she confounded her father by

calling to him in her mother Leda's voice. All who encountered Helen foretold a bright and wonderful future for her.

She was only twelve years old when Theseus, King of Athens, egged on by his wild friend PIRITHOUS, kidnapped her and took her to Aphidna, one of the Twelve Towns of Attica. Leaving the bewildered and frightened girl in the charge of the town's ruler, Aphidnus, and his own mother, Aethra, Theseus went down into the realm of the dead with Pirithous to help realize his friend's mad scheme to abduct Persephone. The plan failed horribly, of course, and the two men were cast by a furious Hades into stone chairs where they stayed imprisoned in the underworld until Heracles passed by during his Twelfth Labor and rescued Theseus.[56] While they were trapped there, Helen was rescued by the DIOSCURI, as her brothers Castor and Polydeuces were often called,[57] and restored to her family in Sparta. She had come to rely on Aethra, however, so the older woman accompanied her to Sparta, not as her keeper now, but as her slave woman. Quite a comedown for Aethra, who—besides being the mother of the great Theseus, slayer of the Minotaur and King of Athens—was in her own right the daughter of King Pittheus of Troezen and a one-time lover of the sea god Poseidon.[58]

THE LOTTERY

After the Dioscuri rescued their sister from her imprisonment in Aphidna, a much closer guard was put upon Helen. As she moved from girlhood to young womanhood, she was forced to endure the presence of sentries outside her door day and night and the company of an entourage of serving women, chaperones, bodyguards, and duennas, led by Theseus's mother Aethra, whenever she wanted to go for so much as a walk around the palace.

Beauty may seem like one of the greatest of blessings, but it can be a curse too. Some are born with a beauty that seems to turn people mad. Fortunately there are very few of us like that, but our power can be unsettling and even eruptive. This proved the case with Helen. Her mother Leda and her father Tyndareus (her *mortal* father, at least) were soon made aware that every unmarried king, prince, and warlord in the Peloponnese, and a good many from the

---

56. See *Heroes*, page 101.

57. Meaning "sons of the god," specifically "sons of Zeus": the words *Zeus*, *Deus*, and *Dios* are kindred, or "cognate," as a linguist might say. The appellation *Dioscuri* is commonly applied to the twins despite only Polydeuces being Zeus's true biological son.

58. And a prospective bride of the hero Bellerophon. See *Heroes* (pages 125, 262, and 309) for the full stories of Aethra, Pittheus, Bellerophon, Theseus, and Pirithous.

mainland, islands and furthest-flung outposts of the Greek world, were lining up for her hand in marriage. A huge throng of eager, powerful suitors began to fill up Tyndareus's palace, along with their noisy and hard-drinking retinues. They would have been delighted enough to win the hand of so eligible a princess from so great a royal house under any circumstances, but Helen's beauty was now so celebrated and sung around the known world that whoever took her for his wife would win a new and matchless kind of prestige and glory, not to mention the unique privilege of being able to wake up to that ravishing face every morning.

Among the most powerful and insistent suitors were the Spartan royal family's permanent houseguests of the time, Atreus's sons Agamemnon and Menelaus, but they were far from alone in their assiduous courting of the beautiful Helen. Ajax of Salamis[59] joined the queue for her hand, as did his half-brother Teucer. DIOMEDES of Argos[60] arrived at the palace, as did IDOMENEUS, King of Crete, Menestheus, King of Athens,[61] Prince PATROCLUS, heir to the throne of Opus (a kingdom on the east coast of mainland Greece), PHILOCTETES of Meliboea, IOLAUS and his brother Iphiclus, rulers of the Thessalian Phylaceans, and many other clan chiefs, elders, princelings, minor nobles, landowners, and hangdog hopefuls. Far too many to mention.[62]

One high-born and respected ruler who did *not* come to Sparta to woo Helen was ODYSSEUS of Ithaca. This prince was reckoned by all who knew him to be the wiliest, cunningest, and most guileful young man in all the Greek world. Odysseus's father was the Argonaut LAERTES, ruler of Cephalonia and its outlying islands in the Ionian Sea.[63] Odysseus's mother ANTICLEA was a granddaughter of Hermes by way of the thief and trickster AUTOLYCUS.[64] Laertes had given his son Odysseus rule in Ithaca, one of the islands in the

---

59. Son of Telamon, and often called Telamonian Ajax, or Ajax the Mighty, or Ajax the Great.

60. No relation to Diomedes of Thrace, the owner of the flesh-eating mares that constituted Heracles's Eighth Labor . . . (see *Heroes*, page 75).

61. He had been installed in the place of Theseus by Castor and Polydeuces when they swooped on Attica to rescue Helen.

62. The total number of suitors, if you combine those listed by such sources as Apollodorus, Hesiod, and Hyginus, comes to forty-five.

63. The name "Ionian" is potentially confusing, since these waters are off the west coast of Greece and nothing to do with the land of Ionia, which is what we would call Asia Minor, now Anatolian Turkey . . . all the way across the Aegean to the east, the land where Troy is situated. Odysseus's Roman name is Ulysses . . . which is odd, since the Romans didn't really have much use for the letter "y." Ulixes is another Latin spelling. Most sources suggest that Odysseus *was* one of the applicants for the hand of Helen, but I stick to my guns in saying that he was not, and perhaps you will see why as the story unfolds.

64. See *Mythos* (page 222) for stories of the wicked Autolycus. Some sources give SISYPHUS— an equally twisty-turny trickster (see *Mythos*, page 219)—as one of Odysseus's ancestors.

Cephalonian archipelago over which Laertes held sway.[65] While it was far from the most fertile or prosperous of the Ionian isles, Odysseus would not have swapped Ithaca for all the wealth and wonder of the Peloponnese. Ithaca was his home and he loved every jagged rock and scraggy bush of it.

Friends and enemies alike were agreed that Odysseus had inherited more than enough of the rascally duplicity and mischievous cunning of his grandfather Autolycus and his great-grandfather Hermes. The enemies stayed away, distrusting and fearing his wit and wiles; the friends leaned on him for counsel and stratagems. He was infuriatingly crooked and duplicitous if you disliked and distrusted him, deliciously crafty and clever if you needed him.

It was in the latter spirit that a fretful Tyndareus sought him out. "Odysseus! Look at the state of my palace. Every bachelor from the islands, highlands and lowlands has crowded in, begging for Helen's hand. I have been offered brideprices that would make your eyes pop. There are idiots who think I'm lucky to have such a daughter, but they simply haven't thought it through. They don't seem to realize that if I give her to one suitor I will almost certainly earn the implacable enmity of all the others."

"There is no doubt," said Odysseus, "no doubt at all, that those who do not win Helen will take it badly. Very badly indeed."

"The whole Peloponnese will froth with blood!"

"Unless we put our heads together and think."

"*You* do the thinking," said Tyndareus. "When I try, I get a headache."

"An idea does occur," said Odysseus.

"It does?"

"Oh yes. Simple and obvious. It is guaranteed to work, but comes at a price."

"Name it. If it stops civil war and leaves me in peace, then it's worth whatever you demand."

"I want the hand of PENELOPE in marriage."

"Penelope? My brother Icarius's Penelope?"

"The same. She is promised to a prince of Thessaly, but I love her and she loves me."

"So that's why you are the only one who hasn't been hanging around Helen's rooms with your tongue hanging out, is it? Well, well. Congratulations. Solve my problem and you can sail her to Ithaca on the next tide. What's your idea?"

"Call all the suitors together and tell them this . . ."

---

65. Cephalonia, or Cephallenia (Kefalonia to today's Greeks), is the largest of the Ionian islands and was named for Cephalus, a lover of Eos the Dawn (see *Mythos*, page 250) and father of Odysseus's father Laertes.

Tyndareus listened as Odysseus outlined his plan. He needed to hear it run through in detail three times before he finally understood. He embraced his friend warmly.

"Brilliant!" he said. "You're a genius."

Tyndareus gave commands. Horns and drums sounded. Slaves ran through the palace in bare feet, calling on the guests to convene at once in the great hall. The suitors answered the summons filled with nervous excitement. Had a decision been made? Had Helen chosen? Had her parents chosen for her? After a final fanfare and roll of the drums, Tyndareus, Leda, and a blushing Helen appeared on the high balcony. The great press of kings, warlords, clan chiefs, princelings, generals, nobles, landowners and hangdog hopefuls below fell silent.

Odysseus sat on a stool in the shadows, smiling. How would the suitors respond to his plan, he wondered. They would be forced to accept. Of course they would. Reluctantly at first, but accept they must.

Tyndareus cleared his throat. "My friends. Queen Leda, Princess Helen, and I are most touched by the ardent interest you have shown in forming an . . . intimate connection with our royal house. So many of you, and all so fine, so noble and so eligible. We have decided that the only way to settle this matter fairly is . . ."

He paused. A creaking of leather and a clinking of brass as fifty men leaned forward to hear.

". . . by lottery."

A great groan went up. Odysseus's smile broadened.

Tyndareus raised a hand. "I know, I know. You fear that the odds are against you. Or perhaps you fear that the *gods* are against you? For if the winner is decided by lot, he is elected not by me, nor by the queen, nor by Helen herself, but by Moros and Tyche,[66] from whom fate and fortune, good or ill, always derive."

The suitors appeared to see the justice of this rather—to Odysseus's mind—sententious point, and muttered their consent.

Tyndareus put up his hand for silence. "One more thing. There is a *price* to be paid for a lottery ticket in this draw."

Mutters now of discontent. Odysseus hugged himself.

"Not, I assure you, a price in gold or goods," said Tyndareus. "The price we require is an *oath*. Applicants for the hand of Helen will only be allowed to draw their lots if first they swear by all the gods of Olympus and on the lives of their children and grandchildren that, no matter who wins, they will abide

---

66. The Greek personification of chance.

uncomplainingly by the result. Furthermore, they pledge themselves to defend Helen and her lawfully recognized husband from all who might come between them."

A silence fell as the suitors absorbed this. It was brilliant, of course. Tyndareus could never have thought of such a scheme himself. Who but Odysseus of Ithaca had the wit to propose an idea so simple and so perfect? The lucky winner of Helen's hand could now feel safe forever. The unlucky losers, however resentful or disappointed, would be able to do nothing about it without breaking a sacred oath. An oath witnessed by the most formidable gathering of the powerful ever gathered in one place.

With grumbling assent the suitors fell one by one to their knees and swore, before the gods and upon their honor, to protect and defend whichever of their number drew the winning ticket from the great copper bowl that even now was being carried into the hall.[67]

The winner of the draw was Prince Menelaus. This delighted Tyndareus, who told Odysseus that he read in such a pleasing result the benevolent intervention of the gods.[68]

"He is just the right age. I like him. Leda likes him and Helen has always liked him. I think he will make her happy. Surely Apollo or Athena guided his hand when he drew his ticket."

"We must hope not," said Odysseus. "When the gods play so deep a part in our affairs, we should count ourselves cursed."

"You are a cynic, Odysseus," said Tyndareus.

Just then Agamemnon approached, favoring Odysseus with a dark glare. "Your bright idea, I suppose?"

Odysseus inclined his head. Agamemnon was no more than a prince in exile, a king without a country, yet he had that about him which commanded respect. He brought with him wherever he went an atmosphere of strength and weight. A powerful aura of authority.

Agamemnon was younger than Tyndareus by almost twenty years, yet the Spartan king always felt flustered in his presence. "I hope you're pleased for your brother?"

All three men looked across the hall to where Menelaus and Helen now sat enthroned, accepting the congratulations and loyalty of the losing suitors.

---

67. In truth I cannot say what form the lottery took. It will not have been written tickets—perhaps plaques with the symbols of each suitor's royal house inscribed; perhaps it was a blind draw of pebbles, all but one of which were black, for example.

68. In some versions of the story there is no lottery. The suitors swear the oath and then Tyndareus chooses Menelaus (who is not there, but represented by his brother Agamemnon).

◈ Menelaus, King of Ancient Sparta

"They look like the kind of young lovers that artists depict on their plates and jars, do they not?" said Odysseus.

"It isn't right," said Agamemnon darkly. "She should be marrying *me*. I am the older and—with all respect—the better man. There are plans afoot. Before long I will have recaptured Mycenae. If Helen were mine, she would find herself queen of the greatest kingdom in the world."

A preposterous claim, Odysseus thought. And yet barked out with a gruff certainty that somehow convinced.

"Oh yes," said Agamemnon, as if sensing Odysseus's doubt. "My prophet CALCHAS has assured me that great victories lie ahead of me. And Calchas is never wrong. I've nothing against my brother. Menelaus is a fine fellow, but he is no Agamemnon."

The embarrassed Tyndareus shot Odysseus a look of mute appeal.

"Has it not occurred to you," said Odysseus, "that Helen has a sister? She may not have quite the same degree of beauty—no mortal does—but Clytemnestra can surely be counted among the loveliest women in the world. Had Helen never been born, Clytemnestra would be the stuff of poetry and song."

"Clytemnestra, eh?" said Agamemnon, rubbing his beard ruminatively. He glanced in the direction of Helen's sister. Clytemnestra was standing with her mother Leda and surveying the crowd clustering around Helen and Menelaus with a look of coolly ironic self-possession. She had never expressed the least hint of rancor or envy for the hysteria that her sister's beauty generated.

Agamemnon turned back to Tyndareus. "Is she promised?"

"No, indeed," said Tyndareus eagerly. "We have been waiting first to get Helen off our . . . That is to say, we had thought first to find a match for Helen . . ."

"Go on!" said Odysseus, daring to nudge Agamemnon in the ribs. "Marry Clytemnestra! What could possibly go wrong?"

The lottery for the hand of Helen of Sparta represented a momentous turning point in the history of the Greek world. It seemed to betoken the passing of power from one generation to the next and to promise the arrival of a new age of stability, growth, and peace. Tyndareus abdicated the throne of Sparta in favor of his new son-in-law Menelaus.[69] Agamemnon raised an army to invade Mycenae and, as he had assured Tyndareus and Odysseus he would, drove his cousin Aegisthus and uncle Thyestes from the kingdom, installing himself on the throne with Clytemnestra as his queen. Thyestes died in exile on Cythera, the small island off the southern tip of the Peloponnese.

Agamemnon—as all who had watched him grow up guessed he might, and as his seer Calchas had prophesized—proved himself a most brilliant and effective warrior king. He absorbed, annexed, and overwhelmed neighboring realms and city-states with astonishing speed and skill. His ruthless generalship and natural gifts of leadership earned him the soubriquet *Anax andron*, "King of Men." Under his rule Mycenae rose to become the richest and most powerful of all the Greek kingdoms, such that it might almost be called an empire.

But what, meanwhile, of Peleus and Thetis, whose wedding had been so strangely interrupted by Eris and her Apple of Discord?

---

69. Timelines are, as ever, exasperating when it comes to myth rather than history. Certain lines of narrative render very problematic the calculation of the ages of the protagonists or any consistent ordering of historical events. Some suggest that Menelaus took the throne of Sparta only after the deaths and catasterization of his twin brothers-in-law Castor and Polydeuces.

THE SEVENTH SON

Six sons had Thetis given Peleus, but the famous prophecy that a son by her would grow up to be greater than his father had no chance to be proven, for every one of her six babies died very early in their infancy. No, that is not quite true. To say that they died is misleading. It would be more accurate to say that—from Peleus's point of view at least—they disappeared. He could not understand it, but he was too sensitive to push a clearly distressed Thetis for details. Babies died more often than they lived, after all. He knew that. Six in a row seemed extreme, but it wasn't for him, a mere man, to inquire too deeply.

The reasons were not beyond his understanding because he was a mere man, however; they were beyond his understanding because he was a mere *mortal* man.

In desperation, Thetis, now pregnant with their seventh child, visited her father, the sea god Nereus.

"It is so very upsetting," she said. "I have done *everything* correctly, I am sure I have, yet still the babies burn."

"I beg your pardon?" said Nereus.

"Peleus is a fine man and a good husband," said Thetis, "but he is mortal."

"Certainly he is mortal. But what's this about burning?"

"I shall live forever. Forever is such a long time. If I am to have a son by mortal Peleus, the son who is said to be destined to rise to such greatness, then I could not bear for him too to be mortal. He would be gone in a flicker of time. I will hardly get to know him before he grows old, then decrepit, then dead. I have accepted that this will happen to Peleus, but I want my great son to live forever."

"But any child of yours by a mortal father must, of course, be mortal too," said Nereus. "It is the way of things."

"Ah, but not if I make him immortal! The Oceanids told me that there is a way. They assured me it would work. But I fear they may have misled me."

A shining sphere rolled down Thetis's cheek. They were in Nereus's great undersea grotto, in scale and grandeur a structure second only to the palace of Poseidon himself. When Thetis wept above the waves she shed salt tears like all creatures of land and air, but when she wept below the surface her tears were bubbles of air.

"You consulted *Oceanids?*" said her father. "Oceanids know nothing. What rubbish did they tell you?"[70]

---

70. As mentioned before, Oceanids were children of the primal Titan of the sea, Oceanus. The children of Nereus were Nereids. Perhaps it was to be expected that there might be rivalries between these divinities. Nereus's wife Doris was herself an Oceanid, of course, so the rivalry was presumably of a familial kind.

"They said that to immortalize a human child I should smear it with ambrosia and then hold it over a fire. I did exactly as they said six times, but each time . . . each time . . . the baby just screamed and burned up and died."

"Oh you silly, silly, silly child!"

"What they said was wrong?"

"Not wrong, no, but *incomplete*—which is as bad as wrong, worse perhaps. Yes, slathering a baby in ambrosia and then roasting it over flames will certainly confer immortality, but first you have to make the child *invulnerable*, don't you see?"

"Invulnerable?"

"Of course."

"Oh," said Thetis, the truth dawning. "Oh! Yes, I should have thought of that. First invulnerable and only *then* the ambrosia and the flames."

"Oceanids!" said Nereus with contempt.

"Just one thing," said Thetis after a pause.

"Yes?"

"What exactly is the procedure for making a child invulnerable?"

Nereus sighed. "The STYX, of course. Full immersion in her waters."

You will remember—which is to say you will be entirely forgiven for not remembering—that Peleus had inherited the throne of Phthia, the kingdom of the Myrmidons in eastern mainland Greece. It was there that Thetis and Peleus lived, and it was thither that she now rushed after her conference with Nereus, in time to give birth to her seventh child, yet another son. Peleus was pleased, naturally he was pleased, but his warm paternal pleasure was greatly diminished by the anxiety he felt when he saw the excitement, joy, and optimism with which Thetis celebrated this new birth. After six early deaths it seemed folly to invest so much love and hope.

"This time all will be well, I'm sure of it," she said, hugging the baby to her. "Beautiful LIGYRON. Have you seen how bright his hair is? Like spun gold."

"I shall go and sacrifice a bull," said Peleus. "Perhaps this time the gods will be merciful."

That night, while Peleus slept, Thetis took the young Ligyron from his cot and made her way with him down to the nearest entrance to the underworld. Styx, the river of hate, which ran through Hades's realm of the dead, was herself an Oceanid, one of the three thousand children of the Titans Oceanus and Tethys. Her waters were cold and black—literally Stygian black. Thetis knelt down and dipped the naked Ligyron into the river. To ensure that the swift current did not bear him away she held him by one ankle, clutching the heel of his left foot between finger and thumb. She counted to ten and then brought

◈ Thetis dips Ligyron (Achilles) into the River Styx.

him up and wrapped him in a blanket. The shock of the icy water had woken Ligyron, but he did not cry.

Back in her chamber in the Phthian palace she laid him on a table and looked down into his eyes.

"You are invulnerable now, little Ligyron," she told him. "No one can hurt you. No spear can pierce your side, no club can break your bones. Not poison nor plague can do you harm. Now I shall make you immortal."

She warmed a handful of fragrant ambrosia in the palms of her hands before rubbing it all over Ligyron.[71] The child gurgled happily as the unguent was smeared over his skin. When she was sure that his whole body was covered she took him to the hearth, where a good fire was blazing.

This time. This time it would work. Her boy would never die.

Thetis leaned down and kissed Ligyron on the brow, tasting the familiar sweetness of the ambrosia on her lips. "Come, my darling," she breathed, holding him over the flames.

---

71. No one is agreed on the exact composition of ambrosia. The idea that nectar was the drink of the gods and ambrosia the food is suggested by references in Homer, but other writers in classical antiquity had it the other way round, with ambrosia as the liquid and nectar as the solid. Most are agreed that it smelled sweet and fragrant and probably contained an element of honey. The word "ambrosia" itself seems to have derived from one that meant "immortal" or "undead."

"*No!*"

With a yell of fury, Peleus reached into the hearth and snatched the child from the fire.

"You unnatural witch! You mad, cruel, diseased—"

"You don't understand!"

"Oh, I understand. I understand what happened to our six other sons now. Leave. Leave the palace. Go! Go . . ."

Thetis stood up to face her husband, her eyes ablaze with anger. Peleus stealing up behind her had been a shock, but she was a Nereid and not minded to reveal any hint of weakness.

"No mortal dares tell me to go. *You* leave. *You* go."

Ligyron, in Peleus's arms, began to cry.

Peleus stood quite still. "I know you can kill me too if you choose. Well, choose then. The gods will see what kind of a creature you are."

Thetis stamped her foot. "Give him back to me! I'm telling you, you don't understand what I was doing."

"Go!"

Thetis screamed in frustration. Mortals. They weren't worth the effort. Very well. She had failed to complete the process of immortalizing her son. Ligyron would die, like all humans. She had better things to do than descend to a vulgar brawl. She should never have involved herself with weak mortal flesh in the first place.

In a swirl and swim of light she disappeared.

HOLDING THE BABY

Peleus stood for some time, the infant Ligyron flushed and gulping in his arms. It seemed incredible to him that any mother, divine or human, could undergo the burden and pain of pregnancy and childbirth and then . . . and then do what Thetis had done. Consign her children to the flames. She must be demented. Sick to the very soul. Perhaps, over the years, the warning of the prophecy had become garbled. It was not that a son of hers would live to be greater than his father, it was that a son of hers would never live at all.

He looked down into the eyes of his seventh son. "Will you live now and grow up to outshine me, Ligyron? I'm sure you will."

It was to the cave of his grandfather and savior, Chiron, that Peleus now took the child. The very cave in which he and Thetis had been married in front of all the gods on the day when Eris rolled the golden apple.

◈ The Education of Achilles

"You were my tutor," said Peleus to the centaur, "and you raised Asclepius and Jason. Will you now do the same for my son? Be his instructor, guide, and friend?"

Chiron bowed his head and took the baby in his arms.[72]

"I will return for him when he is ten years old," said Peleus.

Chiron did not like the name Ligyron. It meant "wailing and whining"—and Chiron made the assumption that it had been given to the baby as a kind of mocking nickname. All babies wail and whine, after all. It was likely that, had things gone forward in the usual way, Peleus and Thetis would have found a different, more dignified name for their son. After some thought, Chiron settled on ACHILLES.[73]

---

72. The torso, head, and arms of a centaur were human; they were four-legged horses from the waist down only. Hence they could talk and use their hands like any human.

73. Apollodorus thought that Achilles meant "lipless one" (*a-cheile*)—a gloss that Sir James Frazer (author of the pioneering 1890 work of myth and folklore *The Golden Bough*) deemed "absurd." Some writers, like Robert Graves and Alec Nevala-Lee, feel "lipless" is appropriate for

And so it was that Achilles spent the first part of his upbringing in Chiron's cave, learning music, rhetoric, poetry, history, and science, and later, when he was deemed old enough, in his father's palace in Phthia, where he perfected his skill at the javelin and discus, charioteering, sword-fighting, and wrestling. At these last, the arts of war, he showed quite astonishing aptitude. By the time he was eleven no one in the kingdom could catch him on the running track. It was believed that he ran faster than Atalanta herself,[74] that he was swifter indeed than any mortal who had ever lived. His speed, eye, balance, and matchless athletic grace endowed him with a glamour, an aura, that thrilled and captivated all who came into contact with him, even at so very young an age. He was Golden Achilles, whose glorious and heroic future was assured.

When this paragon was about ten years old and newly transferred from Chiron's cave to the Phthian royal court, King Menoetius and Queen Polymele of the nearby kingdom of Opus sent a message to Peleus. Polymele was Peleus's sister and Menoetius had been a fellow Argonaut back in the days of the quest for the Golden Fleece. They asked Peleus if he might take in their son Patroclus, who had accidentally killed a child in a fit of rage, and must now grow up exiled from Opus to atone for his crime. Young Patroclus, that one temper tantrum aside, was a balanced, kindly disposed, and thoughtful youth, and Peleus was all too happy for Achilles to have his cousin as a companion. So it was that the two boys grew up together, inseparable friends.

THE CAST

Let us remind ourselves of who is who and where they are.

In Troy, Hecuba and Priam have added to their family with—among many other children[75]—the sons DEIPHOBUS, HELENUS, and TROILUS, and the daughters Iliona, CASSANDRA, Laodice, and POLYXENA. Their eldest boy, Prince Hector, has married the Cilician princess ANDROMACHE; while Paris, the "stillborn son" (as word was put out), whom no one in Troy suspects to be

---

an "oracular hero"—though why they think Achilles is "oracular" I cannot quite work out. Other interpretations of the name include "sharp-footed" and, perhaps by extension, swift-footed—a quality associated with Achilles by Homer and many others. Also "distressing to the people," or maybe "whose people are distressed"—a meaning that Homer also plays with, in a punning way that neither proves nor disproves that this is the true origin and "meaning" of the name. It's a derivation game philologists have long played and it is hard to give the palm to any clear winner. As with all names and titles, common use erodes both connotation and denotation and the name *becomes* the named and vice versa. Achilles, in every sense, stands alone.

74. See *Heroes*, page 231.

75. As many as *fifty* sons by Hecuba and previous wives, if you add the various sources together.

alive, moons around with his flocks and herds on Mount Ida, quite unable to forget the strange dream he had that sunny afternoon: Hermes, an apple, a scallop shell, goddesses, and that *face*—a face so beautiful that Paris knows he will see it in his dreams forever.

That face belongs to Helen, now Queen of Sparta, married to Menelaus. The couple have been blessed with a daughter, HERMIONE, and a son, NICOSTRATUS. Helen is attended by her bondswoman, Theseus's mother Aethra.

Agamemnon rules in Mycenae with his young wife Clytemnestra. She has borne him three daughters, IPHIGENIA, Electra, and Chrysothemis, and a son, Orestes.

On the island of Salamis, Telamon reigns with his wife Hesione (the Trojan princess he brought back with him when he and Heracles sacked her father Laomedon's Troy). They have had a son, Teucer—a prodigiously gifted archer—who gets on perfectly well with his huge half-brother Ajax—Telamon's son from his first marriage.

Telamon's brother Peleus rules in Phthia without his estranged wife Thetis. Their son Achilles, always accompanied by his friend Patroclus, is growing up to be remarkable.

Odysseus, having satisfactorily settled matters for Tyndareus, has sailed with his bride Penelope back to Ithaca.

If all that is clear in our minds, we can travel back east across the Aegean Sea and revisit Troy.

PARIS COMES HOME

By the time the eighteenth anniversary of the death of Priam and Hecuba's second-born came around, the guilt, shame, and sadness that they felt for his killing was in no way diminished or assuaged.

It had been the custom to hold funeral games in honor of the lost child every year on the day of his supposed birth and death. No one in Troy but Agelaus the herdsman had any knowledge of the king and queen sending their own baby to die on a mountainside. As far as the world was aware, a young prince had been stillborn. Such things happened. It was a rare couple whose children all survived to adulthood.

Paris himself, living with the mountain nymph Oenone on the high pasture slopes of Ida, knew that these special funeral games had been going on for as long as he could remember, but he had no inkling of his unique personal connection to them, that they were memorializing his death. As for the visitation of Hermes and the three goddesses . . . Well, it was known that if you fall asleep in the meadows of Ida, Morpheus could sometimes come and blow the scent of poppies, lavender, and thyme into your nostrils, causing strange and vivid phantasms to rise in the mind like mirages.[76] Paris had decided that Oenone need not know about this particular dream. Some summers since, she had borne him a son, CORYTHUS, and while Paris had never given her any reason to doubt his love for her, he had a feeling that she might look with disfavor on his story of three goddesses, a golden apple, and a lovely mortal woman called Helen. So he had kept the peculiar vision to himself. That face, though . . . oh, how it haunted him.

One afternoon, a few days before the annual funerary games were due to begin, an officer and six soldiers arrived on Ida to take possession of the prize bull whose beauty Paris had, months earlier, boasted to be matchless. The boast that had caused the apparition of Hermes and the whole bewildering episode.

Paris could not understand why a company of soldiers would want to take the animal.

"He belongs to me and my father Agelaus!" he protested.

"This bull, like all the animals on Ida, like you yourself, young lad," replied the officer with lofty disdain, "is the property of his majesty King Priam. It has been selected to be first prize in the games."

Paris ran to tell Agelaus of the fate of their favorite bull but he couldn't find him. How dare King Priam take it? Yes, it was technically the property of the royal house, but how could a cattle herdsman do his job properly without a breeding bull? It annoyed Paris to think of some arrogant athlete winning this noble beast, an animal for which a town-bred Trojan could have no possible use. Doubtless, after the games had ended, the great beautiful bull would be sacrificed. A needless waste of valuable stock.

It was infuriating. Paris bet he was faster and stronger than any pampered city youth. He pictured himself running, jumping, and throwing against the best that Troy could offer.

A voice suddenly whispered inside his head.

Why not?

Why shouldn't he go down, enter these games, and win his own bull back? The competition was open to all, surely? But years ago, when he was still a boy, Agelaus had made Paris swear an oath never to go to Troy. Paris had innocently asked what the city was like and whether they might visit one day. The ferocity of his father's response had astonished him.

"Never, boy, never!"

---

76. Morpheus was the god of dreams. His name is connected not just to the *morph* of "morphine" but also to the *morph* of "morphing" and "metamorphosis." After all, dreams are transformations, shiftings of shapes, meanings, and stories in the head.

"But why not?"

"Troy is bad luck for you. I . . . heard it said by a priestess. At the temple of Hermes where I found you as a baby. 'Never let him go through the gates of Troy,' she told me. 'There's nothing for him there but ill luck.'"

"What sort of ill luck?"

"Never you mind what sort. The gods have their reasons. Not for us to know. Swear to me that you'll never go there, Paris? Never enter the city. Swear it to me."

And Paris had sworn.

But, the voice inside Paris said, the games were held *outside* Troy. On the plain of Ilium between the River Scamander and the city walls. He could go down, compete, win the bull, and return with it—all without breaking his promise to Agelaus.

Down the hillside Paris skipped, following the soldiers and the bull. He caught glimpses of glittering bronze and gleaming stonework through the trees as he descended, until finally all the turrets, towers, banners, battlements, ramparts, walls, and great gates of Troy came into view. Close behind the soldiers and the bull, Paris crossed over a wooden bridge that spanned the Scamander and took in the magnificent sight.

Troy was at the height of her glory. The riches that came from the trade with the east showed not just in the mass, solidity, and smoothness of the city's masonry, but in the shining armor of the soldiery, the richly dyed clothes of the citizenry, and the healthy, well-nourished complexions of the children. Even the dogs looked prosperous and contented.

Everything was in preparation for the games. Alongside the running track, a full stadion in length,[77] areas for discus, javelin, and wrestling had been marked out. Groups of people were streaming out of the smaller side gates of the city. Tradesmen and entertainers awaited them. Musicians played. Dancers spun about clashing finger-cymbals and making whirling patterns in the air with brightly colored ribbons. Food sellers had set up stalls and were shouting the names and prices of their produce. Dogs ran up and down, barking with excitement at the welcome outburst of color, aroma, noise, and spectacle.

Paris approached an important-looking individual who was standing at the entrance to the running track and asked how he might put his name forward to enter the games. The official indicated a line of young men who were queuing up in front of a low wooden table. Paris joined them and after a short while he was issued with a token and pointed to the athletes' enclosure, where he stripped down with the others and began to warm up.[78]

---

77. About 630 feet . . . or 192 meters in today's money. Our word "stadium" derives from the unit of length, which was also used to describe the sprint race itself.

78. He didn't strip right down. It wasn't until the mid-eighth century BC that full nudity became compulsory for athletic events. An idea introduced by the Spartans, probably. *Gumnos*

A whip-crack and a shout. The crowd pressing up against the enclosure parted as a pair of chariots swept through, driven by two smooth, well-groomed, and athletic young men.

"Prince Hector and his brother Deiphobus," whispered the competitor next to Paris. "The finest athletes in all the Troad."

Paris looked the princes up and down. Hector, heir to the throne, was tall and undeniably attractive and well made. He nodded and smiled as he stepped out of his chariot and handed the reins to a slave, laying a hand on the man's shoulder and appearing to thank him. With an almost shy wave, he acknowledged the cheers of the crowd and joined Paris and the other athletes. His brother Deiphobus jumped down from his chariot, but let the reins drop to the ground, and passed through the press of people, making no contact and meeting no eyes. He looked fit and well-muscled, but there was something arrogant and contemptuous in his bearing that Paris took against from the first.

The crowd turned at the sound of a fanfare. Paris saw a line of heralds on the very top of the city walls. Below them a great gate opened.

"The Scaean Gate!" whispered the athlete at Paris's side. "It can only be the king and queen themselves."

Paris expected a great chariot or carriage to sweep out, accompanied by heralds and outriders. At the very least there would be a procession carrying the royal couple on a litter or divan, like those favored by rulers in the east. He did not expect to see a middle-aged couple step out, arm in arm. More like an ordinary man and wife out for a morning walk, Paris thought, than a great ruler with his consort. A loud cheer went up, which the couple acknowledged with nods and warm smiles.

"Is that really King Priam?" Paris asked the athlete next to him.

By way of answer the athlete fell to his knees, as did all the other competitors, the princes Hector and Deiphobus included. Paris knelt too and watched as Priam and Hecuba reached the dais set out for them, commanding a view over the field.

King Priam raised his arms to signal that everyone should stand. "Eighteen years ago," he called out, "a prince was born to us." His voice was strong and clear. "The child never had the chance to breathe the air, but he is not forgotten. Queen Hecuba and I think about him every day. Today all Troy thinks of him. Today his memory is honored before the gods." He turned to the competitors. "Be strong, be fair, be proud, be Trojan."

---

is the Greek word for naked—hence "gymnasium," a place in which to be naked. Modern gym management insists on a modicum of clothing these days and won't listen to any arguments about the real origins of the word—I've given up trying and usually wear at least a little shred of something when I work out these days.

The athletes all around Paris beat their chests and cried out in chorus five times, "Strong! Fair! Proud! *Trojan!*" hitting the last word with greater and greater emphasis each time. He realized this must be a custom and joined in, feeling a shiver of excitement and a thrill of belonging as he thumped his rib cage and yelled out the words.

Trojan! Was there a finer thing to be?

A ram and a ewe were sacrificed. A priest released into the air eighteen doves, one for each of the years that had passed, Paris was told, since the death of the young prince.

Paris threw himself into the games with unbounded enthusiasm and energy. He was in the finest flush of youth, his body honed from years of chasing and rounding up calves, piglets, kids, and lambs, seasoned by the mountain air, and fed on the best mutton stews, goat's milk, and wild-thyme honey. He triumphed in each event as it came, much to the amusement of the crowd, who instantly took to this unknown, but wildly good-looking and boyishly eager, competitor. The only two in the field who came close to threatening his lead were the two royal princes. During the course of the tournament, Paris was told that one or other of the two had been crowned victor at these games for each of the past seven years.

Hector didn't seem to mind being bested by the young stranger, but his brother Deiphobus grew more and more sullen and annoyed as the afternoon wore on. The cheers that rose up from the spectators every time Paris beat him were especially galling. It was all the more unfortunate, therefore, that when lots were cast for the wrestling, the final event of the afternoon, Deiphobus should find himself drawn against this presumptuous interloper.

"I'll bloody teach the peasant not to frisk about like he owns the place," he growled to Hector. "The cocky runt won't know what's hit him."

"Go easy on him," warned Hector. "Show some grace, eh? The people are on his side, and whatever the outcome he will be the overall victor."

The style of fighting for the event was called *pankration*, or "all the strengths"—it was said that its no-holds-barred fusion of boxing and wrestling was invented by Theseus when he defeated the wrestler king Cercyon of Eleusis.[79] Deiphobus was confident that his innocent opponent would be unprepared for the savage kicking, nose- and ear-biting, eye-gouging and scrotum-twisting that were all permissible.[80] But Deiphobus himself was unprepared for the way Paris skipped around him, always out of reach. Daring to smile too. The more

---

79. See the Labors of Theseus in *Heroes* (page 272).

80. In the later, classical, age such scoundrel behavior was forbidden, but in these earlier times few holds were barred.

Deiphobus roared and lunged, the quicker Paris seemed to leap backward. The spectators howled with laughter.

"Stay still, damn you!" shouted Deiphobus. "Stand and fight!"

"All right," said Paris, nipping in and sweeping a foot under Deiphobus. "If that's what you want . . ."

One moment Deiphobus had been standing up, the next he was flat on his back with a country nobody kneeling on him, pinning his shoulders to the ground.

"Had enough, have you?" said Paris, laughing down, one hand raised up to the crowd in salute. Young girls pushed forward and screamed their approval.

This was too much. Deiphobus scrambled to his feet with a yell of wounded pride, calling out for his servant to throw him a sword.

"I'll teach you a lesson you'll never forget!" he snarled, catching the hilt.

But Paris was too quick for him. He took to his heels and ran toward the city walls, still laughing. He knew he could outrun Deiphobus over any distance. He had already proved it in three different foot races.

"After him!" cried the enraged prince.

"Oh, leave it," said Hector. "The boy won fair and square."

"He mouthed blasphemies into my ear," said Deiphobus. "He said foul things about our mother."

This was a lie, but it was enough to energize Hector, who called out, "Stop that man!"

Still laughing, Paris ran on, not knowing where he was going, but filled with the pleasures that victory and exertion bring, laughing and loving life. He could hear the clamor of the chase behind him, but he did not doubt that he could dodge, dive, and duck his way out of trouble. Without thinking he darted through the great open gateway and into the city itself. He slowed to marvel at the maze of lanes and alleyways all around him. So this was Troy. Courtyards, shops, fountains, squares, streets, and people. So many people. It was dazzling and bewildering. He turned round and around, feeling like Theseus in the Cretan labyrinth. He could hear the hue and cry behind him growing louder. He chose a straight and narrow street and ran hard along it until he arrived at stone steps leading up to a pair of gilded gates. Too late he realized that the gates were barred shut and that he had reached a dead end. With the noise of his pursuers growing behind him, he rattled the gates and shouted.

"Help! If this is some temple, I beg sanctuary in the name of all the gods! Help, help!"

The gates opened and a beautiful young priestess emerged from the shadows and descended, holding out a hand.

"Come . . ." she said.

Paris reached up, but the moment his hand touched hers, she drew back with a gasp, her eyes widening in horror.

"No!" she said.

"Please, I beg!" cried Paris, looking over his shoulder. Deiphobus and Hector, swords drawn, were at the head of a veritable river of supporters, spectators, and excitable dogs and children.

"No!" repeated the priestess. "No! No! No!" She shrank back into the shadows, slamming the gate behind her.

Paris banged his fists on the great wooden panels of the portal, but Deiphobus was on him, teeth bared, and roaring with fury.

"Hold him up, Hector. Let's see how much his impudent head laughs when it flies from his shoulders."

Hector, the taller of the two, lifted Paris bodily and held him. "You really shouldn't have upset Deiphobus," he said. "If you apologize humbly, I'll make sure you aren't parted with more than an ear for your troubles."

Deiphobus had raised his sword.

A voice rang out, loud and sharp. "Stop! You can't kill your own brother!"

Deiphobus and Hector turned. Paris turned too and saw his father Agelaus pushing himself through the crowd.

"Set him down, my lord Hector! Set your brother down!"

One side of the crowd parted to let Agelaus through. Another side parted to let King Priam and Queen Hecuba through. Agelaus saw them and dropped to his knees.

"I couldn't do it, your majesties! I couldn't kill that child. And I'm glad I didn't. Look at him. You should be proud of him."

The story tumbled from Agelaus. The crowd fell silent.

Hecuba was the first to embrace the stunned Paris. Priam clasped him close and called him "son." Hector punched him affectionately on the arm and called him "brother." Deiphobus punched him—markedly harder—on the other arm and called him "brother" too. The crowd cheered and cheered as the royal party turned and made their way to the palace.

Behind them, the golden gates at the top of the temple steps opened and the priestess stepped out, wailing and waving her arms as if possessed by some demon.

"Take him away, away from the city!" she cried. "He is death. He will bring destruction to us all."

If anyone heard her, they paid no attention.

The priestess's name was Cassandra, and she had chosen a holy calling over the life of a princess. The most beautiful and gifted of the daughters of Priam and Hecuba, she had devoted herself to this temple of Apollo in Troy. It was her ill luck to have caught the eye of the god himself, who—captivated by her beauty—gave her the gift of prophecy. More a bribe than a gift. He moved in to take her into his arms.

"No!" Cassandra said at once. "I give myself to no one, god or mortal. I do not consent. No, no . . . !"

"But I gave you as great a gift as any mortal can have," said Apollo, outraged.

"That's as may be. But I never asked for it and certainly never agreed to give you my body in return. No. I refuse you. No."

Apollo could not take back the gift—it was an adamantine law that no immortal could undo what they or another immortal had done[81]—so, in his fury, he spat into Cassandra's mouth just as it was rounding for a repetition of the word "No." The spit was a curse. It meant that Cassandra's prophecies would always go unheeded. No matter how accurately she foretold the future, no one would ever believe her. It was her fate to be ignored.

What the brief touch of her brother Paris's hand had told her, we cannot know. What she saw now in her mind's eye, we can only guess. Perhaps it was the same image of flames that had come to Hecuba in her dream eighteen years earlier. We leave Cassandra on the steps of the temple, wringing her hands and wailing with despair.

81. They could augment or supplement, but not undo.

◈   Cassandra

THE GODS LOOK DOWN

The impulse that had sent Paris down the hill, following the prize bull—did that come from him or from a god? A voice inside his head breathed, *Why not?* Why not go down and enter those games and win back that bull? *Why not?* Was it Paris's own voice, his own ambition and youthful impulse, or was it divine inspiration?[82]

Aphrodite had promised him that, if he gave her the golden apple, she would give him Helen. Paris's acceptance into the royal palace at Troy was a delightful excitement for the young man, a change in his life he could never have dared to hope for. But it was a development that seemed more to fulfill Hera's promise of power and principalities than Aphrodite's promise of love. Being a prince in a palace was charming beyond words, but it brought him no closer to that vision of a face, that promised "Helen."

Or did it?

The gods have their own way of doing things.

Yes, life as a prince was certainly charming. Slaves, riches, and gorgeous clothing, food and drink of a quality he had never tasted before. Trojan citizens fell to their knees when he passed. It was—at first—more exciting and delicious than he could ever have imagined. But it seemed there was a price to be paid for all this luxury, obedience, and status. It seemed princes were expected to know all kinds of things.

The arts of war, for one thing. Paris was a born athlete, as all Troy had witnessed. But now he was expected to translate his natural athleticism into the harsher skills of soldiering. Unlike his brothers Hector and Deiphobus, he did not have the muscular strength and military discipline required of a warrior, but for the moment he got by with his gifts of speed, balance, and coordination. Besides, what call was there for martial prowess? Was there ever a more peaceful city than Troy?

The arts of peace Paris found entirely tedious. Protocol, history, commerce, taxation, diplomacy, law . . . Lessons in these subjects kept him indoors and bored him to distraction.

One afternoon Paris was lying back on the cushions in his father's rooms. Priam's voice had been droning on and on, telling the endlessly complex stories of the great royal dynasties of the Greek world. Paris had mastered the art of setting his face into an expression that appeared keen and interested while his mind wandered elsewhere.

---

82. "Inspiration" literally means a "breathing in"—to the ancients this would imply from a god, Muse, or other external power.

"Your aunt Hesione, I have already told you of," Priam was saying. "My dear sister. I owe her my very life. She bought me from Heracles, who was on the point of cutting my throat, as I have told you. How I would love to see her again. But she was taken off when I was boy, as I also mentioned, by Telamon of Salamis. And there she lives with him. They have a son, Teucer. A Trojan name at least, it pleases me to say. Now, moving across the water to the Peloponnese itself. The Argolid is controlled by the great Mycenaean king Agamemnon, of course. His wife is Queen Clytemnestra. And they have four children . . ."

Paris risked a secret glance out of the window. He could hear men somewhere practicing swordplay. Music drifted up too, the sound of girls singing. He thought of his wife Oenone and son Corythus and a small stab of guilt assailed him. In all decency he should have insisted that they join him here in the palace, but he thought of them as belonging to his old life, along with Agelaus. The old herdsman had quite properly insisted on staying on Mount Ida.

"The sheep and cattle will miss you, my boy," he had said. "And I'll miss you too. But your place is with your real family."

Oenone had been less reasonable. She had shed many tears and made a hysterical scene. Paris felt she could at least have understood his position. He had got his way, however. She and his son were on Mount Ida and he was in the royal palace of Troy. It was how it should be. Meanwhile, Priam was still reciting his endless list of kings, queens, princes, and princesses. What possible use was it for Paris to know all the details of these damned royal families and their infernal interrelationships? The knot of Gordium was not more intricate and insoluble.[83]

"And then we move down to Sparta," Priam went on, "where Agamemnon's brother now rules with his wife Helen. Their father Tyndareus has—"

Paris sat up with a jerk and blood rushed to his cheeks. "What was that name, father?"

"Hm? Tyndareus? A descendant of Perseus, like Heracles, originally he—"

"No, before that. You said a name . . ."

"I have said many names," said Priam with a sorrowful smile. "And I rather hoped that you might remember them *all*. I have been speaking of Agamemnon and Clytemnestra—"

"No, after that . . ."

"Menelaus? Helen?"

"Yes . . ." Paris's voice had gone a little husky. He cleared his throat and tried to sound casual. "Helen, did you say? Who is she exactly?"

---

83. See *Mythos* (page 300) for the story of the Gordian Knot.

Priam patiently went through Helen's pedigree, omitting the story of Leda and the swan. The world had heard rumors of the two eggs that hatched the two sets of twins, but Priam felt no need to endorse mere gossip.

Paris let his father finish and then cleared his throat again. Inspiration had struck.[84]

"I just had a thought, father," he said. "That story you told me about Telamon abducting your sister Hesione. During the time of Heracles?"

"What of it?"

"I don't think it's right that my aunt should be living in Salamis. She is a Trojan princess. How would it be . . . No, it's a mad thought . . ."

"What is a mad thought?"

"Well, you're always telling me about diplomatic missions and royal responsibilities and all that," said Paris. "How would it be if I took a—what's the word?—an 'embassy,' is that it? Or is it a 'legation'? One of those. How would it be if I took an embassy, or legation, to Telamon to see if he would be willing to let Hesione come back home? Here to Troy. I mean, you said you'd like to see her again and—"

"My boy! My very dear boy!" Priam was moved almost to tears.

"Let me take ships to Salamis," said Paris, growing in confidence. "Ships laden with costly gifts—you know, silks, spices, wine, and treasure. I will convey your warm and courteous messages to Telamon and perhaps diplomacy will free my aunt."

"It is a wonderful idea!" said Priam. "I shall see Phereclus at once about putting together a small fleet. You're a good boy, Paris, and I bless the day you were restored to us."

But Paris was not a good boy. He had no intention of sailing to Salamis to negotiate the return of some old aunt for whom he cared nothing. What was Hesione to him, or he to Hesione? Aphrodite had whispered his true destination. Sparta and the promised Helen.

No, Paris was not a good boy.

ANCHISES: AN INTERLUDE

Zeus was angry. Aphrodite had dared to laugh at him. In front of all Olympus. That tinkling and triumphant ripple of a laugh that always set his teeth on edge.

---

84. Once again. Was it inspiration, or was it Aphrodite?

Zeus was King of the Gods, Lord of the Sky, and undisputed Ruler of Olympus. But in common with many leaders he was discomfited by the feeling that everyone, from the muddiest mortal to the most shining divinity, was freer than he was. Less hamstrung, hampered, and hedged in. He was confined by treaty, obligation and covenant on the one side and the constant threat of sedition, disobedience, and rebellion on the other. The other eleven Olympian gods could do more or less as they wished, especially within the realms over which they had dominion. They acknowledged Zeus as their king, but he knew that they would never allow him to wield the kind of unquestioned individual power that his father Kronos and grandfather Ouranos had exercised as their right. Apollo, Poseidon, and the others had dared challenge him in the past, they had even gone as far as binding him in chains, but the one immortal he was most afraid of—more so than of his powerful wife Hera—was Aphrodite.

The goddess of love, a daughter of the primordial sky god Ouranos—and therefore of an older generation than Zeus and the other Olympians—Aphrodite spent most of her time on her home islands of Cyprus and Cythera.[85] But the night before, she had dined with the others on Mount Olympus. She had been in a feisty, combative, and teasing mood.

"You gods all think you are so strong, so powerful, so invulnerable. You, Poseidon, with your trident and your tidal waves. You, Ares, with your warhorses, spears, and swords. You, Apollo, with your arrows. Even you, Zeus, with your thunderbolts and storm clouds. But I am stronger than you all."

Zeus frowned. "I rule here. No one has power over me."

Hera cleared her throat meaningly.

Zeus took the hint. "Unless . . . unless, that is, I choose to submit to . . . wiser heads and sounder judgment," he amended. "As in the case of my dear wife, of course."

Hera inclined her head, satisfied.

But Aphrodite was not to be put off. "Admit it," she said. "I have power over you all. Except Athena, Hestia, and Artemis. Those three are immune."

"Ah. Because of their vow of eternal celibacy," said Zeus. "You are speaking of love, I suppose."

"Look what it makes you do! All of you. Every shred of dignity falls away. In the throes of your desire for the most ordinary and worthless mortals you turn yourselves into pigs, goats, and bulls—in every way. Anything to chase down the objects of your lust. It's too funny."

"You forget who I am."

85. Zeus's aunt, Aphrodite, was born from the seed of the castrated sky god Ouranus: see *Mythos*, page 36.

"Yes, you can shoot a thunderbolt, yet my son EROS and I shoot something much stronger. A thunderbolt might blast an enemy to atoms, but love's dart can bring down whole kingdoms and dynasties—even, perhaps one day, your own kingdom and the dynasty of Olympus itself."

Aphrodite's mockery and her irritating peals of silvery laughter were still ringing in Zeus's ears the next day. He would show her. She underestimated him. She was not the only one with the power to humiliate. Now, he asked himself, what was her weakness?

Aphrodite's weakness—one shared by all the gods (Zeus included, although he did not care to acknowledge the fact)—was vanity. She could never receive enough praise, worship, or sacrifice. Zeus knew that, in common with Apollo and her lover Ares, she had a special fondness for the city and people of Troy.[86] It so happened that a festival in Aphrodite's honor was held at this very time of year at one of her temples on the lower slopes of Mount Ida. She would be sure to attend. Like many of the gods she commonly moved among congregants in disguise, eavesdropping on the prayers cast up to her, reveling in the praise, and occasionally punishing the blasphemies that fell from the lips of her supplicants.

Zeus looked down on Mount Ida, searching for a randomly ordinary mortal. His eye fell on a herdsman lying asleep on a grassy bank: a blameless fellow by the name of ANCHISES.[87]

Zeus sent for Hermes. The messenger of the gods, patron divinity of thieves, rogues, and tricksters, cocked his head to listen to his father's bidding.

"Go to the palace of Eros. Find a way to steal one of his arrows. Then make your way east to the Troad. Once there . . ."

Hermes grinned as Zeus outlined his plan. With a flutter of wings from the sandals on his feet, he flew off to obey.

A few days later, in the foothills of Mount Ida, Aphrodite, in the guise of a country girl, glowed with pleasure as she listened to the prayers of the people moving down the hillside toward her temple. A huge painted image of her, garlanded with flowers, swayed on the shoulders of the crowd as they processed. Behind her, Hermes was urging Anchises forward.

"I don't even know you," the herdsman was saying. "And who is this girl that you claim is in love with me?"

"You'll thank me when you see her," said Hermes.

Aphrodite turned in annoyance—a figure in the crowd had come too close and something sharp had pricked her side. Her gaze rested on the person standing closest to her, a man with soft brown eyes. She was about to upbraid

---

86. Aphrodite was officially the spouse of Hephaestus, the lame god of fire and the forge, but it was an open secret that she and the war god were lovers. Venus and Mars . . .

87. Usually pronounced "An-*kai*-sees."

him when a strange feeling swept over her. What was it about him? The young companion by his side—whose head was bowed and whose features she therefore could not make out—pushed him forward. He stood awkwardly in front of her, his face flushed with embarrassment.

"Who are you?" asked Aphrodite.

"I . . . My name is Anchises."

"Come with me. Come with me now!" said Aphrodite. Her heart was beating fast and the blood was singing in her ears. She led him away from the procession. Hermes watched them go, a smile spreading across his face.

In a secluded wood—hidden from but within earshot of the festival procession—Aphrodite and Anchises finished their love-making.

He looked into her eyes. "You know my name," he said. "May I know yours?"

She told him.

He stared. "But why me? Why me? Why a mortal?"

"I don't understand it myself," said Aphrodite, tenderly tracing her fingers over Anchises's face. "It is a mystery. I was walking along with the crowd and then I . . . Oh!" Suddenly she understood.

Zeus! It could only be the work of Zeus.

"Who was that young man I saw you with?"

"Just some cattle-drover. He met me on the high pasture and bullied me and bullied me into coming down to join the festival. He said there was a girl there . . ."

"That would have been Hermes," said Aphrodite. She pulled Anchises toward her in a close embrace. "He thinks that this is a humiliation for me. I choose to see it as a blessing. I feel your child inside me. A son for you, Anchises. I shall protect him always. But be sure to tell no one about this. No one."

Despite his apparently lowly position herding cattle, Anchises was of royal birth—a cousin of King Priam's.[88] There had been some argument years before, which had led to Anchises storming out of the palace and choosing the life of a herdsman on Ida over that of a prince within the walls. Perhaps Zeus knew this fact about Anchises; perhaps he had overlooked it. Perhaps Zeus's actions had been guided all along by Moros. Even the gods were powerless in the hands of the god of destiny, for certainly the child of Anchises in Aphrodite's womb had

---

88. It is tempting but deceptive to think of the Greeks and Trojans as resembling medieval Europeans—feudal kings and lords feasting in their castles, while peasants and serfs toiled in the fields. In fact, the great and noble counted their riches, status, and importance in livestock and never thought agriculture and pastoral labor beneath them. Just as the biblical King David had been a shepherd, so Odysseus could be seen at the plow, and royally born Anchises was quite content with his cattle and sheep. Homer often used the epithet "shepherd of the people" to describe the kingly role of Agamemnon and other leaders.

a destiny. In the view of some, he was—until the arrival of Jesus, perhaps—the most significant child ever born. His birth, like that of Christ, was attended by asses and oxen—for Aphrodite chose to have her baby on Anchises's home pastureland. They named him AENEAS; like Paris, the boy grew up as a herdsman on the slopes of Mount Ida; and, also like Paris, he was all the time without knowing it a member of the Trojan royal family.

It was natural enough that Aeneas and Paris, as fellow herdsmen of the same age on the same mountain, would meet each other and become friends. When Paris's true identity became known and he moved into the palace, he called for his friend to join him. Just as Agelaus had revealed Paris's identity as a prince of Troy, so Anchises came forward to declare himself Aeneas's father. The disagreement with Priam that had led to Anchises leaving Troy was forgotten and Aeneas was welcomed into the palace as Paris's companion and a valued prince of the blood royal in his own right.[89]

THE ABDUCTION

Priam, as he had promised, instructed Troy's finest shipbuilder and engineer, Phereclus, to construct and provision a vessel suitable for Paris's great mission to bring Hesione home from her captivity on Salamis. Paris appointed his friend Aeneas as the legation's second-in-command. While Phereclus finished work on the flagship, Aeneas saw to the preparation of six smaller vessels that were to sail with them in protective convoy.

The Trojan royal family, headed by Priam, Hecuba, Hector, Deiphobus, and Cassandra, gathered on the quayside to see the small fleet off.

"Paris is not going to Salamis," wailed Cassandra. "He is going to Sparta! Sink the ships now and let him drown. He will return with death for us all, death for us all!"

"May Poseidon and all the gods protect you," said Priam, as priests cast barley grain, seeds, and flowers onto the decks. "Hurry back as soon as you can. Every day you are gone is painful for us."

Once they were out to sea, Paris let Aeneas and the rest of the crew know of their real destination.

"Sparta?" His friend was troubled.

---

89. Some versions of this story say that Zeus struck Anchises lame, or blind, or even dead, for daring to blab of his liaison with Aphrodite. It is hard to see why Zeus would be annoyed by his trick on Aphrodite becoming known, but it is accepted by most sources that Anchises was lame.

"Oh, you're so holy, Aeneas," said Paris, laughing. "Live a little! This will be the greatest adventure of your life."

In Sparta, King Menelaus welcomed Paris, Aeneas, and the deputation from Troy. If their visit was a surprise, he was too well mannered to say so. The quality and costliness of the gifts with which Paris showered them proved that this was a friendly visit—one designed, Menelaus assumed, knowing Priam's reputation, to foster amicable relations and a prosperous trading connection between Sparta and Troy. He and Helen feasted their guests and entertained them lavishly for nine days.

On the ninth day the Dioscuri, Helen's brothers Castor and Polydeuces, received word from Arcadia that had them hurrying off with brief apologies. Some long-standing enmity between them and their cousins.[90] The next day a message came for Menelaus to say that he was wanted for the funeral of his maternal grandfather CATREUS on Crete. Suspecting nothing, he too departed at once.

The way was now left open for Paris and his retinue to loot the palace and abduct the unprotected Helen. They took with them Helen's baby son Nicostratus and her enslaved attendant, Theseus's mother Aethra, but they left her daughter Hermione behind.

So many questions present themselves. Was Helen abducted against her will? Did she fall for Paris in the usual way that people fall for each other? They were both young and beautiful after all, or did Aphrodite—ever mindful of her promise—arrange the whole thing? Certainly, in some tellings of the story, the goddess sent her son Eros to Sparta to pierce Helen with one of his arrows, to induce her to fall in love with Paris. Was Aphrodite also behind the death of Catreus, the sudden event that had called Menelaus so conveniently away?[91] These are questions that have always been asked, and will be asked until the end of time. But what we can say with confidence is that Paris sailed away with much of Menelaus's palace treasure, including the greatest treasure of all—the beautiful Helen.

On his voyage back home to Troy, Paris stopped off at Cyprus, Egypt, and Phoenicia, where King Sidon entertained him hospitably and for his trouble was

---

90. Idas and Lynceus, sons of their father Tyndareus's brother Aphareus.

91. Possibly. Catreus was a son of Minos and Pasiphae (see *Heroes*, page 286, for their story) and the father of Aerope (Menelaus's and Agamemnon's mother); his death at the hands of his own son had in fact been foretold by a prophecy years earlier. Which does not disprove Aphrodite's part in it, but certainly complicates it. The accidental slaying of Catreus by his son Althaemenes did occur at just the right time as far as Paris's and Aphrodite's plans were concerned. So convenient was the timing that the intervention of a divine hand might well be inferred.

◈   The Abduction of Helen

murdered. Paris ransacked the Phoenician treasury and sailed for Troy with his ships laden.

Priam, Hecuba, Deiphobus, Hector, and all the rest of the royal family of Troy were astonished to see Helen, but they were delighted by her sweetness, dazzled by her beauty, and entranced by the treasure ships containing the riches of Sparta and Phoenicia. Paris's new bride was welcomed warmly into the palace.

Cassandra burst in to tell them that the presence of Helen would guarantee the destruction of Troy and the death of them all, but they didn't seem to hear her.

"Blood, fire, slaughter, destruction, and death to us all!" she howled.

"Here's to Helen," said Priam, raising a cup of wine. "To Helen!" cried the court.

"To Helen of Troy!"

THE GREEKS (ALL BUT ONE) HONOR THEIR PLEDGE

Menelaus and Agamemnon had made their way separately to Crete to attend the funeral obsequies for their grandfather Catreus. They returned to the Peloponnese together.

"Come and stay with me and Helen," Menelaus urged his brother.

"Good of you, but I'm anxious to get home to Clytemnestra and the children."

"Just a few days. Paris, the Trojan prince I told you about, he and his retinue will still be there. I'd like you to meet him. A good relationship with Troy is in all our interests."

Agamemnon had grunted his assent and disembarked with his brother at the Laconian port of Gytheio.

When they reached the palace in Sparta they found the royal compound in complete uproar. Servants and slaves had been locked in the cellars while Paris and his men had looted and ransacked to their hearts' content. But it was the theft of his baby son Nicostratus and, above all—above everything in the world—the abduction of his beloved Helen, wife and queen, that struck Menelaus like a thunderbolt from Zeus.

Agamemnon roared with fury. For him this was not a personal loss but something far worse—a slight, an insult, an act of contemptuous provocation and betrayal carried out in what Agamemnon regarded as his fiefdom, his Peloponnese. "I had heard that King Priam was wise," he thundered.

"I had heard he was honorable. Report lied. He is neither. He is dishonorable. In rousing Agamemnon he has proved himself to be a fool." The King of Mycenae was the kind of man who did not mind referring to himself in the third person.

A great horn, metaphorical not real, was sounded around the kingdoms, provinces, and islands of Greece. The kings, warlords, clan chiefs, princelings, generals, nobles, landowners and hangdog hopefuls who had gathered in Sparta for Helen's hand and sworn to defend and honor her marriage were now called upon to make good their pledge.

Homer never calls the allied army that Agamemnon convened "Greeks" and only rarely even "Hellenes." He most commonly refers to them as "the Achaeans," named for Achaea, a region in the north central Peloponnese that was part of Agamemnon's combined lands of Corinth, Mycenae, and Argos,[92] but which was used to denote the whole peninsula, including city-states of the southern Peloponnese like Sparta and Troezen. Like Homer, I'll use "Achaean," "Argive"

---

92. Also called the Argolid, just to confuse us more.

("of Argos"), "Danaan,"[93] or "Hellene" to describe the alliance, but most often just plain "Greek" . . .

And so they came, not only from Achaea and the Peloponnese, but also from Athens and Attica in the southeast of the mainland and Thessaly in the northeast, from the Ionian islands and from Crete, Salamis, and the Aegean islands comprising the Sporades, Cyclades, and Dodecanese. The messengers that swarmed from Agamemnon's Mycenaean palace urged each king to bring as many ships and men as they could muster and to gather at the Theban port of Aulis on the coast of Boeotia which looked east over Euboea across the Aegean to Troy.

In Salamis, Ajax the Mighty obeyed the summons along with his half-brother Teucer, the great bowman. Just to complicate matters, a second significant Ajax answered the call too—Ajax, King of the Locrians of central Greece. He is traditionally known as Ajax the Lesser, which is not to disparage his very considerable valor and military zeal, but to distinguish him from Telamonian Ajax, the Great, whose size and strength were more formidable than those of any man alive, second only to the now immortal Heracles. We shall use the original Greek spelling for the Locrian Ajax and refer to him as AIAS to avoid confusion.

Another of the highly important kings to join the alliance was Diomedes of Argos,[94] a fierce and gifted warrior and athlete in his own right, beloved of the goddess Athena, trusted by Agamemnon (not, as we shall see, an easy trust to win) and a close friend of Odysseus of Ithaca, whose idea, of course, the lottery and the oath had been. Idomeneus, King of Crete, grandson of the great Minos, arrived with eighty ships—as many as Diomedes's Argive contribution. Only NESTOR of Pylos and Agamemnon himself, with ninety and a hundred ships respectively, provided more.

As the weeks passed and more and more allies arrived at Aulis, Odysseus became more and more conspicuous by his absence.

"Damn it," grumbled Agamemnon. "You would think he'd be the *first* to arrive."

"I'm sure he will be here soon," said Diomedes loyally.

But of Odysseus there was no sign. At last, word came through that the worst possible fate had befallen the Ithacan king. He had lost his wits.

"It is true, King of Men," said a messenger, bowing low before Agamemnon. "Stark mad, they say."

---

93. Named after Danaus, a mythical Libyan who was considered one of the founder kings of Argos.

94. It could be pronounced "Di-*om*-ed-eez" (to rhyme roughly with "my comedies"), or "Di-oh-*mee*-deez," as the mood takes you.

"Well, now you see, this is a lesson to us all," said Agamemnon to his brother and the assembled courtiers. "Haven't I always said that intelligence can be more of a curse than a blessing? A brain like that, always whirring and churning, scheming and dreaming, plotting and planning—bound to come to grief in the end. Sad thing. Sad thing."

"And his wife Penelope has just presented him with a baby son too," said Menelaus, shaking his head in sorrow.

Their cousin PALAMEDES pursed his lips. "You can never be sure with Odysseus."

"Yes, crafty bugger, no question about that," said Agamemnon.

"How do we *know* that he's truly out of his mind?"

"Might be play-acting, you mean?"

"I wouldn't put anything past him," said Palamedes.

"No harm in making sure," said Agamemnon. "I can ill afford to do without a brain like his on my staff. Go over to Ithaca, Palamedes. See what's what, what?"

SOWING SALT

Palamedes had always disliked Odysseus. The craft and guile that others admired he distrusted. In his opinion the man was as twisted as a pig's tail. And as shitty. If there were two ways to approach a problem, one straight, the other crooked, Odysseus would always choose the crooked. Agamemnon, Menelaus, Diomedes, Ajax, and the others fell for his surface charm and encouraged the plotting and scheming. They seemed to find it amusing, like parents who show off their child's skill at dancing or mimicry. Palamedes was aware that Odysseus was descended from Autolycus and Sisyphus, two of the most devious cheats and double-dealers the world had ever seen. Which made the god Hermes an ancestor too. But that was nothing: on his father's side Palamedes was a grandson of Poseidon and on his mother's a great-grandson of King Minos of Crete, and therefore a great-great-grandson of Zeus himself. He was no more impressed by Odysseus's pedigree than he was by his trickery.

But when Palamedes and his retinue disembarked on Ithaca they found the entire population grief-stricken and distressed. Their beloved young king really had, it seemed, lost his mind. Penelope and the court were distraught, Palamedes was told. They directed him to the southern shore of the island where they assured him he could see the poor lunatic Odysseus and judge for himself.

Palamedes arrived there to find Ithaca's king at the plow. His entirely naked body was caked in mud. His beard was untrimmed and his hair was stuck through with what looked like straw. He was singing a song in a high, tuneless voice. The words were in no language Palamedes had ever heard before. But that was not the strangest part. His plow was being pulled by an ox and a donkey. Their different speeds, sizes, and strengths were causing the plow to veer wildly as it cut a haphazard and wayward groove through the sand and shingle. Odysseus had an open sack hung around his neck by a halter. He took from it handfuls of salt, which he scattered into the furrow as he plowed, singing his wild song all the while.

"Poor man," said Palamedes's second-in-command. "Sowing salt into the sand. He really is gone, isn't he?"

Palamedes frowned, wondering. Then he called out Odysseus's name. Once, twice, three times, with increasing volume. Odysseus paid no attention. He just sang and sowed his salt as if oblivious to everything else in the world.

Odysseus's parents Laertes and Anticlea looked on, a small group of courtiers at their side. His wife Penelope stood apart from them, a look of tragic suffering on her face. There was a basket at her feet.

A young dog, scarcely out of puppyhood, ran up and down the beach barking furiously as Odysseus turned his mismatched team around and began to plow a return furrow, quite as mad and crooked as the one before.

Without a word of warning Palamedes darted toward Penelope, snatched up the basket and—to the astonishment of his own followers and the horror of Penelope and her retinue—ran out and placed it straight in the path of the ox and donkey.

Palamedes rejoined his companions, panting slightly, but looking very pleased with himself.

"What's in it?" his lieutenant asked.

In reply, Palamedes smiled and pointed.

A baby's head came up from the basket. Penelope screamed. The ox and donkey were heading straight toward it. The baby gurgled quite contentedly, its fists waving in the air.

Odysseus suddenly stopped singing. His back straightened, he called out crisp commands to the straining ox and donkey and steered them away. The churning plowshare missed the basket by a finger's breadth. Odysseus dropped the plow's handles, ran round and lifted the baby up.

"TELEMACHUS, Telemachus," he whispered, covering him in kisses.

"So," said Palamedes, approaching. "Not so mad after all, I think."

"Ah," said Odysseus. He turned to face Palamedes and gave a rueful smile. "Well, it was worth a try . . ."

The young dog that had run up and down the beach barking so loudly now leapt up at Palamedes, snarling and snapping its jaws.

◈   Odysseus feigns madness.

"Down, Argos, down!" said Odysseus, noting Palamedes's discomfort with some amusement. "I'm afraid my dog doesn't seem to like you very much."

Palamedes nodded stiffly and went over to present his compliments to Penelope.

Odysseus watched him go. "And *we* don't like him very much either, do we, Telemachus?" he added under his breath to his baby son. "And we won't forget what he did, will we? Ever."

Penelope grasped Palamedes by the hand. "Promise me that you will not let King Agamemnon believe that my husband is a coward."

"Well, you must admit—"

"But this was all at my insistence! An oracle has prophesized that if Odysseus leaves Ithaca to fight in a war, he will not return for twenty years."

"Twenty years? But that's absurd. You can't have believed such a thing, surely?"

"It was very clear."

"Oracles are never clear. Must have meant twenty months. Or maybe it meant that twenty of his men would be lost. Or that he would return with twenty captives. Something like that. But fear not, I shall pass on your message to my cousin Agamemnon. I depart at once. Ask your husband to make his preparations and join us at Aulis as soon as he can, yes?"

Palamedes left Ithaca delighted to have outfoxed the fox.

But the fox was not one ever to forget or forgive. He vowed that the day would come when Palamedes would pay for what he had done.

For now, there was much to do. His feigned madness abandoned, Odysseus threw himself into the preparations for war with zeal. Two hundred and twenty-eight of Ithaca's fittest and finest volunteered to sail with him and fight under his banner, and within a few short weeks twelve sleek penteconters, freshly painted and fully provisioned, were lined up in the harbor ready to sail for Aulis.

Odysseus gave the signal and his fleet set sail. Looking back from the stern of his command vessel, he took in a last sight of Ithaca, a last sight of his wife Penelope, and a last sight of his son Telemachus in her arms.

From her position on the harbor wall Penelope watched the line of twelve ships grow darker and smaller against the huge white of the sky. Argos barked out at the sea, outraged at being left behind. The barking turned to inconsolable howling as his master and the fleet were slowly swallowed up by the haze of the horizon.

On the way to join Agamemnon, Odysseus stopped off at Cyprus to secure the alliance of King CINYRAS, who had promised to provide a fleet of fifty. It was something of a disappointment when his son Mygdalion arrived at Aulis with only the single vessel that he commanded.

"Fifty were promised!" thundered an enraged Agamemnon.

"And fifty there are," said Mygdalion, launching forty-nine miniature model ships of Cypriot clay, each filled with little ceramic figures representing warriors.

It was a stunt that Odysseus and Diomedes were inclined to shrug off, but if Agamemnon had one defining weakness it was self-importance. To his prickly nature the smallest slights and expressions of disrespect were as sparks to dry straw. We all know people like that. He cursed Cinyras and forbade his name ever to be mentioned again. He was brought round by Cinyras's gift to him of a magnificent breastplate.[95]

---

95. Different sources tell different stories about Cinyras. As a major mythical King of Cyprus he is described by some as a pioneer of copper mining and smelting. The island was a major source of the ore for successions of Mediterranean civilizations. Copper was, of course, especially valued during the Bronze Age (bronze is an alloy of copper and tin): indeed, our word "copper" and the chemical abbreviation for it, Cu, derive from the Latin for the island *and* the metal—*cuprium*. Although the island itself may have got its name from the Sumerian word for

While the fleet at Aulis awaited more and more vessels arriving from further kingdoms and provinces, Agamemnon was prevailed upon by his oldest and wisest counselor, Nestor of Pylos, to consider a diplomatic solution to the problem of Helen's abduction.

Accordingly, messages were sent across the Aegean to the court of King Priam, in turns cajoling, insistent, and threatening. Helen must be returned.

Priam responded to the first wave of demands by pointing to precedent. Abduction was clearly not the crime that Agamemnon seemed to imagine. Had not Zeus himself abducted EUROPA and IO?[96] In the mortal sphere had not great Jason taken MEDEA from her native Colchis and brought her to mainland Greece?[97] And surely King Agamemnon could not have forgotten that the so very noble Heracles had snatched Priam's own sister Hesione from Troy to be the forced bride of his friend Telamon? On that occasion Priam had sent delegations with offers of treasure to Salamis, entreating her return, but they had all been dismissed with haughty contempt. Helen was happy in Troy with Paris. Agamemnon and his brother should accept it. The further, more aggressive messages he ignored.

"So be it," said Agamemnon. "Let it be war."

A more serious blow to the morale of the gathering Greek forces came when Calchas—the priest of Apollo retained as royal seer by the court of Agamemnon and respected especially for his ability to read the future from the flight, behavior, and cries of birds[98]—witnessed one day a snake invading a sparrow's nest and eating the eight chicks and their mother.

"Behold!" said Calchas. "Apollo sends a sign. The snake has consumed nine birds. This is a sign that for nine years we will besiege Troy, winning only in the tenth."

Agamemnon valued Calchas highly, but, like most powerful people, he found ways either to ignore or to exploit unpleasant prophecies.

"How do you know it doesn't mean the tenth week, or the tenth month?" he demanded.

---

bronze, *kubar*. Or from the cypress tree. Or from an old word for the henna tree, *kypros* (henna as a dye yields a coppery color: I dyed my hair that color in a moment of student madness back in 1979, when the world was young and more forgiving). Cinyras, according to Ovid, fathered—by way of an incestuous relationship with his daughter Myrrha—the beautiful Adonis, with whom Aphrodite fell in love, the story Shakespeare retells in his extended poem *Venus and Adonis* (see *Mythos*, page 262).

96. See *Mythos*, pages 168 and 182.

97. See *Heroes*, page 192.

98. This practice, which the Greeks called *oionistike*, was known as "augury" in Rome. Another word for this form of divination is "ornithomancy." Not to be confused with "haruspicy" and "extispicy"—forecasting by the inspection of animal entrails.

Calchas knew what was good for him. "Other readings are indeed possible, my lord king."

"Good. Well, don't go round making depressing forecasts like that again."

"No, indeed, sire," said Calchas, bowing his head. But he too had his pride and could not refrain from adding, "There is one truth of which I am absolutely certain, however . . ."

"Oh yes?"

"There is no possibility of victory against the Trojans unless the greatest warrior alive can be numbered in the Greek ranks."

"Well, I *am* in the Greek ranks. More than that, I'm the *commander* of the Greek ranks."

"With the greatest respect, sire, there is a warrior greater even than you."

"Oh," said Agamemnon icily. "And who might that be?"

"Achilles, son of Peleus and Thetis."

"He is just a child, surely?"

"No, no, he is fully an ephebe now, I believe."[99]

"But unproven. He may be fast in the stadium and know how to throw a pretty javelin, but—"

Calchas drew himself up. "Majesty, it is as clear as anything I have ever seen that Prince Achilles will prove the greatest fighter in our armies, and that without him we cannot hope to prevail."

"All right, all right, damn you," said Agamemnon. "Send for this prodigy."

There was a problem, however. Achilles was missing. No one knew where he was.

The men at Aulis soon heard about Calchas's prophecy concerning Achilles's indispensable place in their ranks, and although Agamemnon was now minded to sail for Troy without him, they were superstitious enough, or respectful of Calchas enough, to insist to the point of outright mutiny that Achilles be found and enlisted. But where was he? Agamemnon summoned Odysseus and Diomedes.

"Find Achilles," he commanded. "Take as many men with you as you need, but don't you bloody well dare to return without him."

---

99. An ephebe was a male adolescent who had reached the age—typically seventeen or eighteen—where he could begin full training in the arts of war.

THE LOVELY PYRRHA

A few years earlier Peleus had been more than a little surprised when Thetis came to see him in his palace in Phthia. The appalling image of her holding the infant Achilles over the flames had never left his mind.

She approached him meekly now, throwing herself down before him, grasping his knees, and waving her long hair over his feet in an act of weeping supplication that would have been excessive in a peasant or slave, but from an immortal was without precedent.

"Please," said an embarrassed Peleus, raising her up. "There is no need."

"I have long owed you an explanation," said Thetis. "You were too angry to listen to me, but now you must hear me out."

When at last he understood how and why his first six sons had been burned and lost, it was his turn to weep.

"How much better it would have been, Thetis, if you had trusted me and told me at the very beginning."

"I know!" said Thetis. "Not a day has passed without my regretting my silence. But now, Peleus, I will share everything with you. All the world knows of the prophecy first made by Prometheus—"

"That any son of yours would rise to be greater than his father? Of course, and you know I have never minded it. And it has been shown to be true. You should see Achilles in the stadium. No other boy matches him in any—"

"You think I don't know?" said Thetis. "I come here often, in many forms, to marvel at his speed and power, his skill and his grace. But there is another prophecy of which you have no knowledge, a vision only I have seen."

"What vision?"

"It has been revealed to me that Achilles has two futures. One is a life of serene happiness, a long life blessed with children, pleasure, and tranquility. But a life lived in obscurity. His name will die with him."

"And the other future?"

"The other life is a blaze of glory such as the world has not seen. A life of heroism, valor, and achievement that outshines Heracles, Theseus, Jason, Atalanta, Bellerophon, Perseus . . . every hero that ever lived. Eternal fame and honor. A life sung by poets and bards for eternity. But a *short* life, Peleus, so short . . ." Tears filled her eyes again. "Naturally, even the first life, the long life of obscurity will be short to me. Ninety winters and summers pass in a flash to an immortal. But the second future . . ." She shuddered. "Less than an eye-blink. We cannot allow it."

"Surely we must give him the chance to choose?"

"He is fourteen years old . . ."

"Even so the choice should be his . . ."

"And there is a war coming."

"War?" Peleus stared. "But the world has never been more at peace. There are no threats to peace from any quarter."

"Nonetheless, war is coming. I feel it. I know it. A war such as the world has never known. And they will come for our son. You must let me take him and hide him."

"Where will you take him?"

"It is best that you do not know, that no one knows. Only then will he be safe."

Achilles embraced his friend Patroclus. "I'm leaving you in charge of the Myrmidons," he said.

"They won't obey anyone but you," said Patroclus. "You know that."

It was true that, despite Achilles's young age, the Phthian army were more loyal to him than they were even to his father, their king.

"Nonsense, I'm just a mascot," said Achilles. "Besides, I'll be back before you know it."

"I still don't understand why you have to leave."

"My mother is not one to be refused," said Achilles with a rueful smile. "She has a strange bee buzzing in her ear. She is convinced there is a war coming and that if I fight in it I will be killed."

"Then she is right to take you away!"

"I'm not afraid of dying!"

"No," said Patroclus, "but you are afraid of your mother."

Achilles grinned and punched his friend on the arm. "Not as afraid as you are."

Thetis took Achilles to the island of Skyros, whose ruler LYCOMEDES was an old friend. His most significant act in history up until this point had been his killing of the hero Theseus.[100]

"I think I know how to hide your boy," Lycomedes said to Thetis. "I have, as you know, eleven daughters.[101] Achilles can be dressed up as a girl and live amongst them. No one will ever think to look for him in their company."

A most fetching girl Achilles made too; but he soon proved that he had crossed the threshold into full masculinity by fathering a child by DEIDAMIA, the most beautiful of the king's daughters. They called their baby son PYRRHUS, after the

---

100. He threw Theseus off one of Skyros's cliffs. See *Heroes*, page 316.

101. Different sources credit Lycomedes with a different quantity of daughters: anything between eight and a hundred.

name Achilles had taken as a girl—Pyrrha, which means "girl of flame"—on account of his red-gold hair.[102]

This, then, was the situation when, some years later, Agamemnon sent Odysseus and Diomedes out from Aulis to scour the Greek world for the lost son of Peleus and Thetis. It was unfortunate—as far as Thetis and her hopes of concealing Achilles were concerned—that Skyros was so close to Aulis, for the island was one of the very first places that Odysseus decided to look.

The moment Odysseus arrived at the palace of King Lycomedes, the wily Ithacan's suspicions were aroused. He was a hard man to deceive, and Lycomedes was not an accomplished liar.

"Achilles?" said the king doubtfully, as if the name were unfamiliar to him, which in Odysseus's view seemed unlikely. Even in Achilles's youth, his fame had spread far and wide. "Nobody here of that name, I assure you."

"Really?" said Odysseus. "I am talking about Achilles, son of Peleus and Thetis. Your *friend* Thetis," he added meaningly.

"You're welcome to look around," said Lycomedes with a shrug. "No one here at the palace but my twelve lovely daughters."

Diomedes and Odysseus entered the large open courtyard where the princesses spent the day. Some were bathing, some strumming on stringed musical instruments, some weaving, some combing their hair. A fountain

---

102. Some sources say Achilles had another son by Deidamia, called Oneiros, which is the Greek for "dream." If true, Oneiros seems to have been disregarded by mythographers, unlike his brother Pyrrhus, whose life, as we shall see, was fully recorded under his later name of NEOPTOLEMUS. While on the subject of names, the issue of Achilles's name while on Skyros is of great interest and worth a diversion. There is a much-quoted passage from Thomas Browne's *Urn Burial* (1658): "What song the Sirens sang, or what name Achilles assumed when he hid himself among women, though puzzling questions are not beyond all conjecture." The questions derived from speculation by the Roman biographical writer Suetonius, but Browne took them up again as a way of (ironically) comparing the real possibility of acquiring the full details of a nonhistorical myth with the near impossibility of piecing together the stories behind the bones, memorial urns, and other articles left behind by *real* life—hence Edgar Allan Poe famously using this passage as an epigraph for his story "The Murders in the Rue Morgue," considered by some to be the first detective story, which is all about piecing together truths. The matters Browne raises are indeed "not beyond conjecture." As for the name Achilles took, well, most writers and commentators go with Pyrrha—the "flame-haired one." But according to Suetonius in his *Twelve Caesars*, the Emperor Tiberius (who loved to twit scholars on these matters, as we noted when discussing Hecuba's lineage) came up with a variety of contenders aside from Pyrrha. Cercysera (or Kerkysera) was one, derived from the Greek for a spinning wheel's distaff, long a symbol of femininity, as in the "distaff side" of a family, and the word "spinster"—although *kerkos* means "tail" or "penis," so some think this name was a later joke, one scholar going so far as to suggest that it comes from *kerkouros*, which means "he who urinates through his tail" (given Tiberius's notoriously dark and sick sense of humor he may well have preferred this option). Another suggested name was Issa or Aissa, referring to Achilles's speed (*aisso* means "I sprint, dash, or dart"). Robert Graves has this to say: "My conjecture is that Achilles called himself Dacryoessa ('the tearful one') or, better, Drosoessa ('the dewy one'), *drosos* being a poetic synonym for tears." Aspetos, meaning "limitless" or "vast," is also suggested by some, although this seems to have been a soubriquet used later, once Achilles's reputation had been made.

played. Songbirds sweetly warbled in their rush cages. It was the very picture of feminine tranquility. Diomedes remained awkwardly on the threshold, uncertain where to look, but Odysseus took his time in surveying the courtyard with narrowed eyes. He turned to Diomedes.

"Go back to our ship and return with twenty of the fiercest and ugliest of our men," he said. "Charge in here with them. Storm the place. No warning, swords out. Make to attack the girls. Be terrifying. Yell and beat your shields."

"Seriously?" said Diomedes.

"I mean it," said Odysseus. "And don't hold back. All will be well. Trust me."

When Diomedes had gone, Odysseus stepped forward and quietly laid his sword on the stone edge of the fountain. Then he stepped back, folded his arms, and waited.

Diomedes may have been puzzled by Odysseus's request, but he played his part perfectly. He and twenty huge, hairy, musclebound soldiers burst violently into the courtyard, swords drawn, yelling the most blood-curdling war cries. The princesses screamed and fell back in alarm—all except one of their number, a pretty, redheaded girl, who snatched up the sword at the fountain's edge and brandished it with a snarl and a roar.

Odysseus stepped forward, smiling. "Hello, Achilles, son of Peleus," he said.

Achilles, sword in hand, breathing hard, looked from Odysseus to Diomedes and the twenty men and back again. Then he laughed and put down the sword.

"Let me guess," he said. "Odysseus, son of Laertes?"

Odysseus bowed.

"My mother warned me that if anyone were able to find me it would be you."

"Are you willing to join us?" Odysseus asked. "To go back to Phthia, bring your Myrmidons, and win glory for Greece? Our honor is at stake, and your presence will surely guarantee victory. Agamemnon, Menelaus, your cousin Patroclus, and a great navy await you at Aulis."

Achilles smiled. "Sounds like fun."

IPHIGENIA AT AULIS

The arrival of Achilles and his Myrmidons put great heart into the expeditionary force. They all knew the prophecies. Achilles would assure victory. He would be their champion, their totem. The boost to Greek morale that his presence gave was much needed: tens of thousands had been languishing in Aulis, kicking their heels while they awaited the order to depart for Troy.

Agamemnon welcomed Achilles with as much cordiality as he could summon. "Now at last we can set sail and get this thing done."

But they could not set sail. No fleet, no matter how mighty, can sail without wind and there was none. Not a breath. Not enough to move a toy boat across the waters of a pond. Not enough to wave a single blade of grass. The vessels that carried the food, arms, staff, servants, and all the provisions necessary for the war required wind to move. It would be an impossible folly for the warriors to row the penteconters to Troy without their supply ships sailing in support.

"Calchas!" roared Agamemnon. "Somebody find me my damned seer."

Calchas bowed low before his king, but was reluctant to speak.

"What's the matter with you? Just spit it out, man. Why no wind? Or don't you know?"

"I know, your majesty, only . . . perhaps if I were to tell you later . . . in private?"

"In private?" Agamemnon looked around. His senior staff—Menelaus, Diomedes, Ajax, Odysseus, and King Nestor of Pylos were all present. "No secrets here. Out with it."

"I . . . it . . . it has been revealed to . . . that is to say . . . the goddess Artemis . . . it is she . . ."

"*Artemis?*"

"She has commanded Aeolus, divine keeper of the winds, to calm the breezes, King of Men."

"But why? Who has offended her?"

"Well . . . it seems . . . that . . . that . . ."

"*Will* you stop opening and closing your mouth like a damned fish and come out with it. Who has been mad enough to offend divine Artemis?"

The distress on Calchas's face was evident and its meaning clear to at least one of the group.

"I think," said Odysseus, "that Calchas is finding it difficult to say *your* name, Agamemnon."

"*Mine?* You *dare* to suggest—"

"He can hardly dare to suggest anything if you thunder at him like that," said Odysseus. "Either you want him to speak or you want to terrify him into silence. You can't have both."

Agamemnon waved his hand testily. "You may speak freely, Calchas, you know that. Bark much worse than bite."

Calchas took a breath. "Do you remember last week, my lord king, you went hunting in the grove southwest of here?"

"What of it?"

"I did mention at the time, if you recall, King of Men, that the grove was sacred to the goddess . . ."

"Did you? Don't remember. What of it?"

"You . . . you shot a stag that day. An *excellent* shot but . . . but it seems the stag was also sacred to the divine Huntress. She is angry, sire."

Agamemnon gave an exaggerated sigh, the sigh all leaders give when they wish to express how they are surrounded by fools and eternally burdened with problems that would break lesser men.

"All right. I see. And I suppose we need to make some sort of sacrifice to placate her, is that it?"

"Your majesty is correct."

"Well, give the orders then! Do I have to do everything myself? Sacrifice what, exactly? What would be appropriate? Another stag? A bull, a goat, what?"

Calchas twisted the hem of his cloak and looked in all directions but toward his king. "She really is very angry, sire. Very angry indeed."

"Ten bulls? Twenty? A whole bloody hecatomb?"[103]

"It . . . it is worse than that, majesty . . . The goddess requires nothing less than the sacrifice of"—the seer's voice dropped to a hoarse whisper and tears sprang to his eyes—"the sacrifice of your daughter."

"My daughter? My *daughter*? Is this a joke?"

Calchas's anguished face put the answer beyond any doubt. There followed an icy silence. Agamemnon broke it with another question.

"Which daughter?"

Calchas twisted the fabric of his cloak even more tightly. "Only the offer of your eldest will propitiate the goddess."

Menelaus, Odysseus, and the others turned to look at Agamemnon. His wife Clytemnestra had borne him three girls. Electra and Chrysothemis were still children, but Iphigenia was approaching early womanhood. She was said to be intelligent, pious, and good-natured.

"No," said Agamemnon after a long silence. "Never."

"Now just a moment," said Menelaus. "We are all sworn to this venture."

"Then sacrifice your own daughter!"

"The treacherous Trojan brat has already stolen my wife and my son Nicostratus," said Menelaus. "I have sacrificed enough. Remember your oath."

"What has Iphigenia ever done wrong?"

"I know it's a hard thing to ask, Agamemnon, but if Artemis demands it . . ."

Agamemnon was not to be persuaded. "There are other gods. Athena, for one. She favors Odysseus and will always smile on anything he does. Poseidon is

---

103. A hecatomb was a sacrifice of a hundred cattle. One source suggests that Menelaus had promised Aphrodite he would offer her a hecatomb in thanks after he won Helen in the lottery, but that in all the excitement he forgot. Her anger at this slight is given as a reason for Aphrodite selecting Helen as Paris's offered reward at the Judgment on Mount Ida.

on our side too. And Hera. They will persuade Zeus to intervene. Artemis cannot hold up our fleet forever. If we wait long enough all will be well."

But days passed without a hint of a breeze. The hot, stale conditions at Aulis became a breeding ground for disease. As rumors began to circulate among the Greeks, many came to the conclusion that the vengeful Artemis had gone so far as to shoot her plague arrows into their camp. Weeks went by without the wind springing up or the contagion dying down.

Finally Agamemnon yielded to the pressure mounting on him from all sides. "Sail to Mycenae," he said to Odysseus.

"Sail? The whole point is that we . . ."

"Row! Row to Mycenae. You damned well know what I mean. Swim if you have to, but get there. Tell Clytemnestra that you are commanded to bring Iphigenia to us so that she might marry."

"And who is to be the fortunate husband?"

"Achilles," said Agamemnon.

"Really?" Odysseus arched an eyebrow. "And how does the young prince himself feel about this?"

"No reason to bother him with it," said Agamemnon with a wave of the hand. "They're not really going to marry. Whole thing's just a . . . just a . . . What's the word?"

"Pretext? Excuse? Deception? *Lie?*"

"Don't question my orders. Just go."

"But you don't feel," said Odysseus, "that it is almost inevitable that—"

"That what?"

"Well . . . don't you feel that perhaps a better reason might be found for bringing your daughter here?"

"Nonsense. My plan is perfect. What could be better than betrothal to Achilles? He's the world's darling."

"It's only that . . ." Odysseus cast about for the right way to express himself.

"No more prevarication. Go!"

As Odysseus's ship rounded the southern headland of Attica on its way to the Peloponnese, he pondered the quirks and inconsistencies of his fellow men. He could not doubt that Agamemnon was the most brilliant military commander alive. One could only admire the speed, audacity, and resolve with which he had conquered and combined the disparate city-states, kingdoms, and provinces of the Argolid and turned Mycenae into the great power it unquestionably was. Yet how could such an able general be so foolish when it came to questions of personality, emotion, and feeling? It was surely inevitable that Agamemnon's wife Clytemnestra would insist on accompanying Iphigenia to Aulis for the wedding. What mother wouldn't be there for the most ordinary betrothal, let alone a union as glorious as that which was being held out? How could Agamemnon, who was capable of second-guessing the finest enemy commanders in the field, not see this? How would Clytemnestra react when she discovered that she and her daughter had been lured to Aulis under false pretenses—and for the most unspeakable purpose? And how would the impetuous Achilles respond to the use of his name in such a deception? Ah well, not for Odysseus to question, only for Odysseus to watch with his usual air of ironical detachment.

His assumptions were borne out on arrival at Mycenae. The moment "marriage" and "Achilles" were out of his lips the palace was thrown into an uproar of preparation. Iphigenia was overcome with happiness and Clytemnestra with pride. There was nothing Odysseus felt he could say to stem the tide of their inevitable excitement. His facial muscles ached from the fixed smile he forced onto his features. Yes, *wasn't* it the most marvelous marriage imaginable? Achilles was *quite* as handsome as report had put out. *Weren't* the bride and groom the luckiest young people alive? A *triumph* for Mycenae and for Phthia and all Thessaly. How *very* clever of Agamemnon to conceive of such an *auspicious* notion prior to setting off to rescue poor, *darling* Helen.

It was some time before Clytemnestra had supervised to her satisfaction the loading onto her ships of what she judged to be the appropriate number of slave girls, musicians, and cooks, and enough silverware, fine cloth, and wine to create a wedding feast fit for so golden a couple. Odysseus had been forced to wait fully two weeks before her flotilla was ready to follow his ship to join Agamemnon and the becalmed Greek fleet.

But the moment she stepped down onto the Aulis quay, Clytemnestra knew something was wrong. In the hot, still air the harbor smelled appalling. The expressions on the faces of those gathered to greet her presented looks of either dread, hostility, or inexplicable sympathy.

Agamemnon was genuinely surprised to see his wife. "No need for you to have come, my dear," he said, kissing her on each cheek.

"No need for me to come? You silly man. Odysseus said the same thing. What nonsense! As if Iphigenia would not want her mother on hand for the wedding. Why on earth is everyone looking so distraught?"

Within half an hour she knew everything, and a chastened Agamemnon had once more changed his mind about the sacrifice.

"It's no good," he told his senior staff. "The queen is quite right. The killing of such an innocent would be an obscenity. The gods cannot possibly want it."

Menelaus opened his mouth to protest, but before he could do so Achilles had burst into the meeting.

"You dared use *my* name to lure that poor girl here to her death?" he said, choking with rage. "You *dared?* Send her back at once."

"I will not have my decisions questioned by a mere boy," said Agamemnon.

The two men approached each other breathing heavily, but before they could square off Odysseus interposed himself.

"Now, now . . ." he said, "let's not lose our self-control."

Achilles spat onto the ground and departed without a word.

Odysseus was grateful not to be the supreme commander of this expeditionary force. He knew that leadership brought with it nothing but headaches and heartaches. In this case it was clear that, no matter what Agamemnon did, he would suffer. It was natural that all his instincts as a father and husband should revolt violently at the thought of his daughter's death. Yet by now the whole alliance, down to the meanest slave, had learned the details of his killing of the sacred deer and what Artemis had demanded as recompense. Everyone, even his brother Menelaus, was calling on Agamemnon to yield. Iphigenia must die or the whole project to rescue Helen from Troy would fail. What was one life against the honor of so many Greek kings and princes? What was one life against the rising tide of mortality from the sickness infecting the fleet at harbor? What was one life against the prospect of all the Trojan *treasure* that lay in wait for their victorious armies?

That night even Achilles had overcome his fury at being the unwitting instrument in bringing Iphigenia to Aulis and had added his own voice to the chorus clamoring for her death. He felt deeply sorry for the girl, but his Myrmidons were in no mood to loiter in Aulis for a day more than was necessary. Two of his commanders, Eudoros and PHOENIX, had come to see him that afternoon to make him understand the mood in the Myrmidon ranks.[104]

"They love you, Prince Achilles," Phoenix had said, "but they will not hear of Agamemnon defying the wishes of the goddess."

"It is true," said Eudoros. "Artemis is implacable. My mother Polymele was once a votary of hers.[105] She does not forgive. The Huntress must be appeased. There can be no way out. Unless Iphigenia is sacrificed, this whole enterprise will have been in vain."

In the end it was Iphigenia herself who broke the deadlock. "I will lie on the sacrificial stone and gladly give my life for Greece," she said to a horrified and

---

104. Eudoros was a son of Hermes. Prince Phoenix ruled Dolopia, a subject kingdom of Phthia, and had been responsible for raising Achilles when he had removed from Chiron's cave to Phthia. After Patroclus, he was the man Achilles loved most.

105. This was true. The god Hermes saw Polymele dancing for Artemis and was entranced by her grace and beauty. Eudoros was born of their union. Artemis had not been pleased at the loss of her votary. Had Eudoros not been under the protection of Hermes she would certainly have killed him or transformed him into something beastly.

◈ Iphigenia's Sacrifice

disbelieving Clytemnestra. "This sacrifice is my enduring monument; it is to me marriage, motherhood and fame, all those in one. And it is right, mother . . ."[106]

And so it was that, before them all, she was laid out on the altar stone.

Calchas raised a silver knife high in the air—his expression and speed of movement betraying, to Odysseus's mind, rather too much enthusiasm—and called out to the goddess to accept the sacrifice.

Clytemnestra sobbed. Achilles looked away. Agamemnon screwed his eyes shut.

Calchas brought the knife down. But he did not stab Iphigenia, for Iphigenia had disappeared. In the same instant that the knife descended, she vanished. A stag took her place, and it was that creature's hide that the blade penetrated, not the pale skin of Iphigenia.

The stag's blood erupted in a great fountain. Without missing a beat, the blood-spattered prophet turned to the crowd with a shout of triumph.

"Behold the mercy of the Huntress. She spares the girl! She smiles upon us!"

A muted cheer went up. Had Iphigenia truly been spared by the goddess, or was it some kind of trick cooked up by Agamemnon and his priest? But even as the crowd was deciding, Calchas pointed to the trees that fringed the site.

"Look!" he cried out. "She sends us a wind!"

It was true, the air all around was suddenly in motion. "Zephyrus!" cried Calchas.

Not just *a* wind but the West Wind . . . the wind they needed for the speediest passage east to Troy.

"Zephyrus!" cried the Greeks. "Zephyrus! Zephyrus! Zephyrus!"

In the thrill and fever of preparations, Agamemnon never noticed the departure of Clytemnestra and her party.

"Left without saying goodbye," he told Odysseus. "Not to worry. This war will be over soon enough. A little reflection and she'll understand that I had no choice. Besides, the goddess will have spirited Iphigenia back home anyway. She'll be there at the palace to welcome them when they return. Of course she will. Hope your ships are all seaworthy and ready, Odysseus. We sail at dawn tomorrow. Ho for Troy!"

"Ho for Troy," echoed Odysseus. Drily.

---

106. These are the words attributed to her by Euripides in his tragedy *Iphigenia in Aulis*. That play and the story of Iphigenia's sacrifice were the basis of the excellent Yorgos Lanthimos film *The Killing of a Sacred Deer*, starring Colin Farrell and Nicole Kidman.

THE ACHAEANS

And so the largest fleet the world had seen since time began sailed east across the northern Aegean toward the Troad.

In the second book of the *Iliad,* in a section known as the "Catalogue of Ships," Homer takes 266 lines to itemize this great armada. In flowing dactylic hexameters—the metrical line of twelve to seventeen syllables—that he used for his verse, he tells us where the ships came from and who led them. Over the centuries, classicists and historians have delighted in analyzing this list, comparing it to other sources and weighing the likelihood of each penteconter truly being able to hold up to 120 men, as Homer seems to suggest.[107] The arithmetic that emerges from Homer's list gives us an estimation of the forces which puts the total number of ships at something around 1,190 and of fighting men a (more or less) generally agreed 142,320.[108] Scholars apply archaeological, documentary, and historical data (and a deal of guesswork) to make their own estimates.

In some ways all this is not unlike the "Great Game" played by those avid Sherlockians who discuss Holmes and Watson as if they had been real men who truly lived and whose cases as related by Arthur Conan Doyle are to be treated as factual. A fun and fruitful game it is too. So let it be with the Trojan War. How much historical truth lies behind the story of the story I examine in the Appendix (page 240). But even if we believe a great deal of it really did take place, there is much inconsistency to deal with. I have already bellyached about chronology. In the main lines of the story as it has been handed down, there was at least an eight-year gap between the abduction of Helen and the final sailing of the fleet. This messes with the ages of some individuals in ways that I won't even touch on here. Given the intervention of the gods and other magical and supernatural happenings, I have—as mentioned in the Introduction that you so wisely skipped—thought it best to tell the story of the war and its aftermath without attempting to dot every sequential *iota* or cross every chronological *tau.*

It is enough for our purposes to know that the great Achaean expeditionary force consisted of an unprecedentedly vast fleet carrying warriors drawn from

---

107. A penteconter was a vessel rowed by fifty oarsmen. Not all the ships in the Homeric account had so many men at oar, however. Some are described as having twenty; perhaps they were smaller ships, or perhaps thirty of their rowing benches were left vacant. For example, we are told in the "Catalogue" that each ship of the Boeotian contingent held 120 men, which would mean they had an additional seventy non-rowing warriors on board. We know from the *Odyssey* that the Ithacan ships held fifty men each. The counting game is fun if you're that kind of person, but naturally it proves nothing. It's enough for our purposes to know that the fleet was a large one.

108. Sources like Apollodorus and Hyginus, for example, offer slightly lower numbers. Most agree that the total number of fighting men was somewhere between 70,000 and 130,000.

dozens of kingdoms and provinces under the command of the alliance's High King, Agamemnon of Mycenae.

But before we breast the beaches of Ilium with that force, there is an adventure that befell the Greeks on their way there that we should know about. Although none of the chief actors could have realized at the time, it was an event significant enough to prove decisive to the final outcome of the entire campaign. The origins of this episode, like the origins of the great city and civilization to which the Greeks were headed, could be traced back to the greatest of Zeus's mortal children—Heracles.

STRANDED

The Achaean fleet approached the opening of the Hellespont straits and laid up off the island of Tenedos.

"Last stop before Troy," said Agamemnon. "Let the men have some fun before we begin the grim business of war."

The Greeks swarmed over the island holding impromptu athletic competitions, hunting down game and searching out the island's womenfolk.

Achilles was delighted to encounter a most attractive girl bathing in a pool. But before he could make a move on her, a man rushed out from the trees to confront him, brandishing a sword and roaring with anger.

"Well, well," said Achilles. "And what have we here?"

"You trespass on my kingdom, insolent boy."

"Your kingdom?"

"I am TENES, son of Apollo and ruler of this island. Without the decency to ask permission, you savages chase wild animals across our countryside, tearing up our fields and vineyards, and now you dare to approach my sister. You will pay."

Tenes stamped his feet into the ground and gave another roar. But to Achilles the roar was drowned out by an urgent whisper that echoed inside his head. The voice of his mother Thetis.

"Achilles, beware! Kill no sons of Apollo, or Apollo will surely kill you."

Whether she was truly speaking to Achilles, or whether he was recalling words of hers from long ago, he could not be sure. Thetis had been warning him of things ever since he could remember—dangers, revenges, traps, incitements, taboos, prohibitions, curses. All mothers were protective, he knew that. Thetis was unquestionably more protective than most. Perhaps she had once told him that those who kill the sons of gods could expect to be killed by those gods. It was the sort of thing she would say. Achilles was not afraid. He tamped the inner voice down. His hot blood was up. The sight of this self-important islander snarling and shaking his sword at him was intolerable.

A feint to the left, a dance to the right, a dart forward, a sharp twist of the wrist, and Tenes's sword was on the ground without the need for Achilles even to bring out a weapon of his own. One more sharp twist and Tenes's neck was broken and his life extinguished. His sister screamed and ran away.

Meanwhile, a royal party headed by the Atreides[109] had left Tenedos for the smaller neighboring island of Chryse. It was their intent to make a sacrifice there to Heracles, who had himself burned offerings to the gods on the island before his attack on Laomedon of Troy. They were being led to the very spot by one of Heracles's most loyal followers, Philoctetes, son of King Poeas of Meliboea, who had been there with Heracles all those years ago.

Philoctetes had also been present at the moment of the great hero's death. He had watched in helpless despair as corrosive poison from the shirt that once belonged to the vengeful centaur NESSUS ate its way into Heracles's flesh.[110] In his agonized frenzy, Heracles had uprooted trees for his own funeral pyre. When he begged his friends to set it alight, they had all drawn back. Only Philoctetes had had the heart to do it. In gratitude, the dying Heracles bequeathed him his bow and legendary arrows. Philoctetes, tears in his eyes, set a lighted torch to the pyre and watched Heracles's huge and tormented soul leave his huge and tormented body.[111]

The bow had been given to the young Heracles, some say, by the archer god Apollo himself. But it was the *arrows* that really mattered. Heracles had dipped their tips in the venomous blood of the many-headed water dragon, the Lernaean Hydra. These lethal arrows had secured him victory in many subsequent encounters.[112] But now, since his death—or rather, since his raising up to

---

109. A common appellation for the brothers Agamemnon and Menelaus—it means "the sons of Atreus." Noble and royal Greeks liked to address each other in such terms.

110. See *Heroes*, page 110.

111. Sophocles, in his tragedy *Philoctetes*, has Poeas, Philoctetes's father, doing the actual lighting of the pyre.

112. So many, indeed, that one is given to wonder how many arrows there can have been. He must have knelt beside the Hydra coating arrow tips for hours, or even days, if one is to account for all the damage they were subsequently to do. Some killjoy historians and spoilsport commentators suggest that the Greeks were in the habit of using a mixture of snake venom and excrement to make their arrows and spears either rapidly fatal or slowly and viciously infectious, and that Heracles had probably re-envenomed his arrows many times using this method, rather than relying exclusively on his stock of Hydra-tainted tips. I prefer to believe otherwise. The deadly blood has a direct link to the Hydra's father, the ancient snakelike chthonic monster TYPHON, son of primordial Gaia and Tartarus, and is thereby linked to Python too, the snake slain by the young god Apollo (see *Mythos*, page 97). Pytho, the location of this slaying, was later called Delphi, and its oracle's priestess was known as the Pythia;

Olympian immortality—the bow and arrows were held in the fierce keeping of faithful Philoctetes, who had, in due course of time, numbered himself among the great press of noble suitors that gathered in Sparta for the hand of Helen. And so it was that Philoctetes, along with the others, had sworn the oath to defend the marriage and duly supplemented Agamemnon's grand invasion force with his own seven ships.

Philoctetes's contribution to the Greek cause appeared to end before it began, however. For in leading Agamemnon and the others to the site where he remembered Heracles making sacrifices all those years earlier, he had the ill luck to tread on a viper, which instantly struck out and buried its fangs in his foot. Within moments the flesh around the foot had swollen up and Philoctetes could barely walk. Diomedes helped him across the island to the boat which should have carried them all back to their ships, but by this time the wound was suppurating and giving off the most terrible stench. Odysseus whispered to Agamemnon and Menelaus that such an infection could not be cured and would risk spreading contagion through the ships. The Atreides decreed that Philoctetes should be left behind. They were considerate enough—considerate in their own estimation if not in that of the outraged Philoctetes—to agree that Chryse was too small and inhospitable for him.[113] And so the hobbling, howling, outraged Philoctetes was abandoned on the neighboring isle of Lemnos which, at this time, was deserted.[114] Command of his seven ships, with their complement of 350 oarsmen-archers, was given to Medon, a half-brother of Aias, Ajax the Lesser.

Philoctetes was to remain on Lemnos, suffering from the agony of a wound that refused to heal and living off the flesh of such birds and animals as he could shoot with his bow and venomous arrows, for the next ten years. Store his name somewhere in the back of your mind, for he will return.

---

it would be the Delphic oracle that commanded Heracles to undertake his Labors. Typhon once fought with Zeus for the very control of the cosmos. While the most important destiny of Zeus's son Heracles was to save Olympus and the gods from destruction at the hands of Gaia's offspring the giants, which he accomplished with the blood of Typhon's Hydra-child envenoming his arrows (see *Heroes*, page 107). In a similar manner Heracles rid the world of many of Typhon's other spawn, and defeated countless further adversaries; and then, through the cruel irony of the shirt of Nessus, that same venom caused his own agonizing death. The destiny of those very arrows, as we shall see, was to determine the course of the Trojan War too. What this rambling excursion is trying to suggest is that the Hydra venom is woven through the tapestry of Greek myth, from beginning to end, like a serpentine thread. The painful symmetry of its final use to end the Trojan War and bring down the curtain on the Olympian Age—gods, heroes, and all—calls to mind the *ouroboros*: the serpent that eats its own tail. Typhon was to have his revenge after all.

113. Indeed, it seems that Chryse (the "golden island") was small enough to be wholly submerged by a rise in sea level around the time of the Roman Empire. An amateur archaeologist in the 1960s claimed to have found its underwater ruins, temple and all.

114. A deserted island, according to Sophocles at least. Perhaps after Jason had fathered the Minyae (see *Heroes*, page 171), they left Lemnos and sought habitation elsewhere.

"Now," said Agamemnon, "let the signals be sent. The fleet strikes out at dawn tomorrow."

The word spread from deck to deck across the ships.

"Troy!"

"Troy!"

"*Troy!*"

ILIUM

ARRIVAL

The topless towers of Troy gleam in the sun. From the city's walls the sentries and watchmen cry out and sound their horns. They have seen a sight to strike fear into the bravest heart.

Far out to the west, the horizon that separates the sea from the sky has turned black. The soft bar of haze that every day, until this day, has separated the sea from the sky is now a broad black line, stretching left and right as far as the eye can see. As the Trojans watch, the line thickens. It is as if Poseidon is pushing up a new island or a new continent.

Soon they realize that the black line is not a great cliff rising from the sea. It is an unimaginably huge fleet of ships approaching line abreast. Hundreds upon hundreds upon hundreds of them.

The Trojans have readied themselves for war. For month after month they have been making their defensive preparations. All Troy knows that the cursed Achaeans are coming, but the scale of the fleet, the sight of it . . . For that, nothing could prepare them.

Hector and Paris climb to the ramparts at the first sound of the horns.

"How many?" says Paris.

Hector looks. It has been no more than an hour since Eos flung wide the gates of dawn for her brother Helios to drive his chariot through. The Titan of the sun is already high enough in the sky for his rays to set the sea sparkling. Through the haze, Hector sees flashes in the far distance as sunlight strikes prows and masts and hulls and dipping oars.

"They will be close enough to count before long," he says. "Come. Time to make sacrifices and then . . . we arm."

While we wait for the fleet to arrive and for the Trojans to prepare and make their offerings to the gods, there is also time to consider the question of which gods the Trojans make those offerings to. To the same gods as the Greeks? Have the gods chosen sides?

OLYMPUS

The gods have been growing more and more excited by the spectacle of the gathering mortal storm. They have watched with fascination and mounting excitement as the Achaeans made their preparations and set a course for the Troad.

The Olympians enjoy the mauling and brawling of their playthings, their little human pets. They thrill to mortal war. They are as fired up and involved as Elizabethan nobles wagering on the outcome of a bearbaiting, or Regency lords ringside at a cockpit in the East End, or Wall Street bankers at an illicit downtown cage fight. "Slumming it," nineteenth-century sprigs of the nobility called such excursions into the mud and blood of the commonality. The appalling appeal of the dirt and its heady threat of violence. And like those sporting aristocrats, the gods have their favorites. Rather than wagering with gold, the immortals stake honor, status, and pride on the outcome. Also like those sporting aristocrats, the gods—as we shall see—are not above nobbling the runners and riders they disfavor and unfairly assisting those they support.

By quieting the winds and demanding the sacrifice of Agamemnon's daughter Iphigenia, Artemis, the divinity of the hunt and the bow, had held up and dispirited the Greeks at Aulis, which gives us a clue as to where her loyalties lie. She and her twin Apollo favor the Trojans, and over the coming years they each will do what they can to advance that cause. As will their mother, the ancient Titaness Leto. Aphrodite has naturally been on the Trojan side ever since Paris awarded her the Apple of Discord (and perhaps before, when she coupled with Anchises and bore his child, Aeneas). Ares too, the god of war and Aphrodite's lover, has aligned himself with Troy.[115] These four Olympians will prove hugely powerful allies for the Trojans.

The Achaeans can look to support from Hera and Athena, who still smart from the insult of being spurned, as they see it, by Paris. Besides this, Athena has always had a special fondness for Diomedes and Odysseus and will always watch over them. Hermes favors Odysseus too,[116] but the slippery messenger god's first loyalty is always to his father Zeus. Poseidon, ruler of the sea, takes the Achaean side, as does Hephaestus, god of fire and forge—perhaps for no other reason than that his unfaithful wife Aphrodite and her lover Ares prefer Troy. Naturally Thetis, for the sake of her son Achilles, will always do what she can to advance the Greek cause.

Hades could not care less who wins: it is enough that the conflict will fill his underworld with new dead souls. He hopes the war will be a long and bloody one.

---

115. In Homer's account certain minor gods, often associated for obvious reasons with Ares, are also numbered on the Trojan side. They are Phobos (Fear and Panic) and Deimos (Dread)—in reality they are little more than personifications of the human emotions that naturally run high in battle. Eris too, goddess of strife and discord, whose golden apple led to Helen's abduction, is sometimes counted in the Trojan ranks. The river god Scamander naturally aligns himself with Troy and will have a role in trying to repel the greatest of the Achaean warriors.

116. As mentioned, Odysseus is a great-grandson of Hermes through his mother Anticlea, a daughter of Hermes's son Autolycus.

Dionysus takes no active part but is satisfied by the knowledge that libations of wine will be poured, wild dances held, and sacrifices made in his honor during the periods of feasting and revelry which must inevitably punctuate the crises and climaxes of battle.

Demeter and Hestia, goddesses of fertility and the hearth, are the two Olympians with the least interest in or connection to warfare of any kind. Their concern is with the women and children left at home, with the grieving families, and with the workers and slaves who labor in the fields and vineyards, with those—as a phrase from our time has it—who keep the home fires burning.

Zeus, ruler of heaven and king of all the gods, what of him?

Zeus likes to think himself a wise and benign onlooker, a disinterested spectator far above the fray. He accepts the role of referee and grand arbiter. He has instructed the other Olympians not to interfere, but he will turn a blind eye when they do. He will not be above being persuaded to make interventions himself. His own mortal daughter Helen is, of course, the *proschema*, the *casus belli*, the flame that has lit the fuse; this might be thought to lead him to side with the Trojans, but Zeus has skin in the Achaean game too. His beloved son Heracles was responsible for installing Tyndareus on the throne of Sparta[117] and for the sacking of Laomedon's Troy. Another son, Aeacus, is the grandfather of three of the Greek alliance's most important warriors—Ajax, Teucer, and Achilles. Zeus has lost count of how many other of his descendants are numbered among the Greek (and indeed Trojan) forces. But he believes himself to be magnificently neutral.

Some historians and mythographers have put forward the notion that the Trojan War was initiated by Zeus as a deliberate attempt to end the human project. To wipe mankind from the map once and for all. Or at least to thin out the population, which was growing larger and larger. As it did so, mankind was becoming more difficult to control. Even the immortal gods couldn't engage, relate, interbreed, and command the destinies of so swelling a number of ambitious, inventive, and self-obsessed beings. Why, they were becoming as arrogant and entitled as the gods themselves. And more and more forgetful of their obligations by way of temples, prayers, and burnt offerings. They were forgetting their place. Especially those who were descended from Zeus himself, or from his fellow Olympians. A world stocked with demigod heroes was unstable and dangerous. Heracles had saved Olympus, but maybe another could arise with the presumption and strength to dislodge the gods.[118] Zeus had dispossessed his father Kronos who had usurped *his* father Ouranos. Thetis had

---

117. See *Heroes*, page 107.

118. Bellerophon, for one, had tried to place himself up there: see *Heroes*, pages 124 and 136.

been avoided by Zeus on account of the prophecy that foretold how great any son by her would grow to be. Achilles seemed to be showing the truth of that.

But Zeus had neither the focus, the insight, nor the eye for detail to formulate or drive such a plan to a properly thought-through conclusion. He was more in the mold of the one who maddens the dogs and lets them fight it out, or of the Roman emperor who looks down on the slaves and gladiators, gloating at all the blood and gore that soaks into the sand. He was neither puppet-master nor grandmaster tactician. He hadn't the patience to pull every string. He took no pleasure in surveying the board, fingers pressed to temples, deep in analytical thought, foreseeing every move and countermove. Give a good shake and see what happens, that was his way. Light the blue touchpaper and retire.

Let mankind tear itself to pieces all on its own.

THE TROJAN FORCES

We know that the Achaean expeditionary force is made up of over a hundred thousand men drawn from dozens of the kingdoms, island realms, and provinces that constitute the Greek world. But what of their enemy, the defenders of Troy? Is there no more than one people in one walled city to repel this unprecedented threat?

In reality the Trojan alliance is made up of almost as many disparate elements as the Achaean. Hector and Priam have cemented a coalition of forces from the neighboring states of the Troad and beyond, from as far north as Macedonian Paeonia and Thrace (today's Bulgaria) to as far south as continental Africa. A "Catalogue of Trojans" appears in Book 2 of the *Iliad* alongside the more exhaustive "Catalogue of Ships." Over the course of the war, Prince Aeneas will lead the Dardanian allies;[119] MEMNON of Ethiopia, Zeus's son SARPEDON of Lycia, and PENTHESILEA, Queen of the Amazons, will fight for the Trojans too. Other significant warriors from the coalition will make themselves known as the war unfolds.

Homer seems to suggest that all the Achaeans converse in Greek and that the Trojans—while understanding Greek and speaking it to the enemy on the few occasions when they meet to parley or exchange messages—have to contend with allies who "bleat like sheep" in *hundreds* of languages, which means that Hector and his fellow generals are forced to rely on interpreters in the field to relay their

---

119. In some sources, the Dardanians are the original inhabitants of the country around the city of Troy and governed by the junior branch of the Trojan royal family headed by Anchises and Aeneas.

messages and instructions. Modern philology proposes that the Trojans in reality spoke a Hittite language called Luwian.[120] We will allow the convention begun by Homer and continued by Shakespeare and almost all playwrights, historical novelists, and filmmakers since. Unless a particular moment in the story calls for different tongues, all the participants understand each other and speak the same language. Happily for us it is *this* language. The one that you are reading now . . .

THE EMBASSY

The Greek flagship was a sleek black Mycenaean penteconter fronted by a brightly painted prow. On board were Agamemnon's senior staff of advisers. With the enemy coast now in sight, Agamemnon's mind raced ahead, picturing the beachhead and drawing up plans for the first assault, but Nestor of Pylos urged him to stay his hand. The High King had had enough of delay, and took no pleasure in being interrupted by anyone, but he always found time for Nestor, who was known to be the wisest man in the Greek world. He was certainly the oldest of Agamemnon's close counselors, and while the King of Men could be impatient, impulsive, and stubborn, he had sense enough to know that good advice cost nothing and might sometimes save a deal of trouble. Nestor convinced him that before he committed to an all-out attack, it would be prudent for the fleet to lay off at some distance and send forward a single ship with an embassy to King Priam, offering him a final chance to return Helen.

"They will have observed by now," said Nestor, "that a force of unprecedented size is bearing down upon them. Priam is accounted a sensible man. He will see the value of an honorable concession."

Menelaus, Odysseus, and Palamedes were chosen to lead the delegation.

"But demand more than just Helen," Agamemnon commanded. "Our expenses in equipping for war must be met too. Priam must open his treasury to us."

The sentinels on the watchtowers of Troy saw a ship break from the line and make its way alone toward the shore. The white flag of Eirene, goddess of peace, fluttered from its mast. A Trojan named ANTENOR—who was to Priam what Nestor was to Agamemnon, a wise and trusted counselor[121]—was sent to meet this embassy.

As it awaited news, the Trojan court found itself divided. Hector and Deiphobus, egged on by a hotly furious Paris, convinced Priam that Agamemnon's

---

120. Sometimes called the more pleasing "Luish."

121. And a distant relative too: at least according to sources later than Homer.

and Menelaus's outrage at Helen's flight from Sparta was fake, confected, in reality no more than a pretext for aggression.

"The Atreides couldn't care less about Helen," said Hector. "They want the spoils of war."

"Hear the legation out! Hear them out!" said Cassandra.

"Hector is right," said Deiphobus. "The Hellenes have cast envious eyes across the Aegean for years."

"Hear them out or Troy falls."

"It's our gold and treasure they want." "Hear them out or Troy burns!"

"They're not taking Helen away from me," said Paris.

Cassandra started to weep. "If Helen is not returned, we all die! Every one of us in this room."

"Besides," said Hector, "no city has ever been better defended. No army better prepared. Troy is impregnable."

"We should at least make them welcome," said Priam, "and listen to what they have to say."

Helios had slipped below the western horizon by the time the truce ship dropped anchor off the Troadic coast. Odysseus, Menelaus, and Palamedes, attended by pages, came ashore in a small tender, where they were met by Antenor, who greeted them with great respect and unfeigned civility. Under protective guard, the party made their way across the plain of Ilium, over the River Scamander, through the high Scaean Gate, and into the city, where they were led to Priam's palace. Crowds of Trojans lined the streets and watched in silence as they passed by.

The handsomeness of Menelaus was noted.

"But nothing like as beautiful as Paris," murmured the women.

"But who is the man smiling as if he knows a great secret?" others wondered. The whisper went round that it was Odysseus of Ithaca, and some hissed. Word of his duplicity and cunning had reached Troy.

Priam and Hecuba greeted the deputation with solemn dignity. The Trojan princes were polite, but cold. Paris and Helen stayed away. After feasting, music, and formal praise poems sung in their honor, the Greek party were taken to Antenor's house, where they would spend the night, before returning to the palace in the morning to begin the formal discussions.

"You are welcome under my roof-tree," said Antenor. "Sleep well, and let us pray to the gods that tomorrow our talks will prosper."

Back at the palace, Priam sought out Helen in her private apartments.

"Paris not here?"

"He is making plans," said Helen. "He worries that Menelaus and Odysseus will somehow persuade you to give me up."

"That is what I came to ask you about. Is it truly your wish to stay?"

"Paris is my husband and this is my home."

"No part of you would rather go back to Sparta with Menelaus?"

"Not the smallest part of me."

"That is all I needed to know."

In fact, Paris had slipped out of the palace and made his way to the house of ANTIMACHUS, a well-born but far from affluent courtier who owed Paris more than he could ever hope to repay. He had been entrusted by Priam to lead the negotiations with the Greeks.

Paris pressed gold into his hand. "Not only is your debt forgotten," he said, "but there is more gold to come."

"If?" said Antimachus.

"If," said Paris, "you persuade the negotiators to stop their ears to Achaean lies and false promises. And there is more gold than you have ever seen or dreamed of if the Achaean dogs now asleep in Antenor's house never make it back to their ship alive."

Menelaus had found it a torment to be inside the city, so close to Helen yet forced by the requirements of diplomacy to hold his tongue and temper. As he had lain in bed trying to sleep he had considered stealing out of Antenor's house and making his way to the palace. If he found the vile Paris lying next to his adored wife, he would slit the coward's throat. No, he would beat him to death with his fists. Beat him and beat him and beat him . . .

With this delicious scenario playing in his mind—fists crashing and smashing Paris's pretty and insolent face into a mush—the sound of urgent banging at the door jerked him awake.

Antenor was a seasoned courtier. Courtiers do not survive long enough to be seasoned unless they maintain an efficient network of spies and informers. Antenor's spies had followed Paris all the way to Antimachus's house and overheard every word of his plot against the Greek legation.

"I am ashamed of my own people," he said, hurrying Menelaus and the others into his hallway. "We are not all so treacherous. But it is no longer safe for you to remain in the city. I urge you to come with me."

Under cover of night he led the Greeks back to their boat.

When they reached the flagship and relayed the news of Paris's murderous intent, Agamemnon roared in fury; but in his heart of hearts he was not displeased. An all-out campaign against Troy would bring him glory such as no man—not Jason, not Perseus, not Theseus, not even the great Heracles—had ever won. Gold and treasure and slaves and eternal fame. The gods might even raise him to Olympus. He could not confess it even to himself, but had the peace mission been successful, he would have been hugely disappointed.

There was another advantage to the embassy's failure. Word of Paris's secret plot spread from ship to ship like wildfire, filling every Achaean heart with fury. If energy and morale had been sapped by the seemingly endless preparations and the succession of dark portents that had hung over their enterprise since the beginning, this confirmation of Trojan perfidy was just what was needed to inflame the passion and reinforce the commitment of every member of the invasion force.

BEACHHEAD

At dawn the following morning Agamemnon commanded that the signal be sent down the line. The oarsmen bent their backs and the fleet advanced.

Each ship had a prow, or beak, painted in bright colors and usually carved into a figurehead. On Agamemnon's flagship the head of Hera, Queen of Heaven, glared out with imperious scorn. Other ships showed the faces of gods and divinities local to their kingdom or province.

Picture the sight of a thousand hulls fizzing to a stop in the sand, beaks grinning, glowering and scowling; hear the sound of tens of thousands of warriors banging their swords on their shields and yelling out their war cries. Enough to curdle the blood.

But Hector, shining in his armor, splendid in his chariot, led the Trojans out of their city, over the bridges that spanned the Scamander and toward the invading Greeks, calling out encouragement.

Agamemnon's flagship slid to a halt on the beach and dropped her anchor stone from the stern. Achilles climbed up onto the prow's peak.

"Follow me," he yelled, pointing his sword toward the dunes. "We can be inside the city before the sun sets."

Agamemnon was being fitted into his armor at that moment. It annoyed him to have the grand moment of his own landing on enemy territory upstaged. He was about to bark a terse counter-order when the seer Calchas shouted at Achilles to stop.

"I have foreseen that the first man to step down onto Trojan soil will be killed," he said. "If that man is you, Peleides,[122] then our cause is lost before it is begun."

"There are more prophecies to my name than there are days in a year," said Achilles with disdain. "I am not afraid. Besides, that isn't soil—it's sand."

---

122. "Peleides" means "son of Peleus"—I shan't use this formulation much. Homer and the other poets of the Trojan War use it all the time, and of every hero. Diomedes is *Tydides*, Odysseus *Laertides*, etc. As we know, Agamemnon and Menelaus are the *Atreides*.

But whether it would have brought his death or not, Achilles was to be denied the moment. Before he could spring down, a voice behind him cried out, "I'll be the first to fight!"

A young man leapt from the ship.

"Who was that?" shouted Agamemnon.

The young man turned with a broad smile and beckoned to the rest. They recognized the face of Iolaus, leader of the Phylacean contingent.[123]

The sight of him, so young, so cheerful, and so confident, inspired the others. They swarmed down from their ships to join him, in turn putting heart into the troops up and down the line. Within moments the whole beachhead was filled with Greek warriors beating their shields and crying, "Hellas! Hellas! Greece! Greece!" They streamed up the dunes and followed Iolaus onto the plain. The war had begun.

Iolaus threw himself into the ranks of Trojans massed on the plain to meet the Greek advance. He killed four, and wounded a dozen others, before the enemy around him suddenly melted away and he found himself facing a tall warrior alone. The warrior's helmet obscured his features, but the cries of "Hector!" from the Trojan ranks made it clear to Iolaus who his opponent was. He put up a fierce fight, but was no match for Hector's skill and strength, and in a blur of sword strokes, feints and parries, was quickly cut down. He died where he fell. Calchas's prophecy had been fulfilled. The first Achaean to touch Trojan ground had died.

Two of Iolaus's Phylacean contingent pulled his body back toward the Greek line. Hector let them go. He admired courage, but above all he respected the custom, so profoundly serious for Greeks and Trojans alike, that the dead be given up to be cleansed and burned or buried by their people. For their corpses to be left above ground to rot was the greatest dishonor that could befall them. Such sacrilege shamed both sides. The war that was to rage for so many years would see unspeakable violence, barbaric acts, and monstrous bloodletting of the most cruel and merciless savagery; but there were, nonetheless, conventions and rituals to be observed, and their importance cannot be overstated. As time will show.

From that moment on Iolaus was given the name PROTESILAUS—"the first to step forward."[124] For generations and generations, long after the war, shrines and statues to him were erected and venerated around the Greek world.

---

123. Pronounced "I-owe-lay-us"—not to be confused with Heracles's nephew of the same name (see *Heroes*, page 67). The "Catalogue of Ships" records him as having brought forty vessels.

124. Pronounced "Pro-teh-si-*lay*-us": kind of end-rhyming with Menelaus and Iolaus.

His brother Podarces took over command of the forty ships that the Phylaceans had brought to the alliance.[125]

With Protesilaus's body safely behind the lines, the battle was now joined in earnest. Achilles and Hector were in the thick of it, but it was a Trojan by the name of CYCNUS who swiftly emerged as the most fearsome warrior on the field. He roared forward, hacking to the left and right with his sword.

"I am Cycnus, son of Poseidon," he yelled, "and no spear, sword, nor arrow can pierce my skin."

The slaughter he inflicted began to turn the tide of battle, and it looked as if the Greek cause was lost almost before it had begun. It really did seem to be true that he was invincible. Teucer's arrows bounced off him; Ajax's spearpoints glanced away too. Achilles, entirely unafraid, exulting in the fighting, ran straight at him with a whooping cry, shield up. The force of this sudden rush and the shield smashing into his face knocked Cycnus to the ground. Achilles was instantly on him, grabbing at the fallen man's helmet straps and twisting them

125. Confusingly, Podarces was also Priam's original name, as you may recall. It means "helping with your feet," "running to the rescue," "swift-footed." Variations of it are used by Homer as an epithet for Achilles, whose speed as a runner was unequaled.

◈ Greek Armada landing at Troy, as depicted in Wolfgang Petersen's 2004 film.

tighter and tighter around his throat until the life was strangled from him. His hide might have been impenetrable, but like any mortal man he needed to breathe.

While for the most part Poseidon favored the Achaean cause, Cycnus had been his son, and he did not forget him now. No sooner had the last choking breath left his body than he was transformed into white swan which rose up high above the battlefield and flew away, westward. Away from Troy.[126]

The Trojans took this for a sign and turned and ran for the sanctuary of their city.

Agamemnon ordered no pursuit. "Time enough soon," he said. "We know now we have their measure. First we attend to our dead, send up sacrifices to the gods, and make all the proper preparations."

THE BATTLE LINES HARDEN

The Achaean fleet could not remain stretched out so thinly along the beachhead, out of sight from the central command vessels in both directions and open to attack from Trojan raiding parties. But to cluster the ships close was to render them even more vulnerable. Above all to fire. Agamemnon had conducted enough campaigns by sea to know that lines of shipping could be sitting targets for flaming pitch or oil. Fire was able to spread from deck to deck with terrifying speed. He instructed each contingent of the fleet to go deeper into such protected inlets and creeks as they could find, or further out to sea. Twenty-four-hour guards to be posted on all moored ships. The punishment for falling asleep on sentry duty to be death.

Next, the construction of a defensive stockade was undertaken. Behind this outwardly pointing palisade of sharpened stakes the Greeks could set up a secure encampment. Temporary, of course—Troy would be theirs within a week, two weeks at most—but there was no reason to be slapdash about things. For most of the time, the Aegean's tides were as gentle as the lapping of a lake, but Eurus, the East Wind, had been known to buffet and blow with destructive force when his temper was up. Only Agamemnon's flagship and the vessels of the most important leaders were to remain close in to the stockade. The supply ships with their slaves, servants, sutlers, craftsmen, priests, cooks, carpenters, musicians, dancers, and other essential camp-followers could shuttle back and forth between land and sea as required.

---

126. *Cycnus* means "swan," as in our word "cygnet." Phaeton's lover had the same name and was turned into a swan, too, when the gods took pity on his grief after Phaeton's death.

Nestor and Odysseus between them devised a rudimentary signaling language of handclaps, horns, flags, and fires by which some element of ship-to-ship, ship-to-shore, shore-to-shore, and shore-to-ship communications could be established. Tents were erected for senior generals and their retinues. The campaign would be over too quickly for the miniature settlement to need to grow much more.

Agamemnon was content. Morale was high.

Across the plain of Ilium stood a great city ready to repel any assault and weather any siege. Over the past year, under the supervision of Priam and Hector, Troy's already mighty walls had been reinforced and a network of secret tunnels and inland waterways dug. Seaports and trading stations could be reached by river as well as by tunnel. The city was in no danger of being starved into submission. Watchers on the ramparts had a full 360-degree field of vision from which to survey the land around and warn of incoming hostile troops.

Within the city walls every household had been given three huge *pithoi*, or storage jars, each one as high as a man, with the capacity to hold enough grain, oil, and wine to support a small family and its servants and slaves for a year. A spirit of determination and fellowship bonded Trojans of all ranks and classes together, united in unshakable loyalty to their city and royal house and in their detestation of the foe.

Priam was content. Morale was high.

STALEMATE

We have the benefit of relatively recent history to know that confident expeditionary forces and confident defenders, each armed with equal technologies, resources, and tactical intelligence, can quickly become entrenched in insoluble stalemate. We know how wars that each side believed would soon be decided can stretch out over months and years. The Greeks and Trojans were perhaps the first to discover this unhappy truth.

Agamemnon and his generals soon realized that Troy was too big to encircle in a siege and the Trojans too wise to be coaxed out for one great decisive battle.

Months went by. The passing of the first year was marked with songs, sacrifices, and games. Then another year was over. And another. The period of stalemate, from Protesilaus planting his feet on Trojan soil to the full engagement of the armies, lasted an extraordinary nine years. There was a fear that to make the first move was to create a weakness—a bind that chess players call *zugzwang*.

During this time the Achaean stockade naturally grew more and more set, solid, and substantial. The encampment under its protection added more tented accommodation and weatherproofed huts, more supply lines and more features of what could only be called town life. Makeshift markets, drinking dens, and shrines soon became indistinguishable from the kinds the Greeks knew back home. The pathways that ran along between the ships and the stockade turned now and then into side tracks, or opened up into areas for assembly, until they began to resemble civic roads, streets, and squares. In time they were given names. Corinth Avenue. Thessaly Street. Theban Way. An air of permanence descended.

The support structure that fed this great encampment was of a complexity that could never have been achieved through one conscious act of design. Only the slow evolution of need could build out such an intricate entity. With its nerve center, veins, arteries, and sluicing drains, the Greek camp took on the qualities of a living organism; and like any living organism it needed continual sustenance.

The city of Troy itself might have been unassailable, but there was nothing to stop Achilles, Diomedes, Odysseus, Ajax, Menelaus, and the others from leading war parties to raid, scavenge, and maraud the countryside around. Wine, grain, livestock, slave women—all were fair game, all could help feed the great encampment. For nine years the Trojan War was more plunder than thunder.

These raids were the specialty of the Myrmidons. Homer relates that under Achilles's relentless and ruthless direction they sacked more than twenty cities and coastal towns over the course of the nine years. One such raid was to have far-reaching and fatal consequences. We will come to it soon enough, but first we should look at the few other episodes of significance that took place during this stagnant period.

PALAMEDES

You will remember Agamemnon's cousin Palamedes, the man who saw through the feigned madness of Odysseus? There was never any love lost between the two men. Odysseus was not above nursing grievances, harboring grudges, and plotting slow revenges. Things came to a head after Agamemnon had sent Odysseus north to Thrace under instructions to return with as much grain as his ship could carry. When he returned with nothing more than a pitiful quantity of olive oil and sour wine, Palamedes had mocked him in front of his own men.

"The great Ithacan, the master tactician, Odysseus the brilliant, Odysseus the wise and wonderful. So reliable. So resourceful."

Odysseus kept his temper under control and replied icily. "We all bow to Palamedes when it comes to intellect and ingenuity. Doubtless he could have done better."

He did not expect the riposte that came.

"Of course I can. Anyone can. Anyone who isn't scared off by Thracian barbarians shaking their spears."

"Prove it."

Much to Odysseus's chagrin, Palamedes *had* proved it. He sailed off in a ship of his own and, in a few weeks, returned, loaded to the gunwales with fine-quality grain and fruit.

Over the next months, Odysseus stewed and studied, brewed and brooded, all the while keeping a cheerful outward demeanor. Palamedes was liked by the rank-and-file soldiers, not least because he had devised dice and board games, which had started a craze among the troops up and down the line.

One evening a group of Mycenaeans came to Agamemnon. A dead Trojan spy had been found in the Greek camp. His body had been searched and a note found, apparently from King Priam to Palamedes.

"The information you have shared with us has been priceless to Troy's cause. The gold we sent you is but a small measure of our gratitude."

Palamedes, hands bound, was brought before Agamemnon. When shown the note, he laughed and denied all knowledge.

"A cheap and obvious plant. Either the Trojans want to sow confusion or some enemy of mine is making a clumsy attempt to incriminate me."

"I agree," said Odysseus, nodding with sympathy. "There may be little affection between us, Palamedes, but I have never thought you capable of such base treachery."

Palamedes bowed, a little surprised and disconcerted to receive support from this quarter.

"Yes, but the seal is unquestionably Priam's," said Agamemnon.

"Poo, easily forged," said Odysseus. "Besides, even if it *is* Priam's seal, that's as much proof of Trojan trickery as it is of Palamedes's guilt. I think you'll find our friend is innocent. There'll be no secrets traded for gold."

"Well, it's soon settled," said Menelaus. "Let Palamedes's headquarters be searched."

Odysseus shook his head with displeasure. "Such a mistrustful course of action can only . . ."

"Search away," said Palamedes. "I've nothing to hide."

To the shock and disgust of all, and the pained distress of Odysseus in particular, a large hoard of Trojan gold was found buried in the ground right behind Palamedes's tent.

Agamemnon would settle for nothing less than a public execution by stoning. Palamedes died protesting his innocence, punished further by his last sight: Odysseus shaking his head and pursing his lips in sorrowful disapproval, before—when he could be sure that no one else could see him—favoring Palamedes with a wide smile and a triumphant wink.

News reached Euboea and Palamedes's father, King Nauplius, who was horrified by the thought that his son could have been guilty of the unspeakable crime of treason. He had another son, Oeax, who convinced him that Palamedes had been the victim of a plot to frame him. His popularity and ingenuity had posed a threat to the cozy cabal of Agamemnon, Menelaus, Odysseus, and Diomedes, Oeax said.[127] Odysseus had surely been the spider at the center of the whole ugly web of conspiracy. He had never forgiven Palamedes for exposing his feeble pretense of insanity on Ithaca. Or for showing him up over the matter of the Thracian raids.

Miles away from the Troad, across the wide Aegean, there was nothing either Nauplius or Oeax could do to avenge the death of Palamedes. For now. But Nauplius, son of Poseidon, was quite as capable of biding his time as Odysseus had proved himself to be.

TROILUS AND CRESSIDA

Another story that comes down to us concerning these years of stalemate is that of Troilus and CRESSIDA, immortalized not by Homer, or Virgil, but by two great English-language poets who lived much, much later—Chaucer and Shakespeare. Their versions are based on a combination of classical and medieval sources and their own imaginations.

In the simplest and earliest tellings, Troilus is established as the youngest of Priam's and Hecuba's sons. Still in his teens and, it is generally agreed, of remarkable personal beauty, he tries to take an active part in the skirmishes and minor engagements that were the stuff of the war's early years, but is kept back by his family in deference to a prophecy which tells that Troy will never fall to the Greeks if Troilus lives long enough to reach the age of twenty. The Trojans

---

127. There was a common belief later that Palamedes, besides devising board and dice games, had "invented" all the consonants in the Greek alphabet except *beta* and *tau* ("b" and "t"). Unhappy math students can blame him for *pi* and *sigma* . . .

are determined to keep him from harm, therefore, and ensure that nothing should stop him from attaining that age, thereby securing the safety of their city.[128] Unfortunately for them, Athena whispers the substance of this prophecy to Achilles, who ambushes Troilus while he is out riding with his sister Polyxena. They flee for protection to a temple of Apollo. Achilles, who has no time for the niceties of sanctuary, chases them inside, where he cuts off Troilus's head and, in the frenzy of his bloodlust, butchers the body. Polyxena he spares. She looks into his eyes and he into hers. There seems to be a connection between them. That connection is to come to a crisis much later.

The brutal murder of Troilus was seen as crucial in hardening Apollo's opposition to the Greek cause and to feeding his hatred of Achilles in particular. It was not in the nature of the Olympian gods to overlook such sacrilege committed on their holy ground.

In the later stories a romantic element is added. Troilus is still young and beautiful, but now he has fallen in love with Cressida, the daughter of Agamemnon's prophet Calchas.[129] A forbidden love affair across enemy lines blossoms—encouraged and enabled by the Trojan courtier PANDARUS. Homer represents Pandarus as a mostly honorable and courageous leader of men (although susceptible to being manipulated by interfering gods, as we shall see); in Chaucer he is amiable enough as an avuncular go-between; but in Shakespeare he is portrayed as a whispering flatterer, a distastefully prurient matchmaker and pimp.[130]

Calchas persuades Agamemnon to sue for his daughter's return. At this time (in Shakespeare's version at least) the Greeks hold captive the senior Trojan lord Antenor, savior of Menelaus and the earlier Greek deputation, and so an exchange is negotiated: Cressida for Antenor. But Diomedes falls for Cressida and she, in turn, falls for him. Troilus hears of this betrayal and vows revenge on Diomedes. Strangely, in Shakespeare's play—which is considered one of the most problematic and beguilingly odd of his entire canon—neither Troilus nor Cressida suffer the usual fate of star-crossed lovers. The play ends with the killing of Hector and an address to the audience from Pandarus in which he

---

128. Troilus's name can be seen as combining *Tros* and *Ilus*, the names of Troy's two founding kings. Other interpretations see it as a diminutive, i.e., "Little Troy," or perhaps a fusion of *Troi-* and the verb *luo* which means, among other things, at a stretch, "destroy"—or at least "dissolve" or "disintegrate"—and, in its middle voice (a special Greek verbal mode), "ransom."

129. In these versions Calchas is not a Greek, as otherwise represented, but a treacherous Trojan who has defected to the Greek side.

130. His name lives on in the English word "pander," which derives from his representation as a procurer and sexual matchmaker. To pander to someone is to accommodate their tastes, to gratify their desires.

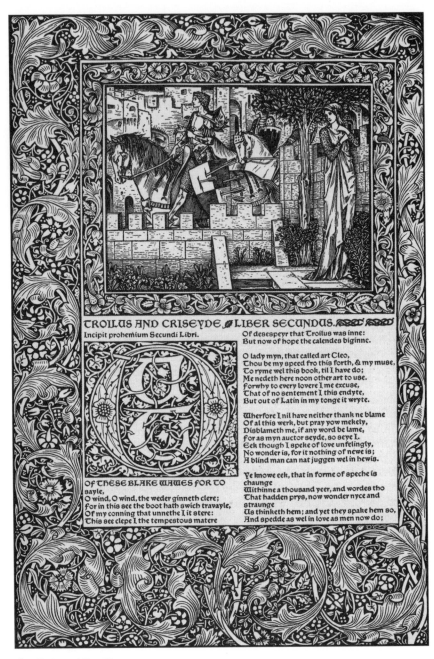

Troilus and Cressida

bemoans the lot of the "bawd" (pimp) and bequeaths the audience his venereal diseases. Troilus and Cressida are left alive and their story is entirely unresolved.

AENEAS, ACHILLES, AJAX, AGAMEMNON—THE RAIDING PARTIES

Among the various sorties undertaken by Achilles and his Myrmidons was an attack on Mount Ida, the mother mountain of the Trojans. Until he and his flocks were violently preyed on by Achilles, Aeneas had mostly stayed out of the war. The loss of his livestock and the laying waste of his pastureland drove Aeneas and his father Anchises to Troy, where he remained, fighting alongside his cousins Hector, Deiphobus, Paris, and the rest, until the final moments of the conflict.

Ajax did his share of rustling and raiding too.[131] One story tells of his attacking the kingdom of Phrygia, south and east of the Troad, and bearing off the king's daughter TECMESSA, with whom he developed a fond and fruitful relationship. Another rather touching episode describes Ajax and Achilles becoming so wrapped up in a board game that they are oblivious to an encroaching band of Trojans.[132] Only the intervention of Athena saves them from certain death. In these circumstances divine assistance is often rendered by the god or goddess in question creating a thick fog as cover for the escape of their favorites.

The most consequential of Achilles's raids took him to the city-state of Lyrnessus, in Cilicia, to the south of the Troad. Here he slaughtered the king and all his sons, but spared a princess of the royal house named BRISEIS.[133] She was added to the great train of captives pulled along by the marauding Achaeans as they made their way around the provinces of Asia Minor, looting and burning. He razed the city of Chryse to the ground too, capturing—among others—CHRYSEIS, the daughter of CHRYSES, a priest of Apollo.[134]

---

131. Just to remind you: unless otherwise stated, plain "Ajax" refers to Telamonian Ajax—Ajax the Great. If Ajax the Lesser appears, he will be called "Aias."

132. The board game is given variously as *pessoi* or *petteia*—*pessoi* being the Greek for "pieces" or "men," as in chess pieces or chessmen. Indeed, the game is sometimes represented as having been played on a checkerboard and has been thought of as a forerunner of draughts (checkers). This is the game believed to have been invented by Palamedes.

133. It's an important name, so worth thinking how you might pronounce it in your head, which always makes names easier to read. "*Briss*-ace" is probably the most straightforward pronunciation, or "*Briss-ay*-iss"; though some would prefer "*Bryce*-ace" or "*Bryce-ay*-iss."

134. *Chrys-*, which prefixes all the names here, is from the Greek for "gold"—as in chrysanthemum, literally the "golden flower."

When the raiding parties made it back to the Achaean encampment, the booty from the sacked towns—including its human content—was counted and divided up. Agamemnon was given the pick of the women and chose Chryseis to be his personal slave. Achilles took Briseis as his prize. Other treasure and slaves, male and female, were apportioned first to the great kings, princes, and generals, next to their subordinates, and then all the way down to the ordinary fighting men, who cast lots for what and who remained.

Into the tenth year, then, nothing had been achieved by either side. The Trojans had failed to dislodge the Achaeans and the Achaeans were no closer to taking back Helen than they had been when Protesilaus fell on that first day of fighting.

Things were about to change. A tepid war was about to catch fire.

CHRYSEIS AND BRISEIS

Sheltered some way from Agamemnon's command post, the Myrmidon ships and tents had become the center of Briseis's existence. Now the property of Achilles, she moved around the camp in mourning for the loss of everything and everyone she had known and loved in Lyrnessus. Patroclus, Achilles's friend and sometime lover himself, liked and admired the young princess and did what he could to comfort and console her.

"Achilles is more than fond of you," he would say. "When all this is over, he will take you back to Phthia as his wife and queen. Wouldn't you like that?"

To which Briseis would only smile in sorrow and shake her head.

Meanwhile, Agamemnon was enjoying the fruits of his own pillage and plunder, having chosen the beautiful Chryseis to be his personal slave and attendant.

Chryses, the priest of Apollo and father of Chryseis, left the smoking ruins of his home city of Chryse and made his way by ship to the Greek encampment.[135] At the heavily guarded entrance to the stockade he begged to be allowed through for an audience with the Achaean commander. The guards led him to Agamemnon's enclosure. Throwing himself down on the ground before the throne, Chryses grasped Agamemnon's knees, as was the custom when beseeching favors from the mighty.

"Our city is named for the gold that once enriched us. Only return my daughter, great Agamemnon, and what treasure I still possess will be yours."

---

135. Christ, what a criss-crossing crisis of Chryse names . . . It is worth noting, however, that this scene—the painful embassy of Chryses—is where Homer begins his *Iliad*.

◈ Achilles and Ajax playing dice during the siege.

Agamemnon pushed the old man's hands away. "All that you have we can take whenever we choose," he said. "And as for Chryseis—she is mine. A lawful prize of war. She pleases me and will grow old in my service. At the loom by day, in my bed by night."

The guards and attendants sniggered. Chryses dropped his head and clutched again at Agamemnon's knees.

"In the name of mercy, dread king . . ."

"Enough, old man!" Agamemnon kicked him away. "Your snot and slime disgust me. Leave now or be taken prisoner yourself."

Chryses was driven back along the shore toward his ship, dogs at his heels. The wild children of the camp chased after him throwing stones, jeering at his pitiable distress. There on the sand he fell to his knees and cried up to his divine protector.

"Apollo Smintheus, lord of mice and men! Golden god of archery and augury. If ever my service and devotion have pleased you, avenge me now on these brutal Danaans. In mocking your devoted priest they mock you. Avenge me and avenge your honor. An arrow of yours for every teardrop of mine."

Apollo heard his prayer and answered it at once. He stormed down from Olympus, a quiverful of plague arrows at his back. He shot them first into the animals—the mules, horses and dogs—before turning them on the Achaean men, women and children.[136] For nine days the deadly arrows rained down into the ships and along the whole beachhead. Contagion in a military camp strikes more fear than fire, ambush, or any threat of enemy attack. The spread of the disease seemed unstoppable. The Achaeans were forced to pile up more and more corpses to burn. The stench of death was everywhere.

On the tenth day Achilles, alarmed by the depredations in his own Myrmidon division and by the rapidly deteriorating spirit and morale of the entire army, summoned the prophet Calchas to a meeting of the principal generals—himself, Agamemnon, Menelaus, Odysseus, Diomedes, Idomeneus, Nestor, and Ajax.

"Calchas," said Achilles, "you are gifted with the sight that looks into the dark purposes of the immortals and the unwinding of Fate. Tell us why we are being punished with this rain of death. Which god have we offended and how do we put it right?"

Calchas clasped and unclasped his hands. "Speak!" said Achilles. Calchas shook his head unhappily.

"Are you saying that you do not know?"

"Dear son of Peleus, I can see all too well," said Calchas; "but there are those here who will not want to hear the truth. If I speak openly I fear that it will enrage one who is powerful enough to have me killed for revealing what I know."

"Anyone who dares threaten a single one of the silver hairs on your head will have to deal with me first," said Achilles. "That I swear. You are under my protection. So speak freely."

Calchas took courage from this. "Very well, then," he said. "It is clear what has happened. Shining Apollo has answered the prayers of his servant Chryses, whose daughter King Agamemnon refuses to return. This plague is his punishment for our treatment of one dear to him." He turned nervously toward Agamemnon. "Asking no ransom, you must return Chryseis to her father, King of Men. When you have done this, and made sacrifices to Apollo, only then will the pestilence lift."

Agamemnon stared in disbelief. "I beg your pardon?"

"As long as Chryseis stays in your retinue, the sickness will continue to rage."

---

136. That the plague struck the animals before the men is a pleasing Homeric detail. In truth it is not uncommon for plagues to jump species: from marmots to fleas to rats to humans, and so on. These kinds of "zoonotic" transmission still take place today, as we know to our cost.

"Every time I ask you for a prophecy," said Agamemnon, his color rising, "Every single bloody time, it's nothing but gloom and doom. Your counsel is always for me to sacrifice something, *my* daughter, *my* gold, *my* retinue . . . Me, always *me*. Never any other king or prince, always *me*. Why should I lose Chryseis? She is beautiful, wise, clever, and capable. She means more to me even than my own wife Clytemnestra back in Mycenae. I deserve her. She is mine by right. And now you dare tell me to give her up for nothing. Not a scrap of recompense? I should strangle you for your impudence."

"By all means, majesty," replied Calchas smoothly, "but you might recall that Achilles has just promised to protect me. That might be something you want to turn over in your mind before you raise a hand in anger."

Achilles placed himself in front of Calchas, arms folded. The High King's foul temper was fully on display now, but he retained enough of a sense of self-preservation to hold himself back from a physical confrontation with one he knew could best him in all the arts of close combat. Besides, in his heart of hearts, he knew that Calchas was probably right. As he always was. But the combination of the contemptuous gleam in Achilles's eye and the realization that he would have to surrender Chryseis was more than he could bear. To be so humbled in front of not just every senior prince and general of his army but their guards and staff officers too—this was an unendurable assault on his pride and dignity. The news of it, doubtless exaggerated to make him look even more foolish and impotent, would spread across the encampment quicker than wildfire, quicker than the damned plague itself.

"Very well," he said at last, in what he hoped was a tone of measured, even bored, magnanimity. "Odysseus, take a ship and return the girl to her father. But as compensation I must be allowed to take another girl to be my body servant. That is only right, is it not?"

The others nodded their heads in assent.

"That is fair," said Menelaus.

"Good," said Agamemnon. "Then I choose the girl that Achilles moons over, Briseis—is that her name?"

"Oh no," said Achilles. "Never."

"Am I not supreme commander of the Achaean armies? Why should I always be the one to give up his treasure for the common good? I shall take Briseis. It is decided."

Achilles exploded with rage. "You pig-eyed sack of drunken shit!" He drew his sword and fired his foam-flecked fury right into Agamemnon's face. "You bastard son of a mongrel bitch . . . How dare you? I've come all this way to help you win back *your* sister-in-law. The Trojans have never done me any harm, but my Myrmidons and I risk our lives every day for you and your brother. When have I ever seen you in armor risking death? I should strike you down like the treacherous, whining, stinking, cowardly dog you are."

And Achilles might indeed have dealt Agamemnon a fatal blow, there and then, had not the voice of Athena sounded deep inside him.

"For my sake, Achilles, and for the sake of the Queen of Heaven herself, who loves you and Agamemnon equally, put up your sword! Believe me, the day will come when a glory will be yours such as man has never known—if only you can find the courage to walk away now."

Achilles took a deep breath and sheathed his sword. In a lower voice, all the more dreadful for its quiet intensity, he said, "Take Briseis from me and that is the last you or the armies of the alliance will ever see of Achilles or his Myrmidons."

Agamemnon had no such voice of divine calm and reason sounding inside him.

"Sail away, little boy!" he yelled. "We can dispense with your glamour, vanity, and show. We don't need you or your pretty Myrmidons. You may be gold, and we poor ordinary men may be of bronze, but ask any soldier out there which metal they'd rather have for a sword blade or a spearpoint—fine gold or base bronze. Sail away, and leave this war to real men."

Before the inflamed Achilles could answer, Nestor stepped forward, arms upraised.

"Please, please, please!" he said. "If Priam and Hector could hear you now, they would laugh with joy and triumph! They would laugh and cheer! For the two greatest men of our armies to be at each other's throats is a disaster for the noble cause to which we are all sworn. Listen to me. I have seen more years in this world than the two of you combined. I have fought the wild centaurs of the hills with Pirithous and Theseus. I was in the hunt for the untamable Calydonian Boar and the quest for the Golden Fleece of Colchis, side by side with every hero you have ever heard of.[137] Believe me when I tell you that infighting like this is a graver threat to us even than Lord Apollo's plague. Agamemnon, great lord! Show your power and wisdom. Give up Chryseis—"

"Haven't I already said that I will do so?"

"—and agree not to seek to replace her with Achilles's prize. Achilles, fall on your knees before your supreme commander. The royal and divine scepter in his hands tells us that Agamemnon is our king of kings, anointed by Zeus.[138] Recognize this. If you embrace each other, we cannot lose."

---

137. See *Heroes*, pages 310, 225, and 166.

138. The scepter was made by Hephaestus himself, master craftsman of the gods. He gave it to Zeus, who gave it to Hermes, who gave it to Pelops, who gave it to his son Atreus (father of Agamemnon and Menelaus), from whom it was taken by his twin brother Thyestes, from whom

"Yes, yes, that's all very well," said Agamemnon, before Achilles could reply; "but this spoiled brat has set himself up against me. He thinks *he* is the key that will unlock Troy and release Helen. An army needs a clear understanding of who commands. We will do better without him and his petulant tantrums."

"And you *will* do without me!" said Achilles. "Hear me proclaim this, you loathsome turd from the ass of Typhon. From this moment on, I declare myself out of your war. The gods themselves could not persuade me to lift one finger to help bring your brother's precious wife out of Troy. She's nothing to me—and you, King of Pigs, are less than nothing to me. The day will come when you crawl weeping to me on your knees like the trail of treacherous slime you are, begging for me to fight. And when that day comes, I will laugh in your face."

Achilles stalked out, head held high. Silence fell over the assembly. Agamemnon gave a sharp bark of contempt.

"We are well rid of him. Now, to work." Chryseis was fetched and accompanied Odysseus back to her father's city of Chryse on a ship loaded with cattle and lambs for sacrifice, as directed by Calchas. Next, Agamemnon summoned two of his heralds, Talthybius and Eurybates. "Go to Prince Achilles's headquarters and order him to hand Briseis over to you. Tell him that, if he refuses, I will come and fetch her myself."

The heralds bowed and made their way, gulping with trepidation, along the shore to where the Myrmidon ships were beached. In front of them stood the cluster of tents and huts belonging to Achilles and his personal staff.

Achilles welcomed them with something approaching warmth. "Come in, come in. I know why you're here. Don't be afraid. I have no quarrel with you. Patroclus, fetch Briseis. You'll take some wine with me, gentlemen?"

The heralds broke into relieved smiles. When Achilles chose, he could dazzle with unforced charm.

Patroclus found Briseis and told her of her fate. She dropped her head.

"I'm sorry, princess," said Patroclus. "What must be, must be. He does not want to let you go. We will see what we can do to get you back. He will miss you. I will miss you."

Patroclus watched Talthybius and Eurybates escort Briseis away toward Agamemnon's enclosure.

The moment the heralds had departed, Achilles dropped his outward show of indifference. Without telling Patroclus where he was going, he abruptly left the tent. Once outside, he broke into a run, flying over the wet sand along the

---

it was finally wrested by Agamemnon. Pausanias, the second-century AD traveler, tells us that the scepter survived down to his own time, when it was worshipped as a god by the people of Chaeronea. It was kept in the priest's house, and people brought it offerings of cake every day. I wonder if Chaeronea was known for the plumpness of its priests?

line of shipping, skipping over the mooring cables with all the astonishing speed and grace of which he alone among mortals was capable. He did not stop until he had reached a deserted part of the shore, where he sank down on his knees and cried out into the waves.

"Mother, come to me! Help your miserable son."

A splash, a flash, and Thetis stepped from the waves and rushed to embrace her beloved boy.

Motherhood was hard for Thetis to bear. The knowledge that she would live forever and her son for a brief burst of mortal time was a constant torment. To see him so unhappy, and for this to cause unhappiness for her, was an experience for which she had no defense. Empathy did not come naturally to immortals and, when it did, it came as pain.

"What is it, Achilles, my love?"

Out it came: all the anguish and despair, all the rage at the injustice, betrayal, insult and ill-use. If Thetis thought he was making too much of a small thing, she gave no indication. Mothers never do. All she saw was his misery and despair.

"Outrageous, wicked, monstrous," she murmured, stroking his golden hair. "But what can I do?"

"Zeus owes you," Achilles said. "Go to him. Tell him to send Trojans swarming over the Achaean camp, killing and killing without mercy. I want the Achaean army pinned against their ships like herded cattle. And slaughtered like herded cattle. Let Agamemnon see what disaster falls when he insults Achilles. The Greeks must lose everything. I want them humbled. I want them broken.

 Briseis leaves Achilles.

146

Brought down into the dust. How dare he take Briseis away from me? How dare he? How *dare* he? Let the armies of Greece be pushed into the sea. Their ships can go up in flames and I will cheer. Let him come whimpering to me, sobbing for forgiveness, and I will spit into his beard."

AGAMEMNON'S DREAM

Thetis cooled her son's burning brow, sang to him, and only left him when she was sure he would do himself no harm. She took herself up to Olympus to seek the aid of Zeus, throwing herself before his throne and grasping his knees in supplication.[139] The King of the Gods heard her out. He loved her well and wanted to grant the favor that, as Achilles had rightly said, he owed.[140] But he feared the wrath of Hera, his wife.

"She has never forgiven Paris for awarding the apple to Aphrodite. You know how she hates Troy and all Trojans. If I gave them any victory over the Greeks, even if it were to please Achilles and bring Agamemnon to heel and a final Greek triumph closer, I would never hear the end of it."

"But you will help?"

"I bow my head," he said, doing so. "You know that is a sign that my word is given and can never be broken. I will find a way. Leave this with me."

Thetis left and plunged herself into the ocean. Zeus sat and plunged himself into thought.

His solution was cunning in the extreme. That night he sent a dream to Agamemnon, a dream that took the form of Nestor.

"King of Men," said Dream Nestor. "The Sky Father is pleased to send me as a messenger with the news that tomorrow is The Day. After so many long years, the hour of Argive victory is finally come. If you raise your army and go all out to fight tomorrow, the walls of Troy will fall. Know this as the word of Zeus."

Agamemnon awoke and spread the news for all the armies of the alliance to arm themselves and prepare for a great victory. If Nestor was surprised and

---

139. Homer rather endearingly suggests that Thetis had to wait twelve days before she could get an audience with Zeus, because he and the other gods had traveled overseas to feast with the Ethiopians . . .

140. Thetis had been personally instrumental in saving Zeus from a rebellion started by the other gods, who had tried to shackle him and usurp his power. Thetis broke the chains and summoned the hundred-handed Briareos (also known as Aegaeon), the fiercest of the three HECATONCHIRES (see *Mythos*, page 22), up from Tartarus to sit by Zeus's throne and scare off the rebels. So Zeus certainly did owe Thetis this favor.

puzzled to have starred in a dream without his knowledge, he kept the fact to himself.[141]

The Trojans, meanwhile, were also preparing. Their spies in the Greek camp had told them the welcome news of Achilles's withdrawal from combat. Hector and Priam took this as a sign that the Greek army would be demoralized and ripe for attack.

Paris armed himself in front of the mirror, admiring what he saw. Now he stalked through to the front line of Trojans gathering on their side of the River Scamander and looked across to the enemy.

The Greek army was emerging from their ships and tents like bees from a hive: thousands and thousands swarmed through the stockade and massed in formation on the plain.

For the first time in ten years, true battle lines were forming. Following Nestor's advice, Agamemnon gave orders that they should line up according to region, tribe, and clan. To have the men fighting shoulder to shoulder with their comrades, kinsmen, and neighbors would be of boundless help with morale and fighting spirit, Nestor said.[142]

The front lines of the Achaean forces were led by Odysseus on the right flank, with Nestor's son ANTILOCHUS as his deputy. Aias and Idomeneus of Crete headed the left.[143] The center was commanded by Diomedes and Ajax the Great.

King Agamemnon, pricked and shamed by Achilles's accusation that he never fought, was parading majestically up and down in full battle armor in front of the whole Greek line. No one could doubt that he looked magnificent. Every inch the supreme commander. The sight of him, and of the towering Ajax in particular, caused Paris to turn and head back through the Trojan lines. His brother Hector stopped him at the Scaean Gate.

---

141. In Book 2 of the *Iliad*, Agamemnon first tests the Greek armies by saying they are free to go home, fully expecting them to cry out as one that they would rather stay and fight. To his dismay they hurl themselves into the ships and only the combined rhetorical skill and persuasive power of Odysseus and Nestor (the real Nestor) persuade them back from the brink of desertion.

142. A principle that was adhered to as recently as the Great War of 1914–1918. Lord Kitchener thought along the same lines as Nestor. Soldiers would fight more cheerfully and with greater resolution if they were alongside those they knew, he ruled. But a crucial difference between the Bronze Age and the Steel Age soon became apparent: as local regiments were decimated by the slaughter, telegrams began to arrive bearing news of casualties that touched neighboring houses, streets, villages, and counties. Whole communities were blighted by the losses, and morale on the home front suffered accordingly.

143. Aias—Ajax the Lesser—may have been a short man, but Homer makes it clear that no one in all the Greek armies surpassed his skill with the spear. And what he lacked in height he more than made up for in bravery.

"Damn you, Paris, we are here for you," he called out. "*You* are the one who defied the sacred laws of guest friendship and took Helen from Menelaus. You brought her to live among us. We bowed to your demands that she stay. It is for *your* honor and *your* pride that Trojan blood has been spilled this last ten years. And now you think you can turn tail and run away like a frightened kitten?"

Hector's voice was loud enough to be heard by many Trojans. The rank and file worshipped Hector, but had grown to dislike Paris, whom they thought haughty, vain, and arrogant. All show and no go. Too petty and too pretty to be trusted, that was the view in the lines.

Paris flushed to the roots of his hair. "You're right, brother," he said with an unconvincing laugh. "Of course it would be wrong to run. I was going to our father the king to tell him my plan."

"What plan?"

The idea came fully formed into Paris's mind even as he spoke. "As you say, the quarrel is strictly between me and Menelaus. So, let it be decided by us."

"Meaning?"

"Meaning, let me stand as champion for Troy and face Menelaus in single combat. If I win, Helen stays and the Greeks depart. If I lose, they can take her back to Sparta. And all the treasure I brought along with her too," he added in a burst of magnanimity.

Hector put a hand on his shoulder. "I misjudged you, brother."

The jeers in the Trojan ranks changed to cheers as a flushed and emboldened Paris now strutted up and down before them. He had thrown a leopard skin over one shoulder, hoping to evoke a reminder of the great heroes of the past who had adorned themselves in just this fashion. Jason on the way to Iolcos, perhaps, or even Heracles in his signature costume of the hide of the Nemean Lion.

When the offer of single combat was relayed to the Greeks, Menelaus was only too pleased to accept the challenge. The ranks of Troy and Greece cheered with combined relief and excitement. They spread themselves out on the plain like a crowd of holidaymakers settling for a great picnic.

Helen, alone in her chambers, sensed the change of mood in the city. She heard shouts of delight and fanfares coming up from the streets below. She left the room and went over to the city walls to see what was happening. Priam was already up there on the ramparts and called down to her to climb the steps and sit with him. He was sitting with some of the courtiers who were too old to fight, Antenor amongst them. When they saw Helen coming up, they bent their heads and whispered to each other.[144]

"Her beauty pierces the heart, doesn't it?"

---

144. They were "chirruping like grasshoppers," Homer says.

"When she's out of sight, you forget those looks. But the moment you see her—sweet Aphrodite! That there could be such beauty in a mortal woman."

"For all that, I wish she would leave Troy forever and take the curse of that beauty away with her."

Priam rose to greet Helen and the courtiers moved away. The old king was fond of his daughter-in-law and had never upbraided her for the death and disaster her presence had brought on his people.

"Sit with me, my dear. Paris and Menelaus are about to decide the whole affair between themselves."

"Oh!"

Some women might have been delighted by the thought of men fighting over them, but Helen was not one.

"See the Greeks down there," said Priam. "I have to confess they look quite splendid. Tell me, who is that tall one with the orange-colored plume to his helmet? So powerful and commanding. A king surely?"

Helen looked down. "Oh, that is Agamemnon himself. He has aged a little since I last saw him."

"So that is the 'King of Men,' is it?"

"My brother-in-law, as was," said Helen in a low voice. "May the gods forgive me."

"Hush now. That broad-chested fellow over there, he looks familiar. Where have I seen him before, I wonder?"

"Oh, that's Odysseus, son of Laertes."

"Of course. I remember him. When he and Menelaus came to sue for peace at the beginning . . . Was it really ten years ago? And is that a great tree or a man looming over him?"

Helen laughed. "That is Ajax of Salamis."

Helen scanned the Greeks below, searching for two faces in particular. "I wonder where Castor and Polydeuces can be," she said. The last time she had seen her brothers had been in Sparta. They were called away during Paris's fateful visit. Something about a sordid cattle feud with their cousins up in Arcadia. Helen wondered if Aphrodite had been behind that too, for it had been their absence—along with Menelaus suddenly having to depart for the funeral in Crete—that had allowed Paris to ransack the palace unopposed and take her to Troy so easily.

Priam did not reply. He was shocked that Helen did not know what had happened to her brothers.

The world knew that they had gone north to settle the cattle business with their cousins and that Castor had been treacherously killed. The inconsolable Polydeuces had prayed to Zeus that he might die with his beloved twin. In reply

Zeus had allowed Polydeuces to accompany Castor by day to the realm of the dead, while at night they shone in the sky as Castor and Pollux, the inseparable stars of the constellation of the Twins—Gemini. As guiding stars in the night sky they had become an indispensable aid to shipping.[145]

Priam had assumed that Paris would have told Helen this news when it had reached Troy. Perhaps he had been afraid of how she would take it. She had loved her brothers the Dioscuri with all her heart.

And so they sat—Helen pointing out the Greek characters she remembered, even mimicking the voices and mannerisms of their wives. Priam smiling and gently nodding.

Whatever trance Aphrodite had put Helen in at the beginning had certainly cleared and she felt nothing for Paris now. Nothing but contempt. He had kept her as a prize, pressed himself upon her, paraded her when it suited him, and boasted of his ownership of her beauty, but he had never shown her any personal affection or given her the least sign that he loved or even respected her. His younger brother Deiphobus was much the same. When others weren't close by, he watched her with lustful eyes and spoke to her as if she was a whore. Priam, Hecuba, and Hector were different. They always treated her with nothing but kindness and honor.

As Helen and Priam looked down, Menelaus and Paris emerged from the ranks of the opposing armies. The thousands upon thousands of excited warriors roared their approval and beat their weapons against their shields. Helen had never heard a sound so loud. She felt the very walls of the city tremble.

SINGLE COMBAT

Menelaus and Paris had armed themselves well. With horsehair-crested helmets tucked under their arms they hefted their great bronze shields, layered with tough hide. The tips of their ash-wood spears had been freshly sharpened and flashed in the sunlight.

Prince Hector came forward with his own helmet outstretched. Into it he dropped two stones, one white and one black. Holding the helmet high, he cried out, "White for Prince Paris, Black for King Menelaus!"

The crowd hushed as he gave the helmet a violent shake. The white stone jumped out.

145. Fishermen believed that the phenomenon we know as St. Elmo's fire was also a manifestation of the Dioscuri.

"Prince Paris to make the first throw."

This was to be no wild and ugly brawl but a ritualized duel. Agamemnon on his side, and Priam on his, had slaughtered oxen and goats to the gods. They and their priests were determined that this moment—the moment that, one way or the other, would see the end of the war—should be conducted in as dignified and honorable a manner as could be managed.

The massed ranks of both sides were less able to contain their excitement. A carnival atmosphere had arisen. They would be going home. No matter what happened, they would be going home. The two men now striding apart from each other were the absolute heart of the issue—Menelaus, Helen's husband, and Paris, her lover. While the average soldier cared little who emerged victorious, there was the not inconsiderable matter of the spoils, for Paris had promised that if he lost he would hand over not just Helen but a great haul of treasure too. Most of it would go to the great kings and princes, of course, but enough would filter down to the rank and file.

When Paris and Menelaus had walked away from each other for what Hector judged to be the correct number of paces, he called out for them to stop. They turned. Silence fell. Paris took his spear, pulled back his arm and threw . . .

The crowd gave a great gasp as the spear's long shadow sped toward its target. The tip struck the very center of Menelaus's shield with a loud thump, but the armor of tough hide bent the point back. A fine shot, but not a wounding strike. The Greek contingent sighed with relief, the Trojans groaned with disappointment.

Now it was Menelaus's turn. He hefted the spear, feeling the balance.

To give Paris credit, he did not shrink back or cower. He stood firm and erect. Menelaus took aim and let his spear fly. It too struck the shield full center, but this time the spearpoint punched through. Paris turned with a deft athletic movement at the last moment. The tip did not pierce him, but it did graze his side. Hearing Paris's sharp involuntary cry and seeing the blood, Menelaus sensed victory. With a wild yell, he closed at speed, swinging his sword down onto Paris's helmet. There was a loud crash, but it was the sword that shattered, not the helmet.

As a stunned Paris staggered backward, Menelaus grabbed at the helmet's horsehair plume and pulled hard. Paris fell to his knees in the dust and Menelaus began to drag him along the ground by the chin strap. He would have throttled the life from him, just as Achilles had strangled Cycnus all those years ago when the Achaean ships first made landfall, had not the goddess Aphrodite intervened on behalf of her favorite. She broke the straps and Menelaus jerked backward, grasping an empty helmet.

Aphrodite now caused Paris to disappear in a swirl of dust and confusion. Menelaus called out his name but could not see him. No one could see him. He had been spirited away to his bedchamber in the palace, safe behind the walls of Troy.

The crowd roared its frustration and disappointment.

Inside the palace Aphrodite appeared before Helen and commanded her to go to Paris, to tend to him and make love to him.

"My true husband Menelaus has won," said Helen. "Why should I go to the coward Paris? If you love him so much, go to him yourself. *You* stroke his brow. *You* make love to him. I hate the very sight of him."

Aphrodite's face transformed into a twisted mask of fury. "Don't you dare disobey! Make an enemy of me and discover just how hated you will be by Trojans and Greeks alike. No woman in history will have such abuse, scorn, and punishment heaped upon her head as I will make sure is heaped upon yours. Go!"

Helen shivered at the violence of Aphrodite's rage. The sight of divinely radiant beauty turning so quickly into a Gorgon scowl of such screeching ugliness would have frightened even the mighty Ajax. Wrapping the shining white shawl tight around her shoulders, Helen made her way to Paris's rooms.

He was sitting on the bed, gingerly touching the scratch on his side and wincing.

"So the mighty warrior has returned from his great and glorious triumph, his terrible wounds gushing with blood," said Helen with disdain. "All these years you've been telling me how you would spit Menelaus like a roast duck with your spear. How much stronger, and faster, and wilier, and braver you were . . . And now look at you . . . *pathetic.*"

"Menelaus was helped by Athena!" Paris complained. "I'll get him tomorrow. For the moment, let us make love you and I . . . Come, come to bed."

Menelaus, meanwhile, was yelling up at the Trojan battlements.

"Had enough, Paris? Had enough? Victory then is ours! This very day we take Helen and my son Nicostratus and sail away from this pestilential town forever. For *ever!*"

Helen was sure that the cheering from both sides must have been the loudest noise a massed group of mortal humans had made since the world began.

Down on the plain the soldiers of both sides were crazed with joy.

Home! thought the Greeks. *Home!*

Peace! thought the Trojans. *Peace!*

But Hera's hatred of Troy demanded more, far more than this. It demanded the complete destruction of the city, its razing to the ground.

On Olympus she and Athena would give Zeus no rest.

"The matter is not decided, and you know it," said Hera.

"How can it be left like this, father?"

"It is absurd."

"It settles nothing and only dishonors each side."

"It dishonors the gods. All of us, but most especially you, Zeus."

The combined persuasive powers of wife and daughter were too much for him to resist and Zeus bowed his head.

"Go, then," he said. "If you must."

Athena took herself off to the walls of Troy where, disguised as Laodocus, the warrior son of Antenor, she sought out the Trojan archer Pandarus. She whispered to him that eternal glory would be his if he raised his bow and shot Menelaus, who was still striding up and down calling up for Paris to face him like a man.

Pandarus took careful aim and fired. The arrow would have pierced Menelaus's armor and reached a vital organ, but quick as lightning, Athena was there to deflect it,[146] and the tip stuck into the flesh of his leg instead—not a fatal wound, but serious enough for the blood to spout and for Menelaus to fall to the ground.

The Greeks roared with fury at this flagrant betrayal of the terms of the truce and the armies now clashed in earnest. For the first time in more than nine years, real battle was joined on the plain of Ilium. The River Scamander—sometimes called the Xanthus, the Yellow River—would soon be flowing red.

DIOMEDES V. THE GODS

The injured Menelaus had his wound healed by MACHAON, a son of Asclepius, who applied a salve mixed by the centaur Chiron himself.[147]

Meanwhile, the battle exploded into a full, violent frenzy. The shooting of his brother seemed to bring out the true leader in Agamemnon, who was everywhere in the fray, roaring on encouragement to his generals, Odysseus, Ajax, and Aias, and Diomedes.

The last named, Diomedes, King of Argos, son of Tydeus, was filled with especial fury and valor. This was his hour, his *aristeia*. He blasted his way through the Trojan ranks like a cyclone. Pandarus, high up on the walls of Troy, shot at

---

146. "Like a mother flicking a fly from her sleeping child," says Homer.

147. Machaon was one of the sons of Asclepius. The divine healer, you will remember, had, like Achilles, been tutored by the centaur Chiron.

him and wounded him; but with barely a grunt Diomedes had his friend and companion Sthenelus pull the arrow out.

"You'll have to do better than that, you coward, Pandarus," he yelled, before diving into the fight once more, slaughtering to the left and slaughtering to the right.

The Olympians were caught off guard by the sudden eruption of violence. After all these years of stalemate, it astonished the gods to witness the two sides now hurling themselves at each other, swords hacking, chariots thundering, arrows and spears flying, and the air filled with war cries and the screams of the injured and dying. And the sight of Diomedes rampant caused even the god of war to blink with wonder. But Ares, always on the side of the Trojans, came to and threw himself into the thick of the fighting, tossing Greek warriors aside and making his way inexorably toward Diomedes, whom he would have felled, had not Athena shouted at him to desist and let the mortals be. Ares stumped off to the banks of the Scamander to sulk.

No one had ever seen a warrior as entirely and terrifyingly energized as Diomedes was that day. He was *enthused*—a word whose literal meaning is "to be filled with the spirit of a god" (*en-theos*). If there were such a word in English, we might say that Diomedes was "engodded"—Athena being the god in question. She even gave him the power to discern the immortals themselves.

"Engage with any of them if you need to," Athena whispered to him, "any but Aphrodite. She is not a battle deity and should be left alone."

Diomedes killed two sons of Priam—and Pandarus too, who in an excess of confidence had come down from the walls of Troy to join the battle at ground level. At least a dozen senior Trojans fell before Diomedes's blaze of violence. It looked as if the inspired Argive now had Prince Aeneas, leader of the Dardanians, at his mercy too. Diomedes raised over his head a boulder that two strong men could never have been able so much as to move and brought it down on Aeneas, who tried to twist aside. The boulder missed his head but smashed his hip. Diomedes unsheathed his sword, and was all ready to finish him off, when Aeneas's mother Aphrodite interposed herself. Diomedes in his unquenchable bloodlust and frenzy attacked *her*, cutting the wrist where it joined her hand. Silver-gold ichor poured from the wound and Aphrodite fled squealing to the riverside where her lover Ares was still brooding.

"That Diomedes is mad!" she said to him. "In this mood he would take on great Zeus himself! Lend me your horses and let me fly to Olympus to be healed."

In the meantime Aeneas, shrouded in a mist created by Apollo, was ministered to by Apollo's twin, the goddess Artemis, and their mother, the Titaness

Leto. When this was done, Apollo called over to Ares and told him to stop staring into the river like a moody adolescent and enter the fray.

"Diomedes is destroying our best Trojan fighting men! Off your ass and into battle."

Pricked and shamed, Ares now waded in on the Trojan side, and the whole tide of battle began to turn. Diomedes may have slain many Trojans, but Ares set about killing twice as many Greeks.

Athena flew to Olympus and entreated Zeus to let her and Hera join in. "If Ares is allowed to help the Trojans, then we must be allowed to help the Achaeans."

Zeus groaned and shook his head in despair. This was exactly the situation he had feared and most hoped to avoid. A full divine intervention in what he had intended to be a purely mortal affair. But once more he bowed his head in agreement.

Athena charged into the Trojan ranks, her Gorgon aegis flashing.

"Hey, Diomedes!" she called across to him. "Are you warrior or weasel? Look, there's Ares in the thick of the fighting. Dare you take him? Dare you take on the god of war himself?"

With a blood-curdling roar, Diomedes hurled his spear straight into Ares's guts, into his very bowels.

A shudder swept the ranks of both armies as a howl of pain like no other sound ever heard emerged from the wounded war god. Only Diomedes had been given the power to see the immortals, of course. To the warriors on both sides

◈ The Combat of Diomedes

the sound was as mysterious as it was appalling. For a brief moment the fighting stopped as everyone looked around them in horrified wonder.

Ares flew screaming up to Olympus to be healed. Zeus was unsympathetic. The war god had always been his least favorite child. He grudgingly saw to it that his wounds were tended to; but when Athena and Hera also returned to Olympus, he was only too pleased to declare all such future interventions forbidden.

"I have never seen such a display," he said. "Are you Olympian gods or wild children? I am ashamed of you. From now on you take no part in the fighting. We leave the mortals to sort it out for themselves without our direct aid. Understood?"

Exhausted, and for the moment shamed, the gods bowed their heads in submission.

Zeus had not, however, forgotten his promise to Thetis.

HECTOR AND AJAX

Now that Ares was out of the fight, the Greeks were able to press on right up to the walls of Troy. Diomedes led the charge, supported by Ajax, Odysseus, Agamemnon, Menelaus, Aias—even old Nestor pushed through, sword swinging back and forth with a strength that belied his years.

Hector saw that the Trojans were losing ground and that the city could soon be taken. He knew that it was up to him to stem the tide and saw that there was just enough time for him, with Aeneas fighting close at his side, to bring the Trojan army into the city, close the gates, and prepare properly for a counterattack.

At the royal palace Hecuba embraced him and offered a cup of wine and a little rest. Hector pushed the cup away.

"Thank you, Mother, but if I take any wine my mind may slow and my resolve weaken."

He took the staircase up to Paris's and Helen's apartments. "Polishing your armor, brother? Yes, I would say that's about your style."

Paris flushed. "Don't mock me, Hector. I may not have your skill and valor, but when it comes to it I can fight and I will. I go now to sharpen my sword and spearpoint. I'll catch up with you quickly."

Helen watched him leave. "You are fighting harder than anyone," she said to Hector after Paris had gone, "and risking your life for what? All for my sake, worthless as I am. And, of course, for the sake of your pitiful brother Paris and his vanity. I would rather never have been born than bring this all on you."

Hector looked into the loveliest human face there had ever been. "Please," he said, "don't upset yourself. I do what has to be done. No one in our family blames you, Helen. They know what you have suffered since you have been wrenched from your home. My father and mother have welcomed you. You are a princess of Troy. You are my beloved sister. We fight for your honor and for our own. We do so gladly and with pride."

At the Scaean Gate Hector found his wife Andromache, who was holding their baby son in her arms.

"Hello, little Scamandrius," said Hector, gazing down at the sleeping child, whom the rest of Troy called ASTYANAX, "lord of the city." "How fine he looks. Like a star."

"Oh, Hector!" said Andromache. "Must you fight? I don't want my son to grow up without a father. Achilles killed my father, suppose he or Diomedes kills you?"

"We are born with our fate and no one has ever avoided theirs," said Hector. "Besides, how could I live with the shame of knowing that where so many of my brothers and fellow Trojans have risked their lives I slunk home and hid? Death is better than dishonor. I fight for you and Scamandrius too. If we give in now, the Danaans will sack the city and kill us all anyway. And you would be taken off to be a slave in some Greek household. That I will not allow."

Hector's helmet caught the sun. The flash from its polished bronze woke Astyanax, who opened his eyes. The sight of the great plume of the helmet's crest nodding down into his face made him scream out in fear. Andromache and Hector laughed. Hector removed the helmet, picked the child up, and kissed him.

"Grow to be a finer man than your father ever was, Scamandrius," he said, swinging him high in the air before returning him to his wife's arms. "And never fear, my darling Andromache. I will not die. Not today."

Nodding to the gatekeeper, he strode out—Paris ran to catch up, gleaming in his fine armor.

"Here we are, brother," said Paris. "I said I'd be quick, didn't I? Hope I didn't keep you waiting."

Hector smiled. "You're impossible to stay angry with. I know you are brave and willing and able to fight, but it breaks my heart when I hear others heaping scorn on you. Let's do such work today that both our names will live on for so long as men have tongues to sing."

Arm in arm the brothers stepped from the city and out onto the plain where the battle raged.

Instantly they launched themselves into the fight, each bringing down a notable Achaean warrior.

Athena and Apollo, watching, cast each other sidelong glances.

"I suppose you want to swoop in and bring victory to your beloved Argives," said Apollo. "And what's to stop me doing the same for the Trojans?"

"Our father has forbidden us . . . Let us halt the bloodshed and do something wise instead . . ."

"Such as?"

Athena told Apollo her plan and he bowed his head. "It shall be as you say . . ."

Priam's son Helenus, the seer and augur of the family, now heard a voice whispering in his ear. He went immediately to find his older brother, who was right in the heart of battle, hacking away at his enemies.

"Hector!" he said, pulling him aside. "Listen. The gods have spoken to me—to spare bloodshed each side should nominate a champion."

"What?" said Hector, panting. "We tried that . . ."

"Why not try again? The match between Menelaus and Paris decided nothing. Your life against whomever the Greeks choose? One on one?"

Hector thought quickly and then raised his voice above the din to issue the challenge.

"Hear me, soldiers of Hellas!" he cried. "Send me your best warrior to be your champion. If he defeats me, he may take my armor and weapons but must return my body to Troy for cleansing and burning. If I defeat him, I shall strip him of his arms and armor but leave the body for you to take and purify. This issue will settle all. Can we agree?"

Menelaus spoke up at once, offering to be the champion once again, but Agamemnon silenced him.

"You have fought hard enough, brother. The gash in your leg is still healing. Besides, great warrior that you are, you are not the equal of Hector. On height alone you are outmatched."

Nine other leading Greeks—Agamemnon himself, Diomedes, Idomeneus, the Great and Little Ajaxes, Odysseus, and three more all stood up. Each scratched their name on a stone which they threw into Agamemnon's helmet. Agamemnon shook the helmet and out jumped the stone bearing the name of Telamonian Ajax—Ajax the Mighty.

A great cheer went up, for the Achaeans had come to believe that this giant of a man was all but invincible. His size and strength were unsurpassed on either side. Ajax armed himself and raised up his huge tower shield, which was composed of seven layers of thick hide finished with a final layer of hammered bronze. You or I could no more have lifted that shield than we could lift a mountain.

Once again the armies parted to create an arena.

Ajax and Hector faced off against each other. Hector won the honor of throwing first, and his spear penetrated the first six layers of hide on Ajax's shield but was turned away by the last. Next it was Ajax's turn, and his spear punched through Hector's shield and would have pierced his flesh had not Hector turned away just in time.

The soldiers on each side were too absorbed to cheer. They shivered in the knowledge that they were watching history. History of such profound importance that it would become the stuff of legend. The grace and speed of Hector against the power and strength of Ajax.

Now they closed with each other again. Ajax pierced the shield of Hector once more and got through a glancing blow to his neck, nicking the soft skin. Hector hurled a huge rock, and Ajax replied with a boulder twice its size that brought Hector to his knees.

Ajax moved in, and then looked up at the sky. "The light fades," he said, putting out a hand to Hector and helping him to his feet. Their duel was suspended. With princely gallantry Hector presented Ajax with his silver sword and Ajax knelt to offer Hector his war belt. They could not know it, but Hector's silver sword and Ajax's war belt would each play a huge and tragic part in the drama to come.

Thus their single combat was honorably ended. The day's intense fighting was over too, but the war was no closer to being decided than it had been on that first day more than nine years earlier.

THE TIDE TURNS

That night in Troy, in the council chambers of Priam's palace, Antenor urged that Helen be returned. This Paris point-blank refused to do.

"I will return the treasure I took from Sparta and Mycenae, and add treasure of my own too, but Helen I cannot and will not give up."

This offer, when conveyed by messengers under truce to the Achaean camp, was turned down.

The next day the war continued on the plain. In answer to Thetis's repeated requests that Zeus honor his promise to punish Agamemnon, the King of the Gods rained down thunderbolts on the Greeks.

With the Achaean armies in disarray, only Nestor held firm, charging through the Trojan lines again and again in his chariot. The example of this man,

◈　The Duel of Ajax and Hector

twice the age of the next oldest commander, filled the Greeks with a new and desperate courage, but Nestor was finally put out of action when an arrow from Paris pierced the brain of his chariot horse. Diomedes rescued him and put him in his own chariot. A great moan of disappointment and fear arose from the Achaean ranks.

The whole invasion force was turning tail and racing across the plain back to their ships. Agamemnon was not equal to such a reverse. He raised his head to the sky, tears streaming down his face.

"You abandon us, great Zeus? All those signs and portents that drove us to believe that we would prevail, and now this? At least let my brave men escape death. If we must be defeated in war, then so be it, but this massacre is not just. Not just. Not just."

Zeus, who was torn, as ever, between pleasing Hera and Athena, pleasing Thetis, and pleasing his own instinctive admiration for the heroes on both sides, was distressed to see Agamemnon, King of Men, sobbing like a child. He sent a great eagle, which soared over the battlefield, grasping a baby deer in its talons. The Greek army, reading this as a good omen, rallied.

Now Teucer of Salamis, the greatest bowman on either side, went to work: under the cover of his half-brother Ajax's shield he started sniping at enemy warriors, one after the other. Eight royal or noble Trojans fell to his arrows, but not the prize of Hector. He did get Hector's driver Archeptolemus, however— but this just maddened Hector, who leapt down from his chariot and came at Teucer with a rock, pounding it down on the archer's chest before he could loose off another shot from his bow. Ajax came charging forward to the rescue. He barged Hector away, scooped Teucer up, and ran with him over his shoulder to the Achaean lines, pursued by a roaring Hector and what seemed like the whole Trojan army.

The entirety of the mighty Greek expeditionary force was now crouching behind the stockade, its sharpened stakes their last desperate defense against the Trojan hordes.

Agamemnon rose up, still in tears, still blaming Zeus for abandoning their cause.

"Let us go back home," he wailed. "We are beaten. We will never take Troy. They have us pinned to the sea. They are close enough to hurl fire. We should take to our ships and leave."

Diomedes stood up. "I cannot believe that our commander has so little faith in himself or in us. The gods have given the King of Men everything. Wealth such as not even King MIDAS of Phrygia knew. A glorious name. The best land, the best family—everything has come to him in his life, and now, at this one reverse, he squeals like a child and begs to be taken home. Well, you go home, Agamemnon. But I am staying. Sthenelus is with me, I think?"

"I am!" roared Sthenelus, banging his spear butt on the ground.[148]

"Who else?" demanded Diomedes.

Nestor stood. "I stay," he said. "King of Men, dry your eyes and consider! Troy has rallied because Hector, their greatest warrior, their noblest prince, their finest fighter, is encouraging them by his example and his warcraft. We have one warrior who is more than his match—faster, fitter, stronger, abler in every regard. But he sulks in his tent, refusing to put on his armor and fight with us. Why? Because you took Briseis and insulted him. Can you not see that you should put this right?"

Agamemnon bowed his head and beat his breast with his fists. "I was a fool!" he cried. "The son of Thetis and Peleus is worth a division on his own. My pride and my temper got the better of me. But I shall put it right. By the Olympian Twelve, I swear I shall put it right!"

---

148. From the old royal house of Argos and a loyal companion of Diomedes.

Suddenly he seemed filled with an intoxicating mixture of remorse, resolve, and determination—as passionate in his desire now to be generous to Achilles as he had been earlier to humiliate him.

"I shall send gold, a dozen of the finest horses, seven slave women, and, of course, this Briseis whom he values so much. You can tell him, in all truth, that I have not slept with her. And furthermore," Agamemnon's voice rang with strength and confidence now, "furthermore, when we take Troy, Achilles can have the pick of the treasure. And when we get home, I will give him seven cities from my empire and he may choose either of my daughters to be his bride."

The Achaean ranks cheered. This was a most magnanimous concession. No one could refuse such an offer. By all the sacred Hellenic codes of honor, Achilles was bound to accept.

THE EMBASSY TO ACHILLES

Odysseus and Ajax were appointed as Agamemnon's spokesmen, along with old Phoenix. His inclusion was Odysseus's canny idea. After the young Achilles had left the cave of Chiron, Phoenix had been chosen by Peleus to raise him. It was known that Achilles loved the old man almost as fiercely as he loved Patroclus. The three delegates made their way to the main tent of the Myrmidon enclosure, where they found Achilles playing a silver lyre and singing a song that told of the feats of great warrior heroes of long ago. Patroclus, who had been listening, rose to welcome the deputation. Achilles bid them eat, drink, and say what they had to say.

When Agamemnon's regret, apologies, praise, and bountiful offers had been made to him, Achilles made a face of disapproval.

"I know," said Odysseus quickly, "that the very generosity of Agamemnon makes you despise him the more. I understand that. But forget Agamemnon; we can agree that he is a bad and foolish king. Bear this in mind instead: when you bring down Hector, and all Troy lies open to us, your glory and fame will be such as no man, not even Heracles, ever won."

Achilles smiled. "I have known for some time, Odysseus," he said, "that if I fought against Troy my name would live forever as an imperishable and unequaled hero. So my mother has told me. She has said also that, should I choose, I could turn away from this war and my fate would be to live a long, prosperous, and happy life."

"But obscure," said Odysseus. "Obscure and unsung."

"Obscure and unsung," agreed Achilles. "And of the two futures open to me, that is the one I have now chosen. So go back to Agamemnon and tell him that I am no longer angry with him, that I accept his apology, but that I choose not to fight in his cause. If Hector were to come close to the ships of my Myrmidons, then, and only then, would I take up arms in their defense. That is all I can promise."

The three ambassadors left, knowing that this last offer was of little value to the Greeks. The Myrmidon ships were as distant from the center of the beachhead as could be.

When the party returned to the command headquarters, Odysseus relayed the words of Achilles's refusal. Agamemnon took it all in with a grim smile.

"Yes. I suspected as much. The rest of us are bound by custom and by codes of honor. Achilles alone among men is bound only by what his personal pride demands. Well, well. We are not downhearted."

From tears of rage and disappointment to a sudden staunch resolution, thought Odysseus. That's our King of Men.

NIGHT PATROL[149]

Agamemnon and Menelaus found themselves unable to sleep that night. They awoke the other senior commanders.

"What we need," said Agamemnon, "is for someone to get behind the Trojan lines and see what they are planning for tomorrow. Diomedes, select someone to go with you."

Diomedes touched Odysseus on the shoulder and the two men vanished into the night. The Trojans were camped and sleeping all over the ground they had won on the Achaean side of the Scamandrian plain. Crawling forward on their stomachs, Diomedes and Odysseus inched their way silently toward the Trojan lines. They heard footsteps and stopped. A man was approaching.

"Pretend to be dead," Odysseus breathed to Diomedes. They froze where they were.

When the man—who was dressed in wolfskin, with a cap of weasel-fur set upon his head—passed them by, they rose up and seized him.

"Please, please!" the wolf man whimpered. "Don't hurt me."

---

149. This episode, which forms Book 10 of the *Iliad*, is considered by many scholars to be the work of someone other than Homer. It certainly is capable of being left out without in any way changing the story, which is not true of the other books in the epic. Its casual and somewhat gleeful cruelty might be thought of as a later addition, put there to please less sophisticated audiences. I include it and you can judge.

"Sh! Who are you?"

He stammered out his name. "DOLON. I mean you no harm."

Odysseus put a knife to his throat. "Speak."

"Only spare my life. I'll tell you anything."

"We'll spare your life, I promise," hissed Odysseus. "Only speak quickly. And quietly. I have shaky hands and this blade against your throat might just slip and find its way into your windpipe if you aren't quick, clear, and concise."

"I promise, I promise!" The words tumbled from Dolon in a hoarse and panicked whisper. "It's all Hector's fault. He promised me a treasure beyond price if I spied on your camp."

Odysseus smiled to himself. So Hector had had the same idea as Agamemnon, had he? Sending spies behind the enemy lines.

"What 'treasure beyond price'?"

"Achilles's horses and golden chariot."

"Balius and Xanthus?" said Odysseus. "The horses Poseidon gave to his parents? No man alive but Achilles can control them. A little rat like you would be mashed under the wheels of the chariot in seconds. Besides, what makes Hector think he will ever take possession of them?"

"He fooled me," Dolon whined. "I see that now. But my father, Eumedes the herald, he's rich. He'll ransom me. Only please . . . don't hurt me."

"Just tell us what important moves are being made in the Trojan camp tonight?"

"W-well—King RHESUS has arrived with his white horses."

"White horses? What's so important about them?"

"It is said that if the horses of King Rhesus of Thrace enter Troy, the city can never fall. He will ride them in tomorrow and victory will be ours."

"And which way is the Thracian camp?"

"Th-that way."

"Very good," said Odysseus approvingly. "While I hold you, my friend Diomedes will cut your throat as quickly and—"

"But you said—"

"That I would spare your life? And so I did. For five minutes, which is all it was worth."

One swift, clean cut from Diomedes and with a gargling choke Dolon fell dying to the ground.

"Strangest thing," said Odysseus; "that knife must be a lot sharper than we thought. Look at that, you almost sliced his head off."

The pair of them stole through to the Thracian camp, killed the sleeping King Rhesus and a dozen of the guards, before driving the white horses toward their own lines to the cheers of the Achaeans.

AGAMEMNON AND HECTOR RAMPANT

At daybreak Hector rode up and down before the Trojans shouting encouragement.

"We have them at our mercy, my friends!" he assured them. "Nothing can stop us now!"

Hundreds of Greeks fell before the onslaught Hector led, but this was the moment when Agamemnon revealed his fearsome attributes as a fighting man. He might have had his faults as a king and leader, but this morning of his *aristeia*, his glory, he revealed to all that he was a warrior of extraordinary courage. In a remorseless push he drove the Trojans back over the River Scamander, killing two of Priam's sons and many other Trojans besides. Hector commanded the main army to fall back to the Scaean Gate in order to regroup for an immediate counterattack, but his brother Helenus urged him to wait.

"Zeus has revealed to me that the time to strike back is when Agamemnon suffers a wound that will put him out of action. It will happen. Only be patient."

As Helenus spoke, Agamemnon speared Antenor's son Iphidamus straight through with one deadly lunge. He bent down and stripped the body of its armor, to the cheers of the watching Greeks. As the Achaean king held the armor aloft in triumph, Iphidamus's brother Coön charged out of nowhere, screaming for revenge, and stabbed at Agamemnon with his sword, slashing open his forearm. Without so much as a wince or a blink Agamemnon drew his own sword and decapitated Coön with one stroke. Now enraged, Agamemnon kept on fighting and fighting, but the loss of blood from the wound to his arm forced him to turn back with a stagger to his own lines.

Hector saw this and knew that it was time. With a great cry he led a charge into the Greek ranks, killing six men in one quick blur of brutality. Diomedes and Odysseus led the fightback until Diomedes was shot in the foot by an arrow from Paris, putting him out of action for the rest of the day. Then Odysseus was wounded, and would have died out there on the field of battle, had not Menelaus and Ajax rescued him. Ajax was a man possessed. Bellowing like the Cretan Bull, he stormed through the Trojan lines, slaughtering as he went. The soil of the plain of Ilium was sodden with the red blood of Greeks and Trojans.

Hector forced Ajax and the Greeks back to their stockade and trenches. Five divisions of the Trojan army, led by Hector, Paris, Helenus, Aeneas, and Sarpedon, now pushed through for the final *coup de grâce*: an attack on the Greek shipping behind the defensive palisade.

The senior Greeks, wounded as most of them now were, met in hurried conclave. Agamemnon, having started the day so well, started to panic again and called for the Greeks to sail away before the ships could be set on fire. Odysseus shouted him down.

"The ships stay—if the fighting men on the plain and in the ditch see the fleets disperse, they will lose heart."

The Trojans surged on, pushing and pushing toward the ships, which Ajax the Great was now defending almost single-handedly. The Trojan vanguard reached the vessel from which Protesilaus had leapt nearly ten years earlier. Ajax wielded a massive pike and skewered any Trojan who came near, but on and on came wave after wave of Trojans—such numbers could not be indefinitely repulsed, even by a warrior as mighty as Ajax.

Things were going very badly for the Greeks indeed. Hector was inspired. He was unstoppable. What could stop the Trojans now?

THE PSEUDO-ACHILLES

Patroclus ran back from the fighting by the ships to appeal to Achilles.

"Look at this child, running in tears to its mother and tugging at her apron. Don't tell me there's bad news from home?"

"We must do something! They're on the brink of victory."

"Oh, is that all? I thought perhaps your father had died back in Phthia. Or mine."

"For pity's sake, Achilles. We must intervene; we must, or the Trojans win!"

"If I intervene, then *he* wins. What that man did to me. The contempt. The deliberate humiliation. That can never be forgiven."

"But Achilles . . ."

"I said I would defend our Myrmidon ships against Hector if he came this far, but he has not."

"Then at least let me fight in your place," pleaded Patroclus. "I beg you, let me stand in your armor at the head of the Achaean lines. They will think I am you and will rally for sure."

Achilles stared. "By heaven, you're serious."

"Believe it. I'll fight in any event, in your armor or in mine. It makes no difference: I'm going out there."

Achilles smiled at the force of his friend's earnest insistence.

At that very moment Hector finally got the better of the exhausted Ajax, snapping the head from his pike. Ajax fell back and Hector shouted for torches to be thrown into the ship, Protesilaus's ship. The shouts of alarm from the Achaeans, and the whoops of triumph from the Trojans, decided Achilles.

"Very well, you can take my armor, but not my sword, nor my spear. And you shall have fifty Myrmidons from each of my fifty ships. They have been bridling and fretting at being unable to fight. But only in defense of the ships, mind. Don't even think of trying to hack your way up to Troy. You wouldn't be safe from Apollo. He'll guide the arrows of the archers that patrol the city's high ramparts. Just the beachhead. Promise me?"

"I promise!" shouted Patroclus excitedly, skipping off to rouse the Myrmidons and equip himself for battle.

And so it was that Patroclus now appeared in the shining armor and helmet of Achilles, at the head of two and a half thousand fierce, fresh, and fanatical Myrmidons. The impact on the battle was instant and extreme.

"Achilles! Achilles!" cried the Achaeans in triumph.

"Achilles! Achilles!" howled the Trojans in terror.

Emboldened by the cheers around him, confident in the armor of his boyhood companion, friend, and lover, Patroclus was a man transformed. His whirlwind of killing lit a fire of frenzied passion along the Greek lines. The enemy was cut to pieces in large numbers as the tide of battle turned again and the Trojans tried to escape the beachhead and flee over the River Scamander, back toward the safety of their city. But Patroclus now pinned them and trapped them between the stockade and the sea, and he, the Myrmidons and the whole of the revitalized Achaean forces began to turn the ground red with the blood of slain Trojans.

Zeus watched in impotent horror as his son, the Lycian king Sarpedon— grandson of the hero Bellerophon and the most powerful and heroic of Hector's allies—was speared through the chest by Patroclus.

"Fight on, my beloved Lycians!" cried the dying Sarpedon. "But don't let the Greeks dishonor my body."

A savage struggle now erupted over his corpse. The Myrmidons tried to strip it of its armor while desperate Trojans, led by their Lycian allies, swarmed in to retrieve it. Hector smashed the skull of Epigeus the Myrmidon and Patroclus killed Sthenelaus, one of Hector's closest friends.[150] The body of Sarpedon was heaped over with discarded armor, broken swords, and other corpses as the battle raged around. Finally the pressure on the Trojans was too great and once again they streamed in panic for the city walls. The Greeks shook the armor of Sarpedon in the air and shouted their taunts at the distraught Lycians.

---

150. Not to be confused with Diomedes's fellow Argive, Sthenelus.

Patroclus, now at the height of his *aristeia*, roared with exultant, triumphant bloodlust. As far as everyone else knew, this was the great Achilles, roused at last and wading through blood to the victory that was somehow understood to be his birthright.

Now there was nothing between Patroclus and Troy except . . . the god Apollo. Enraged by the sight of this single ordinary mortal threatening the city and people he had sworn to protect, the god repulsed one, two, and three waves of attack from Patroclus. At the fourth, swelling up in majestic fury the god warned him.

"You are not destined to sack Troy. Not even your beloved Achilles is marked out for that honor. Stand back, Patroclus."

As Patroclus gave ground, Apollo took the form of Hecuba's brother Asius and urged Hector to charge forward and win the initiative. Hector mounted his chariot and drove against the Achaeans, scattering them from his path as he thundered forward.

Patroclus threw a rock at Cebriones, Hector's driver, killing him instantly. There now followed a desperate duel for that body, a duel that descended into a gruesome tug of war between Hector and Patroclus. Patroclus and the Myrmidons won the corpse and stripped it of its armor. The Trojans came for him in three waves, and Patroclus killed nine in each wave. He seemed invincible—but it was now that Apollo lost patience and struck Patroclus, again and again. He knocked him off his feet, shattered his spear, stripped the shield from his arm, wrenched off his breastplate and struck the helmet off his head.

The helmet, the famous helmet of Achilles, rolled along the ground and Patroclus's face was revealed.

For a second there was stunned silence, then a great roar arose from the Trojans. They knew it was not Achilles who had been butchering them like lambs, but Patroclus, and the knowledge stung them into action. Young EUPHORBUS launched a spear at Patroclus. It found its mark. With the spear buried in his side, Patroclus stumbled and wove his way back toward the Greek lines. Hector finished him off with a spear thrust that pierced his bowels and came out of his back.

"You think you killed me, Hector," Patroclus gasped. "But it took the god Apollo to do that. Euphorbus was next. You, famous Hector, noble Hector, were just the third. All you did is finish me off. I die knowing that your fate will be settled by one greater than any . . . by my Achilles."

Hector put a boot on the dead Patroclus's chest, pulled the spear out, and kicked the body over.

If the scrapping over the corpses of Sarpedon and Cebriones had seemed fierce, they were as a playground scuffle next to the frenzied animal savagery of the fight for possession of the body of Patroclus.

Menelaus rose to an *aristeia* of his own. He had fought bravely enough against Paris in the duel between them and in the skirmishes that had followed. How long ago those first engagements seemed. He was now fully recovered from the wound inflicted by the arrow of Pandarus, and he fought like a maddened tiger for possession of the corpse. He repaid Euphorbus for his first strike on Patroclus by spearing him through the throat; but when Hector came forward, he withdrew, calling on Ajax to help him out.

Hector began to strip Patroclus of his armor—the armor of Achilles—but GLAUCUS the Lycian, Sarpedon's cousin and friend, stopped him.[151]

"Take that body back to the Greeks and demand Sarpedon's corpse in return."

Hector shook his head. "The time for such courtesies are over. He killed too many of us. Our kinsmen. Your king. All Troy will want to take their revenge."

"Do it, prince, or I march every Lycian away from Troy and leave you to defend it on your own."

It is worth stopping here to remind ourselves of just how important to each side it was that those who died on the field of battle be accorded proper funeral rites. The *kleos*—the fame and glory they earned with their valor and martial prowess—would ensure that their names lived for ever in history, for generation after generation. The honor of having the corpse cleansed and burned on a consecrated pyre with all due songs, prayers, and obsequies constituted the first step to the realization of this *kleos*. It was believed too that there was no possibility of a soul departing life in peace and entering the underworld unless the corpse was covered by earth. Those who died of illness, or any cause other than the wounds of war, could not expect the cleansing and ceremony, no matter how important they had been in life, but they might at least be given the dignity of a handful of dirt over their body. Unseemly and uncivilized as the dogfights that erupted over a dead soldier's mangled remains might appear to us, we should understand that to the Greeks and Trojans those dead bodies were living symbols of the imperishable reputation of the heroic souls that had inhabited them. As much as their companions fought to rescue, reclaim, and honor the bodies of their fallen friends, their foes would fight to keep, mutilate, and defile them, and to take their armor as a prize of war or as treasure to be ransomed from the fallen's family and friends.

---

151. Like Sarpedon, Glaucus was a grandson of the great hero Bellerophon, tamer and rider of the winged horse Pegasus: see *Heroes*, page 128.

For Glaucus and his Lycians not to take back the body of Sarpedon, their kinsman and king, would constitute an unconscionable stain on their honor.[152] So they needed to take possession of Patroclus's corpse to use as a bargaining chip for the return of Sarpedon's. They had made it clear to Hector that he must do everything he could to effect the exchange—Patroclus for Sarpedon. The Lycian alliance was too important to Troy to be put in jeopardy, so Hector agreed to give them Patroclus's body. But the arms—the spear, helmet, breast-plate, shield, and greaves—they were a prize that Hector believed he deserved and might in all conscience keep back for himself. Accordingly, he took off his own armor and put on that of Patroclus—that of Achilles. The helmet he gave to one of his men for safe keeping. He could not risk wearing it, for he might be mistaken for Achilles and face attack from his own side.

The fight for the body of Patroclus that now ensued was among the bloodi-est and most violent passages of arms of the entire ten-year war. Homer's pitiless lingering on the savagery of this high noon of slaughter reveals how desperately important the issue was to each side. Had they known it was but a rehearsal, or at best a kind of gentle prologue to what was to come, they might all have given up in despair.

Aias and Idomeneus joined with Ajax and Menelaus and placed themselves at each corner of Patroclus's corpse, like mourners at a catafalque, but what savage, relentless mourners! They repulsed wave after wave of wild and determined Trojans led by Hector, who like Death himself, threw himself at them time and time again. With all this violence raging above him, Hippothous the Trojan managed to crawl in low down and tie a leather strap around Patroclus's body. He was in the act of dragging it toward Troy when Ajax spotted him and speared him through the helmet. The brains burst from the entry wound, flooding his helmet like wine filling a copper bowl. His friend Phorcys stepped up to reclaim *his* body, but was instantly disemboweled by Ajax's raking spear-point. Hector on his part struck down as many Achaeans as he could, splintering skulls, slicing off arms, heads and legs like some great scything machine. More Greeks moved in to encircle the body, Ajax roaring at them not to yield an inch. The Trojans pressed in on a rolling tide of death, led by the implacable Hector. All the banked-up tension, the disappointed hope, the losses, the betrayals, the fear and frustration exploded with such force and fury that the gods trembled to see it.

Peering through the fencing of the stockade, Achilles could see the clouds of dust and hear the clashing din, but he was not able to interpret what he saw and heard. Antilochus, son of Nestor, came running along the sand toward him in

---

152. Hence the story of ANTIGONE: see *Heroes*, page 257.

◆   The Body of Patroclus

tears to break the news that Patroclus was dead and that it was his corpse that formed the focus of the fighting.

Achilles broke down completely. His despair overwhelmed him. He scrabbled at the ground for dirt and rubbed it all over his beautiful face. He tore his hair and howled with absolute and uncontrollable grief. Antilochus knelt beside him and grasped each hand—as much to stop Achilles harming himself as to show his sympathy and support.

Thetis heard the wild cries of her son and came up from the ocean to comfort him. But he was inconsolable.

"I have lost the will to go on," he said. "Unless I can kill Hector in revenge for Patroclus I will have nothing to live for."

"Oh, but my son," said Thetis, "it is foretold that if Hector dies your death will come straight after."

"Then *let* me die straight after!"

"And Agamemnon?"

"Forget him. What is treasure, or Briseis, or honor, or anything next to the life of the one I loved best and dearest, my beloved, my only Patroclus? Patroclus, oh Patroclus!"

Achilles threw himself down and howled his despair into the dirt.

Meanwhile, the battle for the body of Patroclus continued to rage. Hector had been driven off three times by Ajax and Aias, but his fourth attack would have prevailed had not Hera sent IRIS, the rainbow messenger of the Olympians, to Achilles to urge him to give a sign that he was ready to fight once more. Although Achilles wore no armor, the mere sight of him, standing high on the embankment, bathed in an unearthly light, and uttering the most piercing and monumental battle-cry was enough to scatter the Trojans. Three times Achilles yelled his terrible war cry. The Trojans and even their horses were filled with fear. In triumph the Achaeans bore the body of Patroclus back to their camp.

But Hector was by no means done and he tried to chase the Greeks down. His friend POLYDAMAS urged him to stay back.[153]

"Achilles is back in the fight, my prince. We must secure ourselves behind the city walls."

"Never. We are *winning*, Polydamas! The time for being cramped like frightened prisoners inside the city is over. We'll withdraw no further than the other side of the river. We camp on the plain and tomorrow we launch our final assault on the Greek ships. We have them on the run! I sense it."

All night the Achaeans mourned the loss of Patroclus, with the distraught Achilles leading the funeral songs.

---

153. Who happened to share Hector's birthday—one of those rather charming details in which Homer specializes.

Meanwhile, on Olympus, Achilles's mother Thetis visited Hephaestus and begged him to make new armor for her son.

"He will fight tomorrow, come what may, so please, Hephaestus, as you love me, he needs the finest armor ever worn. Will you work all night in your forge? For me?"

Hephaestus was married to Aphrodite, of course, who was on the Trojan side, but like Zeus he adored Thetis and owed her much.[154] When Hera had given birth to Hephaestus, her first son by Zeus, she had taken one look at him, dark, hairy, and ugly—far from the radiant godlike child she had hoped

---

154. Homer tells us that by this time Hephaestus had a new wife: Charis (also known as Aglaea), the youngest of the Three Graces.

 The Shield of Achilles

for—and hurled him down from Olympus.[155] Immortal as he was, the infant Hephaestus might never have made it to full maturity and godhead had he not been rescued by Thetis and the sea nymph Eurynome and taken to the isle of Lemnos, where he was raised. It was here that he acquired his peerless skill as a metalworker and craftsman.

He embraced Thetis warmly and shuffled to his forge. Overnight he labored at the furnace. Before the first flush of dawn he had created what many held to be his masterpiece—the Shield of Achilles. Five layers thick, two of bronze, two of tin and a central core of solid gold. On its glittering surface, rimmed with bronze, silver and gold, he portrayed the night sky—the constellations of the PLEIADES and HYADES, Ursa Major and ORION the Hunter. He delicately beat out whole cities, complete with wedding feasts, marketplaces, music and dancing. In marvelous detail he depicted armies and wars; flocks, herds, vineyards and harvests. All human life beneath the heavens. By dawn he had finished and was able to present Thetis with not just the shield but a four-plated helmet with a crest of gold, a bright breastplate and—to protect the legs from the knee down—shining greaves of light, flexible tin. Nothing more beautiful had ever been made for mortal man.

That morning Achilles stood on the shore sounding his piercing and devastating war cry, to awaken the Myrmidons and all the warriors of the Achaean alliance.

It was here that he and Agamemnon finally faced off, watched by Odysseus and the other senior Greeks.

"Was it worth it, great king?" said Achilles. "All this death on account of our pride? Enough. I swallow my rage."

Agamemnon, instead of bowing his head and embracing Achilles, let loose a long rambling speech of self-justification. Zeus sent him mad, took away his sense of judgment. It wasn't his fault. He reiterated the offer that Achilles had already refused.

"Please now, take Briseis, take all the treasure you want. When this is over, take one of my daughters as your wife."

"I want nothing but slaughter and revenge," said Achilles. "I have sworn not to eat or drink until my Patroclus's death is avenged and Hector lies bleeding in the dust."

"Very commendable too," said Odysseus. "But don't you think that, even if you won't eat, your Myrmidons will fight all the better with a good meal inside them?"

---

155. He bounced off the mountainside, injuring his leg, and giving him the permanent limp with which he is associated. See *Mythos*, page 77.

Unromantic as it was, Achilles saw the justice in this very practical suggestion.

Briseis, released by Agamemnon, made her way toward Achilles's enclosure. When she saw the lacerated body of Patroclus laid out there, she broke down and threw herself on him, sobbing.

"No one else treated me so well. Oh, Patroclus. Sweet, sweet Patroclus. You protected me. Only you showed me respect and kindness."

Odysseus, Nestor, Idomeneus, and Phoenix all begged Achilles to eat and strengthen himself for what was to come, but he refused. His mind had turned to home. Had his father Peleus died by now, or would the old man have to bear the news of his nephew Patroclus's death?

"And of my death too, no doubt," he said. "And what of my son Pyrrhus on Skyros? Will I ever see him again?"

Such thoughts sent everyone's mind to their families back home and a silence fell over the camp.

"Enough of that," said Achilles. He strode into his tent to arm. Hephaestus's armor awaited him.

When he emerged, the Achaean camp gave a cry of wonder. The marvelous shield glittered, the helmet flashed. This was the sight every Greek had longed to see. Achilles, with the great ash spear and silver-hilted sword of his father Peleus.[156] Achilles, stepping into his chariot. Achilles, ringed in a halo of fire and ready to lead them to glory. A great cheer went up. The Achaean army shivered with anticipation. They could not lose now. Hector and Troy were doomed. This was not a man. Nor a god. This was their Achilles, something more than either.

The Myrmidon captains ALCIMUS and AUTOMEDON harnessed and yoked the snorting, prancing Balius and Xanthus, Poseidon's wedding gifts to Peleus and Thetis. Standing in his chariot, fueled by a rage such as could be quenched only by blood, Achilles gave one more great cry, cracked his whip, and thundered toward Troy, the Achaean host surging like floodwater behind him.

THE ARISTEIA OF ACHILLES

Never had such fighting been seen. Never such glory won. Never such crazed and bloody slaughter.

---

156. You might remember that Peleus's sword had been given to him by Zeus, that Acastus hid it in a dunghill when he left Peleus to be killed by marauding centaurs, and that Chiron helped Peleus recover it. Later, as a wedding present, Chiron had given Peleus a spear possessing miraculous properties—as we will see in due course. That sword and that spear (like the horses Balius and Xanthus) had been passed down to Achilles.

The gods knew this was a day that would live forever. Zeus cast thunder, Athena and Ares clashed, Poseidon shook the earth with powerful tremors.

Achilles hunted Hector, calling on him to come and fight. It was Aeneas who first emerged to face him.

"You, Aeneas! Shepherd boy," sneered Achilles. "Do you think if you kill me, Priam will leave you the throne of Troy? He's got sons. You're a nobody."

Aeneas was unafraid and launched his spear. The tip pierced the bronze and tin layers of Achilles's great shield only for it to bury itself in the soft core of solid gold. Aeneas lifted a huge boulder and Achilles rushed in, sword drawn. One of them would surely have died there and then had not Aeneas vanished in a great swirl of dust. Poseidon, favoring the Greeks as he did, had nonetheless rescued Aeneas, whose destiny he knew to be momentous.

"So," cried Achilles, staring around. "I'm not the only one the gods love. Never mind, there are plenty of Trojans left to kill."

And indeed there were. Whirling about, Achilles charged into the Trojan ranks and swiftly killed Iphition, Hippodamas, and Demoleon, a son of Antenor.

POLYDORUS, Priam's youngest surviving son, although forbidden to fight by his father, had been unable to resist entering the fray. When the boy suddenly found himself face to face with the greatest of all the Greeks, he turned and fled. But he was too slow. Achilles speared him in the back.

Hector heard his younger brother's shrill screams and hurled his own spear at Achilles, but a gust of wind caused it to fall short—or was it, as Homer suggests, blown back by Athena?

Finally! Hector was in his sights. Achilles closed on him with a terrible series of screams, but once more the gods intervened and Hector disappeared in a cloud of mist. This time it was Apollo who denied Achilles his kill.

The enraged Achilles cut down more Trojans. Homer is as merciless and implacable in his descriptions as Achilles was in his killing. Dryops: speared through the neck. Demuchus: knee smashed and cut into pieces. The brothers Laogonus and Dardanus: speared and chopped. Young Tros, son of Alastor: liver split open and butchered. Mulius: a spear through one ear and out the other. Echeclus, the son of Agenor: head split open, a curtain of blood running down his face. Deucalion: speared, spitted, and decapitated.

Achilles: his *aristeia*. A pitiless orgy of blood. An unstoppable cyclone. A raging wildfire. His blood-spattered chariot wheels rolled over the dead. The soaked earth was saturated with dark blood as he pushed the Trojans toward the River Scamander. In quick succession he killed Thersilochus, Mydon, Astypylus, Mnesus, Thrasius, Aenius, and Ophelestes, before dispatching Lycaon, another of Priam's sons, and tossing the body into the river. Scamander, his waters now choked with the corpses of men and horses, begged him to stop. Achilles only laughed and slaughtered yet more Trojans, pitching their bodies into the water. Boiling and frothing with indignation, Scamander called on Apollo to slay Achilles and grant the Trojans victory. Achilles heard the river god's anguished plea; enraged, he dived in and attacked the water.

For a moment Scamander was stunned into stillness by the madness of a mortal man daring to take on a river. But he shook himself, rose up, and forced his current into furious foaming whitewater rapids. Achilles was swept away. He reached up for an overhanging elm and pulled himself out of the water, but Scamander wasn't finished. He sent a giant new swell after him, a great tidal bore of rushing water that even the swift Achilles couldn't outpace. The wave crashed down on him. Struggling and close to drowning, Achilles called out in despair.

"Don't let me die here, like this. Let me at least face Hector, win or lose. If nothing else grant me a hero's death at his hands."[157]

The gods heard him. Hera instructed her son Hephaestus to release a fire, which spread along the riverbank. She herself fanned it with winds until the river so hissed and seethed and boiled and steamed that Scamander screamed in agony, letting go of Achilles, who scrambled out and back onto the plain to resume his killing.

Priam looked down from the walls of Troy and saw his army routed not only by Achilles and the Myrmidons but by a newly invigorated and energized Achaean army behind them. He ordered the gates open to receive his fleeing soldiers. Achilles, howling like a mad dog, raced toward the gates. Antenor's son Agenor, though terribly afraid, launched a spear at him—a good aim, but the tip bounced off the newly minted tin greaves on Achilles's legs, and, without so much as checking his stride, Achilles stormed after him. Apollo spirited the real Agenor away and took his form, taunting Achilles and leading him all over the plain of Ilium, giving the stampeding Trojans time to pour into the city.

Apollo-Agenor then disappeared with a laugh, and a furious Achilles turned to vent his wrath on Troy.

---

157. Homer has Achilles in his desperation conjure the image of a peasant struggling to ford a stream. "Don't let me be swept away like some farm boy trying to cross a flooded river with his pigs," he cries out.

ACHILLES AND HECTOR

King Priam looked down at the inspired, enraged, and implacable Achilles running like the wind toward the city. Hector was standing outside the Scaean Gate, ready for the final encounter. Priam and Hecuba called down, begging him to take shelter inside. The old king tore at his hair as the vision arose in his mind's eye of the fate of his city and the Trojan people if Hector were to be killed.

But Hector would not be persuaded. He knew that the time for listening and for withdrawing into the city had been the night before, when Polydamas had urged that they all take shelter within the walls. In his pride Hector had refused, and so many great Trojans, so many brothers and dear friends, had been cut down. The only way he could redeem himself for his recklessness was by killing the man responsible. Achilles.

And there he was now, Hector's nemesis, his affliction and his curse, racing toward him like an avenging angel and shrieking that horrible war cry. Hector turned cold at the sight of a man who had become a raging wildfire. Golden, aflame with unquenchable violence, Achilles charged him.

Hector turned and ran. Great, noble, and courageous as Hector was, the sight of this terrible angel of death was too much even for him. He turned and ran.

Achilles chased him. Three times they circled the walls of Troy.

Zeus felt for Hector. He liked him and was disposed to intervene on his behalf. Athena rounded on him.

"Father, Hector's fate is decided. You know it is. First you forbid us to get involved with the mortals and alter their doom, now you want to intervene yourself and avert Hector's?"

Zeus threw up his hands. "You're right. You're right."

"May I at least go down and ensure that all unfolds as it must?"

Zeus consented with a mournful bow of the head and Athena flew down to Troy. Taking the form of Hector's brother Deiphobus, she materialized at his side, pledging to fight alongside him.

As Achilles closed in, Hector turned and called out to him.

"Very well, son of Peleus, no more running. It is time to kill or be killed. But one word. If I win, I swear before Zeus that I will respect your body. All I will do is strip it of your glorious armor before returning it undefiled to your people. And you pledge to do the same if you prevail?"

Achilles snarled with contempt. "I have no interest in deals. Hunters make no deals with lions. Wolves make no deals with lambs."

With that he hurled his spear. Hector dropped into a crouch and it shot overhead, burying itself in the earth behind him. Unseen by Hector, Athena retrieved the spear and returned it to Achilles.

Now it was Hector's turn. He took aim and launched his spear. It was the best and strongest throw he had ever made. The point homed in on the very center of Achilles's shield. But the shield held and the spear glanced off.

"Another spear," said Hector, putting out his hand for Deiphobus to rearm him, but Deiphobus was nowhere to be seen.

Hector knew at once that his moment had come. Drawing his sword, he launched himself at Achilles. Achilles lowered his head and charged.

Hector was wearing the armor he had stripped from Patroclus. Achilles's old armor. Achilles knew it intimately, every fold of it.

As the two warriors closed the gap between themselves, Achilles's mind raced faster than his body. Hector's approach, shield forward and sword raised, seemed to come in slow motion. Achilles aimed his spear at the spot where he knew the leather did not quite overlap the bronze, exposing bare skin and leaving the throat open, just where the collarbone met the neck.

Achilles thrust and Hector, Prince of Troy, the hope and glory of his people, came crashing down, mortally wounded.

With his dying breath Hector begged Achilles once more. "My body . . . return it to my people for burning. Don't take it down to your ships to be eaten by dogs . . . My parents will pay a ransom for me such as has never been paid . . . only, please . . ."

Achilles laughed savagely. He had no shred of respect, mercy, tenderness or human feeling left in him.

"The dogs and birds can have you!"

"Mocking me, you mock the gods," Hector gasped. "Your end will come soon enough. I see you at the Scaean Gates, brought down by Apollo and Paris . . ."

Hector died.

Achilles bent to strip the corpse of its armor. His old armor. The armor in which Patroclus had fought and died.

Emboldened by the sight of Troy's greatest warrior lying dead in the dust, Achaean soldiers now pressed forward in ever greater numbers, each anxious to have their own stab at the body of the great Hector. In thirty years they would show their grandchildren the flakes of blood on the tips of their spears and swords and boast of their part in the downfall of the great Trojan prince.

Achilles took the belt from around the corpse's waist—the war belt Ajax had given Hector when they had exchanged tokens after their duel. How polite and gentlemanly that confrontation had been. And how very long ago.

Achilles tied one end of the belt around Hector's ankles and the other to his own chariot. Taking up the reins he drove his team back toward the ships, dragging Hector behind him.

The grief of Priam and Hecuba watching their son's body bouncing so cruelly on the rocks and stones of the plain of Ilium on its way to the Argive ships was more terrible to look at than any sight of the war thus far. Their glorious son dead, and his body treated with such dishonor. No chance for them to cleanse it and prepare it for a noble burning and burial.

Hecuba's anguished sobs reached the ears of Hector's wife Andromache. With a terrible apprehension of what that sound must mean, she ran to the ramparts in time to see her husband's bloody corpse being hauled through the dust.

"Oh, Astyanax," she cried to her baby son. "I am no longer Hector's wife and you are no longer Hector's son. For the rest of time we are widow and orphan."

And the women of Troy wept with her.

◆ Achilles dragging Hector's body around the walls of Troy.

THE FUNERALS OF PATROCLUS AND HECTOR

While he had avenged the death of Patroclus as he had sworn he would, Achilles had not yet finished mourning the loss of his beloved friend. Nor, as we shall see, was his hatred of Hector in any way assuaged.

First, he ordered the construction of a monumentally huge funeral pyre. This was expected. What he did next was not. He had twelve Trojan prisoners of war brought up to the pyre where he cut their throats with no more compunction, and far less ceremony, than a priest slitting the throats of lambs and goats for sacrifice. This was a crime against the principles of proper martial conduct, the codes of honor, and the canons of religion which shocked even the gods.

Now, with Hector's corpse still lashed to his chariot, he dragged it round Patroclus's tomb three times, leaving it face down in the dust.

Patroclus's body was laid on top of the pyre. The Myrmidons cut their hair and laid strands of it all over the corpse, like a shining shroud. Weeping, Achilles sheared off his own golden locks and placed them tenderly in Patroclus's dead hands. He put jars of honey and oil beside the body; lit torches were set to the pyre, and his beloved companion's soul was able at last to fly to the fields of Elysium.

Funeral games were held, a chance for the excited Achaeans to release tension, to remember Patroclus's heroic achievements, and to celebrate the sudden and blessed turn the war seemed to have taken. Just a day earlier it had looked as though their ships would be burned and their cause entirely lost. Now their enemy's greatest champion was dead and their own was rampant, triumphant, and invincible. They could not lose.

Achilles was not yet done with Hector. Every day, standing in his chariot like an avenging demon, whip hand raised, he circled the walls of Troy, dragging the corpse behind. Such implacable fury, such insane cruelty, such open contempt, caused the gods to avert their eyes. After twelve days of this horror, Zeus at last decreed that the sacrilege must end.

That night Priam left the city on a wagon piled high with ransom treasure. His old servant Idaeus whipped the mules on toward the Achaean lines. A young man stepped out in front of them.

"Are you old fools out of your minds? Driving a wagon loaded with gold right into the heart of your enemy's encampment? You'd better let me take the reins. You"—this to Idaeus—"shift over."

There was something about this young man, who told them he was a Myrmidon, that Priam liked and trusted. He was fine-looking, in only the first flush of a beard, but there was a strength and sense of amused self-possession about him that invited confidence.

"You've come for your son Hector, I suppose?" the young man said.

"I have come to collect as much of him as the dogs have left," said Priam. "But how could you possibly know that?"

"Cheer up, old man. You won't believe it, but the dogs haven't touched him. Nor the birds, or the worms, or the flies, and their maggots. You can't even see any wounds. His flesh is uncorrupted. He is as fresh as morning dew. I'd say he looks finer than he did when you last looked down on him from your city's walls."

"The gods be praised," said Priam in wonder.

"Apollo, specifically," the young man said with a grin. Suddenly Priam understood that this was no mortal sitting beside him on the bench, calmly clucking encouragement to the mules as they pressed on into the heart of the Greek camp—this was a god.

When they reached the Myrmidon enclosure, Hermes—for who else could it be but Zeus's divine messenger son?—pulled on the reins and pointed his winged staff toward the central tent.

"You go in there and melt his savage heart."

The Myrmidon captains Automedon and Alcimus were wholly unable to hide their blank astonishment when Priam, King of Troy, entered their tent, fell before the seated Achilles and clutched at his knees like a wretched beggar. He kissed the hands that had killed so many of his sons.

"Achilles, oh Achilles," he said, not caring to wipe away his tears. "Only picture your father Peleus. An old man like me, he has one pleasure left in life, just one. The thought and image of you, his glorious boy. Our children mean more to us than all our thrones and lands and gold. Imagine Peleus, now, in his palace in Phthia. Someone is arriving on a ship to tell him of your death. 'Achilles, the glorious fruit of your loins is dead, my lord,' the messenger cries out. 'His body has been left out for the dogs to chew on. He is befouled and defiled, and those who killed him will not allow him to be burned and buried with the respect and honor that his valor and his nobility deserve.' Can you imagine such a thing, Achilles? How would your father Peleus feel, do you think?"

Achilles caught his breath. Automedon saw tears starting up in his eyes.

"I understand that you felt you had cause for vengeance," Priam went on, never letting go of Achilles's knees. "I bring treasure for you. It is no recompense for the loss of one so dear to you as Patroclus was, but it is a respectful ransom. Offered in hope and love. Perhaps you will take pity on an old man. I had fifty sons, you know that? By Queen Hecuba, of course, and by other wives too. Fifty. So few left to me. The flower of Troy, mowed down. Hector, last of all, defending the land and people he loved. The victory was yours and . . ."

Achilles gently pushed Priam's hands away.

◈ King Priam appeals to Achilles.

"Sit," he said, indicating a chair. His voice was hoarse and he had to clear his throat. "Your courage in coming here. Your honesty . . ."

Alcimus and Automedon watched in awe as the two men fell on each other's shoulders, weeping like children. When they had no more tears to shed, they ate and drank together, quietly finalizing the terms of Hector's ransom and return. They agreed on a twelve-day truce to allow for Hector's funeral rites.

It was just as Hermes had said. Despite the passage of time, despite lying out in the hot sun, despite being pulled roughly through the dirt and sharp stones of the plain so many times, Hector's body was pristine and beautiful.

The Trojan women, Helen, Andromache, and Hecuba chief amongst them, mourned Hector with praise songs. Helen was hit almost as hard as Andromache. She had loved Hector for his courage, his chivalry, and, above all, for his boundless courtesy and all the personal kindnesses he had shown her, a Greek woman come among them bringing nothing but death and desolation. Hector was everything that the vain and hollow Paris was not.

They cremated the body, doused the flames with wine, and interred the ashes in a mound overlooking the city he had given his life to defend. And so the Trojans bade their final farewell to Hector, their greatest of men.[158]

---

158. And so ends Homer's *Iliad*.

AMAZONS AND ETHIOPIANS TO THE RESCUE

The momentum given to the Achaean forces by the presence of Achilles and the absence of Hector might have propelled the war to an immediate end. But at just the moment that the Trojans found themselves being pushed relentlessly back and the city looked likely to be taken, new allies from the east rode in to their rescue in the form of the Amazons, led by their fearsome queen Penthesilea.[159] "Rode to the rescue" is the right phrase here, for the Amazons were the first warriors to fight on horseback. In the rest of the Mediterranean world, chariots were pulled by horses, and horses were mated with donkeys to produce the mules necessary for the movement of supplies; but it was the Amazons, a race of female warriors from the shores of the Black Sea, who climbed on their backs and pioneered mounted warfare.[160] Penthesilea was a daughter of Ares and, by the same divine father, the younger sister of Hippolyta, the great Amazon queen who either married Theseus or was killed by Heracles during the course of his Ninth Labor.[161]

Penthesilea brought with her to Troy twelve fierce Amazon warrior princesses,[162] and she alone accounted for eight hapless Achaean men on her first foray into battle. The very presence of the Amazons spread consternation and alarm through the shocked Greek ranks. None of them had ever engaged with a mortal female in battle, let alone one shooting down arrows at them from horseback.[163] They rallied and summoned the nerve to attack the women with

---

159. "Pen-theh-suh-*lay*-er" is the usual way to pronounce her name. It is thought by many that the name of the *Star Wars* character Princess Leia was inspired by Penthesilea.

160. See *Heroes* (pages 81 and 311) for a more complete description of the Amazons.

161. Many great writers favored the narrative line in which Hippolyta marries Theseus. In *Heroes* I suggest that Antiope marries him, and that Hippolyta was killed by Heracles in a fit of temper. Theseus and Antiope (or "an Amazon") are referred to as a couple in Euripides's *Hippolytus* and Seneca's *Phaedra* (and Racine's *Phèdre*); and, of course, "Duke" Theseus and Hippolyta appear together in Chaucer's *Knight's Tale* and Shakespeare's *A Midsummer Night's Dream*.

162. Quintus Smyrnaeus in his post-Homeric *Fall of Troy* names them as Alcibie, Antandre, Antibrote, Bremusa, Clonie, Derimacheia, Derinoe, Evandre, Harmothoe, Hippothoe, Polemusa, and Thermodosa.

163. There is archaeological and historical evidence to support the idea of a race of horse-riding warriors like the Amazons—and, indeed, for fabulous fighters like the centaurs: riders so at one with their horses that it might seem natural for legend and tall tales to describe them as a single united horse—man creature in the case of the centaurs or as uniquely wild and gifted horsewomen in the case of the Amazons. In both instances the Greeks recognized that such people came from further east even than Troy. We know now, of course, that it was the Mongols from the Far East and then the Magyars who introduced to the West the idea of the horse-mounted bowman.

spears and swords, as if they had been men. Aias, Diomedes, and Idomeneus waded in and accounted for six of the twelve princesses.

The women of Troy, watching from the high walls, were so inspired to see members of their own sex driving the hated Argives back that they determined on joining the fray themselves, until THEANO, a priestess of Athena, warned them that—unlike Penthesilea and her companions, who had been born and bred for battle—they were untrained in fighting and would be certain to be cut down, doing nothing for the Trojan cause beyond adding yet more loss and further cause for lamentation.

Exhorted by the unrelenting Penthesilea, the Trojans beat the Achaeans back toward their ships, where Achilles and Ajax, the two greatest among all the Greek warriors, had remained out of the fighting, still mourning beside the grave of Patroclus. But the sight of their own men being so harried and hard pressed stung them into action. Achilles killed five Amazons alone. Penthesilea hurled spears at Ajax, who was saved only by the strength of his shield and the silver greaves that protected his shins. Seeing this, Achilles turned on her with an angry cry and impaled her with a spear of his own. Her death panicked the Trojans, who turned and fled back to the safety of the city walls.

Achilles roughly stripped Penthesilea of her armor, but when he removed her helmet and saw her face he was struck dumb with wonder. This is how he imagined the goddess Artemis must look. He mourned the death of one so beautiful, brave, and honorable. He wept at her loss. He should have spared her—wooed her, taken her home to Phthia to reign with him as his queen.

Every army, every company, every office, every school classroom, every sports team has its savage joker, its mocking critic. The Greek army had THERSITES, the ugliest (so Homer insisted) and the most cruelly satirical of all the Achaeans.[164] Odysseus had had cause in the past to thwack him with Agamemnon's scepter and threaten to strip him naked and beat him some more if he couldn't control his tongue. But such types never learn their lesson.[165] On this occasion, hearing Achilles mourning the death of Penthesilea, Thersites really did go too far.

"Look at him, the heroic Peleides, mooning over a woman. You're all the same, you great warriors. The moment you see a pretty face, you melt into a

---

164. He was stunted and bowlegged, Homer tells us. According to some sources, this was a result of injuries sustained after being thrown from a cliff by MELEAGER for showing cowardice during the CALYDONIAN BOAR Hunt. Thersites (the name actually seems to mean "audacious" and "brave") plays a significant part in Shakespeare's *Troilus and Cressida* (and, when played by Simon Russell Beale in a memorable Royal Shakespeare Company production, a hilarious one), not caring who suffers from the lash of his vilely abusive tongue.

165. There are those (Robert Graves among them) who have suggested Thersites is usually portrayed as ugly and deformed because he had the guts to speak truth to power . . . It is the powerful who write (or commission) history, of course.

puddle." He spat on Penthesilea's corpse. "That bitch was slaughtering her way through us like Death himself. Good riddance to her."

Enraged, Achilles lashed out at Thersites, striking his head so violently that the man's teeth flew out. He was dead before they or he hit the ground. No one in the Greek camp minded, save his cousin Diomedes, who might well have fought Achilles had the troops around them not begged them to make peace. Achilles, to atone for killing a Greek of noble lineage, agreed to sail to Lesbos to be purified.[166]

The Atreides, meanwhile—Agamemnon and Menelaus—mindful of the appalling carnage that had erupted over the bodies of Sarpedon, Patroclus, and Hector, consented to the Trojan plea that they might receive Penthesilea's corpse. It was borne into the city, where Priam ordered her ashes to be buried alongside those of his father Laomedon. At the same time, the Achaeans fell to mourning over the death of Podarces, speared by Penthesilea. He was the well-loved brother of Protesilaus, the first Greek to fall in the war and his loss was keenly felt.[167]

Now another hero arrived to fight for the Trojan cause: Memnon, King of the Ethiopians, a nephew of Priam.[168] Like Achilles, he was semi-divine—his mother was Eos, goddess of the dawn, and his father Tithonus, the unfortunate mortal who had been granted immortality but not eternal youth.[169] Also like Achilles, Memnon wore armor that had been made by Hephaestus himself. He and his Ethiopians, fresh blood to the Trojan forces, made real inroads against the Achaeans, killing among other notables Nestor's son Antilochus. A grief-stricken Nestor sent one of his other sons, Thrasymedes, into the carnage to recover the body. The old man would have buckled on his own armor and thrown himself into the fighting too had not the honorable Memnon called out to him, urging him to respect his own years and fall back. In his despair Nestor sought out Achilles, who had just returned from his purification on Lesbos. Achilles loved Antilochus and was eager to avenge himself on Memnon. It had been Antilochus, you may remember, who had run so tearfully along the sand to bring Achilles the terrible news of the death of Patroclus. He had stayed to hold

---

166. In Shakespeare's play, Achilles is one of the few characters who actually tolerates Thersites and is amused by him.

167. The "niddering Thersites's wretched corse" (in Arthur Sanders Way's endearingly archaic translation of Quintus Smyrnaeus's *Fall of Troy*), however, was thrown into a pit.

168. The name means "steadfast" and "resolute"—also "patient," and so often used of asses for that reason. The prefix *aga-* is an intensifier meaning "very" or "fully." One might think Agamemnon ill-named therefore, given his impatience and emotional volatility . . .

169. He aged, withered, and weakened so terribly, without dying, that at last Eos took pity on him and turned him into a grasshopper (or cicada, if you prefer). See *Mythos*, page 259.

Achilles by the hands while all that grief, rage, and self-recrimination had poured out. These things form a bond.

The dark Memnon and golden Achilles fought all day in what became the longest man-on-man duel of the war. In the end Achilles's fitness and speed prevailed and he ran through the exhausted Memnon with his sword.

Now the jubilant Achaeans streamed forward to the walls of Troy. Achilles joined them, slaughtering his way through Trojans all the way to the Scaean Gate. Did he recall the dying words of Hector?

"I see you at the Scaean Gates, brought down by Apollo and Paris . . ."

The voice of Phoebus Apollo himself now called on Achilles to turn back, but the blood was singing in the hero's ears. Achilles knew Apollo favored Troy, but perhaps he had forgotten that the god of arrows had a special, personal reason for hating him. Apollo could not overlook the contemptuously blasphemous manner in which Achilles had so brutally slaughtered young Troilus in Apollo's own temple, on his own sacred altar.

Paris sat high up on the walls, looking down at the frenzy of killing. No one could deny that he was among the finest of all the Trojan archers. His aim was always true, and if his bow was well tuned he could send an arrow further than any man—with the exception of his cousin Teucer, who fought on the Achaean side.

But with such a confused melee beneath him, there was surely little chance that Paris would be able to pick out a single man. He saw Achilles, though—how could he not? So many men were falling down all around him, and that *armor . . .*

Paris nocked an envenomed arrow and raised his bow.

Would the shot he prepared to unloose be his own work or that of Apollo? Apollo was the god of archery, so anyone who fired accurately might say, "Apollo guided my hand with that one," just as even now a writer often says, "The Muse was with me that day."

The feathers of Paris's arrow were drawn level with his eye. So many men were getting in his way as he tracked Achilles's movements. He breathed in and out softly. The first requirement for a sniping bowman was patience.

Achilles reared over a panicking young Trojan. The Trojan fell. Achilles stood exposed in Paris's eyeline. He let the arrow fly.

THE ACHILLES HEEL

Achilles was already turning as the arrow flew from the bow. Looking down, Paris's page, whose job was to keep passing fresh shafts to his master, thought that the arrow had fallen short and buried itself in the ground. But Paris gave a cry of triumph, and now the page saw that the arrow had indeed struck Achilles, low down, on the back of the foot. It had pierced the flesh of his left heel. This was the heel that Thetis had held him by when dipping him as a baby in the River Styx. The one vulnerable place on all his body.

Achilles staggered. He knew instantly that his hour had come. But his spear was still in his hand, and even as the venom spread through his body he thrust and thrust at the Trojans that began to surround him, coming at him in quick, stabbing charges, like jackals circling and snapping at a wounded lion. Four, five, six he speared and hacked before his legs buckled under him. Even as he breathed his last breath he killed more Trojans.

Terrified by the sight of a mortally wounded man with such implacable strength and will, most held back, unsure that such a man could really die. That priceless armor was irresistible, however, and they began to creep uncertainly forward. Then a terrible roar caused all but the bravest to scatter and run.

 The Wounded Achilles

Ajax, huge, towering Ajax, charged through, bellowing with grief and rage. He took up a station by the body, cutting to pieces any who dared come too near. Among those who fell before his wild defense was Glaucus, the Lycian lieutenant of Sarpedon; his body was rescued by Aeneas.

Paris loosed off a volley of arrows at Ajax. The thought of accounting for him *and* Achilles in the same hot hour was thrilling to him. He could almost hear the cheers of the admiring Trojans who would bear him in triumph to the temple of Apollo . . . The angle was wrong, however—Ajax was too near the city walls—so Paris stood on the highest part of the battlements and took careful aim downward.

Ajax saw a flash from up high and swayed aside as an arrow sped past, missing him by a hand's breadth. When he saw who it was that had fired, he gave a mighty roar and hurled a great granite rock. It flew up and struck Paris on the helmet. The hard bronze saved him from death, but the force of the missile stunned him and sent up a great ringing in his ears. Enough for one day, he thought, and dropped down out of sight.

Odysseus helped Ajax convey the body of Achilles back to the Greek camp. Both sides were now given over to sorrow and lamentation. The Trojans and their Ethiopian and Lycian allies mourned the loss of Memnon and Glaucus, the Achaeans wept for Achilles.

Once more the Myrmidons cut off locks of their hair to make a shroud for the corpse. Briseis laid her own shorn tresses on the pyre and tore at her own flesh in the violence of her grief.

"You were my day, my sunlight, my hope, my defense," she cried.

Incense, sandalwood, scented oil, honey, amber, gold, and armor were heaped up on the pyre. Trojan prisoners were executed. Agamemnon, Nestor, Ajax, Idomeneus, Diomedes, all groaned and keened openly and beat their breasts. Even Odysseus was seen to weep.

The smoke rose in the air and the cries of every soldier, servant, and slave mingled to make a noise louder than the greatest clamor of the war. The smoke and the sound reached Olympus where the gods wept too.

Golden Achilles, the son of Peleus and Thetis, was gone from the world. His death meant more than the loss to the Achaeans of their foremost warrior and champion. Humanity had lost a mortal of greater glory than had ever been known. Wild, petulant, headstrong, stubborn, sentimental, and cruel as he could be, his leaving marked a change in the human world. Something great had gone that could never—and would never—be replaced.

The vulnerability, the flaw that every human has recalls the first Achilles heel. Every great champion ever since, in war and in sport, has been a miniature of Achilles, a simulacrum, a tiny speck of a reminder of what real glory can be. He could have chosen for himself a long life of tranquil ease in obscurity, but he knowingly threw himself into a brief, dazzling blaze of glory. His reward is the eternal fame that is both priceless and worthless. In our world all athletes know that their years are short; they understand too that they have to be mean, passionate, merciless, and unrelenting if they wish to rise to their own kind of lasting fame. Achilles will always be their patron and their guardian divinity.

We each of us know, or have known, someone with a glimmer of Achilles's flame in them. We have loved and loathed them. We have admired them, sometimes even shyly worshipped them, often needed them.

We recognize that if we had ever encountered the real demon demigod Achilles, we would have feared and dreaded him, hated his temper, despised his pride, and been repelled by his savagery. But we know too that we could not have helped loving him.

THE ARMOR OF ACHILLES

As the body of Achilles burned and the Achaeans mourned the loss of their hero, Thetis stepped from the waves of the sea and joined them in their tears. Funeral games were held, with prizes from Achilles's vast collection of treasure distributed to the winners. After the last race was run, Thetis addressed the senior Greeks.

"The greatest prize of all has yet to be awarded. The shield, breastplate, greaves, and helmet that Hephaestus made for him. The sword and spear of his father Peleus. Only the bravest and best is worthy of these great objects. Of those who fought for and rescued the body of my beloved boy, who is the most deserving? I shall let you all decide."

Everyone instinctively looked toward two men—Ajax and Odysseus. They had been the warriors at the heart of the fighting over the dead Achilles.

Ajax stood. "Let the kings of Mycenae, Crete, and Pylos be the judges," he said.

Odysseus looked across at Agamemnon, Idomeneus, and Nestor, and nodded. "A perfect choice," he said.

"We consent," said Agamemnon.

But Nestor put up his hand. "No, my lord. I do not consent, and nor should you, and neither should King Idomeneus. This is an intolerable burden to put on us. How can we be asked to choose between two men that we love and value so highly? The prize is too great. Whoever wins our vote will rejoice in his possession of the most valuable treasure the world has seen. Whoever loses will simmer in fury. They will hate and resent us. No, Odysseus, it's all very well to shrug, but I think I know something of human nature. How can you have forgotten the destructive madness that erupted when Achilles and the King of Men squabbled over their prizes, Chryseis and Briseis?"

They turned toward Thetis for guidance, but she had disappeared. No one had seen her leave, but gone she was.

Agamemnon sighed. "Well, what do you propose?" he asked Nestor. "She has bequeathed the armor and stated the terms of the bequest."

"Rather than us being put in the position of having to decide," said Nestor, "why don't we ask the Trojans?"

"What?"

"We have plenty of prisoners here. They've had every chance to rate the bravery and strength of our fighters. Surely the best way to determine the most valuable among us is to ask our enemy whom they most dread meeting on the field of battle?"

Agamemnon smiled. "Ingenious. Let it be so."

When the Trojan prisoners of war declared that they regarded Odysseus as their most feared adversary, the Greeks let out a collective groan. They were afraid that Ajax would prove the sorer loser.

They were right. Ajax exploded with instant indignant fury.

"This is a joke! *Odysseus?* A greater warrior than me? How can you possibly believe that? Didn't you all see me fighting over Achilles's body? I killed a dozen Trojans. Odysseus slunk in to pull the corpse free, I'll grant you that. But only when I had made it safe for him to do so. He's all talk. He's all scheming and contrivance. He's not a warrior. He's a coward and a weasel and a . . . a rat and a . . . sniveling dog . . ."

"I expect I'm all kinds of animal, Ajax," said Odysseus with a smile, "but I think I do know how to fight. I seem to remember winning the wrestling match in the games we held for Patroclus's funeral.[170] I seem to remember killing more than my share of Trojans over the years."

"You didn't even want to come here!" yelled Ajax. "We all know how you pretended to be mad so that you could oil your way out of your oath. If it wasn't for Palamedes seeing through your deception . . . Oh, and yes, we all know who framed Palamedes, don't we? We all know who hid gold by his tent so that he'd be taken for a—"

"Dear me, Ajax. And you accuse *me* of being all talk! Who was it who sailed for all those months in search of Achilles? Would *you* have found him, identified

---

170. This is duplicitous Odysseus at his most mischievous. Actually, according to Homer, Achilles intervened in the fight before two of the Achaeans' most valuable warriors could tear themselves to pieces. The fight was declared to be a draw.

him, persuaded him to fight for us? Give me leave to doubt it. You're a big fellow, Ajax, and very strong, but our most valuable asset? I don't think so."

Odysseus's smiling modesty was more than Ajax could bear. He stormed from the meeting, leaving behind a stunned and sorrowful silence.

"Dear me," said Odysseus. "What a pity. I've always liked Ajax, you know. My deputy Eurylochus will stop by to transfer the armor to my ship. I'll see you all for supper later on?"

Ajax, meanwhile, stamped off to his tent, convinced that he had been deliberately snubbed and insulted.[171] So maddened with jealous rage was he that he arose in the night, insanely certain that Agamemnon, Menelaus, and Odysseus were his enemies. He stole through the camp intending to set fire to their ships. Reaching their quarters he stabbed them and their retinues to death in a wild frenzy of killing.

Then Ajax awoke to find himself in the camp's livestock enclosure, surrounded by dead sheep, their throats cut, blood running in rivers.

Distraught at the madness that had overcome him and terrified at how close he had come to murdering those he truly held most dear, Ajax stumbled to a lonely part of the shore, planted his sword—the silver sword of Hector—in the sand and threw himself upon it.[172]

His body was found by Tecmessa, the captive Phrygian princess with whom Ajax had lived and by whom he had fathered a son, Eurysaces.[173] When she saw the terrible wound—out of which Ajax's entrails had spilled—she stripped off her own clothing to cover the sight. All the Greeks were desolated when they learned that their beloved giant had died in so pitiable a fashion. Odysseus seemed shaken too and told anyone who would listen that he would happily have

171. Quintus Smyrnaeus's *Fall of Troy* puts it like this (in Arthur Sanders Way's translation):
    So Aias, his fierce heart
    With agony stabbed, in maddened misery raved.
    Foam frothed about his lips; a beast-like roar
    Howled from his throat.

172. The second formal duel between Greek and Trojan heroes, you will recall, the one between Hector and Ajax (the first being the aborted confrontation between Paris and Menelaus), ended with a courteous exchange between the two combatants: Ajax gave Hector his war belt and Hector presented Ajax with the sword which was to be the instrument of his suicide. The belt, which Hector wore from the day of the duel forward, was used by Achilles to lash Hector's body to his chariot and drag it so cruelly through the dust. These gallant tokens became emblems of the worst and most tragic elements of the war. Achilles's first set of armor—worn by Patroclus and Hector—the wondrous second panoply forged by Hephaestus, the war belt of Ajax and the sword of Hector: they all seem to have been imbued with ill luck. The story of Troy resonates with curses, of course, and these symbols offer a sense that everything to do with all-out war is by its very nature accursed.

173. The boy was named after Ajax's great shield. He went on to rule in Salamis. Sophocles wrote a play about him which has not survived. His tragedy *Ajax*, which presents the hero's madness and suicide, does exist, however, and is still performed, translated, and adapted from time to time.

given the armor to Ajax had he known the poor fellow was going to take it all so badly. It was notable, however, that his regret did not extend to offering the armor to Tecmessa and Eurysaces. Perhaps he had already calculated that he would need it for a greater purpose, soon to come.

Agamemnon and Menelaus ruled that, while the suicide was tragic, it could by no means be regarded as a warrior's death. It warranted no cleansing, no great pyre, no ceremonial burning. The body must, according to the code by which they all lived and fought, be left on open ground.

Ajax's half-brother Teucer was horrified by the thought of wild dogs scavenging the corpse and whipped up such anger in the ranks against the ruling that the Atreides were forced to relent. Ajax had been greatly loved by the men; and, it should not be forgotten, he was a cousin of Achilles.[174]

So it was that Telamonian Ajax, Ajax the Great, was cremated with full honors. His charred bones were sealed in a gold coffin that the soldiers buried in a great mound by the banks of the River Simoeis at Rhoiteion, where for many hundreds of years the tomb remained a popular place of pilgrimage for visitors from all over the Mediterranean world, until the sea finally washed it away.[175] We honor different kinds of courage and achievement: the golden glory of an Achilles is marvelous, but the unquestioning loyalty, tireless courage, and massive steadfastness of an Ajax is no less to be admired.

PROPHECIES

"Achilles and now Ajax!" said Menelaus, wringing his hands. "They were our sword and our shield! It's my fault, my fault, all my fault."

"Now, now," said his brother. "No one is blaming you."

"I am blaming myself, Agamemnon! I have asked too much. All for Helen. So many dead. It is time for us to board our ships and leave. We must sail home."

Before a disgusted Diomedes could reach for his sword, Agamemnon turned on Calchas with a snarl.

"Ten years, you said. Ten years. Nine full years have gone by and the tenth is nearly over, and still we have not taken Troy."

---

174. They were both the grandchildren of Aeacus, who had two sons, Telamon and Peleus, you will remember. You. *Will*. Remember.

175. According to the historian and geographer Strabo, a statue of Ajax from the tomb was looted by Mark Antony and given to Cleopatra. Pausanias, on the other hand, records meeting a Mysian who told him that when the tomb was being washed away, among the bones of Ajax they recovered were his kneecaps, which were "just the size of a discus for the boys' pentathlon."

"We will, great king, it is foretold that we will," said Calchas. "But we must have Achilles's son with us. Without him there can be no victory."

"Achilles's son?"

"'Pyrrhus' he was called when he was born. He answers to the name 'Neoptolemus' now. He is not yet bearded, but I know that he is already a great warrior. He lives on Skyros with his mother Deidamia. I have seen that without him we cannot hope to prevail."

Agamemnon stamped his foot in frustration. "There's always 'one more thing,' isn't there? One more little detail that is suddenly revealed to you. Why have you never mentioned this boy to us before?"

"The vision of him and his place in things was only vouchsafed to me this morning," replied Calchas imperturbably. "I cannot command the gods to disclose all their plans at once. They have their reasons."

Agamemnon sighed. "Very well. Odysseus, Diomedes—you'd better sail for Skyros immediately and bring back this Pyrrhus, or Neopotamus, or whatever his damned name is. Meanwhile—what the hell is that noise?"

The sound they had all heard was the clamor of the newly energized Trojans beating their swords against their shields. They had been reinforced by yet another powerful ally. EURYPYLUS of Mysia had just this moment arrived with a full contingent of fresh fighting men, and morale within the city had grown high once more.

In a strange episode that preceded the whole war, the Greek expeditionary force had invaded Mysia, mistaking the city-state in the northwest for Troy itself. Achilles had speared its king TELEPHUS, a son of Heracles and the father of this Eurypylus. The wound was not fatal, but it festered. Achilles was persuaded to use the same spear (the spear of his father Peleus) to heal it, fulfilling a prophecy. In gratitude, Telephus promised not to involve Mysia in the coming war. Arriving to aid Troy now, his son Eurypylus was breaking that promise but satisfying his own deep love of adventure. Paris, Deiphobus, and Helenus, the senior surviving Trojan princes, could not have welcomed him more warmly. One by one the whole court was shown, and allowed to handle, Eurypylus's fabled shield. It was as huge and heavy as a cartwheel and divided into twelve sections, each depicting in intricately worked bronze one of his grandfather Heracles's Labors. The central boss portrayed the great hero himself, club in hand, and clad in his celebrated costume of the hide of the Nemean Lion.

Not only could Eurypylus boast this illustrious lineage, but he outshone even Paris in looks. Odysseus, who had encountered him during the attack on Mysia, described him as the most beautiful man he had ever seen. Beautiful or otherwise, he could certainly fight. Had it not been for the combined skill and courage of Teucer and Aias, the Achaeans would have been routed and Achilles's son Neoptolemus might have reached the Troad too late to have been of any help.

It had been on the island of Skyros, years earlier, that Odysseus and Diomedes had sought out King Lycomedes and found the young Achilles hiding as a girl. Arriving on the island for a second time, now to seek out his son, they were amazed to be shown into the presence of a young replica. The same flame-colored hair, the same proud bearing and flashing eyes. The lofty, self-confident air with which one so young grandly insisted the visitors state their business struck Odysseus as more comical than commanding.

"Do we have the honor of speaking to Achilles's boy Pyrrhus?" he asked.

The boy flushed. "I am not a *boy* and I do not answer to that foolish name," he said. "You may address me as Prince Neoptolemus."

"I may," said Odysseus, "but that remains to be seen. For now I'd like to speak to your mother."

The mockery in Odysseus's tone was more than Neoptolemus could bear. His hand flew to his sword hilt. Diomedes quickly stepped forward and gripped his wrist.

"I apologize for my friend Odysseus," he said. "He means no harm."

Neoptolemus gaped. "Odysseus? You are Odysseus of Ithaca, son of Laertes?"

The arrogant manner was instantly cast aside and replaced by a rush of youthful excitement and something akin to hero-worship. He took them both at once to see his mother.

Deidamia was still in mourning for Achilles and declared herself entirely opposed to the idea of her son fighting in the war that had killed his father and made a widow of her.

"I forbid it!" she said. "And so does your grandfather."

King Lycomedes nodded his head gravely. "You are too young, my boy. Perhaps in a few years."

"I've trained in the arts of war every day since I could walk," said Neoptolemus with some heat. "No one on this island can best me. And the oracle has declared more than once that it is my destiny to go to Troy and win great glory there."

"But it's too soon, my boy!"

"I'm ready. Ask anyone."

Odysseus had discovered that the general view on Skyros was that Neoptolemus was every inch his father's son. He had much of Achilles's skill, strength, and speed and all—if not more—of his hot temper and insatiable lust for killing.

"We would not come for Prince Neoptolemus," said Odysseus, "if we did not think him more than capable of looking after himself."

"If he goes," said Deidamia, "it will break my heart."

Neoptolemus hated to see his mother distressed and seemed now to waver.

Odysseus read the situation at once. "Your father's armor is mine by right," he said. "Forged by the hand of Hephaestus himself. I have brought it with me. If you agree to join us I will, of course, bestow it upon you."

"The Myrmidons will follow you anywhere," added Diomedes. "They only await your place at their head."

Neoptolemus threw his mother a pleading look of such desperate and agonized intensity that her resistance melted. She gave a moan and bowed her head. His face broke into a brilliant smile.

"I'll be back before you know it," he said, hugging her close.

A STRANGE VISIT

Back at Troy, Eurypylus and his Mysian troops, aided by a rampant Aeneas, had pushed the Achaeans over the Scamander and were threatening to pin them to their ships, just as Hector had done before. Agamemnon and Menelaus joined Idomeneus and Aias in a counterattack, wounding Deiphobus, but Aias was put out of action by a well-directed rock thrown by Aeneas.

The din of battle on the plain could be heard in Helen's suite of rooms high up in the royal palace. She was at her loom, listlessly weaving, as she did every day. Aethra, the mother of Theseus and Helen's old companion, coughed gently to announce that a visitor stood outside, awaiting an audience.

"What is their name?"

"He won't tell me who he is, my dear. Insists on seeing you. Won't take no for an answer."

"Show him in."

Helen was taken aback when Aethra led in a boy no more than fifteen years of age.

"And who might this young man be?"

"My name is Corythus," said the boy, blushing furiously. "I . . . I . . . have a message for you . . . I . . ."

"Why don't you sit down and take something to drink?" said Helen, indicating a seat and nodding to Aethra, who poured wine. "You can gather your thoughts and tell me your message when you're ready. This room is uncomfortably warm, is it not?"

The youth sat down and drank gratefully from the proffered cup. He looked up anxiously at Aethra, and Helen—sensing his unease—dismissed her with a slight movement of her head.

"There now," she said, "we're quite alone and you can tell me your message."

"It's for you to see," Corythus said, passing over a small packet wrapped in the bark of a birch tree.

In some surprise Helen opened the packet and looked long and hard at the tokens inside.

"This is from Oenone?"

Corythus nodded.

"And you are her son by Paris?"

He nodded again and looked shyly down at the floor.

Helen's mind filled with visions of the last ten years. She thought back to her life in Sparta with Menelaus before Paris came. What madness had overcome her? Was it real attraction to Paris or the work of Aphrodite that had led her to leave behind her home, her parents, and most of all her beautiful daughter? Hermione would be thirteen years old now. Had she learned to hate the mother who abandoned her? Hot tears rolled down Helen's cheeks as she thought of all she had left behind and all she had caused. All this death. Even now she could hear the screams of the dying and the clash of arms down on the plain. So many brave men killed and good women widowed. So many parents bereaved and children orphaned. All because of her. If it were not for her, Hector would be alive, Andromache would have a husband and Astyanax a father. And for what? All for a vain, cheating liar like Paris. He had not only ruined her life, and the life of all those in Sparta whom he had forced her to abandon, but he had betrayed his first wife Oenone and this son, this poor, awkward, gulping boy shuffling before her. But she had to be honest. Everything Paris had done, *she* had done. She was cursed. She was death . . .

In the intensity of her grief and distress, Helen fainted to the floor. Corythus tried to call out for help, but his voice stuck in his throat. Not knowing what else to do, he went to her side to feel for a pulse.

At just this moment Paris came through the door. Seeing a young man paying intimate attentions to his wife, he was filled with jealous fury. He took out his sword and cut at the boy, slashing his throat. Corythus died on the spot. In the intensity of his rage Paris would have killed Helen too, if his eye hadn't first been drawn to the bundle of birch bark by her side. When he had understood its meaning and realized that the youth he had killed was his own son, he was overcome with grief and shattered by remorse.[176]

---

176. I can find reference to the version of the Corythus story I have recounted only in Roger Lancelyn Green's *Tale of Troy* and in Book 4 of the poem *Helen of Troy* by the prolific

Helen wanted nothing more to do with Paris. She never spoke another word to the man she looked on as the author of all her woes and all the woes of Troy and Greece. Their relationship was finally, entirely, and irrecoverably over.

Nor had Paris's victory over Achilles showered him in much glory. After all, the poison arrow had been directed, men said, by Apollo. Fine marksman as he was, Paris could never have found so small a target as the great hero's left heel.

The killing by Paris of his own son marked the end of divine support for him. Aphrodite and Apollo, his greatest champions over the years, could not overlook a blood crime so dreadful. Paris's days were numbered.

THE GOLDEN BOY

Beyond the city walls the Achaeans were sustaining terrible losses. Machaon, son of the divine healer Asclepius, was speared and killed by Eurypylus. His brother PODALIRIUS bore the body back behind the lines, where he brought all his arts to bear in a desperate attempt to revive him. But no herb, salve, or incantation could bring Machaon—who had healed so many Greeks himself—back to life. Enraged, Podalirius flew into the fray. His fury and the fighting skills of Idomeneus and Aias pushed Eurypylus back from the stockade, but a

nineteenth-century folklorist Andrew Lang, which I guess must be Lancelyn Green's source and which I further guess is an elaboration by Lang on the more familiar narrative. That is given by the splendidly named *Erotica Pathemata* ("The Sorrows of Love"), which was written in the first century BC by Parthenius of Nicaea, and combines two earlier historians of Troy: Cephalon of Gergitha—a pseudonym under which Hegesianax of Alexandria Trous (*fl.* late third—early second century BC) wrote—and the fifth-century Hellanicus of Lesbos. As the *Erotica Pathemata* (in Stephen Gaselee's translation) puts it:

"Of the union of Oenone and Alexander [i.e., Paris] was born a boy named Corythus. He came to Troy to help the Trojans, and there fell in love with Helen. She indeed received him with the greatest warmth—he was of extreme beauty—but his father discovered his aims and killed him. Nicander however says that he was the son, not of Oenone, but of Helen and Alexander, speaking of him as follows:—

'There was the tomb of fallen Corythus,
Whom Helen bare, the fruit of marriage-rape,
In bitter woe, the Herdsman's evil brood.'"

("The Herdsman," of course, refers to Paris too.)

Lancelyn Green, though, has Helen "read" a message, and Lang talks of "tokens" and (rather confusingly) "runes" . . . I must suppose that if Oenone did *write*, then it would have been in some distant Ionian cousin of Linear B, the Mycenaean syllabic script that had died out by Homer's time, but which preceded the post-Homeric Greek alphabet. Or perhaps the message was written in Linear B's predecessor, the Minoan Linear A—a script that is yet to be deciphered. Linear B was famously unlocked by Michael Ventris and John Chadwick in the 1920s, ten years after Lang's death. Homer never refers to reading or writing in either of his epics, and we have to rid our minds of any notions of messengers bearing dispatches, heralds declaiming from scrolls, or soldiers' letters being sent to and from home. This Andrew Lang version of the Corythus episode depends on some kind of message, however, and your guess as to how these "tokens" were read is as good as mine. Even so, I—like Lancelyn Green—prefer Lang's idea, tokens, runes, and all . . .

quick flanking maneuver caused Agamemnon and Menelaus to become separated and encircled inside the Mysian ranks. Trapped and isolated behind enemy lines, the royal brothers would have been captured or killed had not Teucer waded in to rescue them.

At that moment a great cheer was heard from the shoreline. The ship of Odysseus and Diomedes had returned. With his sure eye for image, Odysseus had instructed Neoptolemus to put on his father's armor and climb high on the prow. Whether it was Athena, Iris, or some other deity who arranged the vision, no one could be sure; but just as Neoptolemus stepped up, a brilliant shaft of sunlight shone down on him through the clouds. The bronze, silver, and gold of the shield flashed. The first Achaeans to see it set up a great cry which spread from the stockade to the fighting on the plain. The Trojan soldiers looked and saw with terror that their arch-nemesis had been reborn.

Shaking the great spear of his grandfather Peleus, Neoptolemus shrieked the blood-curdling war cry of his father Achilles, and the Myrmidons, recognizing it, roared with joy and beat their swords against their shields. Their clamor, depending on whose side you were on, either chilled or thrilled the heart. Neoptolemus sprang down to lead the Myrmidons into battle. Newly energized and inspired, the Achaean army began to repel the Trojan advance. Neoptolemus soon demonstrated not only that he had much of Achilles's athleticism and grace but that he was every bit as violent and bloodthirsty as his father too. As he twisted, swooped, leapt, ducked, darted, hacked, sliced, stabbed, speared, and wove his way through the Mysian lines toward Eurypylus, the Trojans fell back, many convinced that this truly was Achilles new born. When he and Eurypylus finally met, they stamped their feet into the ground and crashed their two great round shields together. Neoptolemus was younger and fresher. Eurypylus was stronger and wilier. He had been fighting hard for days, but never faltered or took a backward step. The long and desperate duel that ensued might have gone either way, but in the end youth and speed won out. Neoptolemus ran round like a hound tormenting a bull until at last his spear found its mark and tore through the older man's throat.

A groan went up in the Mysian ranks as Eurypylus hit the ground. Scenting victory the Achaeans pushed the Trojans right back to the city walls. Neoptolemus fell like a ravening eagle on those not quick enough to escape through the closing gates.

"Now!" he yelled. "Up the walls and avenge my father!"

Linking with each other like a chain of the ants from which they derived their name, the Myrmidons began to swarm up the walls. The panicked citizens on the battlements, men, women, and children, hurled down rocks, bronze cauldrons, stone jars—anything they could find.

Were it not for a great blanketing mist that fell on the city at this most critical moment, the Greeks might well have succeeded in reaching the top of the ramparts and breaking the siege. The Trojans yelled down at them, crowing in triumphant relief.

"Zeus! Zeus!" they roared, convinced that the King of the Gods, the Sky Father, and Cloud-Gatherer himself, had intervened to save them. Certainly the descent of the fog was timely and decisive.

Grumbling and disappointed, unable to see further than the limits of their own outstretched arms, the Achaeans laid their hands on each other's shoulders and shuffled in single file back to the ships, the moment lost.

THE ARROWS OF HERACLES

Once more an agonizing stalemate loomed, and once more Agamemnon turned in frustration to his prophet Calchas.

"What do the swallows and sparrows tell you now, you old fraud?"

Calchas smiled his gentle, sorrowful smile. "Only a foolish leader blames his messengers, and the King of Men, the great one I serve, has never been a fool."

"Yes, well, no one is blaming you, Calchas," said Agamemnon, gritting his teeth. "But you have told us, again and again, that you foresee a clear Argive victory in the tenth year of our campaign. There are not many weeks left. I am sure we would all be grateful for guidance."

"I know now," said Calchas, "that to secure victory we need the arrows of Heracles."

"What?"

"The divine Heracles entrusted to his friend Philoctetes his mighty bow, together with the arrows that he had dipped in the deadly blood of the Hydra."

"Yes, yes, every child in the world knows that, but what do you mean we 'need' them?"

"You may recall, mighty king, that ten years past, when we stopped off on the isle of Lemnos on our way here, Philoctetes was bitten on his foot by a venomous snake."

"Of course I remember. What of it?"

"The wound festered, and it was decided that he should be left on the island lest he infect us all. My lord, the flight of the cranes that rose up from the sands last night told me clearly that we need Philoctetes and those arrows. Without them we cannot defeat Troy."

"But surely the poor man must be dead by now? Alone on that island with such an injury . . ."

"The gods have spared him. I have seen that he yet lives."

Agamemnon heaved the gusty sigh of one much put upon by the weight of office, the malice of chance, and the endless incompetence of underlings.

"Right. Well. So be it." He turned to survey his staff. "Odysseus. You're the one who persuaded us to leave the fellow behind. You and Diomedes go off to Lemnos and fetch him. Why are you still standing in front of me? *Go!*"

On Lemnos, Odysseus and Diomedes found Philoctetes, still in perpetual agony from the wound that would not heal. He had lived all these years in a den of his own making. It was littered with the feathers and bones of birds he had shot with his arrows. Seeing Odysseus, the author of his miserable isolation, he raised his bow. His emaciated arms trembled as he took aim.

"Go on," said Odysseus. "Shoot. I'm sure I deserve it. I put our cause ahead of you. We thought that we had no need of you. We left you to rot. Now we find that we do need you, and I have dared come to beg for your forgiveness and aid. But why should you forgive me? Better we all die here forgotten. Why choose glory and fame in Troy when death awaits us whatever we do? Might as well end it here in this stinking lair as on the field of battle. One way we live forever in posterity—in statues, songs, and stories—the other we are forgotten. But so what? What has posterity ever done for us?"

"Damn you, Odysseus," gasped Philoctetes. "If we do die together here, I'll probably be cursed to spend the afterlife with you endlessly jabbering on in my ear."

"Oh yes, you can be assured that his shade will never shut up," agreed Diomedes. "It would be worse than the tortures of Sisyphus and Tantalus combined. Much better come along with us."

As soon as their black ship dropped its anchor stone at the Achaean beachhead, Philoctetes was carried off and conveyed to the tent of Podalirius, who was delighted to be able to do something to take his mind off the loss of his brother Machaon. He applied a fomenting salve to the suppurating foot. The moment the preparation touched the wound, it foamed and fizzed. Philoctetes screamed and fainted. When he awoke, his foot was whole and the pain gone.[177]

Agamemnon put Philoctetes to work straight away. His poisoned arrows accounted for dozens of ordinary Trojans, but one prize was worth more than all the others put together.

---

177. In Sophocles's tragedy *Philoctetes*, Odysseus takes Neoptolemus to Lemnos with him (Diomedes is not present) and a great psychological game of trickery and deception is played out. Philoctetes refuses to come to the Greek army's aid, but in the end Heracles descends onto the stage as a *deus ex machina*, revealing to Philoctetes that a cure and heroic victory await him in Troy.

A dashing figure in bright armor had ventured out from the city and was killing Greeks with a savage disregard for its own safety. Philoctetes took aim. His arrow flew toward the Trojan warrior, who swayed to one side. The tip of the arrow grazed his throat. The warrior took off his helmet and put a hand to the stinging nick. Hardly any blood at all. It was nothing.

"Paris!" cried Diomedes, clapping his hand on Philoctetes's shoulder. "You've hit Paris!"

The figure in bright armor was indeed Paris. That morning he had burned the body of his son Corythus, the boy he had killed in a fit of misdirected jealousy. Remorse, bitterness, and anger had driven him to a great and savage courage. Even now he shook off the arrow scratch and threw himself back into the fight. But the skin on his neck began to smart uncomfortably. He staggered as sweat broke out on his brow and the blood pounded in his ears. Helping arms lifted him up and carried him toward the Scaean Gate, past the very piece of ground where Achilles had fallen to his own arrow. By the time he was laid down on a bed in the palace, his whole body felt as though it were on fire.

The fever burned and burned and he cried out for Helen in his appalling agony. Helen would not come. Then he called to be taken to Mount Ida.

"Oenone . . . my wife . . . only she can cure me. Take me to her."

Oenone saw him writhing on the litter, but her heart had hardened against him.

"You betrayed me and you killed our son," she said. "You are not worthy to live and I will not lift a finger to save you."

Paris was taken back down to Troy. After three more days of screaming and delirium, his unhappy soul finally left his tortured body.

The Greeks celebrated and few Trojans grieved. Priam and Hecuba led the mourning. Paris's two oldest remaining brothers Deiphobus and Helenus dutifully laid small amounts of treasure on his pyre. Cassandra wailed. Helen kept to her rooms in the palace. Old Agelaus the herdsman came to say farewell to the baby he had left for dead on Mount Ida's summit, the infant he had named and raised as his own, the happy boy who had been loved by all the people of the mountain, the honest, smiling young Paris so contented with life on the green slopes and a blessed marriage to the lovely Oenone. That sweet and silver Paris had long been replaced by something hard and spoiled, tarnished and mean. Aphrodite, Helen, status, treasure, and show had turned his head and soured his heart. And now this pathetic end. If that she-bear had eaten the baby it found on the mountaintop instead of nursing it, how different the world would now have been.

But even as the flames leapt up around Paris's corpse, Oenone pushed through the small knot of mourners and threw herself onto the pyre to be burned with him. Shallow, foolish, and vain as Paris was, she had loved him with all her soul.

His death meant, of course, that Helen could by rights be released now and sent back to Sparta with all the treasure that had accompanied her, so bringing about an end to the war. But Deiphobus and Helenus had fallen completely under the spell of her beauty and would not think of letting her go. It was decided that Helen should marry one of them. She, naturally, had no say in the matter. Deiphobus used his seniority to win her, and Helenus, stung and affronted, slunk from Troy and made his way to Mount Ida to nurse his wounded pride.

Odysseus, at the head of an Achaean raiding party on the hunt for sheep and cattle, found Helenus and brought him to Agamemnon's camp. His bitterness against Deiphobus made him only too eager to tell the Greeks everything he knew.

"If you really want to break Trojans' hearts," he said, "you should find your way into the city—there's a secret entrance I can describe to you. One or two men might be able to pass through it unchallenged, so long as they look harmless. They should go to the temple of Athena and steal the wooden idol we call the Palladium. The Luck of Troy. It fell from heaven at the feet of my great-great-grandfather. While it remains within the city walls Troy cannot fall."

Agamemnon looked across at Odysseus, who shrugged his shoulders with mock resignation. "Come on, Diomedes," he said. "It seems we're needed again."

THE LUCK OF TROY

That very night, cloaked and hooded in filthy rags, Odysseus and Diomedes made their way across the plain and toward the rear of the city. As instructed by Helenus, they found the secret door and—after hiding their swords in the tangle of weeds and long grass at the base of the outer wall—slipped through and made their way along the dark alleyways. Their beggars' disguises ensured that they were not bothered, save on one occasion by stones thrown at them by a group of children.

"You stink!"

Odysseus had insisted they smear horse dung on themselves "for that authentic perfume of beggar."

Helenus's careful directions flew out of Diomedes's head as soon as they entered the mazy network of lanes and dank passages. He hoped that Odysseus was not so baffled.

"Where are we?"

"We should be more or less behind the palace."

"Should? More or less?"

"As long as the moon is above and to our right, we—"

"Tss! There's someone coming!"

Diomedes pulled Odysseus into a doorway as the figure of a woman approached. As she came closer she passed through a shaft of moonlight for just one fleeting second. It was enough. Odysseus stepped out. The woman stopped and stared.

"Odysseus? By all the gods, *Odysseus?*"

"A fine evening, Helen."

Diomedes emerged and stared at Helen, open-mouthed with astonishment. She stared back, equally amazed.

"Diomedes too? Is this it? The moment?" She looked about her. "Is the whole Achaean army in the city? Is my husband here? Is Menelaus here?"

Odysseus put a finger to his lips and pulled her into the shadows. A group of drunken soldiers passed close by, singing loudly.

"Just us," Odysseus whispered. "We're here to steal the Palladium."

"Only we're lost," added Diomedes.

"Will you be Ariadne to my Theseus," said Odysseus, "and teach me how to negotiate this labyrinth?"

Helen's sense of humor got the better of her and she broke into a peal of laughter. "The Palladium? Is this what Agamemnon's mighty war has come to?"

"It's not a joke," said Diomedes. "Helenus told us that without the Palladium Troy will be doomed to fall."

"Well, that's certainly what they believe," Helen said. "I'll help you. This way."

She led them around corners, across courtyards and over rickety wooden bridges until they came to a great square, on one side of which a grand sweep of marble steps led up to a colored frontage of painted columns.

"The temple of Athena," whispered Helen. "The Palladium is inside."

Odysseus and Diomedes entered the temple and Helen stood guard outside. There was silence all around. No one passed by. The sight of two such close friends from her old life had come as an extraordinary shock to her. So sudden, so entirely unexpected. It was like a dream. But a dream that had awoken her from a reality that was far more illusory. Any last hold that Aphrodite had ever had upon her was gone. Deiphobus revolted her and Troy meant nothing. She felt no ill will toward Priam and Hecuba, but she knew now with absolute certainty that all she wanted was to sail home with Menelaus to Sparta. If he would have her.

Odysseus and Diomedes emerged from the temple. Diomedes had taken off his cloak and used it to wrap up the Palladium.

"It's so small," he said, tucking the package under his arm, "and so crudely carved."

"I know," said Helen. "Like all sacred and truly precious objects it is very plain. Only profane things are beautiful."

Odysseus looked at Helen. The bitter self-reproach in that last remark had not escaped him.

"The Atreides will be mightily pleased to hear how you helped us in this," he said.

"Is Menelaus angry with me?"

"Of course not. Be content. This will all soon be over."

"Tell him how unhappy I am. I am unhappy with Deiphobus, who is a pig, but I was unhappy with Paris too. Tell him that."

Odysseus squeezed her hand. "He knows. Now, how in Hades do we get back to that secret door?"

"But I'm coming with you!" said Helen. "Wait while I fetch my son Nicostratus. We'll come with you all the way to the Greek camp and that will be an end of everything!"

Odysseus and Diomedes looked at each other. Could it be as simple as that? They pictured the faces of Agamemnon and Menelaus when they arrived at the stockade escorting the prize of all prizes. Just then a voice rang out.

"Princess Helen!"

They turned. A group of palace guards was approaching. Their captain hurried forward and bowed.

"Prince Deiphobus has sent us in search of you, madam. Who are these men? Have they dared accost you?"

"Athena looks kindly on those who look kindly on beggars," said Helen. "Now begone—off to where you came from," she said to Odysseus and Diomedes, raising her hand and pointing in the direction of one of the five lanes that led out of the temple square.

Odysseus and Diomedes bent low and backed away from her, mumbling thanks.

"And find a horse trough to wash in," she called after them. "You stink like Greeks."

They ran and ran to the end of the lane. Odysseus looked up and around, found his bearings, and soon they were out of the secret door and scrabbling in the grass and weeds for their swords.

As they made their way back to the Greek encampment, the dark magic of the Palladium—or perhaps the dark magic of Odysseus's devious ambition— took hold. A few steps behind Diomedes, he considered how much better it would be for him if he were to arrive at Agamemnon's tent alone. He pictured himself dropping the Palladium casually onto the King of Men's campaign table. "Yes, they came chasing out of the city after us. They got Diomedes in the back and ran off with the Palladium. I pursued, killed them, and retrieved the thing.

No, no, it's nothing. Just wish I'd been able to save poor Diomedes. He was a good man and a dear friend."

All in all, a flawless plan.

Odysseus breathed in, swallowed, and advanced on Diomedes, sword raised. From the corner of his eye Diomedes saw the blade glitter in the moonlight. He turned in time to avoid the vicious downstroke.

The spell broke at once and Odysseus fell to his knees.

"I thought you were my friend," said Diomedes.

"It's that thing!" said Odysseus, pointing at the bundle under Diomedes's arm. "It's cursed."

Diomedes grunted his agreement, but was careful to drive Odysseus forward with the tip of his own sword for the rest of their walk back to the Greek lines.[178] Odysseus was, of course, smart enough to be the first to speak when they arrived. Out tumbled the story of his attempted attack on Diomedes. He told the tale in bewildered tones of wonder and horror as an example of the terrible power of the Palladium. It was decided at once that, rather than keep such an ill-omened object, they should take it to the shrine of Athena that stood in the foothills of Mount Ida, where a guard could be mounted to prevent the Trojans from reclaiming it.

"It is enough that the damned thing has left the city," said Agamemnon, turning toward Calchas. "For now our victory is assured. Is that not the case, Calchas?"

Calchas raised his shoulders with a sweet smile. "So it is written, my lord. So it is written."

"Sometimes," said Odysseus, who knew he still had work to do to regain the trust of everyone around him, "sometimes what the gods write man must rewrite."

"Meaning?" said Agamemnon.

"Meaning, I've had an idea," said Odysseus. "And though I say so myself, it's rather a good one. So good that I suspect Athena herself must have put it in my mind."

---

178. Diomedes knew how invaluable to the Achaean forces Odysseus was, for all his tendencies toward the duplicitous and treacherous. In historical Athens, and all over the Greek world for centuries, the phrase "Diomedes's choice," or "a Diomedean necessity," was used to describe a situation where one is compelled to do something one would rather not do because it is for the greater good—like Diomedes sparing Odysseus, sacrificing his natural desire to revenge himself for the sake of the wider Greek cause.

BEWARE OF GREEKS . . .

DAWN

Every morning when Eos, sister to Helios the sun and Selene the moon, throws wide the pearl gates of her eastern palace, she prays that this new morning will light on a day of victory for Troy. Her husband, Priam's brother Tithonus, had been a prince of the city. It was on the very sands on which the black ships of the Achaean invasion force have lain beached for ten years that she and that dazzling mortal beauty walked during the first days of their love. Their son Memnon had died bravely in battle fighting for the Trojan cause, cut down by cruel Achilles not far from the same shoreline. Eos hates the Greeks and wishes that she could withhold from them the beautifying flushes of coral and peach it is her fate to cast over the vile and the virtuous alike.

Every morning the blear-eyed guards on the ramparts of Troy are relieved by a fresh shift. Every morning the incoming captain asks the outgoing if anything worth reporting on has been observed overnight.

Every morning the answer has been the same.

Until this morning.

This morning, this morning of all mornings, is different.

Eos's work is not yet done and the world is still in darkness when the relief sentries reach the top of the city walls. They are surprised to see the whole night-contingent crowded onto the edge of the battlements, staring out across the plain.

"What is it? What can you see?"

"Nothing!" comes the reply.

"Nothing?"

"I mean nothing. *Nothing.*"

"It's still dark."

"We saw fires earlier. Huge fires, but they've gone out."

The light is starting to leak into the sky and faint outlines are becoming visible. The act of staring and trying to make sense out of the slowly emerging shapes hurts the eyes. But every minute brings a little more definition.

"Why can't I see the silhouettes of the ships?"

"What's the hulking big shape?"

"Wasn't there before."

Far to the east, dawn's gates are fully open and faint streaks now flush across the sky above the city. Slowly, so slowly that it seems the senses are being fooled, an astounding truth is revealed.

The captain of the night guard rushes to the great bronze bell and swings the wooden beam to raise the alarm.

The Trojan citizenry are as well trained as the soldiery. At the sound of the great bell, the people begin to assemble at their agreed muster points. There is no screaming, no bucking and screaming like panicked horses, no freezing into immobility. Hector, who long ago laid down the procedures and drilled the people, would have been proud to see how orderly and unhurried they are at this moment, the first ringing of the bell.

Deiphobus and Cassandra are the first of the royal house to reach the ramparts. Priam himself arrives a little later, disheveled and out of breath. The guard troops are still staring out and have to be jerked into attention by the marshals and heralds attending the royal party.

"What is it?" asks Priam. "An attack? Fire? Ladders?"

"Come look, Father!" yells Deiphobus.

Priam is helped up to the highest point.

Below him the plain of Ilium stretches out. Ten years of war have pocked, pitted, and torn up huge sections of the once fertile land. Priam raises his eyes. There is the River Scamander sparkling in the morning sun and beyond . . .

Priam blinks in disbelief and looks again.

There is nothing.

The Greek stockade has been taken down.

The whole encampment, huts, tents, palisades and all, burned.

He sees the strange hulking outline of something, but cannot make it out.

But the enemy ships have gone, every last one.

Priam is so used to the sight of them fringing the beach that their absence looks like a wound, a terrible scar. The shoreline is naked and exposed without them.

Priam stares and stares, struck dumb with astonishment and something else. Is it fear? He realizes what he is feeling is a small suspicion of a splinter of a shred of *hope*. Dare he hope? The very thought of hope fills him with fear. He has seen and suffered too much to trust hope.

He swings round toward Deiphobus.

"They have . . . Where are they . . . ?"

Deiphobus grins broadly and even dares clap the king on the shoulder. "They have gone home, Father! The Greeks have gone home!" He starts to dance around the dazed old man.

Priam pushes his son away and looks out across the plain again. He turns to his adviser and friend, Antenor.

"What is that—there, that shape looming over the rubble by the shore? My old eyes can't make it out. What can it be?"

Cassandra comes forward and tugs at her father's robes, crying out, "It is death! Death!"

Antenor calls to the captain of the guard. "Send some men out to the Achaean encampment. Tell them to search thoroughly and report back."

Priam speaks to the press of people who have gathered up on the battlements to share the sight.

"It is very chilly up here," he says. "I think it would be a good idea if we all made our way down and had some breakfast while we await further news, yes?"

During breakfast Priam is outwardly calm. He tells Hecuba that he cannot quite believe he is awake.

"Is it possible? After all these years? That they would just leave?"

"It is what we have prayed for, my love," says Hecuba. "Perhaps the gods have finally listened."

"Why now?"

"Why not now? The gods know what this war has done to Troy. To us. You are a good man, Priam. Evil men have lived happier lives and never been forced to bury so many of their sons. Such injustice is an affront to everything. It has taken the gods a long time to set the scales down in our favor, but it is no less than we deserve."

Just then a clamor in the passageway outside tells of the scouting party's return. Their captain bursts in.

"Majesty, they have gone! They truly have gone. Not a Greek left behind. Well, no sire, that is not quite true. There is . . . We came across . . ."

"Get your breath back, young man," says Priam, "and tell us what you found at the Achaean camp."

"The Achaean camp is not a camp. Not anymore. It is dug up, burnt, abandoned. We did find one man there. We left a guard on him because, as well as this one man, we found—" The captain breaks off unable to suppress a great grin. "Sire, you will never guess what we found!"

"Don't play games with your king. Out with it, man!" snaps Deiphobus. "Tell us in plain language what you found."

"In plain language, highness," says the captain, too euphoric to be brought up short by Deiphobus's harsh tone, "we found . . . a horse."

"Well, I'm sure there's nothing so very strange in that," says Hecuba.

"But no!" says the captain, unable to stop smiling. "This is a horse like you've never seen before. A horse"—he points up at the ceiling—"a horse as high as this roof. A horse made of *wood!*"

THE PLAN . . .

When Odysseus described his idea in detail, there were several in Agamemnon's general staff—Neoptolemus and Philoctetes the most prominent among them—who tried to shout him down.

"It'll never work."

"They'll burn it first."

"Wouldn't fool a child."

"Thirty men? And you'll be one of them, will you?"

"I don't think so!"

"Far and away the stupidest . . ."

". . . mad . . . hare-brained . . . suicidal . . . "

Agamemnon raised his scepter and silence fell. "Athena told you this?"

"Every detail," said Odysseus. "I was as astonished as you all are. But she promised me that it will work." He turned to the others. "And yes, certainly I will be one of the thirty men inside. I have no wish for history to count me among the cowards who didn't believe. One of the traitors who spoke against the only plan that can ensure our victory. I will be one of the thirty whom fame will never forget. I expect there to be a fight for places."

The force and conviction of his speech had its effect.

"I came here to do battle against the enemy, not to squeeze myself into the belly of a wooden fire trap," said Neoptolemus.

"I understand how you and Philoctetes, who have known only a few weeks' fighting, still believe that force of arms is the only way," said Odysseus. "But the rest of us are weary of battle and ready to try cunning over killing. Wit over war, you know? Boldness and brains over butchery and blood?"

A grim murmur of agreement from the others silenced the doubters.

"How will we make this thing?" asked Menelaus.

"I suggest EPEIUS," said Odysseus. "He constructed the stockade. As we all know, the best and sturdiest of all the huts and buildings in this camp are those of his design. Back home in Phocis he supervised the construction of temples, ships, and whole towns."

Epeius was called for. He was not the most popular of the Achaean warriors. Many had observed that he was never to be found in the front line where the danger was greatest. He could fight one to one as well as any man, however. He had defeated Diomedes's companion Euryalus in the boxing match that had formed part of the funeral games held for Patroclus. And in those held not long after in honor of Achilles, even ACAMAS—son of the great Theseus, the inventor of wrestling[179]—had been unable to defeat him. If he was surprised to be summoned to this meeting of all the great leaders of the Achaean expeditionary force, he concealed it well.

Odysseus spoke for ten minutes and Epeius nodded as he listened.

"Ingenious," he murmured when Odysseus had finished. "A wooden *horse*, you think? Not an elephant, perhaps?"

There was some laughter at his. Odysseus was quick to laugh too.

"I mean, thirty men . . ." said Epeius. "They will have to breathe, after all."

"Thirty is the smallest number to be sure of success. You can do it, Epeius."

"I will need to build a high wall first to screen what we're doing from the sight of the Trojans and their spies."

"I've thought of that. It should be a rough wooden fence. It should look like a continuation of the stockade. High enough to screen your work, certainly, but a solid wall would excite suspicion."

Epeius nodded. "Well," he said, "I had better get to work. Before anything else, we will need to go to the western slopes of Ida to fell pine trees and transport the timber back here to my site. I shall need mules and men. May I choose whomever I need to work alongside me?"

Agamemnon waved a hand. "Take anyone and anything you want."

When Epeius and Odysseus had gone, Agamemnon turned to Calchas. "We are doing the right thing? I mean, it's one hell of a risk."

"The idea is bold, sire," agreed Calchas, "but something in it accords with a strange sight that caught my eye late last afternoon. I saw a falcon swooping down on a dove. Terrified, the dove flew into the cleft of a rock. For a long time I watched as the frustrated falcon flew around the rock, too big to follow his quarry in. This wheeling about called to mind our armies circling and circling Troy to no avail. But then the falcon stopped and concealed itself in a bush opposite the opening. It waited there, invisible and silent. Then I saw the dove put out its head, look around and take off. Immediately the falcon flew from the bush and fell upon it. The meaning of this came to me at once. Troy will fall, not to speed and strength, but to cunning, my lord king. And then the very next morning Odysseus comes to tell us of his strategy . . ." He raised his palms upward, as if to express his wonder at the imponderably mysterious ways of the gods, the Fates, and destiny.

"Hm," said Agamemnon, sharing an eye-roll with Menelaus.

Epeius fizzed and spun and sparked like Hephaestus as he worked. Rumors flew around the camp that he was expending jewels and precious metals on the detailing for his great wooden beast.

---

179. See *Heroes* (page 272) for more on Theseus and his invention of *pankration*.

"From out of the shared prize chest!" some muttered angrily.

Mostly there was excitement and support for the project. All wished that they could see it more clearly, however. The scaffolding that Epeius had erected to facilitate the construction of the horse was as effective a screen against Greek eyes as the great wooden palisade around the whole project was against Trojan. They heard the sawing and hammering, but could see none of the work in progress.

Odysseus, meanwhile, was clarifying the finer points of the plan for the benefit of Agamemnon and other senior commanders.

"If we simply up sticks and abandon the whole encampment, leaving nothing but the horse for the Trojans to find, they will be wary," he said.

"But I thought that was the whole point. For us to clear out completely?" said Aias.

"Yes, but there must be someone left behind to explain the horse. To allow the Trojans to believe that it is safe for them to bring it into the city."

Agamemnon frowned. "I don't get you."

"And I have just the fellow," said Odysseus, stepping aside and snapping his fingers at the curtain behind him. On this cue a stocky, broad-shouldered man stepped through and executed a short, ironic bow. At the sight of him there was a rumble of surprise and doubt.

"SINON?" said Agamemnon. "I thought you two hated each other."

Odysseus smiled. "There isn't much love lost . . ."

"My cousin Odysseus is a lying, cheating bastard," said Sinon, "and I can't stand the bloody sight of him."

"That much is known," agreed Odysseus. "The part about him not being able to bear the sight of me, that is," he added quickly. "The rest is gross slander born of envy. I simply can't imagine why you're all laughing. The point is that even the Trojans know that Sinon and I are mortal enemies. It makes his treachery all the more believable."

"His what? Explain yourself."

Odysseus explained himself.

"You really are a cunning one, aren't you?" said Agamemnon when he had heard it all. "No one else in the wide world could have come up with anything half as devious."

It sounded more like disapproval than praise.

"Not I, great king," said Odysseus, raising his hands in shocked protest. "Athena. She came to me in a dream and laid out every detail. I am but her puppet, her dumb vessel."

THE HORSE

Priam and his retinue made their way toward the vacated Achaean encampment. As they crossed the Scamander and drew closer, the great wooden horse seemed to grow and grow, its shape rising up in silhouette against the white glare of the sky.

The captain of the guard, having led the scouting party, was now leaning proprietorially again the horse's gigantic left foreleg with that air of proud ownership peculiar to those who have been first to make a great find. At the king's approach he straightened up.

Never had such a thing been seen. In three short days Epeius and his construction team had surpassed themselves. The attention to detail was astonishing. The greater part of the back, flanks, and belly were formed of overlapping wooden staves, like the lapstrakes of a clinker-built boat, every plank curved, turned, and planed true and smooth. To the neck was attached a spangled, purple-fringed mane, tasseled with gold. The eye sockets of the horse were inlaid with beryl and amethyst, setting off a gleam of contrasting colors—rolling, blood-red eyes, rimmed with green. A bridle studded with ivory and silvered bronze flashed and shimmered on the proud head, which was caught in mid-turn, as if some invisible rider had just that moment pulled on the reins. The lips were parted to reveal a jagged row of fierce white teeth.

Priam and the Trojans who stood looking up in shocked amazement could not guess that the horse's great mouth was open not to convey savagery and strength (although it did) but to allow fresh, breathable air to flow through the concealed ducts that ran inside the neck and down into the belly.

The hoofs on each leg were sheathed in tortoiseshell fixed with rings of bronze. From pricked ears to sweeping plaited tail, the effect was of swift majestic life.

In silent wonder Priam and his courtiers took in the sight. Deiphobus stroked the legs, awestruck but puzzled.

"We must destroy it!" cried Cassandra. "Destroy it, burn it, before it destroys and burns us all."

"Remarkable," said Priam at length. "Quite remarkable. You feel as if at any moment Ares himself might mount this great steed and gallop into battle."

"But what *is* it?" said Hecuba. "I mean, what is it *for*?"

"It is for the destruction of Troy," wailed Cassandra.

Polydamas called to his king from under the belly. "Be pleased to come round to this side, sire," he said. "There's something here you should see."

And there they were, letters of gold painted all along the right flank.

"LAOCOÖN, you can read these markings; come forward and tell us what they mean," said Priam, gesturing to a priest of Apollo who was standing close by with his two sons, Antiphantes and Thymbraeus.

Laocoön stepped up and examined the writing. "It says, 'For their return home, the Hellenes dedicate this offering to Athena.'"

"Ah, so it is for the goddess. A gift?"

"Sire, you cannot trust the Greeks, even when they bear gifts."

"You fear this object?"

Laocoön took a sword from one of the soldiers and slapped the flat of its blade sharply against the horse's belly. "I say burn it. I say b-b . . . I say . . ."

But Laocoön was unable to say anything. His mouth opened and closed. Foam started coming up from his throat and he began to twitch and spasm. Antiphantes and Thymbraeus rushed to hold him up.

"Come, father, sit down here," said Antiphantes.

"It is nothing, majesty," Thymbraeus assured the king. "The fit is on him, it happens sometimes."

"Hm. Maybe the gods wanted to strike him dumb for daring to doubt this thank-offering," said Deiphobus.

"We should at least leave it out here, where the Greeks left it," said Priam.

"You couldn't move it into Troy even if you wanted to," growled a voice.

Priam turned to see a bloodied and beaten man, short and powerfully built, who was being held up between two soldiers.

"Shut your mouth, Greek dog!" said one of them, striking him hard across the mouth. "You are in the presence of a king."

"Who is this?"

"He calls himself Sinon, your majesty. We found him hiding in the marshes behind the dunes here. He tried to run away when we approached, but we caught him."

"Let him come forward," said Priam. "He has nothing to be afraid of if he tells us the truth honestly before the gods. I'm sorry, Sinon, my men should have treated you more kindly."

"He was already beaten half to a pulp when we found him, majesty. Says the Greeks did it to him."

"His own people?"

Sinon was pushed down at the king's feet, from where he sniveled and whimpered his replies to the questions—and occasional blows—that rained down on him.

Slowly they were able to piece the whole story together. Odysseus, cursed, vile, cunning Odysseus—Sinon spat every time he had to utter the name—had told Agamemnon that the horse must be built and left on the shore to honor

Athena, who was angry on account of the blasphemous theft of the Palladium from her temple. That sacrilege meant that the Achaean forces had doomed themselves. They could never win the war. Even safe passage home would be denied them, unless they offered the horse to the goddess.

"The Greeks could never win the war?" said Priam. "They believed that?"

"Their prophet Calchas, he said that it was true. That it was time to go home. He said the Trojans had pleased the gods with their honorable and pious conduct, but that we had angered them."

"My very words!" said Hecuba. "What was I saying to you, Priam? The gods understand that we do not deserve to lose our city. I knew it!"

Priam squeezed her hand. "So they really have abandoned the fight?" he asked Sinon.

"Look around you, king. Tents and pickets burned. Ships loaded and hours since sailed for home. Except for poor bloody Sinon, of course."

Priam frowned at the Greek. "So why are you here?"

"Do you remember one of the Achaean generals, a cousin of our chief Agamemnon, name of Palamedes?"

"Of course."

"Well, Palamedes was the one who all those years ago saw through Odysseus—*twah!*"—another violent hawking spit—"and his feigned madness on Ithaca. The coward was trying to wangle his way out of honoring his oath. He never forgave Palamedes for exposing him. So one day, must have been nine or ten years ago . . . close to the beginning of this stinking war . . . one day the body of a killed and captured Trojan was found, and on it a message apparently from you, your majesty, thanking Palamedes for helping the Trojan cause."

"I sent no such message," said Priam. "I barely knew the man."

"Of course not. I saw with my own eyes Odysseus—*twah!*—planting the document. And I followed him later that same day and watched him bury Trojan gold in the ground by Palamedes's tent. The gold was found. Palamedes protested his innocence, but no one believed him, and he was stoned to death as a traitor. I should have spoken out, but Agamemnon and all those close to him—oh, how they love that cunning Ithacan . . . The evil bastard saw the look in my eyes, though. He knew I knew; and I knew my days were numbered. But the years passed and nothing happened. I thought maybe he'd forgiven me. Oh, he knows how to bide his time, that one! Just when I think I'm safe and going home with all the others, home to my town, my wife, and my children, the blow falls. Odysseus—*twah!*—persuades Calchas to tell Agamemnon that, to make the offering of the horse to Athena complete, a sacrifice is needed. A *human* sacrifice. Calchas loves to be the center of attention. Loves to wield the silver knife. Back when we were becalmed at Aulis he convinced Agamemnon he had to sacrifice his own daughter Iphigenia, so this was nothing. You can imagine how eagerly he agreed. The King of Men fell for it, of course. The sacrificial victim was to be chosen by lottery. And guess who arranged the lottery? Who but—*twah! twah! twah!*" Sinon's spitting exploded into a paroxysm of coughing.

"You were chosen?"

"Of course I was. They beat me—see the welts and bruises—then they penned me into a cage like I was some kind of goat. But the gods were watching over me last night. While they were feasting and dancing and singing their blasphemous songs, I broke out. I fled and hid in the dunes. Watched them cut their cables and sail away, leaving me here to the tender mercies of these lovely soldiers of yours."

"Well," said Priam. "That's quite a story."

"'Story' is what it is!" wailed Cassandra. "Lies. Lies cunningly wrapped in truths. Kill him and burn the horse!"

"One thing cannot be denied, Father," said Deiphobus, looking down on Sinon. "The enmity between this man and his kinsman Odysseus is an established fact."

"True, sire," said the captain of the guard. "We've all heard stories of their feuding."

"I've heard them, too," said Antenor. "I believe they share a grandfather in Autolycus, a son of the divine Hermes. But it's well known that they've never been able to abide the sight of one another. Rumors of the plot against Palamedes had reached me too. It all hangs together. I believe this wretched man."

"As do I," said Priam.

"I don't care if you believe me or not," said Sinon. "It's all the bloody same to me."

"You'll address his majesty with respect," said the captain of the guard, delivering a kick vicious enough to make Sinon double up in pain.

"And this horse," said Deiphobus, looking up at it. "You think Athena has accepted it and granted the cursed Danaans favorable passage home?"

"Oh, the horse is a blessing and a protection all right," gasped Sinon, holding his side. "But the crafty bugger has made sure that you could never get the benefit of it."

"How so?"

"He told its builder, Epeius the Phocian, to make sure the thing was higher than the highest of your city gates. Troy can never fall if that horse is inside the walls, but you'll never get it in there!" Sinon fell into a fit of wheezing laughter. "He's foxed you there, all right!"

"Hm." Deiphobus frowned. "Well, what's to stop us from taking it apart, carrying it through and reassembling it inside the city?"

"He thought of that too. See how the staves of wood interlink and overlap? Epeius made sure they are so cunningly fitted one into the other that you'd have to smash the whole thing up. Athena would turn the blessing into a curse if you did that, don't you think? I hate Odysseus—*twah!*—with my heart, soul, and guts, but you've got to hand it to him. Maybe Agamemnon plans to be back in a year or two with a bigger army yet. They couldn't risk letting you make Troy safe under the protection of this charmed horse, now, could they?"

Sinon's savage and gleeful chuckling drove the captain of the guard to strike him hard across the face. Priam was about to upbraid him again when another gasping, hacking sound was heard. Laocoön was coming round from his fit. Supported by his sons, he rose unsteadily to his feet and addressed Priam.

"I beg you, great king. Don't be fooled. This is all part of the Greeks' deception. They *want* you to bring the horse in. Lord Apollo speaks to me, sire, you know he does. I tell you this . . . I tell you this . . ."

His voice trailed off, for Priam and the whole court were staring at him in frozen horror. Or rather behind him. Laocoön could not understand it. Only the sea was behind him. He turned to look, but it was too late.

A pair of huge sea serpents had launched themselves from out of the waves. Either side of Laocoön his sons Antiphantes and Thymbraeus were already being crushed in four colossal tentacles. Two more reached out to coil around him.

The Trojans watched in dumbstruck horror as the serpents pulled their three screaming, thrashing victims into the sea. The men disappeared beneath the waves, a frothing tumult of pleading, outstretched limbs. The whole terrible attack lasted only seconds.

"And so the gods silence doubters!" exclaimed Deiphobus with a wild laugh. "Father, we can get that horse inside Troy and protect our city and our people forever."

"How?"

"Simple. Remove the gates from the widest entranceway—that'll be the Scaean—then demolish the wall around and above it! Just enough to get the horse through. We can board it all up straight away and restore the gates to their former glory soon enough. Oh Father, don't you see? We've done it, we've done it! We've *won!*"

Deiphobus danced around his father like a five-year-old. Soon other Trojans were dancing too. Before long, messages were being sent back and forth between the horse and the city, and half of Troy came rushing out across the plain.

Garlands of bay and wild flowers were cast over the horse's neck. Ropes were tied round the lower portion of the front legs and over the head. Trumpets, whistles, and drums accompanied the dancing Trojans as, with wild joy, they pulled the horse away from the beach, across the plain, over the Scamander's chief bridge, and up to the Scaean Gate.

If anyone saw Sinon slip away back into the dunes, they did not bother to chase after him. He had served his purpose and could do no harm.

THE BELLY OF THE BEAST

Odysseus had heard some, but not all, of what had taken place. When the noise of the world outside did reach him, all the separate sounds were fused into a muffled boom that made picking out individual words all but impossible.

It was hot, dark, and painfully cramped inside the horse. There were thirty of them in there, crammed in as tight as olives in a jar. Epeius's vents and ducts were working, but the air that came through was stale and tasted of wood and tar.

The sudden shocking moment when Laocoön had slammed the flat of a sword blade against the wood next to Odysseus's head had taken him completely by surprise. He had nearly slipped off the narrow wooden bench he shared with nine others. Two more such benches held the other twenty volunteers; all, like him, doing their best not to sneeze, cough, fart, fidget, or shift.

So far as Odysseus could tell, Sinon seemed to be playing his part wonderfully. He made out scraps of the Palamedes story being forced out of Sinon just as they had rehearsed it. He heard the whining tone, the highly convincing shrill edge of contempt and disgust in Sinon's voice. Convincing because Sinon truly did hate Odysseus. No playacting required. He had hoarded insults and harbored resentment for years. Now he could let all that poison out.

Then came a strange and inexplicable moment. An unearthly screeching, as from some terrible demonic creature, followed by choking human screams and a fraught silence. Had they suddenly turned on Sinon? Were they torturing him?

But no, there was laughter next. Laughter and the sound of music. Suddenly the whole inner frame in which Odysseus and the others sat suspended gave a violent lurch. Only the swift, outstretched arm of young ANTICLUS next to him kept Odysseus from being thrown forward off his bench. He breathed a silent "Thank you" to Anticlus. If he had tumbled down onto the secret trapdoor below, he might have burst through, out of the belly, and landed, back broken, in front of a crowd of Trojans. At the very least, the noise of his fall would surely have been loud enough to ruin everything.

The wrenching jerk was prelude to more shaking and shifting. They were on the move. The Trojans were singing and clashing cymbals, and tugging the horse along the ground, there could be no doubt of it.

Epeius had drilled tiny holes, no bigger than the holes made by woodworm, in the horse's side at irregular intervals, just enough to allow thin white needles of light to pierce the pitch-black interior. As the horse was dragged over the uneven terrain, the beams darted about revealing eye-whites, teeth, and the gleam of swords. Odysseus caught sight of Neoptolemus on the bench opposite, grinning across at him.

"You've done it!"

Odysseus pressed his hands down in the air as if to smother the triumphant excitement. "We shall see," he mouthed.

The jogging, grating journey across the plain seemed to last forever. In their time they had all sat on the rowing benches of penteconters, but this was somehow worse. The darkness, the confusion, the terrible possibility that they were being led not to victory but to cruel defeat. At any moment the crunch of axes might come or the furious crackle of fire.

On and on. The scrape and scrabble over rough terrain, the vibrations so violent that Odysseus found himself praying to Hephaestus to keep watch over the horse's tenons, joints, and interior bolts lest they be shifted loose by the incessant jolting and juddering. And all the while the dreadful music: horns, drums, pipes, and screeching, tuneless yells. Odysseus told himself these were the sounds of genuine victorious joy. If the Trojans doubted the horse and planned to destroy it, surely the songs and shouts would have a different tone?

Then the swaying, lurching, and grinding stopped altogether and a relative silence fell. Voices barked inaudible commands. Then came loud banging. Odysseus thought he recognized the sound of demolition and dared hope that the Trojans had begun work on knocking out a space in the wall big enough for the horse to pass through. Hot globes of sweat were dropping from his chin. The tap-tap sound they made as they slapped onto the skin of his bare knees was unbearably loud.

He heard hissing curses of relief and triumph from the men around him as they thanked the gods. They knew what those noises must mean. Odysseus was sure he could identify the smashing of hammers on walls and the splintering cracks followed by deep thumps that could be made only by blocks of stone breaking up and falling to the ground. And then, after so much more time than Odysseus felt he could account for, they jerked into movement once more, this time on smoother ground. The wooden wheels of the horse's hoofs trundled freely over flags and paving stones. The cries and calls boomed louder than before. A scream of joy sounded so close to Odysseus's ear that he almost leapt from his bench again. At first he couldn't understand it. Then he realized that they must be rolling along through a city street. The belly of the horse would be level with the upper story or balcony of some shop or dwelling house. Citizens must be crowded everywhere to watch the passage of this huge and extraordinary artifact, the like of which no one had ever seen before. Where would they take it? To the square outside the temple of Athena, he supposed, the one from which he and Diomedes had abstracted the Palladium.

Odysseus laughed silently. This was all so entirely odd. Perhaps it really had been Athena who had planted this idea. It had revealed itself so completely to him. Just as Athena herself had sprung fully armed from the head of her father

Zeus, so the idea of the horse had emerged complete to the last detail in his head. Right down to the use of Sinon and the need for the Trojans to think that the last thing the Greeks wanted was for the horse to be taken into Troy. How had such a complex notion come to him? Odysseus allowed his head to drop as the thoughts flooded his mind.

"Sinon and I are both descended from the trickster god Hermes, so perhaps it was more his work than grave, grey-eyed Athena's? I have to hand it to my cousin: he not only understood and consented to the plan, he saw the need to be bloody and roughed up when the Trojans found him. "No, you must beat me," he had said. "Break my nose. I wouldn't have submitted meekly to being sacrificed. To having my throat cut. I'd have fought like a lion. It has to look real." Now, there was a sacrifice to the cause. Or perhaps Sinon is one of those warped souls who derives pleasure from pain? Agamemnon promised him a giant share of treasure, of course. When this is all over, Sinon will be one of the richest men in the world. Richest commoners, at least. And his name will be remembered for ever. How strange is our mortal zest for fame. Perhaps it is the only way humans can be gods. We achieve immortality not through ambrosia and ichor but through history and reputation. Through statues and epic song. Achilles knew he could live a long and happy life, but chose blood, pain, and glory over serene obscurity. I don't give a fig for fame. If that smug rat Palamedes hadn't exposed me, I'd be at home with Penelope at this very moment. I'd be teaching young Telemachus how to use a bow and arrow. He is ten years old. *Ten.* How is that possible? He won't know who I am. Does Penelope tell him stories about me?"

Odysseus slept.

HELEN'S VOICES

Helen slept too. She had been lost in turbid dreams when the Scaean Gate was knocked down. The approaching din of music and the frenzied clattering of pots and pans in the streets below forced her awake. The maids, pages, and slave girls were leaning out of the window, bursting with excitement.

Aethra bustled up, a look of wild excitement in her eyes. "Oh, madam my love, come and see, come and see!"

Helen went and saw and thought she must still be dreaming.

The rest of the day and early evening went by like a dream too. Never had she witnessed such crazed celebration and feasting. The wine and grain jars in every storeroom were struck open without a care. The smell of baking bread filled the palace and streets. Outside the city walls she could hear an endless succession of distant bellowing screams as more and more sheep and oxen were slaughtered. The music and the singing never stopped. Troy had turned mad.

Every so often she went to the window and looked out toward the sea. It really was true. Not a Greek ship in sight. How often she had looked and tried to make out which one might have the yellow and black markings of Sparta.

Now Menelaus was on his way home, and she would never see him or her daughter Hermione again. All she had to look forward to were the clumsy attentions of Deiphobus and the sad smiles of Priam, Hecuba, and Andromache. "We don't blame you, Helen. Truly we don't." But truly they must. How could they not?

She did her best to look as happy as the rest of the royal family that night, but the moment she was able to make her excuses she slipped away to her chambers, bolting the door against the drunken intrusion of Deiphobus. Her husband, as she supposed she must call him. Her third and worst. Or fourth, should she count Theseus. That was a lifetime ago. Her brothers had been alive to rescue her then.

From her window she could just see the ears of that extraordinary wooden horse. They were pricked up above the roofline. Really the oddest sight.

When Helen finally fell asleep, Aphrodite came to her in a wild and vivid dream.

"Goddess, I have nothing to say to you."

"Impudent child. Do as you are bid this once and I will leave you to your sour matronly chastity forever after. But for this evening you are mine. I will not see great Troy fall to so mean a trick."

"What must I do?" Helen moaned, tossing her head on the pillow.

Aphrodite told her and Helen rose. For the rest of her life she could never be sure if she had been asleep when she walked and talked that night. She had heard of people who could weave, fetch water, and carry on whole conversations while snared in the coils of Hypnos, so it was quite possible. She certainly preferred to think she had slept through the whole thing.

She stood outside Deiphobus's room, calling his name. He opened the door and smiled a woozily grateful smile.

"My dear husband, I have neglected you." He started to pull her in, but she took a quick step back. "First I must put my mind to rest. That great horse. I don't trust it. Come with me, my love. Let us examine it more closely. Come, come!"

They hurried down out of the palace and through the streets. Some late revelers were winding their way home. Others had fallen drunkenly, and snored where they lay.

"It is too good to be true, surely?" she said. "It all smells of Odysseus to me. Suppose there are men inside? I think maybe there are."

"We looked for signs of an opening," said Deiphobus. "Smooth all round. No trapdoors."

"You don't know Odysseus."

"Then let us burn it down."

"There is a better way. You remember how well I imitate voices?"

"Of course."

Everyone in Troy had marveled at Helen's gift of mimicry. She could reproduce perfectly the voices of Hecuba and Andromache, even Hector's baby boy, the infant Astyanax.

"That's how I'll flush them out. Oh, but it is *huge!*"

The horse loomed above them, its gold tassels, glittering eyes, and silver-bronze fittings gleaming in the moonlight.

"Whoa there, my proud beauty," said Deiphobus with a laugh, jumping up to spank the rump.

Odysseus woke with a start.

He heard the men around him stirring. Something had struck the horse behind his head. A weak slap, but enough to alert them all. And then . . . had he gone mad?

Penelope was calling to him.

"Odysseus, my darling! It's me. I'm here. Come out. It's me, Penelope, come down and kiss me, my love."

He stiffened. This was witchcraft. Penelope had spoken to him in his dreams, but this was waking life. He drew out the dagger from his belt and pricked his thigh with a sharp jab. He was not dreaming. This was real.

There she was again.

"My darling . . ."

Maybe it was a *god*. They could see into the horse and must know who was concealed there. Was this the voice of Aphrodite? Or Artemis, perhaps. One of them trying to save the city they loved.

"Agamemnon, my husband, are you there? It's me, your sweet Clytemnestra . . ."

Odysseus breathed out in relief. It could not be the gods. They, who saw everything, would know that Agamemnon had departed last night for Tenedos with the Achaean fleet and could not possibly be in the horse. He and the rest of the Greek armies should be sailing back by now and be close to the Trojan shore, if not already disembarking and preparing to attack.

Odysseus allowed a sharp "sh!" to escape his lips as a warning to the others to stay quiet.

"Diomedes? It's me, darling man, your Aegialia.[180] Step down, it's quite safe."

Odysseus heard Diomedes, two along from him, swear under his breath but otherwise keep still. More voices came drifting up, pleading, cooing, seducing. The men held firm, until . . .

"Anticlus, my honey, it's your Laodamia. Come down and kiss me. I've so much to tell you. Our son is quite the little man now; you've no idea what he did . . ."

Anticlus let out a cry of surprise. Odysseus pinched his arm and hissed for him to be quiet. Anticlus was the youngest of the thirty men in the horse, brave as a lion but known to be impulsive.

"Anticlus? You know it's me. How can you be so cruel? Don't you love me anymore?"

Anticlus started to call out her name and Odysseus instantly clamped a hand over his mouth and held it there. He could feel the young man's hot breath and muffled attempts to shout. He pressed harder and harder. Anticlus bucked and tried to wriggle free but Odysseus was firm. When he was sure that Anticlus was still and no longer resisting, it was too late. Anticlus was dead. Odysseus had smothered the life from him.

Down at street level Deiphobus was getting bored. He longed to take Helen to bed.

"There's no one there. Let's go back."

He took her by the hand and tugged her away.

As they entered the palace, the dream, or Aphrodite's hypnotic trance, or whatever it had been that had wrapped her in its snare, left her, and Helen was suddenly very aware and very cold and very angry. Deiphobus pulled her toward his apartments and she struck him across the face with all her might and ran up the steps to her own rooms.

"I nearly betrayed them all . . ." she said to herself, despairing. "Haven't I done *enough* harm?"

If there really were men in the horse, then that could only mean that the Greek ships must be lying at sea close by and due to return this very night. She put a lighted lamp at her window, facing out toward the sea. She passed her hands over the flame, hoping that it might make for a signal. Somewhere out there Menelaus would be waiting to come and take her home.

Home! Was there ever such a word?

Inside the horse Odysseus listened hard. No sounds came up from below. He dared to speak in a low voice, just loud enough for everyone inside to hear. To his ears his voice erupted inside the cavernous belly.

---

180. Diomedes's second wife. The name Aegialia, with more than a little disrespect, was latterly given by science to thirty different species of dung beetle.

"So far, so good. It must be the middle of the night by now. Agreed?"

"Agreed," whispered Diomedes. "It is time."

"Epeius, unfasten the trap."

Odysseus heard Epeius drop softly down. There was a scratching sound, followed by a squeaking. An oblong of light opened up below them. Odysseus heard a shuffling scrape, which he knew must be Epeius pulling at the ladder.

Echeon, son of Portheus, gave a cry of triumph and leapt down.

"Wait!" hissed Odysseus. The ladder was not yet in position. Echeon fell straight through. They heard his body hit the flagstones below with a sickening crunch.

"Idiot!" thought Odysseus. When he saw that Epeius had successfully lowered the ladder, he called out in an urgent whisper. "Go down in orderly turns."

They found Echeon in a crumpled heap, neck broken. He had died instantly.

"A bad omen?" said Diomedes. "A sign?"

"A sign that fools fall heavily," said Odysseus. "Now, let's look at you all."

They lined up, stretching their cramped, tortured legs and backs, the twenty-eight survivors of the thirty.

Menelaus, Idomeneus, Diomedes, Neoptolemus, and Aias stepped forward to join Odysseus, the senior commanders separating themselves from the others. Nestor had pleaded to be allowed in the horse too, but they had laughingly told him that his wheezing and the loud creaking of his old bones would alert the Trojans from the beginning. The youngest and fittest had been chosen to make up the bulk of the incursion force.

"You all know what to do," Odysseus said to them, drawing his sword. "To work."

THE END

Sinon had lurked around the dunes and marshes doing nothing much more than gathering firewood and washing his wounds with seawater. He watched Selene ride her moon-chariot across the night sky, and waited until she was precisely aligned with Orion the Hunter overhead, before—as arranged—climbing up to the hillock on which the grave of Achilles stood. Here he lit a beacon for the approaching Achaean fleet. "The horse is safely inside the walls," was the meaning of the fire. "All is ready." Troy lay open, a hive whose honey was there for the taking. All because of him. He laughed out loud. History would call him Sinon the Conqueror.[181]

"More than you ever managed, son of Peleus," he said, spitting on the great stone jar that held Achilles's ashes. "You may have been swifter and better looking than me, but you're dead and I'm alive. Hah!"

Agamemnon's ship was the first to beach, followed swiftly by the others. Sinon joined the warriors streaking across the plain. He could see flames already leaping from the windows of one of the high towers of the city. He hoped that all the important killing hadn't been done. He wanted a royal head for himself. And maybe a captive princess. Some fine lady at least. Something better than a menial slave girl. He deserved everything he could get for taking such a beating in the cause.

There is little one can say to mitigate the horror of what happened that night in Troy, or to excuse the bestial savagery with which the storming Achaeans torched the city and slaughtered its inhabitants.

Odysseus and the men from the horse had already stolen quietly through the streets, cutting the throats of the few sentries who had stayed awake and on duty. One group broke apart the crude makeshift boards that barred the Scaean Gate, another opened the city's other gates. Then, without waiting for Agamemnon's army, they turned inward and went to work.

The Trojans were caught completely by surprise. No compassion was shown. We are used to stories of atrocities perpetrated by victors drunk with violence in

---

181. History has not been so kind. Inasmuch as Sinon is remembered at all, he is remembered as a rat. Dante put him deep in the Fraudulent Circle of his *Inferno*, reserved for liars and deceivers. (Dante is no sentimentalist or hero-worshipper. Diomedes and Odysseus are in that circle too.) There Sinon is, burning up with fever for eternity. Shakespeare mentions him several times, using words like "false," "perjured," "subtle," and "bewitching." Richard, Duke of Gloucester in the famous speech in *Henry VI Part Three* in which he reveals he will be ruthless in his fight for the crown, says:

> I'll play the orator as well as Nestor,
> Deceive more slily than Ulysses could,
> And, like a Sinon, take another Troy.

So at least the villainous future Richard III credits Sinon with Troy's fall . . .

time of war. No matter how much you side with the Greeks and cheer for Odysseus, Menelaus, and the rest, you cannot but be moved to deep sorrowing pity by the plight of Troy and its citizens. We know how brutal soldiers can be. Years of homesickness, hardship, and the loss of comrades while under the constant danger of life-threatening injury harden the heart and stifle the small voice of mercy. We know how the Red Army, for example, raped, looted, and murdered their way into Berlin in 1945. How cruelly British troops tortured and mutilated rebels rounded up after the Indian Mutiny. What the American army did at My Lai in Vietnam. Whatever country we are from, and however proud we may be of our national claims to tolerance, honor, and decency, we cannot dare assume that armies fighting under our flag have not been guilty of atrocities quite as obscene as those perpetrated by the ravening Greeks that night.

The fate of the Trojan royal family was pitiful. As soon as Priam was awoken by the shouts, screams, and clashes in the streets, he knew that Troy was falling. He struggled to put on his old armor, tight around his old man's belly but loose on his shrunken limbs. Sword in hand he stumbled helplessly to the great central hallway of his palace. Hecuba was in one of the open rooms at the side, crouching by the altar of Zeus with her daughters. She called out to her husband.

"Priam, no! Are you mad? You are an old man. You cannot fight. Come here and pray; it's all we can do."

As Priam turned toward her, the ancient, perished leather straps holding up his armor gave way and his breastplate fell to the floor. He looked down and groaned at the wretched sight he knew he made.

Just then his young son POLITES ran in, yelling with fright. Behind him strode Neoptolemus, spear in hand, resplendent in his father Achilles's armor.

"Scared, little boy? This will calm you down."

Slowly, almost lazily, Neoptolemus threw the spear. It flew straight into Polites's chest. The boy grabbed the shaft and looked down in puzzled surprise.

"I think you've killed me," he said, and slipped dead to the ground.

Priam faced Neoptolemus with a wild cry. "You animal! Your father would never have killed an unarmed child in such a manner. I came to him for the body of my son Hector and we wept together. He knew the meaning of honor. Have you none?"

"Honor is for the dead," said Neoptolemus.

"Then let me join them," said Priam raising his spear. "I have no wish to live in a world ruled by men like you . . ."

He threw the spear with all the strength he could muster, but it clattered harmlessly on the floor halfway between them.

⬦ The women of Troy weep at the killing of Priam.

"You run along, old man," said Neoptolemus, striding up, sword aloft. "Run to my father in the kingdom of the dead and tell him terrible tales of his wicked degenerate son."

With the bored indifference of a herdsman readying an ox for slaughter, he grabbed Priam by the hair and pulled him along the ground. The flagstones were slippery with the blood of Polites and Priam's heels skidded on the wet surface. Neoptolemus stabbed Priam once in the side before slicing through his neck with a swift sweep of the sword. The old king's head fell to the floor and rolled to Hecuba's feet. Neoptolemus turned on her and the young princesses cowering behind her, when his attention was taken by the sight of Aeneas crossing in the background, an old man on his shoulders.

"Oh, this is too good to be true," said Neoptolemus, chasing after them with a gleeful shout.

Aeneas had his whole household with him, his father Anchises, his wife Creusa—a daughter of Priam's—his son Ascanius, and his loyal companion Achates. Old Anchises was now too frail and lame to walk, so Aeneas was carrying him on his back. As they hurried out of the main gates of the palace they heard Calchas's voice cry out behind them.

"Neoptolemus! Leave Aeneas. The gods have marked him out. You must not touch him or you will be cursed for all eternity."

Aeneas looked behind him and saw Neoptolemus shrug disappointedly and turn away. The Trojan prince and his small group made it out of the city and on to Mount Ida, where they found temporary refuge in the small shrine to Athena that the Greeks were using to house the Palladium. Aeneas took the sacred object from the altar and kept it with him until his journeying ended many years later on the banks of the River Tiber in Italy.[182]

Menelaus, meanwhile, had also made his way through the royal palace, roaring and killing as he went. He dragged Deiphobus from his bed and ran him through with his sword, swearing and spitting out his rage as he turned from the body.

"Now, where's that bitch? Where are you hiding, Helen? I'm coming for you . . ."

He kicked down doors and threw slave girls aside as he thrust his way through to Helen's bedchamber. He would spit her like a goat. She deserved no better. There she was, cowering in the corner. No, not even with the grace to cower—sitting serenely, awaiting her fate like some chaste votary of Artemis. How dare she not throw herself at his feet and beg forgiveness?

"You . . . you . . ." He choked the words out.

His son by Helen, the child Nicostratus, was crouching beside her. She lifted her face and the eruption of her beauty caused everything to come flooding back. The love he felt for her. The pain of separation. That face still had the power to make his body tremble. Out of sight for so many years, and impossible to recall in all that time except as a lure and a false contrivance. Then one second in the presence of that measureless beauty and he was lost. He dropped the sword and fell to his knees.

"My love, my darling, my queen, my Helen."

Cassandra had rushed to take refuge in the temple of Athena. Most of the wooden houses were already in flames as she tore through the streets, but the temple was built of marble and stone. She passed the wooden horse. The trapdoor swung down, the belly empty. The horse had served its purpose and stood patiently by the temple's steps like any unattended mount.

Inside the temple Cassandra clung to the altar where once the Palladium had stood and prayed to the goddess for protection.

No protection came, only horror.

Aias, Ajax the Lesser, saw her running up the steps. He followed her in and raped her. She screamed, she protested, she warned that Athena would punish

---

182. The further adventures of Aeneas, Anchises, Achates, Creusa, and Ascanius form the basis of Virgil's epic poem, the *Aeneid*, which tells the legend of the founding of Rome.

him, but he only laughed. When he was done, Cassandra ran out of the temple and down the streets, straight into the arms of Agamemnon. The King of Men could not have been more delighted with so beautiful and noteworthy a captive.

"I will enjoy having a Trojan princess as a slave. And so will my wife Clytemnestra."

Shaking, Cassandra howled into Agamemnon's face. "Your wife Clytemnestra? Your wife Clytemnestra? She will stab you with knives. She and your cousin, her lover. They will kill you. Then they will kill me. That is how I will die, and how you will die, poor, foolish, betrayed Agamemnon—Agamemnon, King of Fools."

"Take her to my ship," said Agamemnon, turning away.

Achaean warriors stormed into Andromache's chambers high up in the eastern tower of the royal palace. One of them saw Astyanax in her arms and yelled in triumph. "That's Hector's whore and that is Hector's bastard!" The soldier rushed forward and snatched the baby from Andromache. "Hector killed my brother!"

"Give me back my child!"

The crazed Achaean went to the open window that looked down over the ramparts. "A worthless Trojan brat for a noble Greek warrior!"

He held the baby up in his arms and then, with a manic screech of laughter, tossed it out over the battlements.

Andromache screamed and fell to her knees. "Kill me now," she cried, weeping and weeping. "Throw me down with him. Kill me, kill me, kill me now."

"A valuable prize like you?" said the soldier, grabbing her by the hair. "I don't think so. Someone will pay a fortune for you. Maybe Prince Neoptolemus. You'd like to slave for the son of the man who speared your husband, wouldn't you?"

Scenes like this were played out in every room in every house in Troy over the course of that dreadful night. Rape, murder, torture, plunder, and acts of bestial cruelty that would stand as an eternal stain on the reputation of those responsible. The highest born took the greatest treasure, of course—human and material—but there was enough for all, down to the lowliest spearman, mess-cook, page, and groom. Every villa, cottage, shop, and shack was ransacked and its inhabitants raped, beaten, killed, or captured. Those judged old and useless were stoned, stabbed, or cudgeled to death, thrown into burning buildings, or hurled over the walls.

Amid all the slaughter, two less horrific incidents are worth noting.

Acamas and DEMOPHON, sons of Theseus, joined the war late but had fought valiantly on the Greek side.[183] When Troy fell, their one concern was not killing or treasure but finding and rescuing their grandmother Aethra, the mother of

---

183. Despite Acamas having married Priam's daughter Laodice.

◈   The Sacking of Troy

Theseus.[184] As offspring of the founder king of Athens, the slayer of the Minotaur himself, one of the most venerated and admired of all the heroes who ever was, they might have been forgiven for some show of pride and self-importance. But two more modest and undemanding characters could not have been found in all the Achaean ranks. They asked no special favors, drew no attention to themselves, and lived and fought among their men bravely and dutifully.

As others conducted their orgies of killing and cruelty all around them, they succeeded in tracking their grandmother down and taking her to the safety of their ships, neither seeking nor accepting any other treasure. They were later to apply for Aethra's release from the bonds of servitude, which Helen was happy to grant.[185]

---

184. Just to remind you: many years earlier Theseus had kidnapped the very young Helen with a view to marrying her (see *Heroes* for further details). He left Aethra in charge of her while he went off to find a wife for his friend Pirithous, an adventure that resulted in his being imprisoned by Hades in the underworld. Meanwhile, Helen's brothers, the Dioscuri (Castor and Polydeuces), rescued Helen and—to punish Theseus—took Aethra with them to be Helen's slave. She had remained by Helen's side ever since, first in Sparta and then in Troy.

185. Aethra's long life was an extraordinary one. It spanned the Age of Heroes. As a young girl she had been engaged to marry Bellerophon of Corinth, the hero who tamed Pegasus and rode him to defeat the CHIMERA. Later she was seduced in one intense night by both Aegeus, King of Athens, and the sea god Poseidon. Theseus was the issue of one of these acts of union, but no one is quite sure which . . .

Agamemnon had not forgotten the occasion ten years earlier when Menelaus, Odysseus, and Palamedes had gone to Troy under the flag of embassy to see if an honorable peace could be negotiated. They had stayed as guests at the house of Antenor, who discovered Paris's plan to have them all murdered and conducted them safely out of Troy.

"The household and treasure of Antenor are not to be touched," Agamemnon commanded. "He and his family are to be allowed the same safe passage out of Troy that he accorded my brother."

Those two episodes—the rescue of Aethra and the sparing of Antenor—can be registered as the only lights of clemency and honor that shone during that night of unnameable atrocities.

When Eos next threw open the gates of dawn, her heart burst with sorrow. The flush of light fell on a new and terrible world. The city she had loved was no more. The people were no more. So many members of Troy's great royal house were either slaughtered or in chains. Already the vultures, crows, and jackals were moving into the smoking rubble to feast on the thousands of Trojan dead. The last of the wagon trains of treasure had crossed the Scamander. The Greeks were packing their ships, fighting among themselves, tugging slaves back and forth like wild dogs, claiming and counterclaiming their shares of the spoils.

There was a sickness, a nausea too. Bloated by killing, all they wanted now was to go home. Most of them kept their backs to the ruins, unable to gaze on what they had done.

The gods had watched in helpless horror while the scenes of violence and devastation had unfolded. Zeus had forbidden interference, but he feared he had been wrong to do so.

"What did we see last night?" he asked. "It wasn't warfare. It was madness. Deception, savagery, dishonor, and disgrace. What have the mortals become?"

"Terrible, isn't it? Who do they think they are—gods?"

"There's a time for humor, Hermes, and this isn't it," said Apollo.

"Are you satisfied?" Zeus said, turning to Athena. "Your beloved Greeks have won. Total victory is theirs."

"No, Father," said Athena. "I am not satisfied. There have been violations of the sacred. Abominable crimes have been committed."

"Agreed," said Apollo. "We cannot let them just sail serenely back to domestic life."

"They must pay in full for their profanities," said Artemis.

Zeus sighed heavily. "I wish, all those years ago, Prometheus hadn't persuaded me to make mankind," he said. "I knew it was a mistake."

APPENDIX

MYTH AND REALITY 1

The events told here took place—if ever they really did take place—in a period that historians and others refer to as the Bronze Age. The most significant source for our knowledge of the Trojan War is the poet Homer, who lived—if ever he really did live—in the succeeding Iron Age, the better part of five centuries later. I look at Homer and his period in more detail in the second part of this Appendix. Homer wrote about a time long in his past, when the gods still appeared before mortals—befriended them, persecuted them, favored them, cursed them, blessed them, harried them, and sometimes even married them.

Those who *are* familiar with my two preceding books on Greek mythology, *Mythos* and *Heroes*, may have noticed plenty of discrepancies and chronological inconsistencies. In *Heroes*, for example, I favor the idea that the Olympic Games were established by Heracles. In *Troy*, I have followed another source that identifies Pelops as their founder. These variations are of minor significance, coming down to little more than a matter of choice. The major timelines, however—wring, wrench, and wrestle them as you may—will not straighten out into clean historical paths. How old Achilles was by the time of the last year of the siege of Troy, for example, or what length of time elapsed between the abduction of Helen and the sailing of Agamemnon's fleet—these and many other questions are impossible to resolve. Indeed, when you do settle on one timeline, it invariably ruins another. It is all rather like some kind of nightmarish Jacques Tati art gallery: straighten a painting on the wall and another one immediately drops out of true. To change metaphors, there is a boxing match that any chronicler of these stories is forced to engage in: in the red corner, the need to present a detailed dynastic chronology, filled with consistent relation-ships, backgrounds, and genealogies—and in the blue corner, the need to present the mysteries of a poetical world of myth and miracle whose characters and histories should never be expected to travel obediently along the rails of cause and effect. Over the years, I have come to the view that it is not really a fight, but more a kind of narrative dance in which the deep but complementary pleasures of the real and the unreal can be partnered.

I suppose the point is that there is not too much difficulty or dissonance in us being able to entertain the historical and the imaginative in our minds at the same time. The "knowledge" we have of the gods and heroes is akin to our knowledge of the Roman emperors, or the royal houses of Europe, or, for that matter, the Mafia families of twentieth-century America, but it is also akin to the knowledge we have of fictional characters in Dickens and Shakespeare. Some people would point to the more obvious correspondence with fantasy characters in the Marvel Cinematic Universe, the Game of Thrones kingdoms, Harry Potter's wizarding world or Tolkien's Middle-earth, but this is perhaps not the time for ventilating my thoughts, about the difference between myth and fantasy. The point really is that with myth we can sift and sort details of personality, archaeology, and origins as we would with real lives and histories, yet simultaneously accept and embrace supernatural and symbolic elements of fiction and magic. To quote the newsman at the end of the John Ford western *The Man Who Shot Liberty Valance* (1962), "This is the West, sir. When the legend becomes fact, print the legend."

The involvement or noninvolvement of the gods in the story of the Trojan War is an indicator of how much one might want to treat the story as history and how much as myth. It is perfectly possible to do without the presence of the immortals entirely, as the Wolfgang Petersen film *Troy* (2004) with Brad Pitt as Achilles and Brian Cox as Agamemnon showed very clearly. Not an Olympian in sight. In the course of this book, I have occasionally paused to make the point that it is possible to interpret Homer's description of gods assisting mortals as being metaphorical. When writers or artists of the most rational and skeptical stamp find themselves especially inspired or energized they will often describe themselves as "having had the Muse with them." Greek archers who fired an accurate shot were bound to whisper, "Thanks, Apollo." It's hardly different from boxers crossing themselves before a fight or thanking Jesus after one. Cricketers talk about "Mother Cricket," actors talk about "Doctor Theatre." When Achilles hears the voice of Athena telling him to calm down during his confrontation with Agamemnon, is he really hearing a goddess or is he listening to his own wiser counsels, the better angels of his nature? The beauty of Homer, and of myth, is that you can always take it to be both at once.

This "double determination" of motive allows the real and symbolic to coexist in a way that is precisely Homeric and endlessly rewarding. Humanity cannot let itself off the hook, capricious, foolish, and unfair as the gods may be. The first word of Homer's *Iliad* is μῆνιν *(m nin)*, which is the Greek for "rage." Rage, lust, envy, pride, greed . . . the sins and flaws of humankind energize all of the drama of Troy, but they are balanced by love, honor, wisdom, kindness, forgiveness, and sacrifice. These, it is simple and obvious to say perhaps, are the same unstable elements that constitute the human world today. We live on the same seesaw. Dark human passions of selfishness, fear, and hatred counterbalanced by kindness, friendship, love, and wisdom. The field is still open for someone to portray all that better than Homer, but so far on my journey through life I have yet to see it done.

MYTH AND REALITY 2

It would be impossible to tell the story of the Trojan War without reference to Homer's *Iliad*, long regarded as the first great literary work of the Western canon.[186] The *Iliad* begins with rage and ends with sorrow: the rage of Achilles at Agamemnon's appropriation of the slave girl Briseis and the sorrow of the Trojan people as they mourn the death of their champion Hector. This fractional part of the ten-year siege takes 15,693 lines of verse—each comprising between twelve and seventeen syllables—divided into twenty-four books. The concentrated unity of action, the complex and convincing characterizations, the depictions of such a multiplicity of human emotion and impulse, the cinematic shifts in perspective and point of view, the relentless energy and drive, the unflinching representation of violence, the flashbacks and foreshadowings, the depth, deftness, and daring of imagery—these qualities and more have caused poets, artists, scholars, and readers over the centuries to regard the *Iliad*, along with its companion piece the *Odyssey*, as the supreme works of narrative art to which all others aspire and by which all others are judged. And yet there remains a fundamental question which anyone encountering these works is bound to ask.

Homer and the Trojan War—did they even *exist*?

Now, if you are anything like me, a puzzled frown of concentration will mar the smooth regularity of your features whenever you encounter phrases like "the mid–twelfth century BC"—a little mental arithmetic is almost always needed to give oneself a sense of time's distance, especially when leaping the Year Zero hurdle that separates BC/BCE and our own AD/CE. We can't even seem to agree on how to designate these eras, for heaven's sake. I hope you will find that the timeline does the work of a dozen paragraphs and sheds useful light.

Over the millennia, and the last two centuries especially, so much dissent and disagreement, factionalism, and feuding has enlivened and inflamed the world of Homeric scholarship that the field has taken on some of the characteristics of a kind of religious war. We have seen the Separatists versus the Analysts versus the Unitarians versus the Neoanalysts. A similar schism has obtained (right up to the time of my writing this) in the fevered world of Trojan studies. German antiquarians, classicists, and archaeologists have dominated both realms, with American scholars coming a close second. Academics can get heated and intemperate about the most esoteric and obscure matters, as is well known, but in the case of Homer the stakes have always been high: proving or disproving his existence, definitively describing his modes of creation, and settling the question

---

186. Though whether "literary" is the right word remains a matter for debate.

of how much of what he wrote is fact or fable . . . These can almost be regarded as the secular equivalent of establishing the historical existence of Christ and his crucifixion. So much of who and how we are flows from the idea of Homer. Our culture may be Judeo-Christian in its religious and moral grounding, but it is Greco-Roman to at least an equal degree in these and other domains. If the Greeks and Romans looked back to Homer as the author and founder of so much of their identity—and they did—then it is unsurprising that settling the Homeric Question has long been something of a scholastic Holy Grail for our civilization.

There exist History and Prehistory. Put simply, *prehistory* is what happened in the human world before the development of writing. Prehistory can therefore be studied only by reading not words but *objects*. This study is *archaeology*: the analysis and imaginative reconstruction of ancient buildings and their ruins, the excavation and interpretation of artifacts, relics, and remains. *History*, conversely, is mostly analyzed through documentary records—manuscripts, tablets, inscriptions, and books.

Human prehistory is understood to have begun around three and half million years ago, when our hominin ancestors first constructed stone tools whose archaeological traces we can unearth and examine. Anything before that time we call *paleontology*, where the only indications left behind are fossils. History, on the other hand, is extraordinarily recent. It began not much more than five thousand years ago, with the invention of phonetic scripts in Babylonian Sumer, writing systems that were spread by the trading Phoenicians all around the Mediterranean world, developing into the alphabets we still use today— chiefly Greek, Roman, and Cyrillic. Separately, and a little later, the Chinese and other civilizations further east developed their own, nonphonetic, ideographic systems. That is a sweeping outline; a closer look reveals squiggles and wrinkles as we shall see.

The periods of the prehistorical era are named according to the prevalent *materials* of those ages. The first and longest period (three million years at least) was the Stone Age. Then, around seven and a half thousand years ago, the first metallic age was entered when humankind learned the trick of smelting copper. With the addition of a little tin (and maybe some nickel, zinc, or arsenic if there was any to hand), the alloy *bronze* came into being a couple of thousand years later. Harder and stronger than its constituent metals, bronze could be fashioned into tools, weapons, armor, and ornaments. Another two thousand years or so after this, techniques were developed that allowed the mining and smelting of an even more versatile metal—iron. Stone Age, Bronze Age, Iron Age. There's an argument that, since the late Industrial Revolution, we have been living in the Oil Age, and perhaps now—somewhat distressingly—the Plastic Age.

What we call the Trojan War was fought more than three thousand years ago, around 1200 BC, by Bronze Age Mediterranean civilizations which had arisen in what we today call Greece and Turkey in about 1550 BC (naturally such dates are no more than current best guesses). In western Greece, on the peninsula of the Peloponnese, flourished the city-state and empire of Mycenae.[187] This was the fabled kingdom of Agamemnon. To the east of the Aegean, on the northwest coast of Asia Minor, stood the city of Troy.

The literate era began in the last years of the Bronze Age. Scholars have deciphered some of the forms of writing that existed during this time. The civilizations we are interested in, those of the Greek and Trojan regions of the Mediterranean, used various scripts during the Bronze Age. The Minoan (Cretan) script called "Linear A" is still a mystery to us, but the Mycenaeans used a descendant called "Linear B" which was eventually cracked in the twentieth century. These writing systems developed separately from the Sumerian alphabet-style script which, as we shall see, had yet to reach the Greek world.[188]

Nonetheless, all this should surely mean that the story of the Trojan War is *historical*. Writing existed in its time, the Mycenaeans used it, and thus there should, or could, exist a documentary trail leading directly from the siege of Troy to the present day. In fact this is not the case. Quite soon after the supposed time of the Trojan War (some have even suggested as a result of it), the Mycenaean civilization collapsed, and what are known as the Greek "Dark Ages" descended. The most usual explanation for this collapse is a combination of apocalyptic horsemen: namely, some kind of geological or climate catastrophe, a famine, a plague, and the invasion of the Greek and Mediterranean world by the so-called "Sea Peoples."[189] As a result of these disasters and the abandonment of the great city-states of the Mycenaean Bronze Age, the art of reading and

---

187. Archaeologists sometimes refer to it as the "Mycenae—Tiryns—Pylos civilization"; those being the three great citadels of the empire.

188. Linear A and B used syllabic and "ideographic" signs (like glyphs) rather than the phonetically representative characters (letters) that the Greeks (and we) were later to use in alphabets.

189. Just as the Vandals, Goths, Visigoths, and other Germanic tribes invaded the Roman Empire and ushered in the western European "Dark Ages," so the Sea Peoples conquered Egypt, the Levant, and the Greek islands and mainland, ushering in an early equivalent. No one is quite sure who they actually were: the consensus seems to suggest that they were some kind of loosely federated group of seafarers from the eastern coastal regions of the Mediterranean. Another name for the Greek Dark Ages is the Geometric Age, on account of the style of ornamentation—ceramics and so forth—that emanated from that period. Interestingly, if one thinks of Celtic jewelry and metalwork, the later Dark Ages produced pronouncedly geometric art too . . . The mainland and islands of Greece have long been thought to have also been conquered by a people called the Dorians. Their true identity and origin is as mysterious as that of the Sea Peoples.

writing Linear B was utterly forgotten.[190] For centuries, until the Phoenicians spread their alphabet through trade, the entire region remained nonliterate. This meant that during the Dark Ages a functionally *prehistorical* mode of transmission was the only way any memory of Mycenae and the Trojan War could be passed from generation to generation—not by word of pen, but by word of mouth: the "Oral Tradition." In this window of time (or whatever the dark equivalent of a window is), the stories of the Trojan War were passed down, as of course were the stories of Zeus, Olympus, and the gods, heroes, and monsters of what we call "Myth." Whether those who passed them on thought of one set of stories as historical and another as mythical we can only speculate.

After a full four hundred years of this darkness, things began to change in fundamental and dramatic ways. The Phoenician alphabet evolved into the early Greek alphabet, of which we have records from the vases and inscriptions of the period. Politically and demographically, a large increase in population (perhaps as a result of better and more reliable weather and sea levels) saw the development of the *poleis*, the Greek city-state. This period, known as the Archaic Age, was the precursor to the fully historical Classical Age, the ripely sophisticated time of Plato, Socrates, Euripides, Pericles, and Aristotle. Most Greeks of the Archaic Age remained illiterate, however, and narratives of the past were still communicated by oral declamation rather than writing. It was in this Archaic Age that the figure we call Homer is generally supposed to have lived. When I was at school, one teacher told me confidently that Homer was born in 800 BC, on the northern Aegean island of Chios, and died in 701 BC, a blind old man of ninety-nine. Another teacher maintained, with equal certainty, that Homer was from Ionia, now Turkish Anatolia. Modern scholars regard all of these stories as guesswork at best.

So there we have it. The timeline tells the story far better than my confusing words. The Trojan War took place in the Bronze Age (say 1200 BC), the high cultures of the Bronze Age collapsed and a dark, illiterate age succeeded. The darkness lifted, iron was mined and smelted, writing returned, and the story of the war, as declaimed by Homer, was finally written down a full seven hundred years after the events of that war. And here we are, another two and half thousand years later.

It is worthwhile reiterating that by the time of the rise of the Greek civilization from which we can trace our own descent—that culture of science, mathematics, philosophy, art, architecture, democracy, military, and naval power; a self-conscious culture that wrote histories and plays about its origins and nature—by that time,

---

190. Until the brilliant Michael Ventris (and his collaborator John Chadwick) deciphered it more than three thousand years later, in 1955.

the Trojan War was eight hundred years in the past and Homer three hundred years dead.

Mysteries have faced scholars and archaeologists since the Greeks of the Classical Age finally fixed Homer's two epic poems by writing them down in the more or less agreed texts that we read today. One mystery is how Homer knew so much about events that were already at least four hundred years in his past? How was he able to recount so many details of the siege, of the city of Troy itself, the royal families, the warriors, the lineages, and the events of the war? He had no writing, no archive to go on. For 450 years, in other words, "lesser" Homers must have orally passed down these characters and episodes until he synthesized them and turned them into the first great piece of language-based art of which we are aware. To have done this, we assume, he must have grown up hearing oral accounts of the most varied and complex kind. Homer lived in Iron Age Greece or Turkey, but his works accurately depict Bronze Age warriors.[191]

When it comes to Greek mythology generally, there is a remarkable agreement between Homer's works and those of his near contemporary Hesiod, on whom we rely for the stories of the birth of the Titans and gods, the establishment of Olympus, and so many of the canonical details of Greek mythology.[192] There is little doubt that a fair amount of reverse engineering took place in the literary Classical Age, a good deal of refining, smoothing out of anomalies and contradictions, and the creation of the consistent chronologies and genealogies that now exist. The myths were transformed from rough folk stories into finished literary creations, like rocks polished into gemstones. Staying with that simile, the literate Greeks of the Classical Age may have been responsible for mounting the stories in display cases, but it was Homer and Hesiod who had done most of the shaping, cutting, and polishing.

Plato and Aristotle's lives were nearly as far from Homer's as ours are from the author of *Beowulf*, so it is unsurprising that they and their contemporaries knew so little about who Homer the man might have been. We know from the literature of Classical Greece that the *Iliad* and the *Odyssey* were admired, even venerated works, whose episodes were taken to tell a true history. As a young man setting out to conquer the world, Alexander the Great visited the sites of Ilium and was said to have paid homage to what was then understood to be the

---

191. Including the technology of the time. Archaic Greeks were not interested in or aware of such a thing as archaeology (so far as we can tell). How Homer could have had so clear a picture of bronze toolmaking and armory can only be explained by precise and well-remembered oral transmission over a very, very, long time.

192. Unlike Homer's two epics, Hesiod's works were self-consciously written—"authored," you might say. They were the *Theogony* (Birth of the Gods), the *Works and Days*, and the *Shield of Heracles*. They include tantalizing gobbets of autobiography as well as thoughts on agronomy, timekeeping, and economics. It is generally accepted that even if Hesiod didn't actually write his works down, he at least dictated them to a scribe.

◈ Homer

tomb of Achilles, the hero with whom he most closely identified.[193] Mark Antony reputedly made a present to Cleopatra of the funerary statue of Ajax the Great. Later travelers like Strabo and Pausanias made many tours of Trojan and Mycenaean sites. They all took the stories to be truthful records of historical events.

During the Classical Age, popular sections of the *Iliad* and *Odyssey* were often performed in outdoor concerts attended by ordinary and very enthusiastic citizens. It seems that they believed Homer *wrote* those works down, something that seems strange to us, for we have been brought up with the firm idea that Homer was (if not illiterate) a bard, a rhapsode, a declaimer, and perhaps even an improviser of epic verse, but not a writer. This is a recent view, however.

After our own Dark Ages, western Europe underwent a rediscovery of Greek and Roman civilization, art, and culture, a rebirth that we call the Renaissance. Around 1450, Gutenberg's invention of movable type printing allowed the widespread transmission of classical texts in ways that had been unthinkable in the foregoing centuries of monastic scribes producing books by handwriting. In 1488, printed copies of Homer became available. The impact was enormous, a kind of cultural Big Bang. In Britain alone, poets from Dryden, Pope, Keats, Byron, and Tennyson, and into the modern age were transformed by Homer. Painters, sculptors, and philosophers pored over the pages of the original Greek and of each new translation. But they had no more sense that the Trojan War was a historical event than that Narcissus was truly transformed into a daffodil or that Heracles really did descend into the underworld and emerge with Cerberus slung over his shoulder.

This view changed largely as the result of the bold endeavors and determined showmanship of one man, Heinrich Schliemann. Born in Germany in 1822, Schliemann made, lost, and made fortunes in Russia and the United States. The final fortune he accreted from speculation in the Californian goldfields allowed him, now an American citizen, to devote the second half of his life to his great passion—archaeology. Along with the other great archaeologist of the age, Britain's Arthur Evans, he set about trying to find the great sites of the Greek Bronze Age. Evans concentrated on Crete, and his uncovering of Minoan treasures caused a sensation.

Evans was what we would recognize as a true archaeologist, whereas Schliemann . . . Well, his practices were regarded as somewhat drastic even in his own day. We are all familiar with the gentle, achingly slow digging and delicate brushing that archaeologists insist upon. Every site painstakingly pegged out with string, every layer preserved and minutely cataloged. Schliemann had no

---

193. Alexander is said to have taken a copy of the *Iliad* with him to war, a copy with notes and amendments written in the margins by his tutor, Aristotle.

patience for that kind of thing; he swung his spades with a violent zest that approached vandalism.

Schliemann's obsession from first to last was in finding the "true locations" of Homeric legend. He was to excavate sites in the Peloponnese, where his search for Mycenaean treasures certainly resulted in some spectacular finds. In 1876, a gold funerary mask of stunning beauty and workmanship was unearthed and instantly designated by Schliemann (on no compelling evidentiary grounds) "The Mask of Agamemnon." We now know that this artifact predated the Trojan War, and therefore the life of Agamemnon, by a good four hundred years. Schliemann dug up much of Odysseus's home island of Ithaca too, but it was his work in the Troad that was first to make his name ring round the world. His search for Troy took him to Turkey in the early 1870s, where he concentrated on the area around the town of Hissarlik, a site that had been suggested to him by the British archaeologist Frank Calvert. Here he uncovered evidence of *nine* buried cities. One glad day he happened on a trove of gold that he announced to be "Priam's Treasure," incorporating what he declared were "The Jewels of Helen" (subsequent research has shown them to be a full thousand years older than that).

Boring old historical truth and evidence were more or less irrelevant to this outrageous fudger, fantasist, fabricator, and outright smuggler, but this is not to deny the value of his work, especially the effect of his fanfares of self-publicity on scholarship and the popular imagination. His methods (including the cavalier use of dynamite) were so damaging to the archaeological record that successive professionals have wryly congratulated him on achieving what even the Greek armies couldn't—the complete leveling and destruction of Troy.

Nonetheless, the discovery of so many strata of Hittite and Trojan civilizations was proof at least of a flourishing civilization and a great city, with evidence of devastating fire and siege, consistent with the Homeric canon. In recent times, a pioneering 2001 German exhibition, *Troy: Dream and Reality*, morphed into the British Museum's hugely successful 2019 *Troy: Myth and Reality*, which displayed objects excavated by Schliemann as well as many later discoveries. The experience of walking through these exhibitions sparked, in me at least, a powerful sense of a real people with real lives. The artifacts and the reconstructions of Trojan life of course cannot prove the contention that Troy fell as a result of the abduction of a Spartan princess, but it is worth remembering that many a kingdom or empire in recorded history has fallen on account of marriages and dynastic alliances gone wrong. Another possibility—given the strategic and commercial importance of Troy perched as the city was on the Dardanelles strait, the Hellespont—is that some kind of conflict over tariffs and the passage of commerce erupted between the kingdoms of the western and eastern Aegean. Hard for us to credit it, so sophisticated and wise are we today, but back then the primitive fools could find themselves sucked into trade wars . . . Ha!

Naturally, the nuances and refinements of real scholarship, hard science, and proper archaeology have blunted and refuted many of Schliemann's more far-fetched and exaggerated claims, but his Barnum-like huckstering and show-manship have ensured that the Hissarlik site is looked on with favor, and that—give or take, more or less, all things being equal—the world agrees that the siege and fall of Troy 3,200 years ago might be looked on as historical fact.

I shan't dive with any depth into the matter of Homer's life: the classical Greeks thought he existed, and that he wrote down his two great epic poems; later scholars, in the eighteenth, nineteenth, and twentieth centuries, became convinced (on the basis of close philological and linguistic textual scrutiny) first that these works were orally transmitted, and then that their makeup suggested they were in fact largely *improvised*.[194]

In my opinion, the broken line of transmission from the time of Troy and Mycenae to the Archaic and Classical ages, thanks to the collapse of the Bronze Age with its accompanying loss of literacy, is far from a disaster. It is the intriguing distance, the blend of history, mystery, and myth, the interplay of the particular and the universal that makes the Homeric experience so rich and compelling. The action is played out on the golden horizon between reality and legend, the beguiling penumbra where fable and fact coexist. It is this that endows Homeric epic with the minute, realistic and vivid detailing that so animates and convinces, yet also gives us the glorious symbolism and dreamlike depth that only myth allows, with its divine interventions, supernatural episodes, and superhuman heroes.

---

194. It's a long and fascinating story, the development of this line of thinking. The formulaic nature of so many Homeric epithets and images has inclined scholars to the thought (inspired by a study of extant forms of oral poetry in the Balkans) that the bards (known as *rhapsodes*) used these prefabricated tropes as modules with which they could build the poem's structure as they recited. Think of jazz. The rhapsodes knew the melody and the key, as it were, and could therefore vamp at will.

LIST OF CHARACTERS

GODS AND MONSTERS

OLYMPIAN GODS

APHRODITE Goddess of love. Offspring of *Ouranos*'s blood and seed. Aunt
of *Demeter, Hades, Hera, Hestia, Poseidon,* and *Zeus.* Wife of *Hephaestus.* Lover
of *Ares.* Mother (by *Anchises*) of *Aeneas.* Guest at the wedding of *Peleus* and
Thetis. Awarded Apple of Discord by *Paris* in return for *Helen.* Saves *Paris* from
death at the hands of *Menelaus*; withdraws favor from him after his slaying
of *Corythus.* Wounded by *Diomedes.* Along with *Apollo, Ares,* and *Artemis,* a
protector of Troy. Bewitches *Helen* in an attempt to expose the secret of the
wooden horse.

APOLLO Archer god, and god of harmony. Son of *Zeus* and the Titaness Leto.
Twin of *Artemis.* Half-brother of *Ares, Athena, Dionysus, Hephaestus, Hermes,* and
Persephone. Father of *Asclepius, Hymenaios, Lycomedes,* and *Tenes.* Slayer of Python
and establisher of the Pythia's oracle at Delphi. Builds Troy's walls with
Poseidon; then infects the city with plague when *Laomedon* reneges on payment.
Later, along with *Aphrodite, Ares,* and *Artemis,* a protector of Troy. Answers
Chryses's prayers and strikes down the Greeks with plague. Hater of *Achilles*
for his slaying of *Tenes* and *Troilus*; helps *Euphorbus* and *Hector* slay *Patroclus,*
and *Paris* slay *Achilles.* Withdraws favor from *Paris* after his slaying of *Corythus.*
Blesses and curses *Cassandra.* Guest at the wedding of *Peleus* and *Thetis.*

ARES God of war. Son of *Zeus* and *Hera.* Brother of *Hephaestus.* Half-brother of
Apollo, Artemis, Athena, Dionysus, Hermes, and *Persephone.* Father of the Amazons,
notably *Hippolyta* and *Penthesilea*; of Deimos (Dread) and Phobos (Fear and
Panic); and of *Oenomaus.* Lover of *Aphrodite.* Guest at the wedding of *Peleus*
and *Thetis.* Along with *Dionysus,* a curser of the house of *Cadmus.* Along with
Aphrodite, Apollo, and *Artemis,* a protector of Troy. Wounded by *Diomedes.*

ARTEMIS Goddess of chastity and the chase. Daughter of *Zeus* and the
Titaness Leto. Twin of *Apollo.* Half-sister of *Ares, Athena, Dionysus, Hephaestus,
Hermes,* and *Persephone.* Guest at the wedding of *Peleus* and *Thetis.* Along with
Aphrodite, Apollo, and *Ares,* a protector of Troy. Sensitive to slights: sender of
the *Calydonian Boar*; slayer of *Orion*; preventer of the Greeks sailing to Troy.
But apparent sparer of *Iphigenia.*

ATHENA Goddess of wisdom. Daughter of *Zeus* and the *Oceanid* Metis.
Half-sister of *Apollo, Ares, Artemis, Dionysus, Hephaestus, Hermes,* and *Persephone.*

Bearer of the aegis. Bestows on Troy its protective Palladium. Guest at the wedding of *Peleus* and *Thetis*. Insufficiently charming for *Paris* to award her the Apple of Discord. Along with *Hephaestus*, *Hera*, and *Poseidon*, an abettor of the Greeks against Troy. Dotes greatly on *Achilles*, *Diomedes*, and *Odysseus*. Interferes in *Achilles*'s slaying of *Hector* and *Troilus*, and *Pandarus*'s attempted shooting of *Menelaus*. Inspires *Odysseus* with the idea of the wooden horse.

DEMETER Goddess of fertility and the harvest, of hearth and home. Daughter of *Kronos* and Rhea. Sister of *Hades*, *Hera*, *Hestia*, *Poseidon*, and *Zeus*. Mother (by *Zeus*) of *Persephone*, whose absence in the underworld she mourns for six months each year. Guest at the wedding of *Peleus* and *Thetis*.

DIONYSUS God of dissipation and disorder. Son of *Zeus* and the mortal Semele. Half-brother of *Apollo*, *Ares*, *Artemis*, *Athena*, *Hephaestus*, *Hermes*, and *Persephone*. Suckled as an infant by the *Hyades*. Along with *Ares*, a curser of the house of *Cadmus*. Guest at the wedding of *Peleus* and *Thetis*.

HADES[195] God of the underworld. Son of *Kronos* and Rhea. Brother of *Demeter*, *Hera*, *Hestia*, *Poseidon*, and *Zeus*. Abductor and husband of *Persephone*. Imprisons *Pirithous* and *Theseus* for attempting to kidnap *Persephone*.

HEPHAESTUS God of fire and the forge. Son of *Zeus* and *Hera*. Brother of *Ares*. Half-brother of *Apollo*, *Artemis*, *Athena*, *Dionysus*, *Hermes*, and *Persephone*. Husband of *Aphrodite* and Charis. As an infant, cast out of Olympus by *Hera* and lamed; rescued and tended by *Thetis*. Guest at the wedding of *Peleus* and *Thetis*. Creator of marvels, including the armor of *Achilles* and *Memnon*; the scepter of *Agamemnon*; and the sword of *Peleus*. Along with *Athena*, *Hera*, and *Poseidon*, an abettor of the Greeks against Troy. Boils *Scamander* to make him release *Achilles*.

HERA Queen of Heaven and goddess of matrimony. Daughter of *Kronos* and Rhea. Sister of *Demeter*, *Hades*, *Hestia*, *Poseidon*, and *Zeus*. Wife of *Zeus*, and mother (by him) of *Ares* and *Hephaestus*. Punishes *Aeacus* for being *Zeus*'s illegitimate son. Guest at the wedding of *Peleus* and *Thetis*. Insufficiently charming for *Paris* to award her the Apple of Discord. Along with *Athena*, *Hephaestus*, and *Poseidon*, an abettor of the Greeks against Troy.

HERMES Messenger of the gods, and god of trickery. Son of *Zeus* and the *Pleiad* Maia. Half-brother of *Apollo*, *Ares*, *Artemis*, *Athena*, *Dionysus*, *Hephaestus*, and *Persephone*. Father of *Autolycus*, *Eudoros*, *Myrtilus*, and (some say) *Pan*. Great-grandfather of *Odysseus* and *Sinon*. Inventor of the lyre. Guest at the wedding of *Peleus* and *Thetis*. Enlists *Paris* to judge which goddess merits the Apple of Discord. Enlisted by *Zeus* to teach *Aphrodite* a lesson. Supports *Priam* in recovering the body of *Hector* from *Achilles*.

---

195. Hades spent all of his time in the underworld, so technically he is often not regarded as one of the twelve Olympians.

HESTIA Goddess of hearth and home. Daughter of *Kronos* and Rhea. Sister of *Demeter, Hades, Hera, Poseidon,* and *Zeus.* Helps officiate at the wedding of *Peleus* and *Thetis.*

POSEIDON God of the sea. Inventor (and god) of horses. Son of *Kronos* and Rhea. Brother of *Demeter, Hades, Hera, Hestia,* and *Zeus.* Father of *Bellerophon, Cychreus, Cycnus, Orion, Pegasus,* and (possibly) of *Theseus.* Grandfather of *Nestor* and *Palamedes.* Lover of *Pelops;* helps him win *Hippodamia.* Builds Troy's walls with *Apollo;* then sends sea monster to devour *Hesione* when *Laomedon* reneges on payment. Guest at the wedding of *Peleus* and *Thetis;* the horses Balius and Xanthus his gift to the bridegroom. Along with *Athena, Hephaestus,* and *Hera,* an abettor of the Greeks against Troy.

ZEUS King of the Gods. Son of *Kronos,* whom he overthrows, and Rhea. Brother of *Demeter, Hades, Hera, Hestia,* and *Poseidon.* Husband of *Hera.* Father of the gods *Apollo, Ares, Artemis, Athena, Dionysus, Hephaestus, Hermes,* and *Persephone.* Father of the mortals *Aeacus, Dardanus, Helen, Heracles, Perseus, Pirithous, Polydeuces,* and *Sarpedon.* Progenitor of numerous heroes of the Trojan War, including *Achilles, Ajax, Odysseus,* and *Teucer.* Wielder of thunderbolts. Possessor of the oracle at Dodona. Indebted to *Thetis* for rescuing him from his rebellious Olympian family. Guest at the wedding of *Peleus* and *Thetis.* Bestows ant-people and judgeship of the underworld on *Aeacus; Aphrodite* on *Anchises;* catasterization on *Ganymede* and the *Dioscuri;* divine horses on *Tros;* eternal torment on *Tantalus;* immortality (but not eternal youth) on *Tithonus;* the privilege of awarding the Apple of Discord on *Paris;* a sword forged by Hephaestus on *Peleus.* Not entirely successful in preventing the other OLYMPIAN GODS (or himself) from meddling in the Trojan War.

OTHER GODS AND TITANS

ASCLEPIUS God of medicine. Mortal son of *Apollo* and Coronis. Raised by *Chiron.* Father of *Machaon* and *Podalirius.* Temporarily slain by *Zeus* for his *hubris* in resurrecting the dead; later immortalized and catasterized by him.

EOS Titan goddess of the dawn. Sister of *Helios* and *Selene.* Progenitor of *Cinyras.* Lover of *Tithonus;* mother (by him) of *Memnon.* Begs eternal life for *Tithonus* from *Zeus,* but not eternal youth. Transforms *Tithonus* into a grasshopper.

ERIS Goddess of discord and disarray. Daughter of Nyx (Night) and Erebus (Darkness). Sister of assorted shadowy gods and immortals, including the *Hesperides,* Hypnos (Sleep), the *Moirai* (Fates), *Moros* (Destiny), *Nemesis* (Retribution), and Thanatos (Death). Uninvited and unwelcome guest at the wedding of *Peleus* and *Thetis.* Causes the disagreement between the OLYMPIAN GODS that gives rise to the Trojan War.

EROS Youthful god of sexual desire. Son of *Ares* and *Aphrodite*. Possessor of devastating bow and arrows.

FATES See *Moirai*.

GAIA The primordial earth. Daughter of Chaos. Mother of *Ouranos* and Pontus. Mother (by *Ouranos*) of the first generation of Titans (including *Kronos, Oceanus,* and *Tethys*), and the giants. Mother (by Pontus) of *Nereus*. Mother (by Tartarus) of *Typhon*. Bestower of the Golden Apples of the Hesperides on *Zeus* and *Hera*.

HELIOS Titan god of the sun. Brother of *Eos* and *Selene*. Grandfather of *Medea*.

HESPERIDES The three nymphs of the evening. Daughters of Nyx (Night) and Erebus (Darkness). Sisters of assorted shadowy gods and immortals, including *Eris* (Discord), Hypnos (Sleep), *Moros* (Destiny), *Nemesis* (Retribution), and Thanatos (Death). Keen gardeners; propagators of magical golden apples—including the Apple of Discord.

HYMENAIOS Also known as *Hymen*. Youthful god of wedding ceremonies; one of *Eros's* retinue. Son of *Apollo* and the Muse Urania.

IRIS Goddess of the rainbow and messenger of the gods. Sister of the Harpies. Cousin of the Gorgons.

KRONOS Ancient king of the gods. Titan son of *Gaia* and *Ouranos*. Brother of *Oceanus* and *Tethys*. Father (by Rhea) of *Demeter, Hades, Hera, Hestia, Poseidon,* and *Zeus*, and (by Phylira) of *Chiron*. Overthrower of *Ouranos*. Overthrown by *Zeus*.

MOIRAI The three Fates: *Clotho*, who spins the thread of life; *Lachesis*, who measures its length; and *Atropos*, who cuts it. Daughters of Nyx (Night), and Erebus (Darkness). Sisters of assorted shadowy gods and immortals, including *Eris* (Discord), the *Hesperides*, Hypnos (Sleep), *Moros* (Destiny), *Nemesis* (Retribution), and Thanatos (Death).

MOROS Doom or Destiny. Son of Nyx (Night) and Erebus (Darkness). Brother of assorted shadowy gods and immortals, including *Eris* (Discord), the *Hesperides*, Hypnos (Sleep), the *Moirai* (Fates), *Nemesis* (Retribution), and Thanatos (Death). All-powerful, all-knowing controller of the cosmos. Most feared entity in creation, even by immortals.

NEMESIS Goddess of retribution. Daughter of Nyx (Night) and Erebus (Darkness). Sister of assorted shadowy gods and immortals, including *Eris* (Discord), the *Hesperides*, Hypnos (Sleep), the *Moirai* (Fates), *Moros* (Destiny), and Thanatos (Death). Punisher of *hubris*. According to some, the mother (by *Zeus*) of *Helen*.

NEREUS Ancient shape-shifting sea god. Son of *Gaia* and Pontus. Father (by the *Oceanid* Doris) of the *Nereids*, including *Thetis*. Wrestling partner of *Heracles*. Provider of childcare advice to his daughter *Thetis*.

OCEANUS Ancient god of the sea. Titan son of *Gaia* and *Ouranos*. Brother of *Kronos* and *Tethys*. Father (by *Tethys*) of the *Oceanids*. Grandfather of Atlas, *Prometheus*, *Thetis*, and *Zeus*.

OURANOS The primordial sky. Son of *Gaia*. Father (by *Gaia*) of the first generation of Titans (including *Kronos*, *Oceanus*, and *Tethys*), and the giants. Overthrown and castrated by his son *Kronos*. Progenitor of *Aphrodite* (from his blood and seed).

PAN Goat-footed god of nature and wild things. Son (some say) of *Hermes* and the nymph Dryope. Lover of pipe music.

PERSEPHONE Queen of the Underworld and goddess of spring. Daughter of *Zeus* and *Demeter*. Half-sister of *Apollo*, *Ares*, *Artemis*, *Athena*, *Dionysus*, *Hephaestus*, and *Hermes*. Abducted and married by *Hades*, with whom she spends six months of every year. Target of unsuccessful kidnapping plot by *Pirithous* and *Theseus*.

PROMETHEUS Titan brother of Atlas. Friend of humankind. Foreteller of the greatness of *Thetis*'s son. Guest at the wedding of *Peleus* and *Thetis*.

SCAMANDER River god of the Troad. Husband of the nymph Idaea. Father of Callirrhoë and Teucer. Grandfather of *Ganymede* and *Ilus*. Bestower of great fertility on the plain of Ilium. A protector of Troy. Nearly kills *Achilles*. Boiled by *Hephaestus*.

SELENE Titan goddess of the moon. Sister of *Eos* and *Helios*.

TETHYS Ancient goddess of the sea. Titaness daughter of *Gaia* and *Ouranos*. Sister of *Kronos* and *Oceanus*. Mother (by *Oceanus*) of the *Oceanids*. Grandmother of Atlas, *Chiron*, *Prometheus*, *Thetis*, and *Zeus*. Transforms *Aesacus* into a seabird.

OTHER IMMORTALS

CHIRON Greatest and wisest of centaurs. Son of *Kronos* and the *Oceanid* Phylira. Father of *Endeis*. Grandfather of *Peleus* and *Telamon*. Healer. Tutor of heroes, including *Achilles*, *Asclepius*, *Jason*, and *Peleus*. Hosts the wedding of *Peleus* and *Thetis*. Bestows a spear with miraculous powers on *Peleus*.

ENDEIS Nymph. Daughter of *Chiron* and the nymph Chariclo. Wife of *Aeacus*. Mother of *Peleus* and *Telamon*. Implicated in the death of her stepson *Phocus*.

HYADES Nymphs of North Africa who suckled the infant *Dionysus*. Rewarded by *Zeus* with catasterization.

NEREIDS Sea nymphs. Daughters of *Nereus* and the *Oceanid* Doris. Cousins of *Poseidon*. They include: Psamathe, mother of *Phocus*; *Thetis*, mother of *Achilles*.

OCEANIDS Sea nymphs. Daughters of *Oceanus* and *Tethys*. Cousins of *Poseidon*. They include: Doris, mother of the *Nereids*; Metis, mother of *Athena*; Phylira, mother of *Chiron*; Pleione, mother of the *Pleiades*; and *Styx*.

PLEIADES Seven heavenly daughters of the Titan Atlas and the *Oceanid* Pleione. They include: Electra, mother of *Dardanus*; Maia, mother of *Hermes*; Merope, wife of *Sisyphus*; Sterope, mother of *Hippodamia*; Taygeta, progenitor of *Tyndareus*.

STYX *Oceanid*. Goddess of the river of hate in the underworld. Her waters bestow invulnerability on mortals.

THETIS *Nereid*. Daughter of *Nereus* and Doris. Savior of *Zeus* by summoning the *Hecatonchires* to protect him from his rebellious Olympian family. Savior of the infant *Hephaestus* when *Hera* cast him down from Olympus. Desired by all the gods until *Prometheus* prophesizes her son will be greater than his father. Wrestled into wedlock by *Peleus*; their wedding the last great gathering of the immortals. Protective mother of *Achilles*: attempts, to make him invulnerable by immersing him in the *Styx*, and by commissioning his armor from *Hephaestus*; to cheat his destiny by concealing him under the care of *Lycomedes*; to warn him not to arouse the enmity of *Apollo*; to persuade *Zeus* to tilt the balance of the Trojan War against the Greeks and teach *Agamemnon* a lesson.

MONSTERS AND OTHER CREATURES

CALYDONIAN BOAR Giant baby-eating bane of Aetolia sent as punishment by *Artemis*. Hunted by heroes including *Asclepius*, the *Dioscuri*, *Eurytion*, *Jason*, *Nestor*, *Peleus*, *Pirithous*, *Telamon*, *Theseus*, and (possibly) *Thersites*. Slain by *Atalanta* and *Meleager*.

CHIMERA Fire-breathing snaky-tailed lion–goat hybrid. Offspring of *Typhon*. Sibling of the *Hydra* and the *Nemean Lion*. Slain by *Bellerophon*.

CRETAN BULL Creature of *Poseidon*. Father of the Minotaur. Tamed temporarily by *Heracles*, then terminally by *Theseus*.

GOLDEN RAM Bearer of the Golden Fleece retrieved from Colchis by *Jason*, *Medea*, and the Argonauts, including the *Dioscuri*, *Eurytion*, *Heracles*, *Meleager*, *Nestor*, *Peleus*, *Philoctetes*, *Pirithous*, and *Telamon*.

HECATONCHIRES Gigantic fifty-headed, hundred-handed children of *Gaia* and *Ouranos*. Summoned from the underworld by *Thetis* to protect *Zeus* from his rebellious Olympian family.

HYDRA Polycephalic self-regenerative venomous-blooded serpentine guardian of the gates of hell. Offspring of *Typhon*. Sibling of the *Chimera* and the

Nemean Lion. Slain by *Heracles*. Blood involved in the deaths of the giants and of *Heracles, Nessus,* and *Paris*.

NEMEAN LION Offspring of *Typhon*. Sibling of the *Chimera* and the *Hydra*. Slain, skinned, and worn by *Heracles*.

NESSUS Centaur. Killed by the arrows of *Heracles* for molesting the hero's wife. Obtains his revenge when *Heracles* wears his shirt soaked in *Hydra* blood.

ORION Boeotian giant and hunter. Son of *Poseidon*. Slain by *Artemis* out of jealousy; then catasterized out of remorse.

PEGASUS White winged horse. Offspring of *Poseidon* and the Gorgon Medusa. Half-brother of *Bellerophon*, whom he aids in slaying the *Chimera*.

TYPHON First and worst of monsters. Giant serpentine offspring of *Gaia* and Tartarus. Father of the *Chimera*, the *Hydra*, and the *Nemean Lion*.

GREEKS

GENERATIONS BEFORE THE TROJAN WAR

ACASTUS King of Iolcos. Son of *Jason*'s enemy and kinsman Pelias. Husband of *Astydameia*. Offers expiation to *Peleus* for the slaying of *Eurytion*. Then tricked by *Astydameia* into trying to murder him. Slain by *Peleus* in revenge.

AEACUS King of Aegina. Son of *Zeus* and the nymph Aegina. Given ant-people (Myrmidons) by *Zeus* to assuage his loneliness. Husband of *Endeis*. Father (by her) of *Peleus* and *Telamon*, and (by the *Nereid* Psamathe) of *Phocus*. After death, one of the three Judges of the Underworld.

AETHRA Princess of Troezen. Daughter of Pittheus. Niece of *Atreus* and *Thyestes*. Briefly betrothed to *Bellerophon*. Mother of *Theseus* (by Aegeus and *Poseidon*). Carried off by the *Dioscuri* in revenge for *Theseus*'s abduction of *Helen*. Freed, after long service to *Helen*, by her grandsons *Acamas* and *Demophon*.

ANTICLEA Queen of Cephalonia. Daughter of *Autolycus*. Wife of *Laertes*. Mother (by him) of *Odysseus*.

ANTIGONE Phthian princess. Daughter of *Eurytion*. Wife of *Peleus*; mother (by him) of Polydora. Kills herself having been tricked by *Astydameia* into believing *Peleus* unfaithful. Not to be confused with *Antigone*, Princess of Thebes.

ANTIGONE Theban princess. Daughter of Oedipus. Scion of a much-cursed house. Sentenced to death for trying to bury her brother Polynices after he is killed fighting her other brother Eteocles. Escapes her punishment by committing suicide. Not to be confused with *Antigone*, Princess of Phthia.

ASTYDAMEIA Wife of *Acastus*. Her advances spurned by *Peleus*. In revenge, tricks *Antigone* into committing suicide and *Acastus* into trying to murder *Peleus*. Slain in turn by *Peleus*.

ATALANTA Arcadian princess. Exposed as an infant. Fostered by a she-bear, then raised by hunters. Supremely swift. Votary (and devastating tool) of *Artemis*. Too much of a girl, in *Jason*'s view, to be an Argonaut. Too amazing, in *Meleager*'s view, not to be a *Calydonian Boar* hunter. Awarded the trophy for slaying the boar, with fatal consequences. Tempted by the Golden Apples of the Hesperides into matrimony with Hippomenes. Punished with him by *Aphrodite* for ingratitude, then transformed into a lioness for involuntarily profaning a temple.

ATREUS King of Mycenae. Son of *Pelops* and *Hippodamia*. Brother of Pittheus and *Thyestes*. Half-brother of *Chrysippus*. Kinsman of *Theseus*. Husband of Aerope (sister of *Catreus*). Father (by her) of *Agamemnon*, Anaxibia, and *Menelaus*. Exiled with *Thyestes* for murdering *Chrysippus*. Together they depose *Eurystheus*, then feud barbarically, magnifying the curses already upon the house of *Tantalus* and *Pelops*. Adoptive father of *Aegisthus*, who murders him and installs *Thyestes* on the Mycenaean throne.

AUTOLYCUS Light-fingered son of *Hermes*. Husband of Amphithea. Father (by her) of *Anticlea*. Grandfather of *Odysseus* and *Sinon*.

BELLEROPHON Prince of Corinth. Son of *Poseidon*. Briefly betrothed to *Aethra*. Half-brother of *Pegasus*. Exiled for fatally mistaking another half-brother for a boar. Given expiation by King Proetus of Mycenae, then falls foul of his wife Stheneboea. Slayer of the *Chimera*. Wins the hand of the King of Lycia's daughter and the succession to his kingdom. Crippled by *Zeus* for his *hubris* in trying to enter Olympus. Grandfather of *Sarpedon* and *Glaucus*.

CADMUS Founder king of Thebes. Grandson of *Poseidon*. Brother of *Europa*. Husband of Harmonia. Grandfather of *Dionysus*. Great-grandfather of *Laius*. Forebear of a much-cursed house.

CATREUS King of Crete. Son of Minos. Grandfather of *Agamemnon* and *Menelaus*, and of Oeax and *Palamedes*. Killed by his son in mysterious—and, for the abduction of *Helen*, convenient—circumstances.

CHRYSIPPUS Son of *Pelops* and the nymph Axioche. Half-brother of *Atreus*, Pittheus, and *Thyestes*. Groomed and abducted by *Laius*; then murdered by *Atreus* and *Thyestes*. *Laius* and his line cursed by *Pelops* in revenge.

CYCHREUS King of Salamis. Son of *Poseidon* and the nymph Salamis. Father of Glauce. Gives expiation, Glauce, and eventually his kingdom to *Telamon*.

EUROPA Princess of Tyre. Granddaughter of *Poseidon*. Sister of *Cadmus*. Abducted by *Zeus* in the shape of a bull. Mother (by him) of Minos and Rhadamanthus, Judges of the Underworld.

EURYSTHEUS King of Mycenae. Descendant of *Perseus*. Cousin of *Heracles*. Commands *Heracles* to perform Labors to expiate the murder of his first wife. Deposed by *Atreus* and *Thyestes*.

EURYTION King of Phthia. Father of *Antigone*. One of the Argonauts. Gives expiation, Antigone, and eventually his kingdom to *Peleus*. Receives in return *Peleus*'s spear through his chest during the hunt for the *Calydonian Boar*.

HERACLES Son of *Zeus* and Alcmene. Half-twin of Iphicles. Descendant of *Perseus*. Cousin of *Eurystheus* and *Theseus*. *Zeus*'s favorite human son. Persecuted by *Hera*; later her son-in-law. Father of numberless Heraclides, including *Telephus*. To expiate the murder of his first wife, performs Labors for *Eurystheus*: (1) slaying the *Nemean Lion*; (2) slaying the Lernaean *Hydra*; (3) capturing the Ceryneian Hind; (4) capturing the Erymanthian Boar; (5) cleaning the stables of King Augeas; (6) driving away the Stymphalian Birds; (7) taming the *Cretan Bull*; (8) taming the mares of King Diomedes of Thrace; (9) stealing the girdle of the Amazon queen *Hippolyta*; (10) stealing the cattle of the giant Geryon; (11) stealing the Golden Apples of the Hesperides; (12) fetching Cerberus from the underworld. Bane of *Typhon*'s spawn. Out-wrestler of *Nereus*. One of the Argonauts. Rescuer of *Hesione* from *Poseidon*'s sea monster, and Theseus from the underworld. Sacker of Troy. Sparer of *Priam*. Slayer of *Laomedon* and (perhaps) *Hippolyta*. Installer of *Tyndareus* on the throne of Sparta. Savior of the OLYMPIAN GODS from the giants. Fatally wounded by the centaur Nessus's shirt soaked in *Hydra* blood. Immolated by *Philoctetes*; in return, bestows his bow and *Hydra*-envenomed arrows on him. Immortalized and catasterized by *Zeus*.

HIPPODAMIA Daughter of *Oenomaus* and the *Pleiad* Sterope. First prize in chariot race won by *Pelops*. Repulsed by idea of one-night stand with *Myrtilus*. Mother of *Atreus*, Pittheus, and *Thyestes*. Forebear of a much-cursed house.

IO First mortal woman beloved by *Zeus*. Transformed by him into a cow. Persecuted by the gadfly of *Hera*. Gives name to the Bosporus (Cow-Crossing).

JASON Rightful heir to the throne of Iolcos. Son of Aeson and Alcimede. Kinsman of *Atalanta*, *Bellerophon*, Neleus, and Peleus. Father (by *Medea*) of Thessalus. Raised by *Chiron*. Favored by *Athena* and *Hera*. With the aid of the Argonauts and *Medea*'s magic fulfills the task set him by Pelias to recover the Golden Fleece. His plans to marry into the Corinthian royal family fatally spoiled by *Medea*. Reclaims throne of Iolcos from *Acastus*. Hunter of the *Calydonian Boar*. Slain in a shipyard accident involving the *Argo*.

LAERTES King of Cephalonia. Son of Cephalus. Husband of *Anticlea*. Father (by her) of *Odysseus*.

LAIUS King of Thebes. Great-grandson of *Cadmus*. Father of Oedipus. Raised in exile by *Pelops*. Repays that trust by grooming and abducting *Chrysippus*. Cursed by *Pelops* for his role in *Chrysippus*'s death, augmenting the curse on the house of *Cadmus*.

LYCOMEDES King of Skyros. Son of *Apollo*. Father of numerous daughters, including *Deidamia*. Host of the exiled *Theseus*, then slayer of him in a clifftop quarrel. Guardian of *Achilles* and *Neoptolemus*, but fails to prevent them going to Troy.

MEDEA Princess of Colchis and enchantress. Granddaughter of *Helios*. Aids *Jason* to steal the Golden Fleece, and herself. Cuts a bloody swathe through the royal families of Greece. Stepmother of *Theseus*.

MELEAGER Prince of Calydon. Possible son of *Ares*. Cousin of *Diomedes* and *Thersites*. Posthumous brother-in-law of *Heracles*. One of the Argonauts. Leader of the hunt for the *Calydonian Boar*. Possibly responsible for *Thersites*'s limp. Love for *Atalanta* dooms him to an early death.

MYRTILUS Son of *Hermes*. Charioteer of *Oenomaus*. Bribed by *Pelops* to help him win *Hippodamia*, then slain by him. Curses *Pelops* and his house.

OENOMAUS King of Pisa. Son of *Ares*. Father of *Hippodamia*. Slain by *Myrtilus* and *Pelops* in the chariot race to win *Hippodamia*'s hand in marriage.

OICLES Argive warrior. Companion of *Heracles* at Troy. Slain by the forces of *Laomedon*.

PELEUS King of Phthia. Son of *Aeacus* and the nymph *Endeis*. Grandson of *Zeus* and *Chiron*. Brother of *Telamon*. Half-brother of *Phocus*; exiled after killing him. Given expiation, a wife, and eventually a kingdom by *Eurytion*, whom he accidentally slays during the hunt for the *Calydonian Boar*. Deliberately slays *Acastus* and *Astydameia*, restoring the throne of Iolcos to *Jason*'s son Thessalus. Comrade of *Heracles*. One of the Argonauts. Husband of *Antigone*; later wrestles *Thetis* into wedlock. Father (by *Antigone*) of Polydora, and (by *Thetis*) of *Achilles*. Uncle of *Ajax*, *Patroclus* and *Teucer*. Recipient of a god-forged sword from *Zeus*, the divine horses Balius and Xanthus from *Poseidon*, and a miraculous spear from *Chiron*.

PELOPS Son of *Tantalus*. Made a gods' dinner of by his father; then resurrected by *Zeus*. Beloved by *Poseidon*. Fails to regain his father's kingdom of Lydia from *Ilus*. Winner, in a chariot race, of the hand of *Hippodamia* and of her father *Oenomaus*'s kingdom of Pisa. Briber and slayer of *Myrtilus*. Father (by *Hippodamia*) of *Atreus*, Pittheus, and *Thyestes*, and (by the nymph Axioche) of *Chrysippus*. Fosters *Laius*; then curses him and his house for abducting *Chrysippus*. Exiles *Atreus* and *Thyestes* for murdering *Chrysippus*. Southern Greece known as his "island" (*Peloponnesos*) because ruled by his progeny. Establisher of the Olympic Games. Scion and forebear of much-cursed houses.

PERSEUS Founder king of Mycenae. Son of *Zeus* and Danae. Savior of Andromeda from one of *Poseidon*'s sea monsters. Progenitor of *Heracles*. Slayer of the Gorgon Medusa. Catasterized.

PHOCUS Prince of Aegina. Son of *Aeacus* and the *Nereid* Psamathe. Half-brother of *Peleus* and *Telamon*, who kill him.

PIRITHOUS King of the Lapiths. Son of *Zeus* and Dia. Cousin of the centaurs. Argonaut and hunter of the *Calydonian Boar*. Bosom friend and bad influence on *Theseus*. Together, succeed in abducting Antiope (or *Hippolyta*) and *Helen*; fail in abducting *Persephone*. *Heracles* unable to free him from the underworld.

SISYPHUS King of Corinth. Notorious for his deviousness. Father of *Sinon*. Grandfather of *Bellerophon*. Ravisher of *Odysseus*'s grandmother Amphithea; consequently, thought by many to be *Odysseus*'s progenitor. Condemned to eternal torment in the underworld.

TANTALUS King of Lydia. Makes a gods' dinner of his son *Pelops*. Expelled from Lydia by *Ilus*. Torturously and eternally tantalized in the underworld. Forebear of a much-cursed house.

TELAMON King of Salamis. Son of *Aeacus* and the nymph *Endeis*. Grandson of *Zeus* and *Chiron*. Brother of *Peleus*. Half-brother of *Phocus*; exiled after *Peleus* kills him. Given expatiation, a wife, and eventually a kingdom by *Cychreus*. Comrade of *Heracles*. Argonaut and hunter of the *Calydonian Boar*. Sacker of Troy. Husband of Glauce and *Hesione*. Father of *Ajax* (by Glauce) and *Teucer* (by *Hesione*). Uncle of *Achilles* and *Patroclus*.

THESEUS King of Athens. Son of *Aethra* and Aegeus and *Poseidon*. Kinsman of the house of *Atreus* and of *Heracles*. Husband of the Amazon Antiope (or *Hippolyta*) and Phaedra (sister of Ariadne). Father of Hippolytus (by Antiope or *Hippolyta*) and *Acamas* and *Demophon* (by Phaedra). Inventor of the *pankration*. Tamer (and sacrificer) of the *Cretan Bull*; slayer of the Minotaur; hunter of the *Calydonian Boar*; bane of centaurs. Bosom friend of *Pirithous*. Together, succeed in abducting Antiope (or *Hippolyta*) and *Helen*; fail in abducting *Persephone*. Rescued from the underworld by *Heracles*. Exiled for his fatal role in the tragedy of Phaedra's unrequited love for Hippolytus. Killed by *Lycomedes* in a clifftop quarrel. Unifier of Attica, laying the foundations of Athens's historical greatness.

THYESTES King of Mycenae. Son of *Pelops* and *Hippodamia*. Brother of *Atreus* and Pittheus. Half-brother of *Chrysippus*. Kinsman of *Theseus*. Father of Pelopia and (by her) of *Aegisthus*. Exiled with *Atreus* for murdering *Chrysippus*. Together they depose *Eurystheus*, then feud barbarically, magnifying the curses already upon the house of *Tantalus* and *Pelops*. Employs *Aegisthus* to murder

Atreus and install him on the Mycenaean throne. Deposed by *Agamemnon* and dies in exile.

TYNDAREUS King of Sparta; installed on his throne by *Heracles*. Husband of *Leda*. Father (by her) of the *Dioscuros* Castor and of *Clytemnestra*; raises their half-siblings the *Dioscuros* Polydeuces and *Helen* as his children. Uncle of *Penelope*. Awards the hand of *Helen* by lottery to *Menelaus*; and the hand of *Clytemnestra* more conventionally to *Agamemnon*. Abdicates in favor of *Menelaus*.

GENERATION OF THE TROJAN WAR

ACAMAS Athenian prince. Son of *Theseus* and Phaedra. Brother of *Demophon*. Husband of Laodice (a daughter of *Priam*). Late-joining but valiant member of the Greek host at Troy. Rescuer, with *Demophon*, of his grandmother *Aethra* during the sack of Troy.

ACHILLES Prince of Phthia. Named *Ligyron* at birth. Son of *Peleus* and *Thetis*. Cousin of *Ajax*, *Patroclus*, and *Teucer*. Descendant of *Chiron*, *Nereus*, and *Zeus*. Greatness foretold by *Calchas*, *Prometheus*, and *Thetis*. Immersed in the *Styx* to make him (almost) invulnerable. Raised by *Chiron*, when his parents' attitudes to childcare prove irreconcilable, then by *Phoenix*. Childhood friend, later lover, of *Patroclus*. Briefly explores his feminine side as *Pyrrha*. Father (by Deidamia) of *Neoptolemus*. Greatest of the warriors in the Greek host at Troy; unsurpassed in speed or ferocity. Greatly favored by *Athena*; greatly hated by *Apollo*. Furious with *Agamemnon* at being used to lure *Iphigenia* to her doom, then at having to surrender *Briseis* to him. Refusal to fight ended by the death of *Patroclus*. Borne into battle by *Peleus*'s divine horses Balius and Xanthus. Bears into battle *Peleus*'s famed sword and spear, and a panoply made by *Hephaestus*. Slays numberless foes, including *Tenes* and *Troilus*, and Troy's mightiest warriors: *Hector*, *Memnon*, and *Penthesilea*. Overreaches himself when he attacks *Scamander*. Mistreats *Hector*'s body before taking pity and returning it to *Priam*. Finally slain by *Paris* (with the aid of *Apollo*).

AEGISTHUS Son and grandson of *Thyestes*; conceived by him in order to take revenge on *Atreus*. Adopted by *Atreus*, then murders him and installs *Thyestes* on the Mycenaean throne. Driven into exile by *Agamemnon*. Scion of a much-cursed house.

AGAMEMNON King of Mycenae. Son of *Atreus* and Aerope (sister of *Catreus*). Brother of Anaxibia and *Menelaus*. Scion of a much-cursed house. After exile in Sparta, reclaims his throne from his uncle *Thyestes*. Suitor of *Helen*. Husband of *Clytemnestra*. Father (by her) of Chrysothemis, Electra, *Iphigenia*, and Orestes. Leader of the Greek host at Troy. Perhaps over-reliant on the counsels of *Calchas*. Prepared to sacrifice *Iphigenia* to appease *Artemis*.

Prepared to surrender *Chryseis* to appease *Apollo*. Prepared to seize *Briseis*, despite infuriating *Achilles*; then repents after the death of *Patroclus*. Prepared to award the armor of *Achilles* to *Odysseus*, despite infuriating *Ajax*. Prepared to maroon *Philoctetes*, despite needing him to defeat the Trojans. Prepared to resort to the madcap scheme of a wooden horse to capture Troy. Prepared to take *Cassandra* as a prize of war, despite her warning what it will lead to.

AIAS "Ajax the Lesser," "Locrian Ajax." Prince of Locris. Son of Oileus and Eriope (sister of *Atalanta*). Despite his diminutive stature, one of the leading warriors in the Greek host at Troy; unsurpassed in his skill with a spear. Defender of the body of *Patroclus*. One of the contingent in the wooden horse. Violator of *Cassandra*.

AJAX "Telamonian Ajax," "Ajax the Mighty," "Ajax the Great." Prince of Salamis. Son of *Telamon* and Glauce. Half-brother of *Teucer*. Cousin of *Achilles* and *Patroclus*. Suitor of *Helen*. One of the leading warriors in the Greek host at Troy; unsurpassed in size or strength. Captures *Tecmessa*, then captures her heart. Father (by her) of Eurysaces. Duels chivalrously with *Hector*. Member of the embassy to *Achilles*. Defender of *Teucer*, *Odysseus*, the Greek ships, and the bodies of *Patroclus* and *Achilles*. Slayer of *Glaucus*, *Hippothous*, and Phorcys. Quarrels with *Odysseus* over the armor of *Achilles*; driven mad with jealous rage, kills himself with *Hector*'s sword.

ALCIMUS Myrmidon warrior. Captain and attendant of *Achilles*. Witness of his meeting with *Priam* to ransom Hector.

ANTICLUS Impressionable Greek warrior. One of the contingent in the wooden horse. Susceptible to the charms of *Helen* even through solid timber. Accidentally smothered by *Odysseus*.

ANTILOCHUS Prince of Pylos. Son of *Nestor*. Brother of Thrasymedes. Friend of *Achilles*; brings him the news of *Patroclus*'s death, then tries to console him. Slain by *Memnon*. Avenged by *Achilles*.

AUTOMEDON Myrmidon warrior. Captain and attendant of *Achilles*. Witness of his meeting with *Priam* to ransom Hector.

CALCHAS Priest (and great-grandson) of *Apollo*. Seer of *Agamemnon*. Father, according to some later accounts, of *Cressida*. Prophesies *Agamemnon*'s preeminence; the duration of the Trojan War; the death of *Iolaus*, as the first Greek to land at Troy; and the necessity of *Achilles*, *Neoptolemus*, and the arrows of *Heracles* for victory. Advises *Agamemnon* to sacrifice *Iphigenia* to appease *Artemis*, and to surrender *Chryseis* to appease *Apollo*. Advises *Neoptolemus* to spare *Aeneas*.

CASTOR See the *Dioscuri*.

CINYRAS King of Cyprus. Descendant of *Eos*. Father (by his daughter Myrrha) of Adonis, and of Mygdalion. Pioneer of copper smelting. His promise to contribute warriors to the Greek host at Troy fulfilled to the letter but not in spirit. Appeases *Agamemnon* with a magnificent breastplate.

CLYTEMNESTRA Queen of Mycenae. Daughter of *Tyndareus* and *Leda*. Sister of the *Dioscuros* Castor. Half-sister of the *Dioscuros* Polydeuces and of *Helen*. Cousin of *Penelope*. Wife of *Agamemnon*. Mother (by him) of Chrysothemis, Electra, *Iphigenia*, and Orestes. Unlikely to forgive *Agamemnon*'s plan to sacrifice *Iphigenia* or his plan to bring *Cassandra* home from Troy.

DEIDAMIA Princess of Skyros. Daughter of *Lycomedes*. Lover of *Achilles*. Mother (by him) of *Neoptolemus*.

DEMOPHON Athenian prince. Son of *Theseus* and Phaedra. Brother of *Demophon*. Late-joining but valiant member of the Greek host at Troy. Rescuer, with *Acamas*, of his grandmother *Aethra* during the sack of Troy.

DIOMEDES King of Argos. Son of Tydeus and Deipyle. Cousin of *Meleager* and *Thersites*. Suitor of *Helen*. Husband of Aegialia. According to some, a lover of *Cressida*. One of the leading warriors in the Greek host at Troy. Greatly favored by *Athena*. Dispatched on missions with *Odysseus* to enlist *Achilles* to the cause; to steal the horses of *Rhesus*; to bring *Neoptolemus* and *Philoctetes* to Troy; and to steal Troy's protective Palladium. Wounder of *Aeneas*, *Aphrodite*, and *Ares*. Wounded by arrows from *Pandarus* and *Paris*. Slayer of *Dolon* and *Pandarus*. Nearly slain by *Odysseus*. Rescuer of *Nestor*. One of the contingent in the wooden horse.

DIOSCURI The twin "boys of Zeus": *Castor* (son of *Leda* and *Tyndareus*) and *Polydeuces* or *Pollux* (son of *Leda* and *Zeus*). Brothers of *Clytemnestra* and *Helen*. Cousins of *Penelope*. Argonauts and hunters of the *Calydonian Boar*. Rescue *Helen* from abduction by *Pirithous* and *Theseus*; provide her with *Aethra* as a long-serving companion. Mysteriously unable to prevent *Helen*'s abduction by *Paris*. After *Castor* killed in a family feud, the twins jointly catasterized as Gemini.

EPEIUS Architect and engineer of Phocis. Son of Panopeus. Champion boxer. Builder of the wooden horse; one of the contingent concealed within it.

HELEN "Helen of Sparta," "Helen of Troy." Queen of Sparta and unrivaled mortal beauty. Daughter of *Zeus* and *Leda* (or possibly of *Zeus* and *Nemesis*); raised by *Tyndareus* as his daughter. Sister of the *Dioscuros* Polydeuces. Half-sister of the *Dioscuros* Castor and of *Clytemnestra*. Cousin of *Penelope*. Abducted by *Pirithous* and *Theseus*. Rescued by the *Dioscuri*, who carry off *Aethra* to be her long-serving companion. Sought as wife by *Agamemnon*, *Ajax*, *Diomedes*, *Idomeneus*, *Iolaus*, *Menelaus*, *Patroclus*, *Philoctetes*, and *Teucer*. Awarded by lottery to *Menelaus*; then by *Aphrodite* to *Paris*; then by right of seniority to *Deiphobus*. Mother (by *Menelaus*) of *Hermione* and *Nicostratus*. Her abduction by *Paris* causes the Trojan War. Aids *Diomedes* and *Odysseus* in stealing Troy's protective Palladium. Aids the Trojans by mimicking the wives of the Greeks in the wooden horse. Works her old magic to win back *Menelaus*.

HERMIONE Spartan princess. Daughter of *Menelaus* and *Helen*. Sister of *Nicostratus*. Scion of a much-cursed house. Left in Sparta with her father after her mother's abduction by *Paris*.

IDOMENEUS King of Crete. Grandson of Minos. Nephew of *Catreus*. Suitor of *Helen*. One of the leading warriors in the Greek host at Troy. Defender of the body of *Patroclus*. One of the contingent in the wooden horse.

IOLAUS King of Phylacea. Brother of Iphiclus and Podarces. Suitor of *Helen*. First Greek hero to die in the Trojan War; killed by *Hector*. Known to posterity as *Protesilaus*.

IPHIGENIA Princess of Mycenae. Eldest daughter of *Agamemnon* and *Clytemnestra*. Sister of Chrysothemis, Electra, and Orestes. Her sacrifice advised by *Calchas* to appease *Artemis*. Lured to the Greek fleet by *Odysseus's* promise of marriage to *Achilles*. Offers her life willingly, but apparently spared by *Artemis*.

LEDA Aetolian princess; Queen of Sparta. Wife of *Tyndareus*. Mother (by him) of the *Dioscuros* Castor and of *Clytemnestra*, and (by *Zeus*) of the *Dioscuros* Polydeuces and of *Helen*.

LIGYRON See *Achilles*.

MACHAON Son of *Asclepius*. With his brother *Podalirius*, the chief healer of the Greek host at Troy, and leader of the Oechalian contingent. Salves *Menelaus's* wound by *Pandarus*. Slain by *Eurypylus*.

MENELAUS King of Sparta. Son of *Atreus* and Aerope (sister of *Catreus*). Brother of *Agamemnon* and Anaxibia. Scion of a much-cursed house. While exiled in Sparta, wins the hand of *Helen* and then succession to the throne of *Tyndareus*. Father (by *Helen*) of *Hermione* and *Nicostratus*. One of the leading warriors in the Greek host at Troy. Saved by *Antenor*, *Athena*, and *Teucer* from certain death; saves *Odysseus* in turn. Prevented from slaying *Paris* by *Aphrodite*; not prevented from slaying *Deiphobus* and *Euphorbus*. One of the contingent in the wooden horse. Remains susceptible to the charms of *Helen*.

NEOPTOLEMUS Son of *Achilles* and *Deidamia*. Named *Pyrrhus* at birth. His presence at Troy necessary for its fall; brought there by *Diomedes* and *Odysseus*. One of the contingent in the wooden horse. His lust for killing at least the equal of his father's. Slayer of *Eurypylus*, *Polites*, and *Priam*. Sparer of *Aeneas*. *Andromache* destined to be his prize of war.

NESTOR King of Pylos. Son of Neleus. Cousin of *Jason*. Father of *Antilochus* and Thrasymedes. Inherits his throne after *Heracles* slays his father and eleven elder brothers. Argonaut and hunter of the *Calydonian Boar*. Oldest and wisest of the Greek host at Troy; trusted counselor of *Agamemnon*. His attempts to mediate between the Greeks and Trojans, between *Achilles* and *Agamemnon*, and between *Ajax* and *Odysseus* don't work out quite as planned.

NICOSTRATUS Spartan prince. Son of *Menelaus* and *Helen*. Brother of *Hermione*. Scion of a much-cursed house. As an infant, taken by his mother during her abduction by *Paris*. Reunited with *Menelaus* after the sack of Troy.

ODYSSEUS King of Ithaca. Son of *Laertes* and *Anticlea*. Husband of *Penelope*. Father (by her) of Telemachus. Descendant of *Hermes*, *Autolycus*, and *Sisyphus*. Cousin of *Sinon*. Greatly favored by *Athena*. One of the leading warriors in the Greek host at Troy; unsurpassed in guile or cunning. Devises successful scheme to ensure the peaceful marriage and protection of *Helen*. His ruse to avoid taking part in the Trojan War foiled by *Palamedes*. Later avenges himself by conspiring to have *Palamedes* executed for treason. Implicated in the plans to sacrifice *Iphigenia* and in the marooning of *Philoctetes*. Dispatched on missions with *Diomedes* to enlist *Achilles* to the cause; to steal the horses of *Rhesus*; to bring *Neoptolemus* and *Philoctetes* to Troy; and to steal Troy's protective Palladium. Mediates unsuccessfully in the quarrel between *Achilles* and *Agamemnon*. Saved from certain death by *Antenor*, and by *Ajax* and *Menelaus*. Rewarded with the armor of *Achilles*, to *Ajax*'s insane jealousy. Nearly slays *Diomedes* in his own moment of insanity (or jealousy). Inspired by *Athena* with the idea of the wooden horse. One of the contingent in the horse; accidentally smothers *Anticlus*.

PALAMEDES Prince of Euboea. Son of Nauplius and Clymene (daughter of *Catreus*). Grandson of *Poseidon*. Brother of Oeax. Kinsman of *Agamemnon* and *Menelaus*. Foils *Odysseus*'s ruse to avoid taking part in the Trojan War. Saved by *Antenor* from certain death. Stoned to death for treason on a charge trumped up by *Odysseus*. Inventor of board and dice games, and of the trickiest parts of the Greek alphabet.

PATROCLUS Prince of Opus. Son of Menoetius and Polymele. Cousin of *Achilles*, *Ajax*, and *Teucer*. Raised by his uncle *Peleus* after accidentally killing another child. Childhood friend, later lover, of *Achilles*. Suitor of *Helen*. Treats *Briseis* kindly. Leads the Myrmidons against the Trojans in place of *Achilles*. Slayer of Cebriones, *Sarpedon*, and Sthenelaus. Killed by *Apollo*, *Euphorbus*, and *Hector*. His death avenged by *Achilles*.

PENELOPE Princess of Sparta. Daughter of Icarius, the brother of *Tyndareus*. Cousin of *Clytemnestra*, the *Dioscuri* and Helen. Long-suffering but devoted wife of *Odysseus*. Mother (by him) of Telemachus.

PHOENIX Prince of Dolopia. Son of Amyntor. Befriended by *Peleus* after being unfairly exiled by his father. Beloved tutor of *Achilles*. Heeded by *Achilles* in his quarrel with *Agamemnon* over *Iphigenia*. Not heeded by *Achilles* in his quarrel with *Agamemnon* over *Briseis*.

PHILOCTETES Prince of Meliboea. Son of Poeas. One of the Argonauts. Comrade of *Heracles*: immolates him; in return, receives his bow and *Hydra*-envenomed arrows. Suitor of *Helen*. Bitten by a viper and marooned for ten years on Lemnos. Retrieved by *Diomedes* and *Odysseus*, and healed by *Podalirius*, in order to play his prophesized part in Troy's fall. Slayer of *Paris*.

PODALIRIUS Son of *Asclepius*. With his brother *Machaon*, the chief healer of the Greek host at Troy, and leader of the Oechalian contingent. Salves *Philoctetes's* snake-bitten foot.

POLYDEUCES See the *Dioscuri*.

PROTESILAUS See *Iolaus*.

PYRRHUS See *Neoptolemus*.

SINON Son of *Sisyphus*. Grandson of *Autolycus*. Descendant of *Hermes*. Cousin and mortal enemy of *Odysseus*. Convinces the Trojans to take the wooden horse into their city. His name preserved by posterity as a byword for lying and deceit.

TENES King of Tenedos. Son of *Apollo*. Slain by *Achilles* en route to the Trojan War; his death partly responsible for *Apollo's* fateful and deadly enmity.

TEUCER Prince of Salamis. Son of *Telamon* and *Hesione*. Half-brother of *Ajax*. Cousin of *Achilles* and *Patroclus*, and of *Eurypylus, Hector, Memnon*, and *Paris*. Suitor of *Helen*. Greatest archer in the Greek host at Troy. Slayer of Archeptolemus. Saved by *Ajax* from certain death; saves, in turn, *Agamemnon* and *Menelaus*.

THERSITES Aetolian lord. Son of Agrios. Cousin of *Diomedes* and *Meleager*. Hunter of the *Calydonian Boar*; his cowardice causing *Meleager* to hurl him over a cliff. Ugliest and most satirical of the Greek host at Troy. Slain by *Achilles* for mocking his grief over *Penthesilea*.

TROJANS AND ALLIED PEOPLES

AENEAS Prince of Troy. Son of *Anchises* and *Aphrodite*. Kinsman of *Priam*, and of *Eurypylus, Hector, Memnon*, and *Paris*. Husband of Creusa (a daughter of *Priam*). Father (by her) of Anchises. Greatly favored by *Aphrodite*. Accompanies *Paris* during the abduction of *Helen*. After his livestock seized by Achilles, becomes one of the leading Trojan warriors in the siege of Troy; commander of the Dardanian allies. Preserved from likely death at the hands of *Achilles, Diomedes*, and *Neoptolemus* in order to fulfill a momentous destiny. Rescues his family from the sack of Troy, and the Palladium from Greek possession.

AESACUS Trojan seer. Son of *Priam* and Arisbe. Half-brother of numerous siblings, including *Cassandra, Deiphobus, Hector, Helenus, Paris, Polites, Polydorus, Polyxena,* and *Troilus*. Foretells that *Paris* will destroy Troy. Attempts to kill himself after the death of his beloved, the nymph Hesperia; transformed instead into a seabird by *Tethys*.

AGELAUS Trojan herdsman. Ordered to kill the infant *Paris*; instead raises him as his own son on Mount Ida.

ANCHISES Herdsman, and former Prince of Troy. Grandson of Assaracus, the brother of *Ilus*. Kinsman of *Priam* and his numerous children. Lover of *Aphrodite*, thanks to *Zeus*. Father (by her) of *Aeneas*. Saved from the sack of Troy by his son.

ANDROMACHE Cilician princess. Daughter of Eetion. Wife of *Hector*. Mother (by him) of *Astyanax*. Taken as a prize of war for *Neoptolemus*.

ANTENOR Trojan lord. Kinsman of *Priam*; his wisest and most trusted counselor. Husband of *Theano*. Father (by her) of numerous, mostly ill-fated sons, including Coön and Iphidamus (both slain by *Agamemnon*), Demoleon (slain by *Achilles*), and Agenor (saved by *Apollo* from *Achilles*'s wrath). Foils the plot of *Antimachus* and *Paris* to assassinate the deputation of *Menelaus, Odysseus,* and *Palamedes*. As a result, spared by *Agamemnon* during the sack of Troy.

ANTIMACHUS Trojan lord. Bribed by *Paris* to assassinate the deputation of *Menelaus, Odysseus,* and *Palamedes*. Foiled by *Antenor*.

ASTYANAX Prince of Troy. Named *Scamandrius* at birth. Infant son of *Hector* and *Andromache*. Slain during the sack of Troy.

BRISEIS Cilician princess. Daughter of the King of Lyrnessus. Captured by *Achilles*. Her ownership the cause of his great quarrel with *Agamemnon*. Mourns the deaths of both *Patroclus* and *Achilles*.

CASSANDRA Princess of Troy and priestess of Apollo. Daughter of *Priam* and *Hecuba*. Sister of numerous siblings, including *Deiphobus, Hector, Helenus, Paris, Polites, Polydorus, Polyxena,* and *Troilus*. Blessed by *Apollo* with gift of prophecy. Cursed by *Apollo* so that no one ever believes her. Raped by *Aias*. Taken by *Agamemnon* as his prize of war.

CHRYSEIS Daughter of *Chryses*. Captured by *Achilles*. Taken by *Agamemnon* as his prize of war. His refusal to ransom her punished by *Apollo* with plague. Released, and escorted home by *Odysseus*.

CHRYSES Priest of *Apollo* in Chryse. Father of *Chryseis*. Unsuccessfully pleads with *Agamemnon* to free her from captivity. Successfully pleads with *Apollo* to punish the Greeks for *Agamemnon*'s lack of mercy.

CORYTHUS Son of *Paris* and the nymph *Oenone*. Abandoned by his father when *Paris* resumes his place in the Trojan royal family. Unwittingly murdered by *Paris* when he attempts to reestablish contact.

CRESSIDA Daughter of *Calchas*. Star-crossed lover of *Troilus*.

CYCNUS Impenetrable Trojan warrior. Son of *Poseidon*. Transformed into a swan by his father to save him having his neck wrung by *Achilles*.

DARDANUS Founder king of Dardania. Son of *Zeus* and the *Pleiad* Electra. Brother of Harmonia. Father of *Erichthonius*, Ilus, and Idaeus. Progenitor of the Trojan royal line. Gives his name to the Dardanelles.

DEIPHOBUS Prince of Troy. Brutish son of *Priam* and *Hecuba*. Brother of numerous siblings, including *Cassandra, Hector, Helenus, Paris, Polites, Polydorus, Polyxena*, and *Troilus*. Half-brother of *Aesacus*. Kinsman of *Aeneas, Eurypylus, Memnon*, and *Teucer*. Succeeds *Paris* as husband of *Helen*. Slain by *Menelaus*.

DOLON Trojan warrior. Son of the herald Eumedes. Sent by *Hector* to spy on the Greek lines. Fatally intercepted by *Diomedes* and *Odysseus*.

ERICHTHONIUS King of Dardania. Son of *Dardanus*. Brother of Ilus and Idaeus. Father of *Tros*. Noted horse fancier.

EUPHORBUS Trojan warrior. Son of Panthous and Phrontis. Brother of *Polydamas*. Slayer, with *Apollo* and *Hector*, of *Patroclus*. Slain by *Menelaus*. Reincarnated centuries later as Pythagoras.

EURYPYLUS Prince of Mysia. Son of *Telephus* and Astyoche. Nephew of *Priam*. Grandson of *Heracles*. Nephew of *Priam*. Kinsman of his numerous children, and of *Aeneas, Memnon*, and *Teucer*. Famed for his beauty and his mighty shield. One of the leading warriors and allies on the Trojan side in the siege of Troy. Slayer of *Machaon*. Slain by *Neoptolemus*.

GANYMEDE Prince of Dardania. Cupbearer and beloved of *Zeus*. Son of *Tros* and Callirrhoë. Grandson of *Scamander*. Brother of Assaracus, Cleopatra, and *Ilus*. Abducted by *Zeus*. Immortalized. Catasterized as Aquarius.

GLAUCUS Lycian prince. Son of Hippolochus (son of *Bellerophon*). Cousin of *Sarpedon*. Slain by *Ajax* in the fight for *Achilles*'s body. His corpse rescued from the fray by *Aeneas*.

HECTOR Prince of Troy. Eldest son of *Priam* and *Hecuba*. Brother of numerous siblings, including *Cassandra, Deiphobus, Hector, Helenus, Paris, Polites, Polydorus, Polyxena*, and *Troilus*. Half-brother of *Aesacus*. Kinsman of *Aeneas, Eurypylus, Memnon*, and *Teucer*. Husband of *Andromache*. Father of *Astyanax*. Welcomes first *Paris*, then *Helen*, into Troy. Leading Trojan warrior in the siege of Troy. Duels chivalrously with *Ajax*. Nearly succeeds in destroying the Greeks' ships. Slayer of Epigeus, *Iolaus*, and (with *Apollo* and *Euphorbus*) of *Patroclus*. Slain by *Achilles* and his body mistreated before being ransomed by *Priam* for burial.

HECUBA Queen of Troy. Wife of *Priam*. Mother (by him) of numerous children, including *Cassandra, Deiphobus, Hector, Helenus, Paris, Polites, Polydorus, Polyxena*, and *Troilus*. Her prophetic dream entwines the fates of *Paris* and Troy.

HELEN of Troy. See *Helen of Sparta*.

HELENUS Prince of Troy and seer. Son of *Priam* and *Hecuba*. Brother of numerous siblings, including *Cassandra, Deiphobus, Hector, Paris, Polites, Polydorus, Polyxena,* and *Troilus.* Half-brother of *Aesacus.* Kinsman of *Aeneas, Eurypylus, Memnon,* and *Teucer.* Defects to the Greeks when his suit for *Helen* rejected in favor of *Deiphobus.* Advises *Diomedes* and *Odysseus* how to steal Troy's protective Palladium.

HESIONE Princess of Troy. Daughter of *Laomedon.* Sister of Astyoche, *Priam,* and *Tithonus.* Offering to *Poseidon*'s sea monster. Rescued by *Heracles.* Spared by *Heracles* during his sack of Troy and ransoms *Priam.* Taken home and married by *Telamon*; mother (by him) of *Teucer.*

HIPPOLYTA Queen of the Amazons. Daughter of *Ares.* Sister of Antiope and *Penthesilea.* Possessor of marvelous jeweled girdle. Either a lover of *Heracles* and slain by him, or the wife of *Theseus.*

ILUS Founder king of Troy. Son of *Tros* and Callirrhoë. Grandson of *Scamander.* Brother of Assaracus, Cleopatra, and *Ganymede.* Father of *Laomedon.* Recipient of Troy's protective Palladium from *Athena.* Expeller of *Tantalus* and *Pelops* from Lydia. Troy alternatively named *Ilium* in his honor.

LAOCOÖN Trojan priest of Apollo. Father of Antiphantes and Thymbraeus. Suspicious of Greeks even when they bear gifts. Devoured with his sons by sea serpents sent by the gods to prevent him disclosing the secret of the wooden horse.

LAOMEDON King of Troy. Son of *Ilus.* Father of Astyoche, *Hesione, Priam,* and *Tithonus.* Tricks *Apollo* and *Poseidon* out of payment for building Troy's walls; then *Heracles* when he rescues *Hesione* from *Poseidon*'s sea monster. Later slain by *Heracles* in revenge.

MEMNON King of the Ethiopians. Son of *Eos* and *Tithonus.* Nephew of *Priam.* Kinsman of his numerous children, and of *Aeneas, Eurypylus,* and *Teucer.* Possessor of a panoply made by *Hephaestus.* One of the leading warriors and allies on the Trojan side in the siege of Troy. Slayer of *Antilochus.* Slain by *Achilles.*

MIDAS King of Phrygia. His touch (courtesy of *Dionysus*) turns everything to gold.

OENONE Mountain nymph. Daughter of the river god Cebren. Wife of *Paris.* Mother (by him) of *Corythus.* Abandoned by *Paris* when he returns to Troy. In revenge for *Paris* killing *Corythus,* refuses to heal him of his fatal wound; then immolates herself on *Paris*'s pyre.

PANDARUS Trojan lord. Son of Lycaon. Skilled with the bow: *Diomedes* and *Menelaus* wounded by his arrows. Slain by *Diomedes.* In some later accounts, go-between for the star-crossed lovers *Troilus* and *Cressida.*

PARIS Prince of Troy. Named Alexander at birth. Son of *Priam* and *Hecuba*.
Brother of numerous siblings, including *Cassandra, Deiphobus, Hector, Helenus,
Polites, Polydorus, Polyxena,* and *Troilus.* Half-brother of *Aesacus.* Kinsman of
Aeneas, Eurypylus, Memnon, and *Teucer.* Fated to destroy Troy. Exposed at
birth; raised in obscurity by Agelaus. Husband of *Oenone;* father (by her)
of *Corythus.* Awards *Aphrodite* the Apple of Discord in return for the hand
(and the rest) of *Helen.* Abducts *Helen,* along with *Aethra, Nicostratus,* and the
royal treasury from Sparta. Bribes *Antimachus* to assassinate the deputation
of *Menelaus, Odysseus,* and *Palamedes;* foiled by *Antenor.* One of the leading
Trojan warriors in the siege of Troy. Favored by *Apollo* and *Aphrodite* until he
unwittingly murders *Corythus.* Duels unchivalrously with *Menelaus.* Slayer of
Achilles. Slain by *Philoctetes* with the arrows of *Heracles.*

PENTHESILEA Queen of the Amazons. Daughter of *Ares.* Sister of *Hippolyta.*
One of the leading warriors and allies on the Trojan side in the siege of Troy.
Slayer of Podarces (brother of *Iolaus*). Slain by *Achilles.* Mourned by Greeks
and Trojans alike—except, fatally, *Thersites.*

PODARCES See *Priam.*

POLITES Prince of Troy. Son of *Priam* and *Hecuba.* Brother of numerous
siblings, including *Cassandra, Deiphobus, Hector, Helenus, Paris, Polydorus, Polyxena,*
and *Troilus.* Half-brother of *Aesacus.* Kinsman of *Aeneas, Eurypylus, Memnon,* and
Teucer. While still a boy, and while unarmed, slain by *Neoptolemus.*

POLYDAMAS Trojan warrior. Son of Panthous. Brother of *Euphorbus.* Born
on the same day as his friend *Hector;* unable to persuade him of the need for
caution.

POLYDORUS Prince of Troy. Son of *Priam* and *Hecuba.* Brother of numerous
siblings, including *Cassandra, Deiphobus, Hector, Helenus, Paris, Polites, Polyxena,*
and *Troilus.* Half-brother of *Aesacus.* Kinsman of *Aeneas, Eurypylus, Memnon,* and
Teucer. Defies his father's order not to fight. Slain as he flees from *Achilles.*

POLYXENA Princess of Troy. Daughter of *Priam* and *Hecuba.* Sister of
numerous siblings, including *Cassandra, Deiphobus, Hector, Helenus, Paris, Polites,
Polydorus,* and *Troilus.* Spared by *Achilles* when he sacrilegiously kills *Troilus.*

PRIAM King of Troy. Named *Podarces* at birth. Son of *Laomedon.* Brother of
Astyoche, *Hesione,* and *Tithonus.* Kinsman of *Anchises.* Ransomed by *Hesione*
from *Heracles* during his sack of Troy. Raises Troy to unequaled prosperity.
Husband of Arisbe and *Hecuba.* Father of numerous children, including
Aesacus (by Arisbe), and (by *Hecuba*) *Cassandra, Deiphobus, Hector, Helenus, Paris,
Polites, Polydorus, Polyxena,* and *Troilus.* Uncle of *Eurypylus, Memnon,* and *Teucer.*
Father-in-law of *Acamas* and *Aeneas.* Welcomes first *Helen,* later the wooden
horse, into Troy. Ransoms *Hector*'s body from *Achilles.* Slain by *Neoptolemus.*

RHESUS King of Thrace. Son of the river god Strymon and the Muse Euterpe. Possessor of horses vital to the Trojan war effort. Slain, and his horses captured, by *Diomedes* and *Odysseus*.

SARPEDON King of Lycia. Son of *Zeus*, and Laodamia (daughter of *Bellerophon*). Cousin of *Glaucus*. One of the leading warriors and allies on the Trojan side in the siege of Troy. Slain by *Patroclus*.

TECMESSA Phrygian princess. Captured by *Ajax*, who goes on to capture her heart. Father (by him) of Eurysaces.

TELEPHUS King of Mysia. Son of *Heracles* and Auge. Husband of Astyoche. Father (by her) of *Eurypylus*. Wounded, and healed, by *Achilles* wielding the spear of *Peleus*.

THEANO Trojan priestess of *Athena*. Wife of *Antenor*. Mother (by him) of numerous, mostly ill-fated sons, including Coön and Iphidamus (both slain by *Agamemnon*), Demoleon (slain by *Achilles*), and Agenor (saved by *Apollo* from *Achilles*'s wrath). Advises the women of Troy not to become Amazons.

TITHONUS Prince of Troy. Son of *Laomedon*. Brother of Astyoche, *Hesione*, and *Priam*. Beloved of *Eos*; father (by her) of *Memnon*. Granted eternal life by *Zeus*, but not eternal youth. Turned into a grasshopper by *Eos*.

TROILUS Prince of Troy. Son of *Priam* and *Hecuba*. Brother of numerous siblings, including *Cassandra, Deiphobus, Hector, Helenus, Paris, Polites, Polydorus,* and *Polyxena*. Half-brother of *Aesacus*. Kinsman of *Aeneas, Eurypylus, Memnon,* and *Teucer*. His death required to fulfill a prophecy of Troy's fall. Sacrilegiously slain by *Achilles*, earning him (in part) *Apollo*'s fateful and deadly enmity. In some later accounts, the star-crossed lover of *Cressida*.

TROS King of Dardania. Son of *Erichthonius*. Husband of *Scamander*'s daughter Callirrhoë. Father of Assaracus, Cleopatra, *Ganymede*, and *Ilus*. Recipient of magical horses from *Zeus*. Troy named in his honor.

ACKNOWLEDGMENTS

Without a loving and patient husband, without as perfect a personal as *sister* as ever existed, without a wonderful literary agent, without a stunningly gifted and passionate editor, without a copy editor who never misses anything, without an audiobook producer of the very first rank, without a publishing house that enthuses and encourages, without all these, this book could never have been written.

So thank you Elliott Spencer, Jo Crocker, Anthony Goff, Jillian Taylor, Kit Shepherd, Roy McMillan, and Louise Moore.

PICTURE CREDITS

Artist's Reconstruction of Troy; © by Christoph Haußner, München.

Attic red-figure stemless cup, depicting Diomedes stealing the magic Palladium, a statue of Pallas Athena, from Apulia, late 5th century BC (pottery); Bridgeman Images.

Hercules Rescuing Hesione, Charles Le Brun, Etching, 1713–19; Artokoloro / Alamy Stock Photo.

"We to those beasts, that rapid strode along, drew near, when Chiron took an arrow forth," Gustave Doré, c. 1890; The Print Collector / Alamy Stock Photo.

Procession of Thetis, accompanied by two cupids and preceded by a Fortune, whose sail billows with favorable winds, Bartolomeo di Giovanni, 1490; Lanmas / Alamy.

The Marriage of Thetis and Peleus with Apollo and the Concert of the Muses, or The Feast of the Gods, Hendrick van Balen, c. 1618; ACTIVE MUSEUM / Alamy.

The Judgement of Paris, Peter Paul Rubens, 1638; Prado Museum / Alamy.

Helen of Troy, Antonio Canova; Tades Yee / Alamy Stock Photo.

Leda and Swan, Cesare Mussini; De Agostini Picture Library / Bridgeman Images.

Bust of Menelaus, King of Ancient Sparta, Husband of Helen; Vatican Museum, Alinari / Bridgeman Images.

Thetis dipping Achilles into the Styx, Antoine Borel Rogat; © A. Dagli Orti / De Agostini Picture Library / Bridgeman Images.

The Education of Achilles, James Barry, c. 1772; Paul Mellon Fund / Bridgeman Images.

Cassandra, Daughter of Priam, Prophetess of Fall of Troy; Anthony Frederick Augustus Sandys; © The Maas Gallery, London / Bridgeman Images.

The Abduction of Helen, Guido Reni, c. 1626–31; Louvre / Bridgeman Images.

Ulysses (Odysseus) Feigning Madness, c. 19th C, gravure; © Look and Learn / Bridgeman Images.

The Sacrifice of Iphigenia, François Perrier, 1632–33; Musée des Beaux-Arts, Dijon, France / Alamy.

Greek Armada Lands On Trojan Beach in *Troy*, directed By Wolfgang Petersen, Film Company Warner Bros; © Warner Bros / AF archive / Alamy.

Troilus and Cressida, from the Kelmscott Chaucer, designed by William Morris; Lebrecht Authors / Bridgeman Images.

Attic black-figure amphora depicting Achilles and Ajax playing dice, c.540–530 BC; Vatican / Bridgeman.

The Farewell of Achilles and of Briseis, detail of fresco from Casa del Poeta Tragico, Pompeii, 1st century AD; Museo Archeologico Nazionale, Naples / Luisa Ricciarini / Bridgeman.

The Combat of Diomedes, Jacques Louis David, 1776; Albertina, Vienna / Heritage Image Partnership Ltd / Alamy.

Ajax attacks Hector, detail from the outside of an Attic red-figure cup (The Douris Cup), made by Kalliades, c. 490 BC; Louvre / Bridgeman.

Menelaus holding the body of Patroclus, Loggia dei Lanzi, Florence; History / David Henley / Bridgeman.

Shield of Achilles, Philip Rundell, 1821–22; Royal Collection Trust / © Her Majesty Queen Elizabeth II, 2020.

Achilles dragging Hector's body around the walls of Troy, Donato Creti; Musee Massey, Tarbes, France / Bridgeman.

Roman silver-gilt drinking cup depicting King Priam of Troy appealing to Achilles for the return of his son Hector's body, found in a chieftain's grave at Hoby, Denmark, 1st century BC; Nationalmuseet, Copenhagen / Bridgeman.

The Wounded Achilles, Filippo Albacini, 1825; © The Devonshire Collections, Chatsworth / Reproduced by permission of Chatsworth Settlement Trustees / Bridgeman Images.

Laocoön and His Sons Attacked by the Serpents, Roman marble, 2nd Century BC; Vatican Museums / Agefotostock / Alamy.

The Killing of Priam, Antonio Canova, 1787–90; Fondazione Cariplo, Milan / © Mauro Ranzani / Bridgeman Images.

The Sack of Troy, Jean Maublanc; Besançon, Musée Des Beaux-Art Et D'Archéologie / G. Dagli Orti /De Agostini Picture Library / Bridgeman.

Marble bust of Homer, Hellenistic period (330–20 BC); Musei Capitolini, Rome / Bridgeman.

INDEX

A

Acamas, 213, 235, 263

Acastus, 39–41, 62, 176n, 258

Achaea, 59, 96

Achaean fleet, 116, 132, 226, 231

Achaeans, 96–97, 125–26; encampment at Troy, 132–33; in the Wooden Horse, 222–28

Achates, 233, 234n

Achilles (*formerly* Ligyron): birth and immersion in the Styx, 74–75; heel of, 74, 189–91; renamed Achilles by Chiron, 77, 77n; friendship with Patroclus, 78, 79, 104, 140; hidden on Skyros, 105–6; joins the Achaean fleet, 107; and Iphigenia, 110–12, 114; kills Tenes of Tenedos, 116–17; held back by Calchas, 129–30; first battle of the war, 131–32; raids in the Troad, 134; kills Troilus, 137; raid on Mount Ida, 139–40; and Briseis, 140–47; appeals to Thetis, 146; sulks in his tent, 162–64; lends Patroclus his armor, 167–68; mourns Patroclus, 173, 182; armor of, 174–75, 191–94; joins battle, 176; *aristeia*, 176–78; kills Hector, 179–80; dishonors Hector's body, 180–81; returns Hector's body to Troy, 182–84; kills Penthesilea, 186; kills Memnon, 187–88; shot and killed by Paris, 189–90; in Mysia, 195; tomb of, 248; in *List of Characters*, 263

Adonis, 102n

Aeacus, 35–36, 38, 38n, 124, 194n, 258

Aegean islands, 97

Aegean Sea, 17, 21, 23

Aegeus of Athens, 236n

Aegialia, 227, 227n

Aegina (island), 35, 38

Aegina (water nymph), 35, 37n, 38

Aegisthus, 62–63, 72, 263

Aeneas: birth and friendship with Paris, 93; and the abduction of Helen, 93–94; in the Trojan Alliance, 125, 139; in battle, 155–56, 157, 166, 197; escapes being killed by Achilles, 177; rescues body of Glaucus, 190; escapes Troy, 233–34; in *List of Characters*, 268

Aenius, 177

Aeolia (*later* Thessaly), 38, 39n, 41

Aeolus, 108

Aerope, 62, 94n

Aesacus, 51–52, 269

Aethra, 61n, 66, 66n, 79, 94, 197–98, 224, 236, 236n, 237, 258

Africa, 125

Agamemnon: flees Mycenae for Sparta, 62–63; suitor for Helen, 67, 70–71; and Clytemnestra, 72; king of Mycenae, 72, 79, 88; furious at Helen's abduction, 96; preparations for war, 96–99, 101–3; and Iphigenia, 107–14; sets sail for Troy, 115–16, 119; arrives at Troy, 122; and Chryseis, 140–45; scepter of, 144, 144–45n; dream of victory, 147–48; attack on Troy, 148–49, 152; in battle, 154, 157, 166, 197, 200; offers to fight Hector, 159; in tears, 161–62; appeases Achilles, 162–64, 175–76; mourns Achilles, 190; and the death of Ajax, 194; and Neoptolemus, 195; and the arrows of Heracles, 201–2; and the Wooden Horse, 213–15, 217, 218; death prophesized by Cassandra, 235; saves Antenor, 237; in *List of Characters*, 263–64

Agelaus, 52–54, 79, 80, 81, 85, 88, 93, 203, 269

Agenor, 178

Aias (Ajax the Lesser): King of the Locrians, 97, 118; in battle, 148, 154, 157, 171, 186, 195, 197, 199; heroism of, 148n; offers to fight Hector, 159; the battle for Patroclus's body, 173; and the Wooden Horse, 215, 228; rapes Cassandra, 234–35; in *List of Characters*, 264

Ajax (the Mighty): birth, 37, 37n; son of Telamon, 59, 67n, 79; suitor of Helen, 67; joins the Achaean fleet, 97; in battle, 131, 148, 166, 167, 170, 186; raiding parties, 134, 139; fearsome appearance, 148; fights Hector in single combat, 157–60, 161; war belt, 160, 180; rescues Teucer, 162; embassy to Achilles, 163; rescues Patroclus' body, 171, 173; defends Achilles' body, 190; mourns Achilles, 190; madness and death, 192–94; funerary statue, 194n, 248; in *List of Characters*, 264

Alcibie, 185n

Alcimus, 176, 183, 184, 264

Alcmene, 64n

Alexander the Great, 246, 248n

Althaemenes, 94n

Amazons, 185–87, 185n

Amphitryon, 64n

Anaxibia, 62

Anchises, 89–93, 92n, 93n, 123, 125n, 139, 233, 234n, 269

Andromache, 78, 158, 181, 184, 198, 225, 235, 269

Andromeda, 25n

Antandre, 185n

Antenor, 126–28, 137, 149, 154, 160, 211–12, 219, 237, 269

Antibrote, 185n

Anticlea, 67, 99, 123n, 258

Anticlus, 222, 227, 264

Antigone (daughter of Eurytion), 38, 39–41, 258

Antigone (daughter of Oedipus), 38n, 258–59

Antilochus, 148, 171, 173, 187, 264

Antimachus, 128, 269

Antiope, 185n

Antiphantes, 217, 221

Aphareus, 94n

Aphidna, 66

Aphidnus, 66

Aphrodite: protector of Troy, 17, 123; at wedding of Peleus and Thetis, 46; and the judgment of Paris, 49, 58–59; mother of Aeneas, 92–93; and the abduction of Helen, 94; support for Paris, 152–53, 199; injured by Diomedes, 155; and Helen's dream, 225; in *List of Characters*, 252

Apollo: protector of Troy, 17, 123, 169, 183, 188; revenge on Troy, 24; at the marriage of Peleus and Thetis, 46, 47; grants Cassandra gift of prophecy, 85–86; father of Tenes, 116; and Achilles, 137, 177–78, 188, 199; shoots plague arrows at the Greeks, 142; protects Aeneas, 156; and Hector's fight with Ajax, 159; condemns profanities of the war, 237; in *List of Characters*, 252

Apollodorus (Greek scholar), 67n, 77n, 115n

Apple of Discord, 49, 123

Aquarius (constellation), 19n

Archaic Age, 245

Archeptolemus, 162

Ares, 17, 46, 49, 54–55, 61n, 90, 91, 123, 123n, 155–57, 177, 252

Argives, 96–97. *See also* Achaeans

Argo (ship), 38, 42

Argolid, 35, 35n, 88, 96n, 110

Argos (city state), 22, 35n, 59, 96–97

Arisbe, 51n

aristeia, 155, 166, 169, 170, 177

Aristotle, 245, 246, 248n

Artemis, 17, 35, 39, 46, 90, 108–10, 112, 112n, 123, 156, 237, 252

Ascanius, 233, 234n

Asclepius, 40, 40n, 77, 154n, 254

Asius, 169

Assaracus, 19

Astyanax (Scamandrius), 158, 181, 198, 235, 269

Astydameia, 39–41, 259

Astypylus, 177

Atalanta, 49n, 78, 259

Athena: and the Luck of Troy, 21; at the marriage of Peleus and Thetis, 46; and the judgment of Paris, 49, 58–59; supporter of Diomedes, 97, 123, 155–56; support for the Greeks, 109, 123, 139, 153–54; and Achilles' murder of Troilus, 137; prevents Achilles from killing Agamemnon, 144; and Hector's fight with Ajax, 159; and Achilles' fight with Hector, 177, 179–80; condemns profanities on both sides, 237; in *List of Characters*, 252–53

Athens, 35, 97, 207n

Atlas, 17

Atreides, 117, 118, 127, 129n, 187, 194, 206. *See also* Agamemnon; Menelaus

Atreus, 61–63, 144n, 259

Attica, 35, 66, 97

augury *(oionistike)*, 102n

Aulis, Boeotia, 97, 101–3, 106–7, 110–12, 123, 218

Autolycus, 67–68, 67n, 98, 123n, 219, 259

Automedon, 176, 183–84, 264

Axioche, 61

B

Balius and Xanthus (horses), 47, 165, 176

Bellerophon, 37n, 39, 59, 62, 66n, 124n, 168, 170n, 236n, 259

birds and forecasting. *See* augury *(oionistike)*

blood crime, 37, 37n, 39, 62, 199

board games, 135, 139, 139n

Boeotia, 97

Boreas, 18

Bremusa, 185n

Briareos, 147n

Briseis, 139–47, 162–63, 173, 175–76, 190, 192, 242, 269

Bronze Age, 101n, 148n, 240, 244–46, 248, 250

Browne, Thomas, 106n

Byron, George, Lord, 248

C

Cadmus, 19, 61, 61n, 259

Calasso, Roberto, 64n

Calchas, 71, 72, 102–3, 108–9, 114, 129, 130, 137, 137n, 142–43, 145, 194–95, 201, 207, 214, 218, 233, 264

Calvert, Frank, 249

Calydon, 39

Calydonian Boar Hunt, 144, 186n, 257

Cassandra: daughter of Priam and Hecuba, 78; foretells Paris's role in the destruction of Troy, 85–86, 93; granted gift of prophecy by Apollo, 85–86; prophesizes danger of Helen's presence in Troy, 95, 127; mourns Paris, 203; warns against letting the Wooden Horse into Troy, 211, 216, 219; raped by Aias, 234–35; in *List of Characters*, 269

Castor, 64, 65, 66, 67n, 72n, 94, 150–51. *See also* Dioscuri

"Catalogue of Ships," in Homer's *Iliad*, 115, 115n, 125, 130n

"Catalogue of Trojans," in Homer's *Iliad*, 125

Catreus, 94, 94n, 96, 259

Cebren (river god), 50, 51, 54

Cebriones, 169–70

centaurs, 40, 41, 176n, 185n

Cephalonia, 67, 68n

Cephalon of Gergitha, 199n

Cephalus, 68n

Cercyon of Eleusis, 83

Chadwick, John, 199n, 245n

Chaeronea, 145n

Chariclo, 35

Charis, 174n

Chaucer, Geoffrey, 136, 137, 185n

Chimera, 236n, 257

Chiron, 35, 40–44, 46, 59, 76–78, 112n, 154, 154n, 163, 176n, 256

chronology and myth, 72n, 185, 240, 246

Chryse (city), 139, 140, 145

Chryse (island), 117, 118, 118n

M

Macedonian Paeonia, 125

Machaon, 154, 154n, 199, 202, 266

Magyars, 185n

Medea, 102, 261

Medon, 118

Medusa, 58

Meleager, 186n, 261

Memnon of Ethiopia, 125, 187–88, 190, 210, 271

Menelaus: flees Mycenae for Sparta, 62–63; wins hand of Helen, 67, 70–72; becomes king of Sparta, 82; welcomes Paris to Sparta, 94; and Helen's abduction, 94–96; and the sacrifice of Iphigenia, 108–9, 112; abandons Philoctetes on Lemnos, 118; delegation to King Priam, 126–28; fights Paris in single combat, 149–53; shot by Pandarus, 154; in battle, 157, 171, 197, 200; offers to fight Hector, 159; *aristeia*, 170; and Ajax's death, 193–94; blames himself for the war, 194; and the Wooden Horse, 213; enters Troy, 228; finds Helen, 234; in *List of Characters*, 266

Menestheus, 67

Menoetius, 78

Merops, 51n

Midas, 162, 271

Minos of Crete, 38n, 94n, 97, 98

Minyae, 118n

Mnesus, 177

Moirai. *See* Fates (Moirai)

Mongols, 185n

Moros (destiny), 45, 69, 92, 255

Morpheus, 79, 80n

Mulius, 177

Mycenae, 22, 35n, 59, 62–63, 71–72, 79, 96, 110–11, 244–45, 250

Mydon, 177

Mygdalion, 101

Myrmidons, 38, 41, 59, 74, 105, 107, 112, 134, 139–45, 164, 168–69, 175–76, 178, 182–83, 190, 197, 200

Myrrha, 102n

Myrtilus, 23, 61, 261

Myrtoan Sea, 23

Mysians, 197, 200

myth and reality, 240–50

N

Nauplius, 136

Nemean Lion, 29, 149, 195, 258

Nemesis, 64, 255

Neoptolemus (*formerly* Pyrrhus): birth, 106n; summoned to Troy, 195–97; joins battle, 200; in Sophocles' *Philoctetes*, 202n; sceptical of Wooden Horse, 213; in the Wooden Horse, 222, 228; kills Priam, 232–34; in *List of Characters*, 266

Nereids, 44, 44n, 47, 73n, 256

Nereus, 44n, 73–74, 73n, 255

Nessus, 117, 118n, 258

Nestor of Pylos: joins the Achaean fleet, 97; attempts diplomacy over Helen, 102, 126; trusted by Agamemnon, 126; wisdom of, 126; devises signalling system, 133; reconciliation of Agamemnon and Achilles, 144, 162–63; in Agamemnon's dream, 147–48; advice on battle formation, 148; dissuades Greeks from desertion, 148n; in battle, 157, 160–61; encourages Achilles, 176; death of Antilochus, 187; mourns Achilles, 190; refuses to choose between Achilles and Ajax, 191–92; and the Wooden Horse, 228; in *List of Characters*, 266–67

Nevala-Lee, Alec, 77n

Nicander, 199n

Nicostratus, 79, 94, 96, 109, 153, 206, 234, 267

nudity, 81n

O

Oceanids, 44n, 47, 73–74, 73n, 257

Oceanus, 42n, 44n, 73n, 74, 256

Odysseus: and Helen's marriage to Menelaus, 67–72; marries Penelope, 79; feigns madness, 97–101; finds Achilles, 103, 106–7; brings Iphigenia to Aulis, 108–11; favored by Athena, 123; delegation to King Priam, 126–28; called Laertides, 129n; devises signalling system, 133; and Palamades, 134–36; returns Chryseis to her father, 143, 145; persuades the Greeks against desertion, 148n; in battle, 150, 154, 157; offers to fight Hector, 159; embassy to Achilles, 163–64; kills Rhesus and his horses, 164–65; rescued on the battlefield, 166; prevents the Greek ships sailing, 167; and Achilles, 175–76; and Thersites, 186; mourns Achilles, 190; granted the armor of Achilles, 191–92; and the death of Ajax, 193; brings Neoptolemus to Troy, 195–97, 200; brings Philoctetes from the isle of Lemnos, 202; steals the Palladium, 204–7; plans the Wooden Horse, 213–20; in the Wooden Horse, 222–24, 226–28, 231; in *List of Characters*, 267

Oeax, 136

Oedipus, 61

Oenomaus, 22–23, 61, 261

Oenone, 54, 56, 57, 79–80, 88, 198, 199n, 203, 271

Oicles, 28, 29–30, 32, 261

Olympia, kingdom of, 61

Olympian gods, 12–13, 41, 46, 49, 90, 122–25, 137, 155, 252–54

Olympic Games, 61, 240

Oneiros, 106n

Ophelestes, 177

Opus, kingdom of, 57, 78

Orestes, 79

Orion the Hunter (constellation), 175, 231

Ossa, Mount, 39n

Othrys, Mount, 59

Ouranos, 42n, 43, 90, 124, 256

P

Palamedes, 98–101, 126, 127, 134–36, 136n, 139n, 192, 218–19, 222, 224, 237, 267

Palladium, 20, 21, 24, 34, 50, 204–7, 218, 223, 234

Pallas Athena. *See* Athena

Pan, 46, 256

Pandarus, 137, 154–55, 170, 271

pankration, 83, 214n

Paris: birth and upbringing on Mount Ida, 52–54, 78–79; prize bull of, 54–55, 80–81; judgment of, 56–59; return to Troy, 79–86; abduction of Helen, 89, 93–95, 150; watches arrival of the Greeks, 122; plot to murder Achaean delegation, 128–29; fights Menelaus in single combat, 149, 151–53; unpopularity, 149; joins battle with Hector, 158–59; refuses to return Helen, 160; in battle, 161, 166; kills Achilles, 188–89; welcomes Eurypylus, 195; kills Corythus, 198; Helen's disillusion with, 198–99; killed by Philoctetes, 203; in *List of Characters*, 272

Parthenius of Nicaea, *Erotica Pathemata*, 199n

Pasiphae, 94n

Patroclus: suitor for Helen, 67; friendship with Achilles, 78, 79, 105, 140; and Briseis, 140, 145; and the embassy to Achilles, 163; borrows Achilles' armor and joins battle, 167–69; killed by Hector, 169; fight for his body, 170–73; funeral, 182; in *List of Characters*, 267

Pausanias, 145n, 194n, 248

Pegasus, 59, 170n, 236n, 258

Peleides, 129, 129n, 186. *See also* Achilles

Peleus: kills his half-brother Phocus, 35–37; in exile in Phthia, 38–39; accidentally kills Eurytion, 39; tricked by Astrydameia, 39–41; love for Thetis, 41–45; marriage to Thetis, 46–48; king of Phthia, 59, 74, 79; birth of Achilles (Ligyron), 73–76; agrees to hide Achilles, 104–6; sword and spear of, 176, 176n, 191, 195; in *List of Characters*, 261

Pelias, 39, 39n

Q

R

Racine, *Phèdre*, 185n

Renaissance, 248

Rhadamanthus, 38n

Rhesus of Thrace, 165, 273

S

Salamis (island), 33, 35, 37, 59, 79, 89, 93, 97, 102, 193n

Salamis (nymph), 37, 37n

Sarpedon of Lycia, 125, 166, 168, 170–71, 187, 273

Scaean Gate, Troy, 82, 127, 148, 158, 166, 179, 180, 188, 203, 221, 224, 231

Scamander (river), 18, 18n, 21, 50, 81, 123n, 127, 129, 148, 154, 155, 166, 168, 177–78, 197, 211, 216, 221, 237, 256

Schliemann, Heinrich, 248–50

Sea Peoples, 244

Selene, 44, 210, 231, 256

Semele, 61n

Seneca, *Phaedra*, 185n

Shakespeare: *Henry VI Part Three*, 231n; *A Midsummer Night's Dream*, 185; *Troilus and Cressida*, 136, 137, 186n, 187n; *Venus and Adonis*, 102n

Sidon of Phoenicia, 94

Simoeis (river), 18, 21, 50, 194

Sinon, 215, 217–19, 221, 222, 224, 231, 231n, 268

Sisyphus, 67n, 98, 262

Skyros, 105–6, 106n, 176, 195–96

Sophocles: *Ajax*, 193n; *Philoctetes*, 117n, 118n, 202n

Sparta (Laconia; Lacedaemon), 22, 63, 63n, 66, 67, 72, 88, 89, 93–96, 118, 127, 149, 150, 160, 198, 204, 205, 225, 236n

Sporades, 97

Star Wars (films), 185n

Sterope, 39

Stheneboea, 39

Sthenelus (friend of Hector), 168

Sthenelus of Argos, 155, 162, 168n

Stone Age, 243

Strabo, 194n, 248

Styx (river), 74, 75, 189, 257

Suetonius, 50n, 106n

T

Talthybius, 145

Tantalus, 22, 22n, 61, 62n, 262

Tartarus, 117n, 147n

Tecmessa, 139, 193, 194, 273

Telamon: and Hesione, 28–31, 79, 88–89, 102; and Heracles' sack of Troy, 31–34; and the death of Phocus, 35–37; father of Ajax, 37; and the Argonauts, 38; king of Salamis, 79; in *List of Characters*, 262

Telemachus, 99–101, 224

Telephus, 195, 273

Tenedos (island), 116

Tenes of Tenedos, 116, 268

Tennyson, Alfred, Lord, 248

Tethys, 42, 42n, 51, 74, 256

Teucer (son of Idaea), 18n

Teucer of Salamis: son of Telamon and Hesione, 37; suitor for Helen, 67; skilled bowman, 79, 131, 162, 188; joins the Achaean fleet, 97; descended from Zeus, 124; rescued by Ajax, 162; demands funeral rites for Ajax, 194; rescues the Atreides, 200; in *List of Characters*, 268

Teucrians, 18n

Thalassa, 42n

Theano, 186, 273

Thebes, 19

Thermodosa, 185n

Thersilochus, 177

Thersites, 186–87, 186n, 187n, 268

Theseus, 39, 59, 66, 66n, 67n, 83, 83n, 84, 105, 105n, 144, 185, 185n, 213, 214n, 225, 236n, 262

Thessalus, 41